After Dad

A NOVEL

Ralph Cohen

TATTERSALL PRESS

The following chapters have been previously published as independent stories in a somewhat different format.

"Fired!" in *Connecticut Review*
"Ensign Margot" in *REAL*

For my Ruhama

Acknowledgements

I am indebted to the erstwhile Writer's Workshop West, whose members graciously sat through one manuscript reading after another.

I would also like to thank Dave King for his supportive and incisive editing.

RC

Contents

1. Fired!
Jenny

HE WAS ALWAYS THERE FOR ME, from the very beginning.

Like, the first thing I remember was his head rising above my crib like a curly-haired sun. And I remember myself rising soon after that and flying in circles at a blinding speed, though I knew he'd never drop me.

I remember his big leathery hands smothering my face and brushing back my hair, holding me against his rumbling chest as we walked down the street under a deep-blue sky.

I remember his voice, all flat and reedy, how it filled the house morning and night, and how it ran through my thoughts as if it was my own. It was the voice I heard whenever an adult spoke, and it was the voice I heard on TV.

And whenever I watched TV, it was always his face I saw under the cowboy hats and Superman suits, rescuing people and capturing bad guys. I never questioned how he did it, how he reached so many places and still managed to walk through the front door at night, all rumpled and bleary-eyed. I just found it strange that he had other women beside Mom–a different one for every character he played–and that he never brought them home to meet her. Because I was sure they'd get along just great.

It was also strange that we were never in any of his adventures. They seemed to happen in a world apart, in a place that was impossible to reach. Though sometimes, at the end of a long Saturday, when he was carrying me home half-asleep from relatives, I had the feeling that we'd crossed into that world. That instead of rescuing me from nasty cousins and pushy aunts, he was flying me to the very corners of the earth.

I'd wake up the next morning surprised to be in bed. I'd look around for any signs of where we'd been the night before, but there never were any. He was really good at covering his tracks. I'd usually find him in the kitchen banging away on the stove.

"Who wants the best pancakes in the world?" he'd say. "How 'bout it, Muffin? Golden buckwheat. Good enough only for kings and Kovaceks."

"Don't be stupid, Dad."

I couldn't stand the sight of him in Mom's apron. It was even worse than the business suits he wore during the week, when he pretended to be an architect. I knew, of course, that we had to play along and act like we didn't know any better, that if his identity was exposed, it would only mean trouble. But sooner or later, I figured, he'd have to come clean. I mean, we were his family, after all. We couldn't just go on pretending. He might even need our help in a pinch.

As the months dragged by and nothing happened, I started to take matters into my own hands. Like, one night at dinner, I pushed a bowl of hot soup into his lap. I figured he'd just wink at me and brush it off, and it'd be our little secret. I didn't expect him to jump up howling and run to the sink. Or for Mom to throw me in my room. She could be so dense sometimes.

Another time, I yanked the steering wheel while we were driving in the mountains, and Dad just managed to whip the old Plymouth into a turnout. I got sent to the back seat, squeezed in between my grandmother and my older sister Margot, but that's not what I wanted. I wanted him to make the car fly.

And once, when Mom took me to the company where he worked, I ran through all the rooms and closets looking for the capes and six-shooters that I knew had to be there. Mom got very upset and shook me, right in front of all the people, but it was Dad who really pissed me off. He just stood there like a fool, hanging his head.

After a while, I must've given up. There's a picture of me at my fifth-birthday party with my arms folded and my face in a pout. Mom's trying to get me to blow out the candles, but I refuse to cooperate. I can't see the point, not if my deepest wish isn't going to come true.

And then–wouldn't you know it–a couple months later, it finally did. Though it never would've happened if Mom hadn't gone to the hospital for a few days. And even then, Margot and I had to keep popping out of bed. Dad tried everything to make us stay. He bribed us with shiny new dimes. He threatened to tell our boyfriends, as if he we had any. He even offered to tell us a story, but we kept jumping up and down like our beds were trampolines.

"Who wants to hear a dumb story?" I said.

"Not even a *real* story."

I scrambled under the blanket, but Margot still had a few hops left in her.

"I know why Mom's in the hospital," she whispered, hopping on one foot. "She's going to bring home a surprise."

"No, she isn't, stupid." She thought she knew everything because she was two years older. "Nobody goes to the hospital to bring home a present."

"*You're* the one that's stupid."

I lunged at her and Dad caught me in mid-flight.

"Girls, girls, don't fight over me."

"We're not fighting over *you*."

"You're not?" He clutched at his chest and sank to my bed. "Now I've got a broken heart. I'll never be the same."

"Don't be stupid, Dad," I said. "Tell us the story."

"I can't tell stories to jumping girls."

Both of us now scrambled under the covers, and his face went blank. He wasn't expecting *that*.

"Come on, Dad!"

He rubbed his eyes for a moment, as if he was summoning up memories from deep inside. Then he turned to us with a grin. "Okay, but you have to promise not to tell anyone. These are *secret* stories."

"We promise!"

And that's when he spilled the beans.

He said it all began when he was very young, not much older than Margot, and he was living with his mother and his evil stepfather in upstate New York. Sometimes his evil stepfather would beat him and lock him in his room. But one day, Dad escaped and ran away to the dense forests of upstate New York. Grandma did everything to find him. She hired a band of dwarfs, who sent bowling balls crashing through the mountains, making them sound like thunder. She found a giant, who scraped his huge claw over upstate New York and carved out the Finger Lakes. She sent out the best Indian trackers in the world, trackers so good that they could follow a scent clear across the ocean. But the only ones who even came close were the Daughters of the American Revolution. They walked right past Dad's cave singing "Camptown races nine miles long," though even *they* couldn't find him.

It wasn't until Charles Lindbergh got into trouble that Dad finally came out of hiding. Charles Lindbergh couldn't get his plane off the ground because he was loaded down with too much fuel. So Dad pushed him down the runway, and he pushed him so hard that he ended up in Paris. At first, Lindbergh was pissed–he'd only wanted to go to Canada–but then the Parisians mobbed him and yelled, "Leend-boorg! Leend-boorg!" and he forgave Dad.

People went even crazier in New York. They carried Dad down the middle of the city between all the tall buildings, while the office workers emptied their wastebaskets on his head. On Coney Island, they renamed hot dogs "franks" after his first name, and at Yankee Stadium, Babe Ruth pointed him out in the stands above center field. The Babe tried to hit him a home run, but at the last moment, another fan snatched it away.

Dad was so furious, he never let it happen again. From that day forward, he ran down every home run in Yankee Stadium, even if he was miles away in upstate New York. And he didn't just collect the balls. He'd throw them against his neighbor's garage, driving it back an inch a day. He threw so hard that the balls would burn up in mid-air–and that's when they started stitching them together.

"How'd they stitch them, Dad?" I asked.

But he put a finger to his lips. Margot had fallen asleep. "That's for tomorrow night."

The next night, however, he told us a completely different story–about how he and two buddies couldn't find work during the Depression. So they hit the trains and rode the rails. He showed us how they did it. They'd stop the train with a roundhouse punch and then lasso the caboose so they could glide along the tracks like they were water-skiing.

They rode the rails all the way to California. His buddies continued on down to Mexico, but Dad joined forces with Zorro, robbing from the rich and giving to the poor. He wasn't as fast as Zorro because it was easier to slash a "Z" with a sword than a "D" for "Dad." And he wasn't as successful either. Zorro would hold up the stagecoaches of the Evil Governor of Southern California, which left Dad only the roller coaster at Ocean Park. He never did get much loot–people spent most of their dough before they went on the big rides–but because of him, now people raise their arms on roller coasters and scream.

After a few months, he gave up and rode the rails back across the country. Only this time, he went south to Cuba to try out with the Dodgers at their spring training camp. And while he was there, he developed a curveball that broke so sharply, everybody in the stands flinched. The Dodgers wanted to sign him, but the War had broken out, and Franklin Roosevelt sent him a telegram saying that he needed Dad's help.

Margot had fallen asleep again, so I had to wait to hear about the War.

But the next night Dad took up the story after the Army sent him home from Europe. He didn't stay very long in upstate New York. Within a couple weeks, he came out West again to look up a girl–or actually to tell her off. She hadn't written to a buddy of his during the War, and his buddy had carried a broken heart all across Europe.

After a wild goose chase, Dad found the girl's house in Santa Monica. She wasn't too happy to see him, though. She said she hardly remembered his buddy, and anyway, it was none of his business who she wrote to, and if he didn't like it, he could take a hike.

"Did you punch her, Dad?" I asked.

"No, Muffin, I fell in love with her."

"But she didn't write to your friend."

"Well, that's what happens."

Dad said he and Mom had a whirlwind courtship. Everywhere they went, the wind flapped at their clothes and blew their hats away. Their romance became so famous that Frank Sinatra wrote all his songs about them. Though this other Frank could be annoying at times. He kept following them around and offering Mom a light, or trying to butt in when they were dancing.

To get away from him, Dad took Mom on a little cable car that carried people up and down a steep hill in the middle of Los Angeles. From the top, you could see the ocean, but that wasn't good enough for Dad. He made the cable car fly–and he didn't bring it down until Mom agreed to marry him.

I sat up in bed. "Would you make it fly for me?"

"Of course."

"Where did you make it fly?"

"That's for tomorrow."

But the next day, Mom came home from the hospital, and the stories ended. And she *didn't* bring a surprise. She brought my little brat of a brother.

The house was never the same after that. I had to blast the TV just to drown him out. I couldn't believe something so small could make so much noise. And he smelled constantly–of pee or milk or worse. Though every so often, I'd sneak into his room and bend his feet forward just to see his eyes bug out. His toes could actually touch his shins.

Mom wasn't the same either. She yelled at me constantly, and she even smacked me on the butt, just like Dad's evil stepfather.

Dad, meanwhile, returned to his old life, pretending to be an architect, and while he was gone, I'd dream up ways to catch him off guard, most of which I forgot by the time he came home. Still, I couldn't get his stories out of my head. I kept wondering what the dwarfs looked like when they were bowling in the mountains. Or how he held up the roller coaster at Ocean Park. Or what it was like to ride the rails. And I kept pestering him to take me on the flying cable car.

Then one hot afternoon when Toby wouldn't shut up and my butt was aching because I had to blast the TV louder and louder, the front door opened, and Dad walked in much earlier than usual. It wasn't even dark yet, but he still had that bleary look on his face, as if he'd worked a full day.

"How ya doin', Muffin?" he said softly.

Mom marched in and snapped off the TV. She was about to yell at me again, but then she saw Dad, and her head started back. "What are you doing home?"

"I've been fired."

"Are you serious?"

I was halfway to the TV, but now I ran up to his side. "Were you fired, Dad? Were you really?"

"I'm afraid so, Muffin."

I'd heard him use the word a few times before. Usually he'd hang his head when he said it, and Mom's face would tighten, so I knew it was something awful. I imagined people had to walk through a wall of flames, or they were thrown into a burning pit and left to die. I even had nightmares about it.

But now it had happened to Dad, and he was just fine. I pressed his palm against my face, and it wasn't even singed. I could just picture the shocked looks on his co-workers as he walked through the flames like it was no big deal.

"Were you fired, Dad?" I asked. "Were you really?"

Mom pulled me away. "Jenny, go outside and play."

"Fired!" I yelled as I ran into the back yard. "Fired!"

"Jenny," Mom called. "Jenny, don't…" But her voice trailed off.

I ran around the backyard yelling the word for all I was worth. When I finally came to a gasping halt by our fence, I could hear Mom crying and Toby wailing in the background. Even Margot was mewing like a cat.

I couldn't understand what all the fuss was about. Dad would have to share his powers with us now to keep us safe, but that opened up all kinds of possibilities. Like, I could just see us racing up the tallest mountains in nothing flat, or diving into the ocean like it was a swimming pool. Or knocking the stars about like so many marbles. And wherever we went, people would cheer us, even clumsy Margot, because we'd capture all the bad guys.

I held out my arms and whirled around with my head tilted back. And in no time, I could feel myself lifting off the ground. I didn't need Dad anymore–I could make myself fly.

"Fired!" I cried until it echoed against the neighbors' houses.

"Fired!" until the sky overhead throbbed like a pulse.

"Fired!" until I fell to the ground with the sun blinding me in the face.

2. Ensign Margot
Margot

WHEN I WAS SEVEN YEARS OLD, I developed a terrible fear that the ocean would rise up and swallow us whenever we went near it. I don't know where this fear came from. I just remember that it began soon after my father lost his job as an architect and my parents began to fight. Their arguments would rumble from one room to another like a storm breaking inside the house instead of over it, and sometimes they wouldn't end until my father drove off to Santa Monica Pier or Playa del Rey, where he loved to go fishing. If he wasn't too rushed, he'd take along me and my younger sister, Jenny. Toby was too young then, and my mother refused to go, though invariably she would meet him at the door and tell him he was running away from his life. I thought she meant it literally–that somehow the ocean would steal him away from us–so that was probably wrapped up in my fear as well.

It didn't help that one time her warning nearly came true. We shouldn't have even gone that day, but before I was fully awake, I could hear the arguments thundering down the hall like a distant storm, and then my door burst open, and there was Dad grinning in his punched-up old fisherman's hat.

"Are you ready?" he said.

"Ready for what?" It had to be five in the morning.

"You said you wanted to go. Don't you remember? Last night you couldn't stop talking about it. You fell asleep talking about it."

Jenny squealed and popped up from under his arm. She had on her fishing hat too, the one from Disneyland with Goofy's long snout and floppy ears.

I turned away and pulled the blanket over my head.

But the blanket lifted and Dad's warm hand cupped my face. "Come on, Sugar. The fish are waiting for you. Even now, they're saying, 'Where's Margot? We want Margot to come out and play.'"

"Tell them I'm sick."

"I can't. They won't believe me. They only listen to *you*."

"But it's the Fourth of July. We'll miss all the fireworks."

"No we won't. We won't let a single one get by us." He picked me up and set me on my feet. "We can't go without you, Sugar. You're our sunshine."

"So what am I?" Jenny said.

"You're our rainbow."

Still half-asleep, I put on some old clothes and went down to the laundry room to get my fishing pole, but I wasn't too happy about it. My brother's squalling filled the house like a fog, and at the front door, my mother pulled me aside and told me that if my father left her with a cranky baby one more time, he needn't bother coming home. Then she gave me a big kiss, as if she didn't expect to see me again, and drifted off to the nursery.

I trudged off to our Plymouth and curled up in the back. I was hoping I could fall asleep and wake up in my bed. But as we drove off, Jenny kept pestering Dad with questions.

"Why did Mom say, 'Don't bother coming home'?"

"She meant, 'Don't come home without a fish.'"

"What if we don't catch any? She won't let us in?"

"But we always catch something, Muffin."

"What will we catch today?"

"Oh, mackerel and bonito and yellowtail and maybe a shark for Mom. And a blue whale for Mrs. Weaver across the street."

"Can we catch a blue whale from the pier?"

"No, but we can from the barge."

Jenny got up on her knees. "You mean we're going on the barge!"

"Yep, in Malibu."

"But will a blue whale fit in the car?"

"He will if he sits down and doesn't ask too many questions."

"But he'll be dead, Dad! He'll be dead!"

The thought of catching a whale was frightening enough, but the idea of fishing on the barge sent my heart scrambling into my throat. It was a mile offshore.

I sat up and rested my chin on the top of the front seat next to Dad. "Do we have to go on the barge?"

"Not unless you can cast out that far." He tousled my hair. "Aren't you tired of catching perch and herring? Your pole can handle bigger fish than *that*."

"But what if the barge goes down?"

"On a beautiful day like today!"

Jenny wrinkled her nose. "Margot's a fraidy-cat."

I shoved her head and she came back at me with a roundhouse, which Dad caught at the last moment.

"Look, you're missing it." He turned her around toward the front. "The sky's putting on a show."

Ahead of us, the rising sun had transformed a bank of low-lying clouds into streamers of crimson, gold and rust. Jenny whistled, or tried to. I just shivered. I thought it was the last sunrise we'd ever see. It also made me uneasy to go fishing on the Fourth of July. We passed one fireworks stand after another, most of which were plastered with a sneering red devil, and each time, I was sure we were going the wrong way.

At the last signal before the freeway, we stopped in front of a billboard showing bursts of rainbow colors over the Coliseum.

"Dad!" I cried, making him jump. "Let's go to the fireworks show instead."

Jenny grabbed his sleeve. "Can we, Dad? We'll be good."

He sucked in his breath, something he usually did only around Mom. "But we can go down to Mexico *anytime* and set off fireworks."

"But it's not the same," I said. "It's not the Fourth of July."

The light turned green and he pulled onto the freeway with both of us groaning.

"Those shows are no big deal." Dad turned in his seat to check the merging traffic. "You know why they do it?"

I thought I did, but I shrugged anyway.

"They do it to honor World War II. They give thanks that so many people died. Otherwise there'd be too many of us. It's like one big funeral."

"No, it's not," Jenny said.

It didn't sound like what I'd heard either, but coming from Dad I couldn't ignore it. For the next several miles, as we barreled down the freeway, I turned the idea over in my head, and after a while, I could almost picture it–a million sparks flying up into the night, each one a soul that the War had snuffed out. It kept me so preoccupied that when we came face to face with the ocean, I wasn't prepared for it.

Dad swung right and headed up the coast, and once again, I was confronted by this monster bulging up against the horizon. It was bigger than I'd remembered and much more restless. Everywhere I looked, it was shifting about or changing color or lashing out at the shore. I couldn't understand why anyone would want to go near it, and yet, even at this ungodly hour, people were jumping about in the breakers, letting the water suck them under and spit them out again. From the road, they looked like pale figurines or bits of pink glass, so fragile, you had to wonder why the ocean didn't swallow them whole. Or, for that matter, why it didn't rise up and swallow all of us.

I didn't think about it long. A moment later, I was over the front seat, squeezing in between Dad and Jenny.

"Hey!" Jenny gave me a shove.

Dad drew me against his broad chest and hummed along with *Volaré* on the radio. I wondered if he could feel me cringe whenever the waves crashed against the shore. They sounded like the arguments in our house breaking from room to room.

As we made our way up the coast, I prayed that we wouldn't get there, that somehow we'd get lost and have to go home. But all too soon, we rolled into Malibu. It wasn't much more than a sleepy little town in those days, just a few weather-beaten stores and diners, and a stubby wooden pier that reached out into a wide bay. The pier's entrance was guarded by a stout little tower with an enormous wooden gate, the kind you'd expect to find on the other side of a moat. And at the far end, where the pier widened, two fat buildings stood side by side like sentries watching over the deep. Just the sight of it made me shiver. What could possibly be out there that the shoreline had to be so heavily protected?

Dad parked in a lot by the beach, and led us up a small embankment, and as we stepped onto the pier, the seagulls swooped and cried, warning us away. The pier itself shuddered when the ocean swept against it, and through the cracks between the wooden planks, you could see the ocean thrashing and foaming below us. Dad didn't notice a thing. He had a dreamy look in his eyes, as if he were in another world. He let Jenny run all the way to the end of the pier, where she stood up on her toes and leaned out as far as she could. He wasn't even watching her.

Outside one of the fat buildings, Dad parked me on a bench with our gear and went to buy the barge tickets, and when he came back a few minutes later, I couldn't take it any longer.

"What's the matter, Sugar?" He sat down next to me and brushed away my tears with a calloused finger. "Don't you want to have fun?"

I shrugged as high as I could. For some reason I couldn't tell him I was terrified.

"You know what happens to people when they go out there?"

I shook my head expecting something horrible.

"Each time, they go up in rank."

"No they don't. They're not even in the Navy."

"Sure they do." He bent close to me. "You see that man over there, the one with the grooves by his eyes?" He nodded toward a lanky middle-aged man by the ticket window who had deep, whitish lines on the side of his head. "That means he's a first mate. And see that man with the double chin in the brown leather jacket? He's a commander. And that balding man with gray hair? You know what he is?"

I shrugged.

"A *captain*. And–oh my god. Stand up, stand up!"

We stood at attention and saluted a tiny old man who was doddering toward the end of the pier. He barely had a wisp of hair on his head.

"He's a rear admiral," Dad whispered.

I thought we looked ridiculous, but the old man smiled and saluted us back.

I sat down again. "What will I be when we get back?"

"An ensign."

"And the time after that?"

"A lieutenant junior grade."

"And the time after that?"

"A lieutenant."

"But I don't want to get old and wrinkled."

"But that's the best part, Sugar. You'll never get old. You'll always be a beauty."

"Then how will people know my rank?"

"By the commanding look in your eyes. You'll see." He buffed my hair and rubbed my nose with his.

I wasn't completely convinced, but for the next few minutes, as we walked around the pier, checking out the catch of the other fishermen, I tried to look commanding. I even put a frown wrinkle in my forehead. But when the taxi boat pulled up alongside the pier, shaking it to its foundations, my throat seized up and I could barely catch my breath. As we made our way down a rickety gangplank, my knees wobbled with every step, and when a crewman swung me onto the boat and I started tossing and pitching with the waves, I buried my face in Dad's side.

"Look, Sugar," he wheezed, prying me loose. "Here's a couple of chief petty officers. You don't want *them* to know you're afraid."

I turned my head slightly and saw two heavy-set women with grim faces stepping on board, actually making the boat dip. They were followed by a scruffy group of men with unkempt hair and flapping sleeves. As soon as the men piled on, a crewman cast off.

The boat moved sluggishly at first, bucking like a nervous horse. But after we passed the last buoy, it gained speed and bounded high over the waves, sending up spray on either side. Jenny threw her head back and squealed. I buried my face deeper into Dad.

"Listen," he said, bending close. "Listen to those men over there. You know what they're saying?"

The men who had boarded after us had the same wild-eyed look as Jenny. Whenever we splashed over a big wave or a seagull swooped by us, they shouted like kids. But they spoke in strange words I couldn't understand.

"Why do they talk funny?"

"They're speaking French," Dad said. "They're telling each other they're not on the Mediterranean anymore."

"But why don't they open their mouths all the way?"

Dad chuckled. "Because they're French. They never open their mouths all the way. And do you know why?"

I shook my head.

"Because the French love to kiss and they love to drink wine, and they always want to be ready to do one or the other. Let's see if they do."

I watched them, but I didn't see any wine on board. And the only women were the chief petty officers, and they didn't look like they wanted to be kissed. One of the Frenchmen, a short man with a round, boyish face and thick gray bangs, winked at me. I shuddered and buried myself into Dad again. I didn't want him to kiss *me*.

About halfway out, Dad took us inside the small cabin for breakfast, but I couldn't look at food. I gave my doughnut to Jenny, who got the glaze all over her face. I started feeling sick after that, and spent the rest of the trip curled up against Dad, listening to the boat thump against the waves. By the time we arrived at the barge–a towering black thing in the middle of nowhere–it felt as if every organ in my body had been wrung dry. Dad had to help me onto the boarding dock and up a narrow stairway, while Jenny carried my pole, complaining every step of the way.

"Why do I have to carry her things?"

"Because you're the scout," Dad said. "That's what scouts do."

"No, they don't."

When we reached the deck, I couldn't believe how crowded it was. People stood elbow to elbow, their poles bristling like spines, shouting as they cast out. And the fish they brought up weren't the small creatures we were used to on the piers. These were foot-long demons that whipped about furiously, or even larger blue-tinged monsters that pounded the deck like fists.

Dad led us to the center of the barge and sat me down on a bench outside a cabin, where the smells of bacon and coffee nearly made me gag.

"We're not going to desert you, Sugar. We'll be right here. Just come looking for us when you feel better. Okay? This is the best place. It doesn't rock as much. When you can, walk around a little. That's how you get your sea legs. And try to eat something sweet. It'll make you feel better." He put a baseball cap on my head and laid a Baby Ruth and a Butterfinger beside me. Then he squeezed my chin and disappeared with Jenny into the crowd.

I closed my eyes and tried to pretend I was back on land, but the rolling of the barge made it feel as if I were being lifted by a giant Ferris wheel. Up, up, up I went until I was sure the whole thing would tip over. I grabbed the bench and cried out–but when I opened my eyes, we were still above water. The horizon rocked slowly up and down. A young couple turned to gaze at me. Not far away, a boy shrieked with laughter.

I turned to stare him down, but he wasn't even looking my way. He was running from another boy with a fish. As they reached the cabin, the boy with the fish caught up with the first boy and tried to shove it down his shirt. I thought I was the only one watching, but suddenly, a gravelly voice roared over my shoulder.

"Get the hell out of here with that goddamn mackerel!"

The boys bolted upright, and the fish fell to the deck.

"I said get the hell out of here with that goddamn mackerel, or I'll throw you off the barge! And don't think I won't."

The first boy hurried off, but the second boy picked up the fish and shuffled away clownishly with his head down like a stiff old man. I was sure he'd be thrown off the barge and end up in the water, but the man with the gravelly voice just bent over to light a cigarette.

"They leave the goddamn fish around here," he said, waving the match out. "Leave a big mess. You don't have any fish, do you?"

I shook my head as hard as I could.

"Well, if you do, don't leave 'em around here. I ain't got no time to keep this deck clean. Got too many other goddamn things to do."

He was a short, bony man, with a shock of white hair, a pinched, veiny nose and deep horizontal creases down the length of his face, as if someone had taken a knife and pressed it repeatedly into his forehead, nose and chin. I was sure he was an admiral. He certainly dressed like one, all in white, though his undershirt was graying, and there were yellow splotches on his apron.

"Who left *you* here?" he asked. "You didn't come by yourself, did you?"

"My dad left me."

"Well, that's better than leaving fish. People leave their goddamn fish here like it's a garbage can."

Then he sat down next to me. I nearly jumped up and ran, but I was still too queasy.

"You smoke?" he asked.

I shook my head.

"Good, then I don't have to offer you one." And he laughed, though it sounded more like coughing. "Don't take it up. Goddamn filthy habit."

He took a deep puff on his cigarette, and now he really did cough, whooshing like a car trying to start.

"Smoker's lungs," he said. "Fuck you up every time. So how come you're not fishing?"

"I'm seasick."

He waved his hand at the air, which might have been an answer, or a fly he was swatting. "Hell, nothin' wrong with being seasick. When I first put to sea, I was sick half the time. And when I wasn't, I was drunk." He laughed again and tapped me on the shoulder. "Fact, when I crossed the equator the first time, they gave me my Neptune certificate with a bib. 'To Mr. Puke,' some smartass wrote on it. That's what they called me, 'Mr. Puke.'"

He took such a deep puff that his eyes closed. Then he coughed again for about a minute.

"What do they call you?" he asked. "You got a name, don't you?"

"Margot. I'm an ensign."

"Well, Ensign Margot, I wouldn't worry about the heaves. You can get used to anything. I had this girlfriend once who snored every goddamn night. Loud enough to wake up Jesus and his drinking partners. But I slept right through it after a while. And then I had another girlfriend who used to fart like a firecracker. Stunk up the whole goddamn apartment. Fact, now that I think of it, I never did get used to it. Maybe that's why we broke up. That and the fact I was screwing her sister." He cackled again.

Then he took another deep puff, and when his throat cleared he said, "I wouldn't even worry about it. 'Fore you know it, you'll be rowdier than a swabbie. Put all these assholes to shame." He waved his hand at the people by the railing. "Look at 'em. Buy a barge ticket and think it makes 'em an expert. Christ, every five minutes they're casting out. How the hell you supposed to catch something if your bait's not in the water?"

I followed his gaze up and down the barge, and just as he said, people were constantly lowering their poles behind them and calling out "Low bridge!" or "Tow bridge!" and then whipping the poles over their heads, sending their lines out like tiny white jets. For some naughty reason, the poles reminded me of my little brother's penis, the way the tips flicked up and down.

"Look at those two." The admiral lifted his chin toward the two heavyset women who had boarded the taxi boat after us. Their giant bums flexed against their windbreakers as they frantically worked their lines. "They don't even let the bait get wet."

"They're chief petty officers," I said.

The admiral grunted. "Nothing petty about *them*." He watched the women for several moments. Then he asked, "Your daddy a good fisherman?"

"I guess."

"How long he been fishing?"

"I don't know. Before I was born."

"Well, I suppose he knows what he's doin'. Though probably every fish he catches is bigger than the last. And the ones he don't catch are even bigger." He stared at the women's bums again. "Though you know which one you gotta look out for?"

I shook my head.

He grunted and leaned close to me. "The one that gets bigger *after* he catches it. That son of a bitch'll weigh one thing when he lands it and five pounds more when he gets it ashore. And by the time he tells his first woman, it'll be so big, you'll wonder how he got the goddamn thing in the car."

He laughed so hard, he had a coughing fit and his face flushed. I patted him on the back, but it didn't seem to help. Finally, he cleared his chest with a great heaving moan and his color came back, as if he were coming up for air.

"You watch out for that fish now," he wheezed, and cleared his throat again.

"How will I know which one it is?"

"Oh, you'll know. But it won't do you no good. Nobody'll believe you."

"My daddy will believe me."

"He'll be the last to believe you. Take my word for it.

Don't even mention it. You'll be better off."

He took one last puff and flicked the cigarette butt over the railing. Then he yawned without covering his mouth, closed his eyes and let his head sag into his chest. Within a minute, he was snoring softly.

I looked up and down the barge to see if anyone had caught that fish, but people were casting out so often that it was impossible to tell.

"Excuse me," a woman's voice rang down. "How do we get some service in the cafe?"

The admiral sputtered and opened his eyes. "Yes, ma'am?"

"Can we get some coffee? It looks like the grill is open."

He jumped to his feet, brushing cigarette ash off his lap. "Yes, ma'am, be right there. Just go in, and I'll be right with you. Make you anything you want."

She gave him an icy smile and slipped inside the cabin.

He brushed his apron a couple more times. "Christ, can't even take a goddamn smoke. Well, nice to meet you, Ensign. We friends?"

I stood up, and to my surprise, I didn't feel sick, just like the admiral had predicted.

"Friends." I stuck out my hand.

But he didn't take it. Instead, he grabbed my nose and rubbed it a couple times.

"Look at that. So small you can pinch it off. I bet everything else on you is small too."

I shrugged, feeling my face burn. "I'll be eight in five and a half months."

"Hell, stay seven. That's a good age."

"I can't. I have to be eight sometime. Unless I die."

"Well, you don't wanna do *that*."

The woman called from inside. "We'd like some scrambled eggs too."

"Yeah, yeah," the admiral said, more to me than to her. "Now, you watch out for that fish. And remember what I

said. Don't say nothin'. Won't do you no good anyhow."
Then he cackled to himself and slipped inside the cabin.

It took me forever to find Dad and Jenny. I had to walk
three-quarters of the way around the barge before I spotted
them by the bow. I rushed up to Dad to warn him about the
fish, but as soon as he turned, I knew it was hopeless. He
had that dreamy look in his eyes again.

"Hey, Sugar. Did you get your sea legs?"

I looked down, but my legs didn't seem any different.

"Let's get you baited up."

He led me to a couple of large blue tanks in the middle of
the deck, where dark little fish swam about in clouds.
There were little scoop nets on the sides of the tanks, but
Dad reached in and grabbed a fish with his bare hand. As I
held my breath, he slipped one of my hooks through its
gills–and the fish kept wiggling, as if nothing had
happened. Dad baited two more hooks, and then handed
me the pole, which had suddenly come to life.

I had never fished with live bait before, but I managed to
hold onto the pole until we reached the railing. Dad cast
out for me, dangling the pole over the edge and giving it a
slight underhand flip. As soon as my line hit the water, the
bait fish swam around in tight little circles and disappeared
as the sinker took them down.

"Aren't you supposed to do it overhead?" I said, "and
yell, 'Low bridge'?"

"Only if you want to impress your boyfriend."

He gave the bill of my cap a tug and put the pole in my
hands. And now the three of us stood there as we had so
many times before in Santa Monica and Playa del Rey,
waiting for the fish to bite. The sun rose above the
morning clouds, brightening the water to a crystal blue,
while below us, the waves sloshed playfully against the
dark bottom of the barge. In the distance, the ocean
stretched lazily to the horizon, nudging up against the
pillow-like clouds as if settling in for the day.

I closed my eyes and lifted my head to let the sun warm my face. I thought ahead to the weeks to come, when my skin would turn fashionably dark and I would rise up through the ranks. Before the summer was out, I expected to be a commander or even an admiral. And then I wouldn't let anybody catch fish, especially the ones that grew bigger. I'd just let people cast out and reel back in, like most of them did now anyway.

I ate the Baby Ruth Dad had given me and let the glow of chocolate spread through my face and throat. I found that if I closed my eyes, I could tune out everything around me, including the Frenchmen, who were fishing nearby and giving off blasts of their funny language. Including Jenny, who caught a mackerel and nearly fumbled it back over the side.

I let my line drop all the way down, far below where the fish were biting, so nothing would bother the bait fish. I decided that they deserved a holiday too, and when we were done fishing, I was going to let them go.

But after only a few minutes, our luck ran out. My pole shuddered, and I shuddered with it. Something was tugging at the bait. Under my breath, I begged the fish to go away, and for a moment, it seemed to work. But then my pole bent nearly in half, as if a giant arm had reached up and pulled it down.

"Dad!"

He'd been drowsing too, but now he awoke with a start and grabbed my pole. He handed me his own and pulled me under him to the other side so our lines wouldn't cross. He tried to reel in, but the crank turned very slowly. Then the pole thumped against the railing, so hard, I could feel it through the deck.

"What did you hook?" he wheezed.

"I don't know!"

He let the line run, and then planted his feet firmly and lifted the pole high over his head. Then he lowered it again, reeling in quickly. As he worked the fish, it drew a crowd, and I was pushed farther along the railing until all I could see was the pole arching up and down. But I could hear everyone's comments, and with each guess, my heart squeezed in on itself.

"It's a shark," someone said. "It's gotta be a shark."

"A shark would make a run for it. It's probably a barracuda, a big one."

"Or a hell-fish." I was sure that's what the man said. "They usually dive to the bottom."

I reeled in Dad's pole and set it against the railing. Then I elbowed my way back through the crowd, and when I saw Dad again, I was shocked. His face was flushed and the muscles stood out on his neck like cords. And with each passing moment, new creases seemed to etch their way into his skin. He was rising up the ranks right before my eyes, but way too fast.

"You sure you don't need help?" someone asked.

Dad shook his head. "I've always been a little short of breath."

There were others, though, who did need help. Jenny had to be restrained from leaning over the side. And the Frenchmen were going berserk. In the excitement, one of their poles had fallen into the water, and they were screaming at each other, but without ever opening their mouths all the way.

Finally, I cried out, "Kiss somebody!"

They stared at me. Then the short one with the gray bangs gave the man next to him a loud kiss on the cheek. The other man pushed him away, but their friends laughed.

"He's not so pretty as you," the short man said, "but I don't know you well enough. You are more pretty. *Trés jolie.*"

As we stared at each other, a shout went up from the crowd. We rushed to the railing, and below us, the fish burst through the surface with a great thrashing and foaming, as if the ocean had coughed it up. It twisted about furiously as Dad reeled it in, but he managed to get it high enough for two crewmen to snare it with a hook and a net and heave it over the side. Then it dropped at our feet, thumped once or twice, and lay there gasping, exhausted from its fight.

I could barely look at the thing. It was the ugliest fish I'd ever seen–flat and oval-shaped, with kelp-brown skin on top and milky-white flesh underneath. It stared up at us from two beady eyes that crowded together at the tip of its snout, and it had a mouth that opened sideways, revealing rows of pointy little teeth. Dad put his foot on its back to take out the hook, and its sides curled up like a nasty body part.

I thought the other people would be as disgusted as I was, but they actually sighed and bent down to pet the thing, almost the way our neighbors fussed over my baby brother. Word must have gotten around quickly, because soon there was a steady stream of visitors coming by to see it. Even the admiral happened along and squatted down for a closer look.

"God damn, that's a nice one." As he stood up, our eyes met. "That your daddy's halibut?"

I nodded.

"Well, remember what I said. Don't say a word. Won't do you no good anyhow." Then he cackled and disappeared into the crowd.

One of the crewmen wheeled out a scale, and Dad helped him lift the fish.

"Forty-two pounds," the crewman announced.

The deck whirled about and I found myself on Dad's shoulders.

"It's really her fish," he said to the people who had gathered round. "She hooked it."

They beamed up at me, and a few applauded, but I didn't want any part of it. When Dad set me down, I unscrewed my pole and put my tackle away. Jenny wrinkled her nose in disgust, but as far as I was concerned, I was through with fishing. It was just a dirty, slimy sport, and we probably had no business even being here. We never saw any *other* girls at the places we went.

I spent the rest of the day playing with the bait fish in the big tanks, making them unravel through my hands like bolts of silk, or strolling around the barge checking out the catch of the other fishermen. One man had brought up a creature that was even uglier than Dad's, a shark with knob-like eyes on either side of its head. And a woman had landed a tuna with a tail fin the color of a pale autumn leaf. I prayed that one of these was the fish the admiral had warned me about, but I had a sinking feeling that neither of them was. And I couldn't ask him–he was too busy frying hamburgers–though he did wave to me from the grill.

Late in the afternoon, we returned to the pier, and another man weighed Dad's fish.

"Forty-six pounds," he said.

My heart stopped for a moment. I tried to warn Dad, but he just laughed it off. He even put the fish in the back seat of the Plymouth so he could pull it out of the burlap sack when we stopped at a light. Not only did it stink up the car, but each time he pulled it out, I was sure it had gained a pound or two. At one intersection, Dad cut his finger on the fish's teeth when the light changed suddenly and he had to shove it back in.

He rolled into a gas station to wash the blood off his hands, and as he came to a stop, I was ready to scoot out the door right behind Jenny. But Dad grabbed my blouse from behind.

"Hold on, Sugar. Somebody's got to watch our things."

"But I've got to go *too*."

"We won't be long. Just baby-sit the fish."

I scrunched down in the front seat. The last thing I wanted was to be left alone with that thing. I tried to pretend it wasn't there, but in my mind, I saw it gasping on the barge with those hideous little teeth. And even now, it sounded like it was rustling about inside the burlap sack, trying to escape. I peered over the top of the seat–and there it was, standing on its tail! It turned its snout toward me so it could take me in with those beady little eyes. I tried to scream, but nothing came out.

"Oh, hush up," it said.

"You're dead," I whispered. My heart was thumping in my throat.

"Now, honey, don't talk to me like that." She had a balmy female voice like the nurse at my school. "You listen to what Mr. Puke said. Don't say a word or I'll bite you too, and you won't be able to wash it off."

I struggled with the door handle.

"Where you going, dear? Now, just take it easy."

I went flying out the car and pounded on the door of the men's room. "Dad! Dad!"

He yanked it open, his face turning white. "What's wrong, Sugar?"

"Don't take the fish home."

"But Mom loves halibut."

"Dad, you don't understand."

"Did it bite you too?"

"Almost!"

"I'll put it in the trunk, okay?"

When we got back to the car, the fish was in the burlap sack again, and it certainly *looked* dead. But after Dad put it in the trunk and closed it, I still didn't feel safe. As we were driving on the freeway, I was sure I could hear it banging against the back seat, though it was hard to tell with Dad and Jenny singing "Camptown Races" at the top of their lungs.

I kept imagining what would happen when we got home. I pictured Dad opening the trunk and Mom screaming and the police being called. The arguments would flare up again and the Fourth of July would be ruined, and that would be just the start of our problems. I even let the word *divorce* slip into my thoughts.

But nothing like that happened. When Dad called Mom outside and opened the trunk, her eyes turned soft. She sighed like the people on the barge and squeezed the back of his neck. She put Toby in his arms so she could fetch Mr. Ring, the only neighbor she trusted with our Rolleiflex, and then she had us all gather round the fish to have our picture taken.

Mr. Ring chuckled as he focused the camera. "The fish looks like the newest member of the family."

"It is," Dad said, making me shiver.

The fish did grow bigger, but not the way I imagined it would. Mom cut it into several loaves, and it fed not only us but an endless stream of friends and relatives who came to visit.

It also grew whenever Dad talked about it, gaining about five pounds a week. By the end of the month, when my Uncle Max dropped in, it was up to 62 pounds.

And it grew in another way, a special way, engulfing the whole house so that, for a time at least, the arguments stopped and our lives took on the breeziness of that day on the barge. It didn't last long–the arguments soon came back–but that first night, when we left Toby with a babysitter and went to a fireworks show at a local park, the whole world seemed to sparkle and hiss, to gush into silver and gold. It was just like Dad had promised, we didn't miss a thing. And when they set off the big fireworks, with Jenny in Mom's lap and me in Dad's, all my fears seemed to fly up with them, to burst across the sky in dazzling colors–and give up their souls to the night.

3. A Voice in the Choir
Edgar

EDGAR BARNABY THE THIRD WAS NOT in the mood for suffering fools. He had three burials to do on this brutishly hot day and he had only just finished the first. As Assistant Director of the United Carriage Funeral Home, he liked to bring a certain style and grace to these proceedings, but it was difficult to be graceful when one was running around like a factory hand, and it wasn't his style to work himself to death. That was a fate better suited to the blue-collar types whose neighborhood they were passing through.

He could see them frowning from their windows as the limousine rolled by, and from the other cars when they stopped at an intersection. In their innocence, they probably imagined that he wasn't working at all, ensconced as he was in the passenger seat. But what they mistook for idleness was merely the nature of his professionalism. At the most trying moments, he could make his pale, round face, snub nose and delicate, full lips give off an air of bored somnolence. Women often told him that he reminded them of those dreamy cherubs in Renaissance paintings, to which he generally replied, "Do you mean Al Fresco or Al Cappella?" It rarely failed to get a laugh, and occasionally, it led to bedtime favors. Though as he neared forty, he was hearing this compliment less frequently, suggesting that he might need to enrich his cherubicity. Perhaps, when he was done with today's nonsense, he'd get himself a perm.

"We didn't pass Victory Boulevard, did we?" His assistant's nasal voice had a way of jarring him when he least desired it.

"Matthew, for God's sake, we haven't passed Burbank yet."

"Sorry. I guess I'm screwing up again."

"You're fine, you're fine. Now, just take it easy. We'll get there soon enough."

Matthew wasn't a bad egg. Not overly endowed upstairs, and given to spells of daydreaming in which he completely lost track of where he was. He also had a tendency to stamp on the gas pedal from a dead stop, a habit that was inexcusably gauche in a funerary vehicle. But to the boy's credit, he hadn't smirked when they were first introduced, as did so many of the raw hirelings his father-in-law brought into the firm. Instead, he'd simply taken in Edgar's four-foot-eleven stature and furze of blond hair with a deferential nod. Even better, he'd followed Edgar's instructions from day one as if they were the Lord's commandments, to the point of chauffeuring him around on personal errands, a service that Edgar rather enjoyed, despite the lad's itchy trigger foot. He just wished Matthew would relax between calls. Their time on the road was an opportunity to collect one's thoughts, not obsess over business.

"So what'd you think of the Steinbergs this morning?" the boy asked.

Edgar sighed. "They were decent."

Matthew obviously thought the world of the first family they'd assisted. Smiles and handshakes won him over like a puppy.

"What are the next people like? The Calvaceks."

"It's Kovaceks, Matthew. Always get the name right. And frankly, I haven't had the pleasure."

To forestall further questioning, Edgar closed his eyes and settled deeper into his seat, lowering his head onto his spongy chest. True repose, however, eluded him. Mathew's question had set off a twinge in his gut that was not unlike a touch of indigestion. By rights, he *should* have met the Kovaceks–it was part of his official duties as A.D.–but on the afternoon they'd come calling, he was out teaching the finer points of lovemaking to his wife's best friend, Phyllis Wagman. And Phyllis had been such a good student, so responsive to his touch, so eager to learn, that he couldn't quite bring himself to leave. When he returned to the office toward closing time, he was in such good spirits that he didn't even mind his father-in-law meeting him at the door with his usual gruff expression, though he did wonder if Dutch managed to hold onto his poker face when he broke wind.

"I wanna show you something," the old man said.

Without another word, he led Edgar to the embalming table and drew the curtain aside.

Edgar coughed out a chuckle. "That's a good one."

The corpse was fully six feet tall with blond curly hair, a prominent cleft chin and sky blue eyes. Edgar judged him to be a youthful fifty, but what caught one's attention was the mouth. A winsome smile lit up the man's features, as if he were enjoying a private joke.

"And that's after I worked on it," Dutch said. "You should've seen him before."

"At least he went happy."

"Well, he went. I don't how happy he was." Dutch lifted a curl off the man's forehead. "He must've been popular. People have been calling all afternoon."

"Good for him." Edgar wished the old man would get to the point. He did miss his coffee.

"Turns out he was an architect," Dutch went on. "He was also into theater. Carol says he founded the group that put on those plays in the park."

Edgar raised an eyebrow. So his wife had been in to see the *loved one*. "Did he break a leg?" he asked.

"No," Dutch answered dryly. "He had a heart attack."

Edgar wasn't in the habit of reacting to the clientele, but he found it unseemly that a stranger should win over his wife and father-in-law simply by showing up on the embalming table. He suspected that life's pleasures had come easily to this Apollo.

"He's not starring in anything now," Edgar remarked. "I'd say he's taken his last curtain call."

Dutch grimaced and went to wash his hands. With the old man's back to him, Edgar grabbed the corpse by the jaw and gave it a violent shake.

"Won't do any good," Dutch said from the sink. "I'll probably have to wire him shut."

Even then, the smile endured. Carol had to call the family to see whether they wanted the casket open during the service, which apparently they did. Edgar, for his part, couldn't have cared less. As far as he was concerned, they could have mounted Mr. Kovacek on his feet doing a buck-and-wing. What annoyed him was his newfound status as *persona non grata*. Ever since the Kovaceks had paid their visit, his wife had given him the silent treatment, declining to answer even the simplest question–such as why she refused to have dinner with him–or why she had emptied their bank account. And at the office, the old man had taken to ordering him around like the hired help, demanding, of all things, that he clean up after his embalming work, a task normally assigned to interns. And now here he was saddled with three services in one day! If that didn't amount to indentured servitude, he didn't know what did.

He opened his eyes, and his mood didn't improve when

he noticed Matthew's pupils making lazy circles at the road. The boy was having another daydreaming spell. He'd probably drive half a mile past their turn before he realized his mistake.

Rousing himself to an upright position, Edgar yawned noiselessly, scratched his left breast, and snapped, "Next signal, make a right."

Matthew shot up from his seat as if he'd been yanked by a chain. He whipped his head around and pounded on the brake, nearly sending Edgar through the windshield.

"Matthew, Matthew." Edgar had to fight through a fit of silent giggles. "We're not going to make it on time if you don't pay attention."

The boy's face was as pale as one of their clients. "God, I'm sorry. I'm so sorry. There I go again, screwing up. Always screwing up. One minute I'm here, and the next I'm not. It's like my father said. I'll never amount to—"

"You're fine, you're fine. Just keep moving before we get rear-ended. And make a right at the intersection." Edgar shook his head. The things he had to do just to keep himself amused.

With the boy back among the living, they had no difficulty finding the avenue of the bereaved, though the tackiness of the neighborhood dampened Edgar's spirits once again. The houses were all boxy stucco affairs, given over to bland pastels and aluminum siding. And the asphalt road was straight out of a backwater town, washing up frumpishly onto the front lawns without the slightest consideration of a sidewalk. Edgar could just picture a typical evening here–the neighbors sitting outside in their shapeless muumuus and stained t-shirts, while they listened to baseball games and sipped beer from the can.

The one consolation in their arrival was Matthew's newfound grace at the wheel. The boy glided the limousine past a line of parked cars and onto the latter half of the deceased's driveway as quietly as a shadow. Even Edgar had to grunt his approval.

"Now, remember," he said, reaching for the door handle. "I'll do the talking. You do the smiling."

"No problem."

"Just a second."

He straightened his assistant's tie and brushed a piece of lint from his lapel. They were dressed in identical coal-gray suits, though Edgar was painfully aware that they couldn't have looked more different. With his short roundness and Matthew's lankiness, they resembled nothing so much as an exclamation point. Still, the suits had their uses. Among other things, they tended to put the mourners into an action mode, and with today's tight schedule, they simply had no time to waste.

Upon wiggling his plump frame out of the limousine, however, he couldn't have received a more discouraging reception. From the open door of the Kovacek residence, angry shouts erupted into the sluggish air with the force of sonic booms. The cries drew several heads out of the parked cars like prairie dogs from their holes, and caused an old biddy from across the street to descend partway down her porch steps, as if the situation might somehow require her attention.

Edgar's whole body sagged. His first impulse was to let the family sort things out, the schedule be damned. But the heads from the parked cars were turning in his direction, and the sun was pressing down like a steam iron on high. Sighing, he buttoned his coat, drew in a long breath, and with a resolute wave of his head, motioned for Matthew to follow. Often his appearance alone was enough to patch over family tensions, at least until they reached the grave site, though in his short tenure as A.D., he'd never been tested by a full-blown altercation, and he sincerely hoped that today wasn't the official exam.

Arriving on the small porch, he double-checked the address on the support post and rang the bell. Through the screen door, he could make out two or three figures rigidly facing each other. The histrionics had ceased, but from the tense breathing within, it was apparent that the calm wouldn't last. He rang the bell again and rapped on the screen door, and when that failed to elicit a response–apparently, the whole family had entered rigor mortis–he smiled at Matthew, as if demonstrating a procedure, and let themselves in.

The interior was as tasteless as the outside. Blonde furniture, spongy gold carpet, brass pole lighting. All the allure of Early Rumpus Room. Though none of it was as disheartening as the threesome squaring off in the center of the living room.

In the "far corner," facing his way, stood a blonde female adolescent with her arms at her sides and her fists clenched, as if gathering herself for a throw in wrestling. The girl was rather incongruously dressed in blue jeans, a baseball jersey and tennis shoes, looking for all the world like she'd wandered in off the street.

Opposing her, with their backs mostly to Edgar, was a dowdy middle-aged couple, more properly attired, but hardly material for a fashion magazine. The male wore a navy polyester suit that bulged mightily over his burly shoulders, and the female was an absolute throwback to the War years, complete with gushing curls, pencil-thin eyebrows and lined nylons. She would have done Rosie the Riveter proud, though her dark serge dress and heavy mascara did little to enhance her ironing-board figure and pockmarked face.

As his eyes swept the room, Edgar also took in two small boys watching anxiously from a black sectional sofa, and in the adjacent dining room, a dark-haired girl of 16 or 17 with such large, round eyes and snowy complexion that Edgar's heart tripped off a few quick beats. He would have preferred to put his remarks to the young beauty, the only one showing any composure, but instead he cleared his throat and addressed the burly man–or rather his mountainous shoulders.

"Excuse me. Is this the Kovacek residence?"

The brute swiveled his head and started back. "What was that?"

Edgar closed his eyes for a moment. Some people needed to hear everything twice. "Is this the *Kovacek* residence?"

"Look, pal, I don't know what you're selling, but maybe you can come back another time. We're on our way out."

Edgar took a breath and lifted up on his toes. With certain members of the *hoi polloi*, you had to be steady but firm. "I'm looking for a Ruth Kovacek."

"Well, I'm in charge here, so whatever you got to say—"

"A family member, then?"

"Yeah, I'm a family member, and this is the Kovacek residence. And we're on our way to a *funeral*." The brute gave first Edgar and then Matthew a hard stare, as if the last information should send them on their way.

Edgar had to restrain a smile. Normally, he made the introductions at this point, but he found it more prudent to launch directly into his presentation.

"It appears we have the right place, then. We *are* somewhat ahead of schedule, but we find that if we get off to an early start, it smooths out the process and alleviates any undue harshness to the bereaved. Since you *are* in charge, I assume you know then that we'll be having a short service at the chapel and, following that, we'll proceed directly to the interment. In the meantime, we ask that you inform your driving guests to stay in a close line on their way to the memorial park, and to obey all LAPD traffic laws, including stopping at lights and stop signs. The immediate family, of course, will be accommodated by the limousine, which is now waiting outside to transport you in comfort." He smiled at the man, who continued to stare at him. "*So,*" Edgar continued, "given our full schedule, I'm sure you'll appreciate how important it is to 'get a move on,' as they say. That being the case, if you can make yourselves ready to depart *in…*" with a grand motion, he brought his arm around and gazed down at his Cartier watch, "*…six* minutes, it would be most helpful to everyone involved."

His gesture with the watch usually lit a flame under reluctant feet. And true to form, it did light a flame, only not the one he'd intended.

"Oh!" Rosie the Riveter cried out as if she'd been pinched on her flat behind. "You're our attendants!"

Edgar smiled dryly.

"They're our *attendants*, Max!"

The brute cocked his head to one side, and as Edgar watched, the information seemed to enter his face like fluorescent lighting, flickering at first and then blossoming into full wattage. The man's eyes fairly glowed as his features loosened around a sloppy grin.

"Why didn't you *say* so?" He grasped Edgar's hand firmly and squeezed Matthew's shoulder, as if they were locker-room familiars. "Glad to meecha. Sorry about the confusion. So everything all set?"

"You know, in Baltimore they wear the same kind of uniforms," Rosie the Riveter said. "You know what I mean, not uniforms but suits." She tapped Edgar with a bony finger, making him flinch. "They're like uniforms, but you know what I mean. They wear the same two-button suits back there. I thought out here they'd be different because they tend to go for different styles on the Coast. But then for funerals, you wouldn't expect—"

"Yes, thank you," Edgar interrupted.

"They *are* clean-looking," the woman added.

"Of course. So then, we'll see you outside *in*—" Edgar made another sweeping gesture with his watch "—*four* and a half minutes."

He smiled warmly all around. Not everyone returned it. The dark-haired beauty frowned, as if he'd disappointed her, and the towheaded girl glared with such hatred that he found himself reeling back a step. He returned to the beaming faces of the middle-aged couple, hoping fervently that the brute *was* in charge. Then he nodded to Matthew to follow him to the door.

As they reached it, Rosie rushed up and tapped him on the shoulder. "You know, the man's daughter doesn't want to go." She jerked her head toward the blonde girl. "What do you think of that? Don't you think it's a disgrace?"

The brute stepped forward. "Hon, I don't think—"

"It's okay," she said. "They deal with this kind of thing all the time."

Edgar sniffed. "Yes, we do tend to be all things to all people."

"You see?" She grimaced at her consort and turned back to Edgar. "Her mother doesn't have the strength to argue with her, but I've been trying to tell *this one* that she'll carry a torch for *years*. And I know what I'm talking about. I've seen it happen. You have to face up to your responsibilities or you fall apart. My cousin Harris didn't go to his father's funeral, and he's never gotten over it. He acts like he got the last shot in, but he's not fooling anyone…"

As the woman prattled on, Edgar understood that not only had the family lost its head of household, it had also lost its ability to function. He'd have to be very explicit in his instructions, more so than usual.

"By the way," he said, cutting the woman short. "I should mention that the limousine can carry *six* passengers comfortably–*eight* if there are children. More than that and I would suggest other means of transportation. Also, we ask that there be no potted plants at the service. Cut flowers only. Okay? And umm," he cleared his throat, "no fights on the cemetery grounds. Okay? *Hmm?*"

He raised his eyes at the brute, who shrugged, and then winked at the woman, whose mouth came down on a suppressed emotion. Before she could utter it, Edgar pulled Matthew out the door and made a show of examining his watch again. "We'll see you then in...*two and a quarter minutes.*"

"But what about the girl?" Rosie protested.

"Oh, she'll get over it. They always do."

With that, he escorted Matthew across the front lawn, confident that he'd set the family in motion. As they neared the limousine, however, there *was* a minor hiccup. From the front door, one of the little boys cried out, "The fat one looks like a choirboy!" It was followed by a slap and a sharp reproof from Rosie, along with a high-pitched howl from the boy, all of which Edgar found amusing. Choirboy, indeed!

Just the same, he stole a wary glance at Matthew. Bitter experience had taught him that he could never take a supervisory influence for granted, that it could evaporate in seconds. Though if the little boy's wisecrack had lessened Matthew's regard for him, there was no indication of it in his self-absorbed smile.

Back in the limousine, Edgar had Matthew start up the engine, both to hurry the family along and to get the air conditioning going. He didn't expect the Kovaceks to be ready in two minutes–*ten* was more like it–but even that would get them underway on time. Meanwhile, he rather enjoyed the insularity of the luxury car's interior with its sealed windows, padded seats and muting noises. It was the professional distance that he'd always yearned for, and with Matthew lost in himself, he was able to let his mind wander back to his tryst with Phyllis. Once again, he saw her delicate body flush pink wherever he touched her. And once again, he heard with amusement the sobriquets she dropped on his face like so many adoring petals–*my Jell-O Man, my Jack-in-the-Box, my Humpty-Dumpty*–as he brought her to a breathy climax. It was such a delectable memory, such a charming little reverie–and it didn't go at all with the screams erupting anew from the Kovacek residence.

He opened his eyes in time to see the blonde girl go flying out the door. Matthew lowered his window as if to offer directions, but the girl sprinted past, nearly knocking over a bespectacled gentleman walking up the lawn. The gentleman called to her–"Ginny" or "Fanny"–and then barked an order at Matthew. Edgar didn't catch the words, but he experienced the result. Matthew flung the limousine backwards into the street, spun the tires and went roaring off after the girl.

"Matthew! Matthew!"

They were halfway down the block before Edgar could prevail upon the boy to brake. Even then, they nearly ran the girl over. Only her deft execution of a quick left prevented the front bumper from knocking her flat. As the limo skidded to a halt, the girl sprinted up a neighbor's lawn, hopped a chain-link fence and disappeared into the back yard.

Edgar's heart was racing with the car's engine. "What the hell was *that* all about!"

The boy gaped at him.

"Never mind, never mind. We've got the whole neighborhood at their windows. Start driving–slowly." Edgar looked behind. The bespectacled gentleman was closing in on them. "A little faster."

They reached the end of the street.

"Which way?" Matthew asked.

"Left. Circle the block. We'll make like we're looking for her."

Edgar rubbed his eyelids with his fingertips. How in God's name had they been transformed from a funeral procession into a posse for a runaway teenager? With any luck, they could drive around the block and report back to the family that they'd lost sight of the girl, at which point he'd have to inform Rosie that, yes, it was permissible for a family member to miss a service, and no, it wouldn't be the first time. However, if they didn't move right along, it might be the first time on his watch that a *whole family* missed one.

Unfortunately, his plan fell through as soon as Matthew made the next left. The girl was standing in the middle of the street not a hundred feet away, frozen at the sight of the limousine like the proverbial deer in the headlights.

"Go slow," Edgar said.

They approached the girl, and as they drew closer, she had the good sense to dash across the street and take cover behind a house being built.

Edgar turned about in his seat–and let out a groan. The car they'd parked behind in the Kovacek driveway, a Dodge Dart, was rounding the corner. Edgar couldn't be sure if they'd seen the girl, but he wasn't taking any chances.

"Pull over," he ordered. "We're getting out."

"Where? Here?"

"Yes, here! Now!" He had to put a stop to this nonsense.

As they emerged from the limousine, Edgar couldn't contain himself. "What the hell were you thinking back there? Didn't we agree that *I* was in charge? How did you ever get it into your thick skull—?"

"You're right, I'm sorry. There I go again, screwing up. Always screwing up. Dutch talked about promoting me, but I'm just not cut out for this line of work." Matthew was waving his arms. "I'm just a daydreamer, a goddamn screwed-up daydreamer."

Edgar squeezed the boy's elbow and gently led him up the driveway of the partially built house. With all the other shenanigans, he didn't need another hysteric on his hands.

"Just relax. Dutch doesn't have to know about this. Take a deep breath and hold it."

Even as he consoled the boy, his own irritation was growing. No one had bothered to inform him of Matthew's rise in the organization.

Matthew exhaled. "It's just that the man with the glasses was yelling, 'Catch her! Catch her!' so I thought—"

"That was your first mistake."

"What?"

"Thinking. You don't know enough about this profession yet. That's my department."

"I guess. But the man with the glasses was yelling—"

"Do you know who that gentleman is?"

"No, who is he?"

"I haven't the foggiest. He could be their *meter* reader."

"But he was wearing a suit."

"So he enjoys dressing up for his work. Maybe he has a lady friend in the neighborhood."

Matthew's eyes grew large.

"The point is," Edgar lowered his voice, "if you're going to be a success in this business, you can't abide by their every wish. Otherwise, we'd never get them buried."

Edgar glanced at the street. The Kovacek car had parked behind the limousine. When he turned back to Matthew, his assistant's head was between the bare wooden beams of what would become an attached garage.

Edgar pulled him back. "Not so obvious. The neighbors will think we're looking for a corpse. In fact, don't really look. Just cast your eyes about."

Matthew rubbed the dust from his hands. "Does this happen all the time?"

"Of course. For the three o'clock, we get to chase down a Great Dane. A *canine*, that is, not a Scandinavian."

"Really?"

Edgar inhaled slowly.

The brute stepped out of the car accompanied by a dark-haired woman he hadn't seen before and one of the small boys. When the child lifted his head, Edgar had a shock of recognition. The boy sported the same whimsical grin that had lit up the dead man's face on the embalming table. It was almost as if the deceased had sprung back to life in a younger form.

Edgar squeezed Matthew's arm. "Let me handle this."

He approached the family with his most engaging smile. "The girl's perfectly safe. We saw her in the company of friends. They departed arm in arm."

"She doesn't have any friends," the boy said.

"Toby, shh." The woman stroked the boy's hair.

She had to be the widow. She was an older version of the dark-haired beauty in the house and not a bad-looking specimen herself. Grief, however, had raked deep lines across her forehead and drained the color from her face, revealing the bluish tint of her veins. It also made her small frame quaver, as if she was being buffeted by a wind. Edgar realized that it was only by a great force of will that she stayed on her feet at all.

"Maybe she's under the house," the boy cried. He scampered to the crawl space opening in the back. "Jenny!"

Edgar winced. The last thing he needed was to prolong the excitement.

"You see what happens, Ruth?" the brute said. "You gotta be strict or you'll lose control. It's for her good too."

"Max, please, enough for one day. Toby, don't go crawling under there or you'll get your suit dirty."

Edgar cleared his throat. "We do have a schedule to meet."

"I know you do," the widow said gently. "We won't keep you." To his astonishment, she touched his hand and gave him a little smile. "You have to understand that he meant everything to her."

"He means everything to me too," Edgar said.

His tone hadn't changed when he uttered this nonsense– he was all business–but as the words left his mouth, he experienced a sickening feeling that he'd never felt before, a leaden sensation that churned his stomach and set his cheeks aflame. He turned to Matthew, wondering how he might get the family moving again, and was stunned to see a smirk insinuating itself on his assistant's features. Edgar's cheeks burned deeper–his own face probably resembled a spotted apple in a bed of excelsior–and Matthew broke out into a radiant smile.

Edgar turned on his heel and marched back to the limousine. He dropped into his seat and slammed the door behind him. If the family wanted to spend the rest of the afternoon searching for a troubled teenager, that was fine with him, but he washed his hands of the matter. In fact, they could all go to hell, as far as he was concerned. Not only would this funeral be late, but so would the next one, and Dutch would finally have the excuse he needed to squeeze him out of the firm–and probably the family as well.

He looked up suddenly. The thought had come to him out of the blue, but it made perfect sense. It explained the silent treatment he was getting from Carol, as well as her run on their bank account. It also explained the old man's gruff manner and his insistence that Edgar view the corpse. Dutch wasn't offering Mr. Kovacek as a model of behavior. He was Edgar's pink slip, his walking papers, his busting down in rank. His services as A.D. were no longer needed, and the dead man's feckless smile was Dutch's way of showing him the door.

Edgar let his gaze drift upward to the sky. Above him, Mr. Kovacek's grin hovered like a flashbulb shadow, an inverted rainbow announcing to one and all that the world had developed a new axis and was gyrating out of control. And just as the little boy had suggested, Edgar's part in this new state of affairs would be greatly diminished. He'd be no better than an open mouth in the choir, one more fool among the multitudes, one more cipher filling in the background, all his work come to nothing.

A whimper tore itself from his throat. In God's name,

he'd tried to raise this business to a higher level, to lift it out of the bog of mediocrity and give it a sense of dignity. But fools and numskulls ran it and probably *would* run it to the end of time. Which is why he shouldn't have been surprised at Matthew's promotion. It made all the sense in the world. The boy already had the mindless demeanor. All he lacked were the social banalities.

The doors of the Kovacek car whined, and now the limousine swung open. Matthew slipped behind the wheel, already with the air of a manager about him.

"They still haven't found her," he announced, "but they're leaving anyway."

Edgar sniffed indifferently and looked away. He cared about as much as a fart in a windstorm.

Matthew cleared his throat and waited to be instructed. But Edgar had no more instructions to give As the Kovaceks drove off, the two of them sat in awkward silence staring straight ahead. Edgar suspected that they'd be here all day. The boy was simply incapable of acting on his own.

Not a moment later, however, Matthew reached down and started the engine, chuckling to himself. "Did you see how that blonde girl took that fence?"

"Yes," Edgar hissed. "She has a marvelous set of leg muscles."

Matthew yelped. "That's a good one. Wait'll I tell Dutch. Ha-ha-ha. *A marvelous set of leg muscles.*"

Then he slammed his foot on the accelerator, sending Edgar's considerable stomach deep inside his throat–and the contents even further.

4. Mountain Man
Toby

"HOW 'BOUT WE DON'T GO HOME?" Pa said. "We can fish for food and live in that deserted cabin by the river."

A full moon peered over the granite-faced cliffs, spreading its silver across the mountain meadow and touching a finger to the little river. Above them, the trees whispered their drowsy music, while a gray owl hooted and flew off deeper into the woods.

"And look over there." Pa pointed above the cliffs. Toby caught the last flicker of a shooting star. "We wouldn't have to pay for entertainment. It's all provided."

Pa turned the fish over in the pan, and the sizzle leapt up into the night. "Name your trout. Rainbow or cutthroat."

"Cutthroat," Toby said.

As the moon rose higher, two bandit-eyed raccoons crept from the shadows and sniffed about the campfire.

"Watch this," Pa said.

He held out a marshmallow, and one of the raccoons snatched it with rubbery black fingers. It then whirled about and made a dash for the river.

"They clean everything they eat. Nature's healthiest critters."

A soft splashing reached them.

Pa handed a marshmallow to the second raccoon, and it scampered after its companion.

"Don't forget where you got it!"

Pa's laughter boomed across the meadow, echoing against the trees. Then it grew brittle and thin, as if enclosed in a jar.

"Toby, are you with us? Toby?" Mrs. Darcy peered down at him from where the moon had been. Behind her, the walls of the classroom hardened into a faded pea green. "Toby, are you all right?"

"Sure. Why not?"

His classmates giggled.

"Then maybe you can answer the question. Who established the missions in California? It's on the test tomorrow."

Toby shut one eye.

His teacher leaned closer. "We discussed it yesterday. Father…"

"Father Time?"

The class broke up. A couple of boys laid their heads on the desks and pounded their fists.

"Can anyone help? Shhhh. There's a class next door."

Several hands shot up. A few of the children groaned.

"Ricky."

"Father Serra."

"That's right. Father Junipero Serra. Toby, am I going to have to call your mother again? How can I give you a passing grade if you don't know California history?"

He shrugged.

Mrs. Darcy sighed and returned to the front of the classroom. From the back, her waddle resembled the raccoons in Toby's daydream. She gave the children an assignment for the rest of the afternoon, and then settled into her chair with a thick volume, on the cover of which a startled young woman was being swept into the arms of a one-eyed pirate.

Toby stared down at his desk, but he couldn't read. The tangy aroma of frying trout came back to him, along with the whisper of the pine trees and the rustling of the little river. Somehow he had to get back to the High Sierras, back to the mountain meadow where he and Pa had camped out. The other prisoners might be resigned to their fate, scratching out last words on lined sheets of paper, but Toby had a plan. Tomorrow at dawn, when they were being led to the hanging tree, he was going to make a run for it. He knew where the spare horses were kept, and with a little help from Juan Pimento and his band of Tijuana rustlers, he could be in the foothills in an hour, the High Sierras in two. He just needed to get word to Juan.

Maybe Carla would help. She sat in the back by the open door, and though she'd called him a creep after last week's hoedown, it was all a big misunderstanding. He hadn't meant to kill her pet Brahma bull. He'd only ridden it hard because it had thrown every other rider in the territory. He was sure if he could just look into her pine-green eyes and tell her how sorry he was, she'd take a note to Juan.

He turned in his seat to see how she was holding up, but Ricky the Outlaw intercepted his gaze.

"What?" Toby said. Ricky had muttered something under his breath

"I said, 'I'm going to bash your teeth in.'"

"Why?"

"Because you owe me a dollar."

"I don't owe you anything." Toby turned back to the front.

The desk behind him creaked. "Don't think you're tough just because your old man kicked the bucket. I bet he was a punk like you."

"Shut up."

"I bet he was a punk and got what he deserved. You don't see *my* parents dying."

Toby's throat tightened. He stared ferociously at an ink

drawing of Father Serra holding his hand over a kneeling Indian.

"Hey, I'm talking to you, fag. You better pay up or your ass is grass."

Toby felt a painful snap on the back of his ear. He turned his head to the side. "I don't owe you anything."

"Don't give me that shit."

Toby reached into his pocket and put a quarter on Ricky's desk.

"What's this crap? It's a *dollar*."

"I don't have it."

"Then I'm gonna have to bash your teeth in."

Toby bit savagely at his nails. He stared at his book, but the words jumped all around the page.

A loud bang made his heart kick.

"Pick it up, Toby!"

"Ricky, please." Mrs. Darcy removed her reading glasses. "Everyone's trying to work."

"But he knocked my book on the floor."

"Ricky, if you don't settle down, I'll have to send you both to the principal's office."

Toby picked up the book and returned it to the boy's desk.

"Yuck!" Ricky scraped it against his desktop. "Did you have to get your slobber all over it?"

The other children laughed.

"Ricky!" Mrs. Darcy glared at him and turned back to her reading.

The desk behind Toby creaked. "We'll settle this after school, fag."

Toby swallowed hard and continued to stare at his book. It wasn't the first time he'd been in a tough spot. There was that incident in Dodge City when the Winslow Gang thought they had him cornered. And there was that little episode on the plains when the Kiowa had set a trap, not knowing that a squaw had tipped him off. But he'd never been caught flat-footed before–he'd always had some warning. His only chance now was to fly out the door before Ricky knew what happened.

He stared at the clock, and as the minutes ticked away, he crouched in his seat and tensed his feet, and when the hour struck, he was out the door like the wind. Down the banks of a dry creek he flew, toeing his way past prairie dog holes and scrub brush, running with the surefootedness the Dakotas had taught him, moving so fast that the ground fell away beneath him. In no time, the border heaved into view. It was guarded by enemy troops, but with one good surge, he could—

"I said, 'No running!' Do you know what that means?"

He felt himself being lifted.

"Last week, a boy lost a tooth. Is that what you want?" Miss Benjamin held him by the collar.

He shook his head. He wished she'd let him go. The third-graders were staring.

"Now I want you to go back to your classroom and walk back. *All* the way. And I do mean *walk*." She released him and turned to another child.

Toby stood there for a moment with his throat knotted up. Then he felt a painful snap on the back of his ear.

"Thought you could get away from me, didn't you, fag?" Ricky fixed him with a sneer. "I'll be waiting for you when you get back. And you better have my dollar or your ass is grass."

Toby retraced his steps, but when he reached his classroom, he didn't turn around. Instead, he continued to the edge of the playground and climbed over the chain-link fence, slipping into a wide stretch of desert-like land that cut a diagonal through the neighborhood. The land was home to twin rows of soaring electrical towers, and at the foot of one of these giants, Toby found his ammunition cache and began firing away.

He meant to be ready for tomorrow's showdown. The

whole town would be watching, and it wasn't going to be pretty. When he was done with Ricky, the little punk was going to cry out for mercy, just like the towers cried out when he scored a direct hit. Just like the crows cried out when he made them scatter. And even then, he wouldn't let up. Not until he'd reduced Ricky to a bloody pulp.

He fired away until the sweat stung his eyes and his throat was raw, until the clang of metal ricocheted in his ears. Then he slipped one last stone into his pocket and headed into town. He was ready to take on Ricky this minute. This very second. But the punk was nowhere to be seen. He was only tough in school. Outside, he was just a coward. A sissy. A teacher's pet.

Toby strode up the main street and into the saloon. He found his favorite brew and slapped it on the counter along with his coin. One of the townswomen smiled at him. She probably knew his reputation in these parts.

"So *you're* the one putting these in my Coke machine." The barkeep eyed his coin suspiciously.

Toby felt his cheeks flush. It was one of his plug nickels. He fished in his pocket for his quarter, but he remembered now that he'd given it to Ricky.

"You think I'm stupid?" Mr. Palmieri said. "You think I don't know what you kids are up to? Your father's a smart man. I don't know why you can't be more like him. You kids ought to be ashamed of yourselves, trying to get something for nothing."

The townswoman whispered to the storeowner.

Mr. Palmieri nodded with a grunt. "I'm sorry to hear that, but you know these kids. They're supposed to be honest."

"For God's sake." The woman opened her purse. "How much can a soda cost?"

Toby slipped away and headed for the back. The woman called to him, but he continued out the door. He didn't need her charity. And he didn't need Mr. Palmieri's insults. He'd never stolen anything in his life, not even that time in Woolworth's when Ricky had dared him to slip a Three Musketeers into his pocket. Ricky did things like that all the time, but *he* never did. He just caught hell for it.

In the back parking lot, the sun made his eyes water, and he stumbled into Mr. Palmieri's brand new Mustang. He gave the tomato-red sedan a kick and took out his knife. Old Bess would set things to rights. She always did. And sure enough, within minutes, she'd carved the famous Circle TK brand under the door handle. It meant the car was Toby's now, according to the law of the West, but he didn't feel like taking it yet. Besides, Old Bess wasn't done.

On a slab of wet cement by the front corner of the store, she carved another Circle TK. Then she carved "Carla" and "Ricky" and put a heart around the names, and when Toby stood up to examine her work, he nearly fell over. It looked like Ricky had done it, which was just what the bastard deserved. In fact, Toby ought to carve his name *all over* town. Then people would find out what a punk he really was.

He looked around for the next likely spot, but when he glanced down at the sidewalk again, his heart sank. It should've been *his* name above Carla's. *He* was the one who liked her. He just couldn't tell her yet, not until he ran off to the Sierras and came back in buckskins and scraggly hair, with a rifle in the crook of his arm. Then Ricky would crap in his pants just to look at him. Then people would—

A car honked and Toby dropped the pocketknife. But it wasn't meant for him.

"Don't you know how to signal!" An elderly man in a beige Impala shook his fist at a blue-and-white Falcon.

The driver of the Falcon, a prim, gray-haired woman, raised her middle finger as she completed her turn.

Toby felt the blood rush to his face. He'd never seen an adult use that gesture before, and it made him feel a little gritty inside.

He picked up Old Bess and headed back down the road. It was high time he was getting home anyway. The womenfolk were probably wondering where he was. He could just hear his older sister scolding him when he came in late again. "Where do you go all the time? Can't you be home at a decent hour?" Ever since Pa had left, she'd taking to bossing him around, as if she owned the place. Not that it was any of *her* business what he did. In fact, maybe he wouldn't go home at all. Maybe he'd light out for the Sierras this very day. All he needed was a hand-printed sign, like the one he'd seen some hippies holding on a freeway onramp, and with a couple of rides, he could be up there before nightfall. He could sleep in the deserted cabin he and Pa had found and fish for his food. And when the fish weren't biting, there was always the $20 bill he had stashed away in his drawer. It wasn't the best of plans, but it was better than hanging around here, waiting for Ricky to kick his butt. And it was better than failing another test at school.

He chuckled to himself as he made his way down the road, imagining the blank looks on his classmates tomorrow morning when Mrs. Darcy called his name and nobody answered. "Where's Toby?" people would say. "What happened to him?" It was worth it just for that, even if he *was* daydreaming. Even if he *was* living in Fantasyland, like his sister Jenny said all the time.

And yet, the closer he got to home, the more the idea wrapped itself around him like a deerskin jacket, growing warmer and cozier with every step. By the time he reached his own street, he had to draw himself up and lean on the metal sign pole to steady himself. He understood suddenly that nothing was holding him back. Nothing whatsoever. He just had to make up his mind to go, and no one could lift a finger to stop him.

He gazed around at the neighborhood, at the modest one-story homes that had seemed so imposing all his life. In the harsh light of the afternoon sun, they appeared puny and frail, barely able to contain the lives inside them. And the busy main street, which had once formed the very edge of his existence, looked like nothing more than a way out of town.

With his heart beating in his throat, he waited for the traffic to clear, and then bolted across the street. If he *was* going to light out, he had some unfinished business to take care of first.

Turning down a path known only to scouts, he picked his way around the edge of a steep canyon and cut through a forest so dark it hid the freckles on his forearms. Then he leapt over a chasm that would have made Ricky faint and climbed down the sheer face of a rocky cliff, and before the sun had descended one hand, he was in the secret Dakota burial grounds. It was a place so foreboding, even the U.S. Cavalry avoided it, but Toby wasn't afraid. He strode right down the middle of the trail, daring the Indian spirits to show themselves. He knew they were here. On previous visits, he'd heard the knock of their hammers clear across the grounds, and he'd seen flocks of birds squawking from tree to tree, as if fleeing their approach. But today, it was quiet—even the birds were asleep—and he made it to the center of the grounds without any trouble.

Disappointed, he sat by a spring the beavers had dammed and gazed into the still, dark water. His reflection stared back, a blob of pale features with a thatch of straw-colored hair and ears that stuck out like open wings. No wonder Ricky picked on him. He *did* look like a fag. He jabbed at the water, and his face wavered. Then he wiped his hand on his jeans and turned away.

Across the wide cemetery lawns, the brass markers glimmered in the sun like flattened bookends. It was his first visit here since the funeral, and he found it hard to believe that his father was out there with all the other dead people. Only two Saturdays ago, they'd gone fishing at Playa del Rey, and Pa had buffed his head so vigorously when he brought up his first catch that he still felt the big, rough hand on his hair. He hadn't heard Pa's voice for a while now, or seen him puttering around the house, but Toby's own life hadn't changed all that much. He still slept in his old room and went to his old school, and his mother still asked the same dumb questions at dinner every night. Even the same annoying relatives came by to visit, usually when he didn't feel like having them around. If he didn't know any better, he'd have thought that his father was working late at the office or away on business. What brought him up short was the memory of the casket with the lifeless figure inside. It had looked more like a mannequin than Pa, but he couldn't shake the image from his head.

He followed the flight of a feathery blue damselfly as it approached the fountain and came to rest on a lily pad. He wondered what it felt like to be dead. To lie buried underground and not wake up again. To just stay there forever and ever. Though maybe they didn't have to lie there *all* the time. Maybe they could come and go as they pleased, sort of drift up through the grass when no one was watching.

The damselfly slowly raised its tail, and Toby felt a numbness edging down his spine. He whirled about–but there was nothing there, no horde of grinning faces. Just the gently rolling lawns baking in the afternoon sun. The shadow of an airplane passed over, and the grave markers winked at him.

He turned back to the pond and stabbed at his reflection. It was stupid to be afraid. Besides, outside of the Sierras, this was his favorite fishing hole. He used to come here all the time just to horse around. He'd even brought Ricky once, though the punk had been nervous the whole time. He tried to hide it, but Toby could tell. He kept rubbing his arms and taking short breaths and looking over his shoulder. Ricky thought he was tough, but he was just a sissy. A stupid faggedy bastard little sissy. He was even sorry that he'd brought him here. The punk didn't deserve this place.

Toby swept his arm through the water and brought up a handful of wiggling black tadpoles, some no bigger than marbles. He pitched them onto the cement border, where the heat baked them to a satisfying smudge. Then he pitched out several more handfuls until he had a long, cloudlike shadow arching from the pond. He flipped out the lily pad with the damselfly on it, and he was about to flip out another, when a high-pitched voice jolted him.

"What the hell you doin' there! I just worked on that fountain."

He looked up. A brave in war paint was charging down on him, waving a spear dressed in eagle feathers. The brave cried out again, and as he closed in, he raised the spear as if he meant to hurl it. Toby stumbled to his feet and lit out for the edge of the burial grounds.

Usually he had no trouble eluding Fultzie–the old groundskeeper had a bad limp and was blind in one eye– but Toby didn't have his bike today, and Fultzie was driving a motorized cart. He was also waving a leaf rake, as if he meant to swat him with it, which he nearly did once or twice. Toby just managed to duck under his swing or change directions at the last second, though as he neared the ivy-covered wall, his legs were giving out and he was almost out of breath. With one last burst of energy, he took a desperate leap—

—and as the spear sailed over his shoulder, he clawed his way up the jagged face of the cliff. At the summit, he rose unsteadily to his feet and gazed down into the deep canyon on the other side, down into a river that cut a snake-like path in the shadowy earth far below. He meant to turn around and taunt the brave, but a gust of wind carried him over, and the ground came up suddenly, jamming his knee.

"Goddamn kids!" Fultzie called after him.

A sprinkling of mud fell on Toby's head. And then another before he hobbled out of range.

"Next time you won't be so lucky." Fultzie's cart clicked into gear and drove off. "Keep away from this place."

"Fuck you," Toby wheezed under his breath.

He stayed bent over, gasping for air. The brave had injured him deeply–a knife wound to the bone–but there was nothing to be done for it. He was fifty miles from the ranch and in the middle of the Badlands. And his horse was dead–dead from drinking poison root beer that Mr. Palmieri had pissed in. He'd just have to walk it off and hope that he didn't run into any more hostiles.

Each step brought a stab of pain, but by the time he reached the main road, he could walk without a limp. And when he turned down his own street, he was fairly swaggering. He hogged the center of the road, daring any car to honk him out of the way, but none came, not even Mr. Palmieri's Mustang, which technically belonged to him.

Approaching the ranch house, he could hear the womenfolk watching TV in the living room. He knew he'd have to run their gauntlet, so he headed straight for the stable and pulled open the big door. Ma had warned him not to go in there–the place had been Pa's workshop–but he wasn't going to touch anything. He was just passing through. Couldn't a guy grab his gear?

After a few steps inside, however, the life went out of his legs. He stood stock-still and slowly drew in his breath. All around him, dust motes circled like a gentle snowfall, catching fire here and there in the descending sun as it entered behind him through the open door. The light soaked into the rust-colored plasterboard, turning it a molten red, and glinted off the steely faces of the tools that lined the walls. It came to rest on a handful of sawhorses scattered about the room, each one bent over a mound of wood shavings, as if feeding after a long day's work. One of the sawhorses was still saddled with a two-by-four, a giant handsaw lying across its withers.

Toby was drawn to the handsaw, and when he picked it up, he was surprised that his fingers nearly fit the handle grooves. Though why shouldn't they? Wasn't he the man of the house? Isn't that what everyone said?

He lowered the handsaw to the clamped-down board and cut a shallow line, as his father had shown him. Then he started pumping wildly, shooting spurts of sawdust into the air. After three or four strokes, the blade caught and bent like a bow, nicking his finger.

He threw it to the floor and wheeled about. "I don't have to!"

But there was no one there–only the cloud of sawdust that he'd raised.

He scanned the room. If that tool wouldn't do, then another one would. And sure enough, at the end of the workbench, he found what he was looking for. It was Pa's favorite piece, a tool so noisy and powerful that the neighbors would clap their hands over their heads just to keep their teeth inside their jaws. But Toby wasn't afraid. He plugged it in and pressed the trigger, and though the power saw whinnied and bucked, as if it weren't used to strange hands, he managed to bring it over to the clamped-down board and drove it in, sending its howl flying out the door and bounding over the trees. He drove it in again, and it charged down the street, rattling the houses on both sides. He drove it in a third time, and it plowed deep into the earth, shaking the planet to its core. Then it turned on him–sank its burning teeth into his hand–and he was thrown clear.

He waited for his head to hit, for the floor to come flying up, but he found himself falling as if there were nothing below him, as if he were plummeting from the very rim of the sky. On and on he fell, past his sisters, who came running into the garage and stared with frozen faces. Past his mother, who frantically tore at her blouse and wrapped it around his hand. Past the neighborhood children, who hurried up on stumpy legs with their mouths agape and their eyes wide, and past their parents, who tried to hold them back. He fell past old Mrs. Weaver from across the street, who wailed like a siren and pulled at her stalks of gray hair, and past the paramedics in their starchy uniforms, who bundled him up like a papoose, though even they couldn't break his fall. He tried to tell them–but his mother put a hand to his mouth. He tried to tell them that he had to be in the Sierras before nightfall–he didn't think he could find the cabin in the dark–but his mother whispered in his ear, and as the ambulance drove off, the sun plunged into the horizon, burning it to cinders.

In the darkness, Pa's face bent over him laughing.

"Thought you could get away from me, didn't ya?" He stirred the campfire with a stick. "Throw that in too."

He pointed to Toby's left hand, which was nearly sawn off. Toby threw it in, and the flames leapt up.

Pa placed two fish in the frying pan. "Name your trout. Rainbow or cutthroat."

"Cutthroat," Toby said.

A full moon peered over the granite-faced cliffs, spreading its silver across the mountain meadow and touching a finger to the little river. Above them, the trees whispered their drowsy music, while a gray owl hooted softly and flew off deeper into the woods.

As the moon rose higher, they could make out two ragged figures stumbling toward them in the distance. The men had rifles in the crooks of their arms and three or four rabbits dangling from their shoulders.

Pa waved over his head and the men waved back, hastening their steps.

"Where you headed?" Pa asked when they came into the

firelight.

"Grizzly Gap," the larger of the two said. The man could have passed for a grizzly himself. He had flaring eyebrows and a bulging forehead that looked more bear-like than human. "We're looking for a one-handed scout named Toby."

Pa threw a stick at Toby's feet. "Well, you found him, but he don't come cheap."

The man grunted. "We'll pay. Name your price. I sure as hell ain't going there alone."

Pa pointed to the rabbits. "How 'bout a couple of those?"

The mountain men looked at each other.

"Sure," the skinny one said. "We'll even cook 'em for you. How's that?"

"Sounds fine."

The men dropped their packs and eased up to the fire.

"Boy, it sure is spooky out there," the stout one said. He sighed as he stretched out his legs.

"Well, you're fine now," Pa said.

The skinny one chuckled nervously. "You can say that again." He opened a whiskey tin and passed it around.

When it came to Toby, he took a healthy pull. He didn't fancy going down to the lowlands again. It had taken enough trouble just to get up here. And like Pa said, this was home now. But as the whiskey burned a trail down his gut, he saw how the men kept glancing in his direction. Obviously, they were counting on him.

He threw Old Bess into the ground. Oh, hell, he'd take them. What else could he do? If they'd come all this way just to seek him out, then he couldn't very well say no and leave them to their fate. Not fellow mountain men, anyways. And not here in the darkest of woods.

5. Loci
Jenny

MY FATHER DIED SUDDENLY IN 1966 when I was fourteen, though even now I still find it hard to believe. I'll look up sometimes and expect him to be standing in front of me with that stupid grin on his face. Or I'll hear a laugh like his, and it's like he's right there in the room with me. I know it can't possibly be true, but too many things have happened for me to think that somehow, someway, he isn't around.

Nowadays, I can pretty much deal with his passing, but at the time, it was just a disaster. I kept waiting for him to come breezing through the front door with that gleam in his eyes, or to buff me on the head when I got pissed about something. I thought any day now he'd take us fishing again, or his power saw would fire up and go tearing through the neighborhood, or we'd go to another Dodger game, like he'd been promising all summer. But none of these things happened, and for the longest time, I couldn't understand why.

I refused to go to the funeral. I got into this big fight over it with my aunt and uncle, and went flying out the door just as everybody was leaving. And when I came back to an empty house, I threw away all the refreshments Mom had put out for the guests and locked the screen door so nobody could get in. Then I went down into the garage, which Dad used as his workshop. I was going to bust it up, but before I could, I started bawling and I had to sit on the floor. I kept thinking that even if he did show up, I'd never forgive him. Not if he buffed me on the head a thousand times. Not if we went fishing every day of the week. He just had no business leaving us. None at all. The whole thing was so stupid.

And then, right in the middle of my bawling, I heard this flat chuckle.

I looked up, but the room was empty. It was just me and a beam of sunlight pouring through the small window on the side, lighting up all these dust motes. There wasn't anything outside either when I got up to check, just the blotchy ivy drooping on our fence and the house next door shimmering in the heat. I even climbed up the wall ladder to the loft, but all I found was a bunch of moldering plywood and some discarded tools.

"Dad?"

I said it softly, and then a little louder as I climbed back down. The garage gave off a slight echo, but otherwise there was nothing. Not even a peep. Though I was sure I'd heard something. I hadn't just dreamt it up.

I sat back down against the wall again, only quietly this time. What made it so hard was that the place looked like he'd just left it. The floor was covered with sawdust and wood shavings, and tools were scattered all over the place. There was even a long narrow board clamped to a sawhorse, as if he'd tightened it down only seconds ago. It was almost as if the room was holding its breath, just waiting for him to come back.

I closed my eyes and hugged my knees to my chest. I thought if I could just think about him hard enough, I could bring him back. And in a way, I did. I mean, I could almost sense him moving around the room, like he would sometimes when he was thinking over a new project or looking for a tool or something. I even had the feeling that he could see me sitting there, and any second, he'd come over and buff me on the head and tell me where he'd been. It'd be our little secret, something we wouldn't share with anybody, and just the thought of it made me laugh a little. And right at that moment, when I was laughing, I felt this warmth go charging through me, the way it did sometimes when we'd horse around and get into these wrestling matches, and it made me feel so snug and cozy all of a sudden that I couldn't stay awake. I just conked out right there in the garage.

And when I woke up, the house was full of voices. It sounded like we were having another PTA meeting or as if Dad's acting club had come over for a rehearsal. I even heard him tell a story and laugh about it–or I thought I did. But when I ran up to check, it was just the people back from the funeral. My little brother must've crawled through a window to let everybody in.

I tried to beat it out of there, but my grandmother pulled me down next to her on the sectional, and she wouldn't let me go. And while she slobbered over me, everybody came by to tell me how sorry they were and what a great guy Dad had been and how much they were going to miss him. They told me that I'd have to be 14-going-on-20 now to help my mother, and that I'd have to do something really special with my life to make Dad proud. One woman even said I should find somebody else his age and act like *he's* my father. "The man doesn't have to know. Just pretend that he is."

It really pissed me off–the whole thing, I mean, not just her stupid remark–but there was nothing I could do about it. I just had to sit there and take it till they all went home.

* * *

I couldn't stay away from the garage after that. Mom didn't want us down there, but I'd sneak in anyway and sit against the back wall, and though I never heard the laugh again, if I closed my eyes and breathed in the smells of wood and grease, I could almost always get a sense of him. Sometimes I'd poke around the room and pick up one of his tools, and whenever I did, I'd feel the tiniest spark, as if he'd just put it down. Or I'd sit on one of the sawhorses and swing my legs underneath, like I used to when I was little and I'd come in here to watch him work, and at those moments, I could just picture him whooshing away with the giant handsaw, filling the room with clouds of sawdust. Though most of the times I went down there, I'd just hunch up against the wall like I had during the funeral and think about him. Because if I stayed there long enough–say, until the sunlight slashed through the sides of the big door–I could hear him call to me just above a whisper. "Muffin."

And it wasn't only in the garage. I started to sense him in other parts of the house as well. Like, I could be walking down the hallway, and suddenly, I'd get a whiff of his Old Spice after-shave, as if he and Mom were going out again. Or late in the day, I could be nodding off in front of the TV, and the floorboards under the living room carpet would start creaking step by step, as if he'd just come home from work and was trying to sneak up on me. Or sometimes, when Mom got lazy about making up the bed, there'd be this raunchy odor on Dad's side, as if he'd been farting all night–which there often had been.

And every so often, when I had trouble falling asleep at night, I'd hear the faintest tapping of a typewriter, as if he'd taken up writing again and was working on his one big story, "The Great Hairy Coconut." It was about this six-foot, talking coconut who goes around organizing rebellions, and this jerk of a hunter who tracks him down all over the world and just keeps missing him. Dad thought it was really neat–he even hoped they'd make it into a movie–but when he showed it to us, I thought it was the dumbest thing I'd ever read, and I told him so. I think only Toby liked it, that's how bad it was. But now, when I came to breakfast the next morning, I'd be so disappointed when there wasn't another chapter waiting for us.

I know it sounds like I was flipping out, or as if I was carrying a torch, like my Aunt Maddy said. But I wasn't the only one. I could see it in the others as well, like when this vague smile showed up on my mother's face, as if she was listening to him. Or when my little brother got cranky, which was his way of dealing with too much roughhousing. Or when my sister had a fit for God knows what reason.

I'd even see it in my grandmother when she came to visit. She'd get this annoyed look on her face, as if she'd been complimented for something that she didn't value too highly. As far as I knew, it was a look that she'd had only around Dad.

And I'd see it in people *outside* the family, like when his buddies dropped by for a "pit stop," as Margot called their brief stopovers. They'd sit in the living room with their legs crossed and their faces all polite, while Mom served them coffee and cake, but you could tell by the way they hung their shoulders and winked at each other that they weren't taking it seriously. It was like they were just playing along, just going through the motions, until Dad came barging into our lives again.

And one day, he very nearly did.

It happened on this hot, smoggy afternoon, when all you could do was flake out in front of the TV. Margot and I were watching some putrid adventure movie, and just as the neighbors were coming home from work and the sun was starting to go down, turning the smog into this hazy bronze, Dad's power saw fired up and went ripping through the neighborhood. And for the first couple minutes, Margot and I just sat there staring at each other, as if we didn't know what to make of it. Nobody used the power saw but Dad. I mean, *nobody*. But there it was, tearing into the wood, making the walls and the furniture shake and sending the sawed-off end plunking to the ground. Then it tore into the wood two or three *more* times, and each time you could hear the house kind of sigh and echo in return, and you could hear the whine bouncing back from the end of the street, and you could hear all the sounds of the neighborhood–like some kid bawling a few doors down or a car door slamming or these girls playing four-square in the street–as if they were right on our front porch. As if the power saw had just picked them up and dropped them outside our door, just like in the old days.

Then we heard the screams, and we knew something was up. Though even as we went flying out there, I still expected to find Dad's horsy face in the garage. And I wasn't disappointed. When I turned the corner, all the old features stared up at me from the floor–the pale blue eyes, the heavy eyebrows, the long, sharp nose, the square jaw with the slight cleft–as if he'd never disappeared. As if he'd been there all along. Though his face looked small, almost shrunken. And he seemed so old, so very old. Then he gasped, and I realized it was my little brother down there in the wood shavings. Somehow Toby had come into Dad's face years before his time.

I don't know what would've happened if Mom hadn't been right behind us. Probably he'd have bled to death, because his hand was really gushing, and Margot and I just stood there like a couple of fools. But Mom tore off the bottom of her blouse and used it as a tourniquet. Then she had Margot call an ambulance and sent me to get blankets and gauze. It took me forever because I couldn't find *anything*, and when I got back, it was like half the neighborhood was standing in our driveway. And they weren't just rubbernecking. They were all gasping or yelling at their kids to stay away or having their own private meltdown. Like this old lady who lived across the street from us, Mrs. Weaver. She kept screaming, "That poor boy! That poor boy! First the father and now this." When the medics arrived, they actually thought *she* was the one who needed help. They even wrestled her to the ground to give her some oxygen. But then the neighbors pointed out Toby to them, and they wrapped him up and carted him away. They even got everybody to back up a little and give us some breathing room.

But after they drove off, the crowd still didn't disperse. Everybody had to hang around and discuss it fifty million times. And whenever somebody new came home, they wanted us to tell the story all over again.

I finally went into the house and crawled into bed. I just wanted to drown them out. But there was no getting away from it. People started bringing over food, as if *that's* what we needed. And then these little kids started holding relay races on our front lawn, right outside my window. It was like the whole block had been riled up and couldn't settle down.

Though even with all the chaos–even with Mom calling from the hospital every so often to give us updates–and even with Margot and me working half the night to clean up the garage, while cars honked by at all hours, as if we'd put on a carnival or something–even *then*, I still had this sinking feeling, like a hollowness in my chest, that we'd just missed Dad. That somehow he'd slipped away on us moments before we could get there, and if we'd only been paying attention, we could've caught up with him.

* * *

Toby came through his ordeal okay. He lost his thumb and most of his index finger, and he nearly died of shock, but his status among his buddies rose enormously. When they came to visit him in the hospital, he'd hold up his hand with this huge bandage and say, "Not so fast. Not so fast," like some hero in a western. And he got an autographed baseball with all the Dodgers' signatures on it from this freckly-faced girl named Carla. He was pretty quiet when *she* was there, but he really liked that baseball. He slept with it for weeks, holding on tight with his good hand.

The rest of us, though, were just blown away. Mom took to smoking again, which she'd given up years ago, and she developed these dark shadows under her eyes. And Margot came down with this horrendous cold that just wouldn't go away. It kept her in bed for days. And for the longest time, I couldn't fall asleep at night. I'd lay awake for hours trying to imagine my little brother living the rest of his life with half a hand, and the air around me would stir into these little eddies and grow deeper, but still I couldn't fall asleep. It was almost as if we'd lost Dad again, as if this huge void had opened up on our lives and we'd never be able to cross it.

Then Toby came home from the hospital, and things weren't so great for him either. He spent most of his time in bed playing electric baseball, though he *could've* gone out. He wasn't an invalid or anything. But every time I went through his room to get to the garage, which was the only way in there from the house, I'd see him in his pajamas. Sometimes he'd lock the door behind me just to be a twerp, and Mom would give him hell for doing it, and me for going in there, but it didn't stop either of us.

Of course, that was nothing compared to what Mom did. Not long after Toby came home, she decided to clean out the garage, and nothing I said could stop her. I went around slamming doors for a day, and even Margot tried to reason with her, telling her it was all we had left of Dad. But she wouldn't budge, and within a week, she'd given everything away, including the sawhorses. Then she scrubbed the place so thoroughly, you'd never have known it was a workshop. All that was left was the shadowing on the walls where the tools had once hung.

I still went down there, but it wasn't the same anymore.

It was just a big, empty room without even a trace of Dad. And it was the same with the rest of the house, because while she was at it, Mom decided to clean out *all* of his things, like his clothes and his alligator shoes and even the dumb little gifts he used to bring home from clients. Most of it was junk, like this globe-like lamp that never really worked, or pens with three different colors of ink, or this plastic coin bank with a picture of a George Washington from the dollar bill. When you put in a coin, George would roll his eyes as it went down the slot. I mean, they were really stupid gifts, but still, it was kind of neat to run into them once in a while. It was almost like running into Dad again. I could even hear him saying, "Boy, are you lucky! Are you ever lucky!" as if the person he'd just given it to had been pining away all their lives for nothing else. But after Mom cleaned the house of his things, it was like she'd cleaned the house of *him* as well.

I stopped talking to her after that. I even thought of running away. I was going to hop a freight train and take it to Dad's home town in upstate New York, just like he did when he first came out to California. But for one reason or another, I never got around to it. Instead, I started cruising the neighborhood on my bike, or taking city buses to places I'd never been before. I thought if I could just turn down the right street or stumble into the right part of town, I'd run into Dad again. And every so often, I did–only never quite the way I expected.

Like, I could be walking to school on an overcast morning, and the sun would be barely visible behind the clouds, just this pale little disk poking through here and there in solitary beams. But where it did poke through, it gave me the strongest feeling that Dad was trying to reach me, that this was his way of communicating, even if it was in a strange language that I couldn't understand.

Or I'd be sitting in my English class, and a bus would come wheezing to a stop outside, and I'd be so sure that he'd just gotten off. I'd even go up to the window to check, which didn't go over too well with my teacher, Mrs. Hartley.

Or once in Geometry, when I came in late, Mr. Bernstein squeezed the back of my neck, and I felt this warmth go charging through me, the way it did sometimes when Dad and I would horse around and get into these wrestling matches, and for the rest of the class, I didn't hear a thing. I just sat there waiting for Dad to come barging through the door.

I tried coming in late again, but Mr. Bernstein just marked me down for being tardy, which really pissed me off. I mean, it wasn't like I was one of the delinquent kids or anything–I usually showed up on time. But I couldn't stay mad for long. He just reminded me too much of Dad. Like, he had the same pale-blue eyes and cleft chin, and the same screwy sense of humor. And besides, he was the one who helped me figure out what was going on. Not that he said anything about Dad–all he ever talked about was geometry–but one day, he started lecturing about this thing called loci, which he pronounced "low-sigh," and nothing was ever the same again.

"Okay, people," he said. "How many of you do *not* see a line on the blackboard?" He picked up his yardstick and rapped it on the blackboard, which was completely blank.

Everybody raised their hand but me. I was sure I'd get it wrong again.

But he looked me straight in the eye with that lopsided grin of his. "Jennifer Kovacek, you are a very perceptive person, a true mathematician, and don't let anyone tell you otherwise. Everybody else thinks there's nothing there, but you suspect there may be."

Half the class laughed, thinking it was a joke, and the other half turned to look at me, making me feel like a real fool. But Mr. Bernstein went on as if he was perfectly serious.

"Even if you can't *see* a line, you can still find it, *if* you're given the right conditions. Let's say somebody stops you in the middle of the Quad and says, 'What's the one and only figure that's equal distance between parallel lines?' Well, let's find out."

He drew two lines on the blackboard and then measured off some dots between them. Then he connected the dots like in a children's game.

"*Eureka!*" he said, turning back to the class. "The figure that's equal distance between parallel lines is another line. Now how did we know that? We *didn't*. But we knew where to look."

He did a few more examples, connecting the dots to make other figures, like a parabola, a circle and a ray.

Then he looked me straight in the eye again. "You see how it works? In each case, you're given a set of conditions that can only lead to one figure. It can't be anything else. If it clucks, it's gotta be a chicken. If it quacks, it's gotta be a duck."

Everybody laughed, including me, though I wasn't altogether sure what he was talking about. I figured it was one more thing I'd have to work out on my own.

Still, *some* of it must've sunk in, because on my way home, the whole world started going nuts. Usually I went through the downtown area to avoid the other kids, but as I passed the office buildings, the walls started growing and expanding, as if they were filling up with water. The windows of the dress shops bugged out like fish eyes, and the El Portal Theatre practically brushed me off the sidewalk with its huge marquee.

I hurried out to the open area by the lumberyard, but things weren't any better there. The telephone poles started wobbling, as if they were about to pull loose and fly away, and the railroad tracks looked like they'd curl up right out of their beds. Even the sidewalk seemed to be rising and falling, as if it was breathing, making it hard to walk.

I made a beeline for home, but even *there* it wasn't safe. As soon as I got inside, the furniture started crowding in on me, and the carpet bulged up almost to my ankles. Then Mom came banging through the door, and I nearly jumped out of my skin.

I hid in my room until dinner, and when we sat down to eat, I thought if anybody so much as said a word, I'd freak out. But Mom didn't ask endless questions like she usually did, and Margot was in one of her moods. So we ate in silence for a change. Though the ceiling lamp overhead kept swelling and swelling until I was sure it would burst.

I couldn't fall asleep that night. As I curled up in bed, all the objects in the world seemed to be pressing down on me, closing in with their hard edges and sharp corners, while all I could do was just lay there helplessly. Around midnight, I finally couldn't take it anymore. I got up and went outside and stood by the edge of our front lawn. A passing car honked, probably because I was in my pajamas, but I didn't care. I could actually look at something and not freak out. The sky seemed so soft and velvety, I had the feeling I could dive right into it and never get hurt. Though the stars bothered me a little. I'd never seen them so bright before, especially the ones that made up Orion. He hovered over Mrs. Weaver's house across the street with his right arm cocked and his shield extended and the three stars of his belt glittering like rhinestones. Even the cluster that made up his sheath stood out for once. It was almost as if he was going to pop right out of the sky and come floating down to earth.

Dad had pointed him out to me years ago when I was about six, and as I stood there gazing upward, I could hear him saying, "See, Muffin? The sky is full of characters. You just have to know where to look."

And that's when it hit me. That's when all the lights came on. It was the same thing Mr. Bernstein had said. The stars even *looked* like the dots on his blackboard!

I ran into the house thinking I'd wake up everybody. But Margot groaned when I touched her and pushed me away, and Toby nearly had a whining fit. Even Mom, who normally stayed up late to watch Johnny Carson, turned over when I shook her shoulder. I went around to the other side, but she told me to go to bed. And she wasn't too nice about it either.

It was such a bummer. I mean, it really was. The greatest discovery in the world, and nobody to tell!

* * *

The next morning, they all gave me these bleary looks when I came to breakfast. Mom practically flung my scrambled eggs at me.

"What was so important last night that it couldn't wait? You know how hard it is for me to fall asleep."

"Nothing," I mumbled. "You wouldn't believe me if I told you."

She kept staring at me over her coffee, which didn't exactly put me in a mood to fess up.

Then Toby started singsonging, "Jenny's going nu-uts, Jenny's going nu-uts," until I kicked him under the table and he started howling. Mom got all over me for it, but at least it got us off the subject.

Still, I couldn't keep it to myself forever. I *had* to tell somebody. So when Margot and I were walking to school, I spilled the beans.

"You know why I woke you up last night?"

She covered a yawn. "Not unless you tell me."

"I figured it out."

"What?"

"Why it feels like Dad's still with us."

She gave me the same look Mom had given me over her coffee. It was really starting to get annoying.

"Do you feel that way?" she said. "That he's still with us."

"Don't you?"

"No, not really. When do you feel like this?"

"All the time. Practically everywhere I go. It's like I'm always running into him. I mean, something will happen or I'll be someplace, and I'll have the feeling that he's right there." I was really getting excited. I hadn't told *anybody*.

"Well, I suppose it's natural when someone close to you dies. So what did you figure out?"

"That I'm not imagining it. That it's not just me. It's like loci. Like, all the conditions are there, so that's why we feel him. Otherwise, we wouldn't feel a thing."

"You're not making any sense. What do you mean, it's like loci?"

"Like in Geometry. *Don't* you remember? If you're given the right conditions, only certain things show up, even if you can't see them. And it's the same with people. I mean, if you *feel* somebody's there and the conditions are right, then they are in a way. Like, remember last week, when we went to the movies and we were waiting in line, and that old guy cracked a joke and everybody laughed. Didn't it feel like Dad was there, like he'd just gone to park the car and he'd be right back?"

Her eyes got big for a moment, and I thought she'd say something like, Well, maybe you're right, but did you consider this? or You know what so-and-so says. But she just made a face.

"That's not loci. Loci is when you plot a geometric figure on a piece of graph paper. It's an *exercise*. You measure out these dots and connect them to make hyperbolas and rays and things like that."

"But even Mr. Bernstein said you can't always see them. That they could be right there and you wouldn't even know it."

"He was just trying to be cute and keep everybody awake. Besides, it doesn't mean ..." She gave me that look again. "Look, don't tell anybody else, okay? They'll think you're a nut case."

I put my head down and walked ahead of her.

"And don't get sore about it."

She caught up with me half a block later.

"Do you really think he's here, Jen? Seriously, what do you see? Is it his ghost?"

I spun around, but she wasn't smiling, not even with her eyes.

"*No*, I don't see his *ghost*." I started walking again, but slower this time. "It's like, do you remember Leon, how he used to smoke cigars all the time?" Leon was this funny little man Grandma had married late in life. He used to show us magic tricks, like making his thumb disappear or pulling a nickel out of your hair. "Every time I smell a cigar, it's like Leon's still around, as if not every part of him died. It's like the smallest piece of him survived."

"Okay, but that's *your* projection. That's what *you* feel."

"You're right, forget it. I shouldn't have brought it up."

"No, tell me. I'm really interested."

"Well, don't you have conversations with people when they're not there? I mean, in your head."

"Okay, I do. But that's different."

"And don't you have conversations with Dad?"

She made a face again, but this time her eyes got shiny for a moment. "You know what? You should've gone to the funeral. That's all I can say. I know Aunt Maddy was a pain about it, but if you *had*, you wouldn't think he's still around."

"But what if we react to him? What if half the things we do are because of him?"

"What if people said they saw Martians? Would that make them real?"

"It would if people thought they were. If they reacted to them."

"But it's just a dream world."

"So what are dreams? How do you know when you're dreaming and when you're not?"

"Oh, that's easy. By the sheet test."

"What's the *sheet* test?" I figured it was some egghead thing she'd picked up in school.

"It's when you're asleep and you have to go pee, and you think you do. Then you wake up in the morning and your sheets are wet. That's how you know you've been dreaming."

"Ha. Ha. *Ha.*"

She thought she was so clever, but she didn't know everything. And she didn't stop me from looking for him.

* * *

I started ditching school after that. I'd fake Mom's signature on absence cards and take off whenever I felt like it, and if a teacher asked me about it, I'd just say I was getting hormone shots. Which was really stupid because I was already five-foot-seven. But nobody hassled me, and besides, I didn't go to the beach like a lot of kids. I'd go to places where I thought I'd find Dad.

Like, once I slipped inside this woodworking plant that I passed every morning on the way to school. From the street, you'd hear all this wheezing and howling, as if a whole orchestra of power tools was going at it. But on the inside, it was really wild–all these guys in gray t-shirts running around with their hair in their faces, while these huge machines tore into hunks of wood, turning them into planks and boards and stuff. My clothes started getting sticky from the heat, but I could've stayed there for hours just soaking up the smells of wood and sweat. It was like this manly cologne that washed right over you. Then one of the workers saw me, and they all started pointing and laughing, and out of nowhere, this big guy with a full beard came up to me.

"Can I help you, little lady?" He had this deep, soft voice.

"I just want to watch."

"I'm sorry, but our insurance won't allow it."

"Not even for a few minutes?"

"I'm afraid not." He gave me a little smile. "Now, why would someone bright and good-looking like you want to be in a hellhole like this? There's lots of nicer places I can think of."

I slipped out feeling like a real fool, but I swore I'd go back there one day, even if I had to make up some lame excuse–like I was looking for a certain type of wood or something.

Another time, I skipped a whole day and rode the buses to Santa Monica Pier. It took me nearly three hours because I hopped on the wrong bus at one point and had to backtrack. But finally, I made it. I even found the spot where we used to fish, though the pier wasn't anything like I remembered it. It was just plain and ordinary under this gray overcast sky, and the ocean was practically flat. It barely had barely enough energy to splash up against the pilings. And the only ones out fishing were these old geezers who were dozing off in folding chairs–except for one who kept giving me the eye, as if he wanted to make it with me. On the way there, I'd thought of renting a pole and dropping a line in the water, but after a few minutes, I just gave up and took the next bus home.

Most of the times I ditched school, I'd end up in downtown North Hollywood. It wasn't very big–only three or four blocks long–but just the sight of the office buildings and the dress shops and the people rushing about in business suits gave me the feeling that Dad still had his office there. I'd even check out the registry in the front of his old building to see if his name was on it. And once or twice, I thought I spotted him, somebody with his curly hair or his lanky frame or his easygoing walk. I'd run up to the person out of breath, but it'd never be him, of course. Just somebody who looked a little bit like him.

The one place, though, where I never failed to sense Dad was the El Portal Theatre. It stood near the busiest corner with this huge double-sided marquee, a fancy silver box office in the middle and a row of pearl-gray doors tucked across the entrance like a fancy bowtie. All I had to do was walk by the lobby and catch a whiff of buttered popcorn, and I'd feel as if I was in Dad's lap again, watching *Pinocchio* or *Bambi*, or sitting beside him under this humongous chandelier that hung over the auditorium.

I'd always thought it'd be a neat place to work, and one day on a whim, I just went up to the box office and asked if they were hiring. I was sure the woman inside would tell me to get lost because I was underage, but she just said I'd have to talk to the manager. Then she nodded behind me, and when I turned, I saw this balding, overweight man strolling up the sidewalk with his suit coat slung over his shoulder. He was wearing these flashy gold-and-brown suspenders over a patterned dress shirt.

"Mr. Wade," the woman called. "She wants to know if we're hiring."

He came right up to me and said in a bubbly voice, "So you want to be in show business."

It was really corny, but it was also kind of neat, as if I was auditioning for a part in a movie. He even shook my hand like we were old buddies, though he did look familiar. And then I remembered this girl in my English class who said her father was a theater manager.

"Are you Robin's Dad?" It was really stupid, because now I couldn't lie about my age.

"That I am," he said.

I thought he'd tell me to come back when I was older, but he invited me inside, and just going through the pearl-gray doors without a ticket was a treat. We went upstairs to his office, which was next to the projection room, and through a small window, you could see the huge reels turning round and round and the beam of light streaming out into the auditorium. The walls muffled the voices of the actors, but they still had that echo-y sound that made them seem like they were gods or something.

His office was also kind of neat. It was actually more like a den than a place of business. It had this thick walnut carpeting, a black leather sofa and a wooden wall clock in the shape of a sunburst. There was even a set of golf clubs and a putting mat next to this humongous desk. And on the desk, lined up on the edge like trophies, were all these souvenirs, with this old deflated football sitting in the middle like in the place of honor. Somebody had taken a black marker pen and printed on it "Rose Bowl 1946."

My eyes bugged out when I saw that. "Did you play in the Rose Bowl!"

"When they let me." He nodded toward the side, and there on the wall was this picture of a slim young man in a football uniform. The man was bent over from the waist with his fist to the ground, as if he was going to charge you with his mop of dark hair.

"Is that you!" I was blowing it right and left.

He chuckled. "None other."

I thought he'd tell me to go home now and come back when I'd grown up, but he held his arm out toward the sofa. And when I sat down, he sat right next to me. It seemed a little strange for a job interview, but I figured he was just trying to put me at ease.

"Why don't you tell me about yourself?" he said.

So I did. I told him how I'd always wanted to work in a movie theater, especially the El Portal, and that I'd seen hundreds of movies there, which was more or less the truth. Margot and I used to go every weekend, no matter what was playing. I also told him I'd work anywhere, even in the box office.

"I'm good at counting change. I'm usually the banker when we play Monopoly."

It was really a lame thing to say, but he just tilted his head back, as if he was taking it all in. Then suddenly, he got up to tell a passing usher that he didn't want to be disturbed for an hour. As he closed the door, the usher winked and made a circle with his thumb and forefinger. I thought he was being a smart aleck, but Mr. Wade didn't seem to notice. He was fumbling with the doorknob, as if trying to lock it.

"Sorry about that, Joan." He sat down next to me again.

"Jenny."

"Jenny." He smiled and put his arm behind me on the sofa.

I could smell this beery tang on his breath, and it reminded me of Dad, how he used to drink Hamm's all the time when he watched Dodger games on TV.

"Robin wants to work here too," Mr. Wade said. "I guess she's told you that."

I shrugged. I didn't really know her that well. She was kind of weird, if you want to know the truth. Hardly anybody spoke to her.

He told me that she came home from school every day in tears. She thought all her teachers had it in for her, as if they had nothing better to do. Sometimes she'd lock herself in her room and cry for hours, though he suspected the real problem was his wife. Mrs. Wade had lost interest in their two daughters years ago. She'd been diagnosed with depression, but she refused to get help.

"She's lost interest in me too," he said. Then he smiled and lifted his eyebrows, as if I'd understand.

I didn't know what to make of it. I'd never had an adult open up to me like that. It was like we'd skipped over all the awkward steps of getting to know one another and had just hit it off.

So I started opening up too. I told him how everything had gone downhill after my father died–how my sister bossed everybody around and how my little brother had become a sneak. And then, because I felt so close to him, I even told him about loci–how I sensed Dad everywhere. And he didn't laugh. He didn't even smile. He just nodded and patted my knee. And just like that, my stupid eyes started filling up. I didn't even care about a job anymore. I was ready to drop by once or twice a week just to pal around.

He put his arm around me and gave me a hug, and then he pulled me toward him. I thought he was going to whisper in my ear, but he kissed me on the cheek, and when I turned to say something, he covered my mouth with his and stuck his big old soggy tongue inside me. I tried to push him away, but he shifted on the sofa and pressed his huge belly against me, and he was so strong, I couldn't move. I couldn't even cry out–he had his mouth all over me. Then I heard his suspenders snap open and his zipper come undone, and my heart started pounding like crazy. I couldn't believe it was happening. I mean, whole thing was just unreal. I tried to twist away–I even tried to kick him–but he had me pinned there like a bug. I couldn't do *anything*. Then I felt his fingers crawling under my dress, and I thought, *That's it. He's going to do it. No matter what I do, he's going to do it.* I tried to twist away again–I really went nuts–but it was just impossible. He was just so strong, like a bear or something. All I could do was kind of whimper and brace myself and try to imagine what it would feel like. I even started to bawl a little. And in the middle of my bawling, I heard these tiny screams go off–"Dad, Dad!"–like they were far away or deep inside my head. Though I knew it was useless. Nobody could hear me. Nobody even knew I was there. And then suddenly, the screams got very loud, like they were right next to us.

"Dad! Dad!"

Mr. Wade lifted up–and there was Robin, standing in the doorway. She was out of breath and her face was flushed, as if she'd been running. Between gasps, she started talking a mile a minute.

"You should've seen what Mrs. Drexel did today. She

embarrassed me in front of the whole class. I told you she hates me. She even—"

She saw me now and her mouth dropped open. She jerked her head back and forth from me to her father, and then she ran back out.

Mr. Wade smiled and got to his feet. "Excuse me, Joan. This won't take but a minute." He said it very politely, as if we were still having a job interview. Then he shuffled out the door adjusting his pants.

I laid there on the sofa listening to my heart pounding away. My whole body felt numb, as if I'd had the wind knocked out of me. I kept wondering what I should say when he came back. I even thought of apologizing, as crazy as that sounds. And then suddenly, all these sirens went off in my head, and I realized I had to get the hell out of there. I fixed my clothes and went banging down the stairs and out the door.

I must've run a couple red lights because cars were honking, but I wasn't stopping for anything. I ran right past the other kids, who'd just gotten out of school, and kept on going. I felt like I didn't even belong among them anymore, as if that part of my life was over and done with.

When I got home, I went straight to the bathroom and threw up for about two hours. Mom came to the door and asked if I was okay, but I couldn't answer her. I just kept seeing Mr. Wade and his bald head and his white tufts of hair, and I'd throw up again. When I was done, I went straight to my room and got under the covers.

Mom came in and felt my forehead. "Was it something you ate?"

I shook my head and turned away. I just wanted to be left alone.

Later, I heard her tell Margot through the door that I probably had the 24-hour flu, though I wish that's *all* it'd been. Because it lasted much longer. For *months*, I couldn't stand the sight of suspenders or a patterned dress shirt, and if I saw even the tip of the El Portal Theatre peeking over the rooftops, I'd get sick all over again.

Robin, at least, didn't hassle me about it. She gave me a funny look the next day in English when she dropped off my books, but otherwise she never asked what happened–and I never set her straight.

Which is more than I can say for *some* people. Mom and Margot just wouldn't leave it alone. They wanted to know why I ran out of the room whenever a man came to visit. Or why I squirmed like a maniac if somebody put their arm around me. But there was no way I was going to talk about it. I couldn't even *think* about it.

I'd even freak out around Mr. Bernstein. He'd be making some point in Geometry, and suddenly, his eyes would go dark when he looked my way, as if I had some wild expression on my face. Which I probably did, because I couldn't trust men anymore. Not *any* of them. They all seemed to be crouched down and ready to charge, like Mr. Wade in his football picture.

The worst part, though, was that I stopped sensing Dad. //clHe just disappeared on me. He'd seemed so close all those months, but now it was like he'd vanished into thin air, as if he'd never existed. I even tried sitting in the garage again, hunched up against the back wall, like I had during the funeral, but Mom had filled the place with old furniture and throwaways, and all I got for my trouble was a sore butt.

And then, just when it seemed like things couldn't get any worse, Mom announced at dinner one night that we were selling the house. With Toby's doctor bills and the financial shape Dad had left us in, we couldn't afford to keep it anymore. I probably should've seen it coming–Mom didn't bring in a lot of money as a telephone operator, and Dad's business hadn't done well in years–but still, it hit me like a ton of bricks.

Mom tried to put the best face on it. "Just think," she

said. "We can live in one of those Polynesian apartments with tiki torches and banana trees."

As if *that's* all we'd ever wanted.

Toby burst into tears and ran into his room. Margot went after him, which left just me and Mom. So I got up to do the dishes.

Mom grabbed my sleeve as I went by. "Jen, I really need your help now."

But I yanked my arm away. I was still pissed about the garage.

* * *

Right up to the end, I kept hoping that nobody would buy the place. I thought Toby's accident might save us. The neighbors still talked about it in gruesome details, and every so often, a car would slow down, and the people inside would rubberneck, as if our house was jinxed or something. But within two weeks, the place was bought by this Armenian family with an old grandpa and three little boys. On the day he signed the papers, the father walked us through the house, telling us how he was going to change everything.

"Come back in a year," he said. "You won't recognize the place."

After the escrow closed, Mom tried to put the best face on it again.

"Isn't it neat?" she said. "We're almost out of debt." She even wanted to celebrate with a picnic.

But nobody was in the mood for it. She had to herd us all into the old Dart, and then the car wouldn't start. Margot kept turning the key, but nothing happened. That was supposed to be another reason to celebrate–Margot had just gotten her license–but after she tried several times and all it did was click, she threw her arms down and practically had a fit.

I got out and slammed the door. I figured that was the end of our celebration. But Mom wouldn't give up. She loaded us down with all the supplies and said we were going to walk.

"But it's over two miles!" I said.

"Well, show a little spirit. By the time we get there, you'll have an appetite."

She was trying to be funny, but the whole thing was stupid. We looked ridiculous walking down the street with all our picnic supplies. And besides, it was too late in the season. The leaves had turned, and a wind was blowing, and with each gust, another layer fell to the ground. We practically had to crunch our way through them. By the time we got to the main street, it was just plain embarrassing. Cars started to honk us, as if they'd never seen a whole family out walking before–or as if we were a bunch of hicks just in from the country.

When the sidewalk grew wider, I moved up beside Mom and Margot to complain. I was really going to let Mom have it. But something in her face held me back. There were lines in her forehead and down her cheeks that I'd never seen before. And there was something else, something really strange. She left a gap between herself and the curb, as if she wasn't used to walking on the outside. It was really weird–almost as if she was making room for somebody else–and it just about freaked me out. I thought if she moved even an inch to the side, she'd fall into the gap and we'd never see her again.

I dropped back behind them, but I couldn't get over the haggard look in her face. I kept thinking that it came from the gap she left next to the curb. And that Margot, who was still chewing over her mishap with the Dart, got her unhappiness from being the next closest to it. And I was only partially affected, being the next closest. And Toby, dropping in and out of line to kick a rock or pull off a leaf or chase down the tree squirrels that lived in our neighborhood, was too far away to be touched by it at all.

6. The Also-Ran
Margot

THE PRACTICE SESSION WASN'T GOING WELL. I had all my 3-by-5 cards lined up on the lectern, each one meticulously marked and color-coded, and they made no sense at all. They looked like a child's scribbling, as if some grubby little fingers had broken into the crayon box.

Mrs. Wilson stared at me over her reading glasses. Her thumb came down on the stopwatch.

"Margot, why don't you have a seat and compose your thoughts."

I swept up my cards and headed for the back of the room, and as I slipped into a desk, Richard DeFields, my debate partner, settled on top of the one next to mine.

"It's okay," he said. "I'll carry us."

I looked up into his smug, narrow face. "What do you mean, *you'll* carry us?"

"The judges aren't expecting a brilliant performance every time. They've got to make room for the average people too, the ones who plod along."

"Why, thank you, Richard. Do you mean like the runners-up?"

He yawned without covering his mouth. "Yeah, something like that. Where would we be without them?

They round out the competition."

"Or do you mean like the sidekicks in an Errol Flynn movie, the ones who take all the arrows?"

He laughed. "Yeah, those too. Listen, I don't know if I've got time to tutor you—"

"Oh, don't put yourself out. My God! Your future awaits you."

The girl at the lectern paused. Mrs. Wilson put a finger to her lips.

I gathered up my things and headed for the door.

Richard followed me into the hallway. "You don't have to get emotional about it. I've tutored a number of struggling students."

His words rang in my ears as I stepped outside. It was colder than I'd expected, and as I turned up my collar against the wind, I was surprised that I remembered to do even *that*. Or that I could find my way home without getting lost. Though I did run into some trouble. As I crossed through the park, I stumbled onto an anti-war rally in progress. There weren't many of them, just a scraggly bunch, but they made up for their small number with intensity and aggression.

"We've all got blood on our hands!" a bearded man cried into a bullhorn. "Don't think you can walk away from it!"

He meant me and a few others walking past the edge of the crowd. I hurried away as fast as I could.

When I reached home, halfway down the block, I could still hear their muffled screams inside our apartment.

"What we are committing is murder! Organized *murder*!"

I sank into a chair by the dining room table without taking my coat off. My face was hot, and my eyes filled with tears. I knew I shouldn't take Richard seriously. I should have just added his remark to my Richard file, along with the time he told me Mensa, the egghead society, called him every night begging him to join. But I couldn't help thinking that he was on to something. Here it was halfway through November, well past the deadline for most colleges, and like a fool I'd only applied to the very best. Somehow I'd convinced myself that a Bryn Mawr or a Columbia or a Stanford would accept me–and not only accept me but grant me a full scholarship. And just to show how absurd the whole idea was, I was falling apart in every class. I couldn't even count change anymore. At the cafeteria that morning, I'd actually thought that a quarter and two nickels added up to fifty cents.

The wind shifted, and the shouts of the protestors rattled the windows. "We don't need to conquer Asia! We already own half the world!"

I should have started my homework–I had tons of it, plus Drama practice at 7:30–but all I could do was sit there and stare out the window–at the milky white sky that covered the earth like a shroud.

"You'll have this war on your conscience for generations to come!"

I wasn't the only one staring. From his portrait above the china cabinet, my father gazed back at me in his Army uniform. His eyes were dull and partially closed, and his cheeks hung as if he'd lost a lot of weight. The picture was taken right after the War, and I never understood why Mom put it there. It certainly wasn't the way I remembered him, which was more like an overgrown kid than the melancholy figure in the photograph. Though nothing in this apartment brought him back to me. In our old house, at least, you could always get a sense of Dad, if nothing else, from the way the light poured in through the picture windows he'd hung, or from the cherry wood furniture that he'd built and left behind. But here, in this cramped place, with its factory-brown carpet and faded gray walls, there just wasn't room for him. In fact, there was hardly room for us. Mom slept on the pullout sofa, and Jenny and I bunked together. Only Toby had a bedroom to himself.

The wind gusted again, and the windows vibrated with a girl's outrage. "Are we going to accept their bullshit? Are we just going to lie down and *take* it?"

Suddenly, the front door shook, and my heart shook with it. I was sure they were breaking in. But a moment later, Mom poked her head inside.

"Hi, darling. Did you see the letter from Stanford?"

"What are *you* doing home?" Her shift wasn't over till eight.

"I traded with Alice Lin today. She had to go to a doctor's appointment." She set down a bag of groceries on the table and picked up a pile of mail I hadn't noticed. "This one caught my eye immediately." She handed me an envelope with a big red S in the upper left corner.

I turned it over and put it back down.

"Aren't you going to open it?" She brushed a loose strand of hair off my face.

"They're just acknowledging my application. They won't send out acceptance letters until spring."

"You'll never guess who goes there. Alice told me her daughter Debby got accepted last year. She said they have an excellent pre-law program." She hung up her coat in the guest closet. "You know, if you go to Stanford, we can drive up to see you. It'll be a lot easier than flying to the East Coast." She laughed as she took the groceries into the kitchen. "As if we could afford to fly."

I traced my finger around the edge of the envelope. "Mom, you know, I was thinking maybe I shouldn't aim so high. UCLA isn't such a bad school. It's only two weeks past their deadline. If I write to them, maybe they'll make an exception."

"Are you kidding?" she called from the kitchen. "If Debby Lin can get into Stanford, you shouldn't have any trouble. You're *twice* the student she was. Alice told me she earned only B's."

"But she's a minority. It's easier for her."

"So are you. You're a woman."

"That doesn't count. At least, not in the '60s. I'll be lucky if I make it past the first cut."

The refrigerator door shut and she marched back into the dining room. "What's got into you? You're a *wonderful* student. Any college would be lucky to get you."

I took a quick breath and swallowed hard. "I think I botched the SAT."

"Are you sure? You didn't mention it before." She sat down and studied my face. "Well, even if you didn't do so great, it's just one test. They can't base a entire academic career on *that*."

"But I'm falling behind in *everything*. You should hear me in French. I sound like the village idiot. I can't even conjugate the most basic verbs. And forget about Math or Physics. I'm completely lost. I hardly know what's going on anymore."

She put her hand on my shoulder. "Look, we all have bad days. You just have to keep trying. We've invested too much to give up now."

"Well, maybe *we* have been deceiving ourselves."

She shook my shoulder. "You know what? I'll help you. Let's do the *où ést*'s."

"Mom, we don't do that in French anymore."

"*Où ést*—how do you say *door*? Don't tell me. *Où ést la fenêtre?*"

"That's *window*. Why don't you help Jenny? She's having trouble with loci."

"With who? Oh, I know. *Où ést la porte?*"

"How come we never talk about *your* work?"

"Because I hope to God you never have to stoop that low. Because it'll be a sad day when you have to work as a telephone operator."

"Maybe that's what I'm cut out for. Maybe that's all I can handle."

Her voice rose half an octave. "Margot, what's got into you?" She felt my forehead. "Your eyes look watery. Are you feverish?"

"Mom, you don't understand. For every opening in these schools, there are hundreds of applicants. It's the crest of the Baby Boom. You practically have to be a world-class scholar to get into these places."

"Those kids aren't *any* smarter than you. Most of them can't hold a candle to you. How many of *them* are student body vice president?"

"But you should *see* these kids. One girl in my class studied at the Sorbonne last summer. How am I supposed to compete with *that*?"

"You just have to have faith in yourself."

"It's not about faith. It's about reality. Or maybe it's about you impressing Alice Lin."

Her eyes grew hard and her mouth twitched. She stood up and marched back into the kitchen. A moment later, the water came on full force, and the dishes clattered about in the sink. Jenny should have done them by now, but as usual, my sister was chasing around the neighborhood.

At the anti-war rally, they were singing *If I Had a Hammer*, making it sound more like a hootenanny. I had half a mind to run out there and join them. Maybe I could live like a hippie–beg for change during the day, and then dance all night with flowers in my hair.

I hung my coat in the guest closet and drifted into the kitchen.

"I don't do any of it for myself," Mom said without looking up. "I do it all for you. I just wish I had the same opportunities when I was your age." Her voice broke off.

I picked up the dishtowel and started on the big plates. "So what does happen at your work?"

She grunted.

"No, I want to know."

"It'll put you to sleep."

"See? You *never* tell me."

"What's to tell? All I do is sit there all day and give out numbers. Isn't that exciting?" She turned to me with a mock grin.

"But don't you get funny calls? I've heard all kinds of stories."

"Oh, yes. I get my share of the lulus."

She raised her head to look out the window. Below us, a black miniature poodle scampered down the sidewalk, followed by Marcy, the five-year-old who lived downstairs. Marcy ran so hard, her blonde curls bounced against the back of her neck like springs.

Mom started on the silverware. "If you really want to know, today a little boy called and asked what mountains had snow on them."

"Did you tell him?"

"As if I knew. No, we're only allowed to give out numbers. Then around noon, a woman called because she didn't know what to do with her baby. She'd fed her and changed her, but he wouldn't stop crying. Then a man called and crooned into my ear, *'Are you lonesome tonight?'*" Mom lowered her voice and sang in a phony bass. "Isn't that something? Then just before the shift ended, a young man wanted to know why his wife hadn't spoken to him in three days."

"What'd you tell him?"

"I asked him what number he wanted."

"Maybe they weren't meant for each other."

"Or maybe I should open a counseling service. I'd make a lot more money."

I chuckled under my breath.

The protestors were singing in the park again, this time *Amazing Grace*. We listened in silence, as if they were serenading us.

When they finished, I asked, *"Où ést la neige?"*

"The what?"

"*La neige.* The snow."

"Don't tell me." She held her arms down in the dishwater and gazed into the street.

Below us, Marcy carried her squirming poodle home in triumph. As she neared the building, she put the dog in the crook of an arm and shook her finger at it.

Mom turned to me now with her eyes aglow. *"Sur la montagne!"*

* * *

I'd always been the scholar in the family. "Margot the Bookworm," Dad used to say. But it wasn't like that. I didn't go around with my nose in a book. It was more like playing on the rings at school, the only physical activity I was ever good at. The rings hung down on chains from a maypole-like structure, and the object was to swing up from the lowest one and then loop around from ring to ring. Most kids only made it to the second or third, but I found that if I twisted my body about just so and pushed off against the center pole, I could circle around time and again.

And it was the same with my schoolwork. While the other students might groan or break their pencil leads, I'd coast from one subject to the next, as if the answers were dangling in front of me, just waiting for my grasp.

During my last year in high school, however, I started to wonder if I wasn't taking a lot for granted. What if one day I reached out and there was nothing there? What if I twisted myself all about and found only empty space?

The idea first came to me, of all places, in the middle of the SAT. Just the weekend before, we'd moved out of the house I'd grown up in, and though it wasn't the best of circumstances, I didn't think it would affect me all that much. I'd never sweated a test before, and I had no intention of doing so now. But as the test booklets were being handed out, I couldn't help noticing how nervous some of the other kids were. Their eyes fluttered and their faces blanched, and a few were biting their nails. It made me wonder if I was really so different. Why should the answers fall into *my* lap? Did I really think I was that special? Everyone wanted to succeed as badly as I did.

Then the proctors gave us the go-ahead, and like a self-fulfilling prophecy, I proceeded to make a hash of the test. Terms I'd been familiar with all my life suddenly looked strange. I couldn't remember what they meant by "function" or "tangent" or "Celsius." I wasn't sure if the hypotenuse was the longest side of a triangle or the widest angle. And when it came to the verbal section, I fell apart completely. I had to read every sentence twice, and even then, I lost the thread. We'd been warned that our wrong answers would be subtracted from the ones we got right, but like a fool, I took a stab at everything. By the end of the afternoon, I was covered in sweat and my eyes were fluttering like the nervous kids. I was sure I'd ruined any chance of getting into a top university.

When school resumed on Monday, I picked up right where I'd left off with the SAT. I'd suddenly become one of the dummies. Nothing made sense anymore. French was just a babble of noise. Math Analysis sounded like a foreign language. And Physics had become a joke. During one class, Mr. Capros swung his frail old body around his desk to demonstrate a point about velocity, but all I could focus on were his white eyebrows, which, I discovered, flared upward like a pair of tiny candelabras.

I did try, especially after my talk with Mom, but it was like plowing through sand. Even my extracurricular activities became a chore. In Drama, I had to bluff my way through two performances of *Arsenic and Old Lace*. And in Debate Club, after a couple of disastrous tournaments, Richard decided that he didn't want me as a partner after all, not even as an also-ran. I happened to walk into a lunchtime practice while he was pleading his case with Mrs. Wilson.

"I thought we were trying to accomplish something."

"We are," she said, "but I'm not changing teams in the middle of the season. Besides, it's only been a few months since her father—" She saw me now and smiled, removing her reading glasses.

Richard wheeled about and gave me his professional grin, which was more like a slapstick smirk.

"Look who's getting emotional," I said.

As we retreated to the back to go over strategy, he made small talk to cover up. "Mensa called me again last night. I guess I'll have to join sooner or later. I just don't relish the prospect of dominating their meetings. I've been trying to downplay my intellectual side."

During the practice session, however, it wasn't his intellectual side that came up. Directly outside our windows, in the main quad, a rather unusual event was unfolding. Two boys and a girl had strung up a banner with the words "Food Strike" emblazoned in red over the steps of the Arcade, and they sat under it now, quietly inviting others to join them. No one would have argued the point–we all knew the cafeteria food was lousy–but the idea of a strike was a little too adult for most of the students, and it wasn't long before a crowd gathered and the rowdier kids started taunting the strikers.

Mrs. Wilson carried on as if nothing out of the ordinary was happening, raising her voice now and then to drown out the hecklers. But Richard couldn't sit still. As the noise level grew, he clenched his fists and raked a hand through his hair.

"The roiling masses," he said with a nervous chuckle. "Bread and circuses are never enough."

Then suddenly, shouts broke out and a couple students bumped up against our windows. Outside, we could see food flying and the crowd surging toward the strikers.

Mrs. Wilson marched over to the windows and slammed them shut, effectively muffling the noise. But Richard was unnerved. He jumped out of his seat and paced up and down the back of the room.

"Jesus Christ!" he wheezed, which wasn't the sort of thing you said in high school, at least not in the 1960s. "Next thing you know, they'll burn down the whole damn school."

"I don't think so," Mrs. Wilson said dryly. She nodded to the boy at the lectern and reset her stopwatch.

The boy launched gamely into his presentation, but after a few seconds, an early bell rang, ending the lunch period and dispersing the crowd. We were still gathering up our things when a group of excited freshmen poured into the room, shouting and playfully punching each other, as if they didn't want the melee to end. It looked harmless enough–clearly, they were just having fun–but on my way out, I saw Richard standing in the corner paralyzed. His lips were trembling and his face was pale, and he'd attracted the attention of three or four of the freshmen, who'd formed a circle around him. I went over and pulled him away, and when we reached the door, he nodded, as if to say he could make it from there. But as he shuffled clumsily down the hall, it cost him a few laughs.

* * *

Our report cards came out two weeks later, and as I expected, I received 3 Ds and 3 Cs. My C in Phys Ed didn't count, so my grade point average for the semester was 1.4. With my pathetic score on the SAT, it was obvious I wasn't going away to college.

Mom's face was a stony mask for days. "Let's just hope they emphasize your previous years. And your activities."

I didn't have the heart to tell her that I'd been kicked out of most of my clubs, including student government. With all the protests and rallies going on that year, the school administration was not in a forgiving mood. They did allow me to stay in Debate Club, probably because Mrs. Wilson put in a good word, but Richard couldn't have been too happy about it. He complained so often that even *I* suggested we change partners. Mrs. Wilson, however, wouldn't hear of it.

"You're a team," she said. "Probably our best hope to make the finals."

If we were a team, we certainly didn't act like one. A couple days before the last tournament, Richard handed me a small white pharmacy bag, which I assumed was a peace offering. I'd been complaining about coming down with the flu, and I thought he was giving me vitamins. But when I reached inside, I found a bottle of Midol.

"In case it's that time of the month," he explained. "So your hormones don't get in the way."

I threw the bottle at him, just missing his narrow head.

* * *

It turned out that my menstrual cycle was the last thing he needed to worry about. For some unknown reason, Grant High School had given permission for a war debate to be held at the same time as our tournament. The war debate was to be outside, in the lunch area, while ours was to be in the classrooms as usual. But when I arrived on Saturday morning, there were so many tie-dyed shirts, peasant blouses and fringed leather jackets in front of the school that it looked more like an anti-war rally than anything else. Several people gave me dirty looks, as if they suspected me of being on the wrong side.

I hurried to the classroom where our first debate was to be held and found Richard already there, crouched down in one of the desks. His complexion was a couple shades lighter than usual, and his fingers were practically inside his mouth. He grinned at me and raised his eyebrows, but the rest of his face was frozen. As a rule, we'd go over last-minute strategy before a debate, but he could scarcely mumble hello.

Soon afterward, our judge arrived, a Mrs. Pfeffer, along with our opposing team–a tall, fair-skinned girl and a brainy-looking boy with thick glasses and tufts of unruly hair. Mrs. Pfeffer taught English at Grant, and she made no secret of her disdain for the "freak show," as she called the war debate.

"They should all be sent to boot camp," she declared.

We started promptly at nine, and so did the other debate, with the usual squawks and screeches of a temporary public address system. Richard was up first. His arguments were solid, but his voice was almost inaudible, and he cringed every time the loudspeakers squawked. Also, his build-up at the end, normally quite dramatic, came off rather shaky.

The girl on the opposing team wasn't much better. She giggled in the middle of her presentation, lost her place and gave up about twenty seconds of silence. It was highly unusual, and it left the door open for us.

But the moment I got up to the lectern, I knew I was in trouble. I couldn't find the index cards with my leading arguments. And for one panicky moment, I couldn't remember if I was arguing "pro" or "con." I should have just started talking–anything was better than silence–but my throat seized up and I couldn't go on. I kept thinking that I had no right to be here, that far from being an also-ran, I was a dithering idiot, a complete embarrassment to my school. To make matters worse, my head felt achy from the flu bug I'd been fighting all week.

What saved me was the other debate. Grant's administration must have come to the same conclusion as Mrs. Pfeffer, because while I was up there, a teacher announced over the PA system that the war debate was cancelled.

The announcement was met with boos and catcalls. Someone grabbed the microphone and urged the crowd to "take over this fascist institution."

The teacher grabbed it back. "I want you to all go home now like good citizens."

Obviously, that wasn't happening. The catcalls continued, and the crowd began spreading across campus, becoming rowdier and more obscene as it washed up against trashcans, benches and guardrails. It swept into the open area next to our room, and a few dirt clods hit our windows, making us duck. Richard leapt out of his chair and looked around anxiously, but there was nowhere to run.

And now they broke into our building. We could hear them coming toward us like a wave. Shouts echoed up and down. Lockers clanged. Doors were pounded. A girl next door screamed. Our own door flew open, and three or four of them burst inside.

"Okay, this place is liberated!" The announcement came from a tall blond boy with the longest hair I'd ever seen on a male, nearly down to his waist.

Mrs. Pfeffer rose in a huff and stormed out the other door. "We'll see about that."

Richard cried out and ran to the back, stumbling inside a closet.

"You *better* run," a weasely boy cackled.

"This room is now under our control," the longhaired boy repeated.

"Fine," I said, stepping away from the desktop lectern. "Control it."

"Let's break up the place!" A stumpy girl ran to the lectern and put her arms around it.

I grabbed it from the other end and held on tight. "What good would that do?"

"We have to start somewhere. Demolish this whole fucked-up society." She backed away and looked for something else to grab.

"Breaking things isn't going to help." I stood up too, but I kept an eye on her. "All you'll do is discredit your movement."

"We've already been discredited," the weasely boy said.

"And marginalized," Longhair added. "Nobody cares about the war."

"So how do you explain all the people who showed up today?" I waved my arm at the windows. "You overwhelmed the other side. A few months ago, you couldn't get twenty people to a rally. Now you're packing them in."

"Yeah, and millions of others are sitting on their asses," Weasel countered, "while the government plunders Southeast Asia."

"We've got to bring the war to the people," Longhair said. "They have to understand what's being done in their name–with *their* tax dollars."

The girl made a step toward my tin box with the index cards. I snatched it off the desk.

"What were you doing here?" Longhair asked.

"Having a debate," I said.

His eyes perked up. "On the war?"

"No, on compulsory arbitration. Resolved that the federal government should adopt a program of compulsory arbitration—"

"There's only one legitimate subject," the girl said. "And that's the war. Everything else is bullshit."

"Well, it just so happens that nearly half a million people went on strike last year. The most since 1953." Now that it didn't matter, I was just a fount of information. "And some of those strikes brought essential services to a halt."

"What side are you on?" Longhair asked.

"We argue both sides."

"No, on the war."

"I don't have a side."

Weasel laughed. "You mean, you don't have a conscience."

"You don't care there's a war going on?" Longhair looked puzzled.

"She doesn't have to," the girl said. "She's not at risk."

"I'm not at *what*?"

"You can't get drafted," Longhair explained.

"It's cowards like you who let the fascist pigs run wild." The girl looked like she wanted to spit in my face.

"I wouldn't be so sure," I said. "My father risked his life during World War II just so you could say stupid things like that."

"That was different," Longhair said. "That was a defensive war."

"No, that one sucked too," Weasel put in.

Longhair lifted his chin toward me. "We disagree on that one."

"Yeah, he's a Trotskyite, and I'm a Maoist." Weasel said it as if he were telling me what schools they were from.

"And what are you?" I asked the girl. "A John Bircher?"

Weasel cackled, but the girl wasn't amused.

"I'm a Wobbly," she said, "though I don't suppose you'd know what *that* is."

"Industrial Workers of the World," I said. "Founded by Eugene V. Debs. They wanted to take over the means of production and do away with wages." Suddenly, the facts were just tripping off my tongue.

"You should join us," Longhair said. "You sound like the only one here with any intelligence."

"I resemble that remark." This was from the brainy boy on our opposing team. I'd forgotten they were even there.

"I'm not much of a protestor," I said.

"You don't have to be a protestor. You just have to have a heart."

"Or political awareness," the girl said.

"Here, why don't you take one of our flyers?" Longhair handed me a bright orange leaflet splattered with bold headlines and exclamation points. It reminded me of the underground newspaper that showed up occasionally at our high school. "My name's John. We hold our meetings on Saturday around eight."

"Thanks. I'll think about it." I tried to sound nonchalant, but for some reason, I found his offer very touching, as if he'd given me a rare gift.

"We'll see you there." John nodded to the others, and they flew out of the room like winged messengers.

I was almost sorry to see them go. The classroom seemed empty without them.

"You can come out now, Richard," I called. "The coast is clear."

There was some bumping about in the closet, and Richard emerged with his hair tousled and his face flushed.

"Sorry I had to disappear like that," he said to our opponents. "I've been accepted at MIT, and it wouldn't do to disappoint them."

"I resemble that remark," the brainy boy said. He still thought it was funny. I could see now why Richard hesitated to join Mensa.

The protestors went home eventually without causing too much damage, though not before our own tournament was canceled. It was rescheduled for the following weekend, but by that time, Richard and I had both come down with the flu, which effectively ended my debating career.

* * *

Before the semester was over, I managed to bring my grades up high enough to earn a diploma, but there was little joy in our household. Since early April, after I'd received my last college rejection, Mom had gone around with a shadow behind her eyes. On the day I graduated, she dressed in the same dark outfit that she'd worn to Dad's funeral.

We'd been planning a party afterward at the apartment, and though we probably should have canceled it, we went ahead anyway, inviting some family and friends. Mom served everyone refreshments as if she were the maid, breaking her silence only to yell at Toby when he spilled hot chocolate on his suit.

My Uncle Max tried to liven things up. "Are you still in that Drama group, the Lesbians?"

"It's *Thespians*," I said. "No, I had to drop out."

"So what college are you going to?" My Aunt Maddy beamed as if it were a real conversation starter.

"I managed to get into Valley College, but I might have trouble getting classes. I applied very late."

Mom had been setting out clean ashtrays, but now she stared my aunt dead in the eye. "She could have gone to any school she wanted to. She just threw it away."

"Mom, you know that's not true."

"So why'd you do it? To get back at me?"

"I didn't *do* anything. And I didn't do it to get *back* at you. You make it sound like I lost a train ticket."

"It was right there for the taking," she told my aunt. "Right in her lap. She just didn't want it badly enough."

"Or maybe you wanted it *too* badly," I said. "Maybe you wanted to live your life through me. I can't make up for everything that went wrong in your life. It's not my fault you didn't make it past high school."

The slap wasn't so terrible–it only stung for a moment. What hurt was the look in her eyes. It was the same look she used to give Dad at his most shiftless moments.

I don't remember how I got out the door. I just remember running up the street with tears in my eyes until I reached the park. I threw myself under the nearest tree and swore I'd move out that night. I'd pack my things after she went to work and move in with a friend, and she'd never have to see me again. She could just worry about Toby and Jenny, and forget I ever existed.

If I'd wanted to be alone, however, I couldn't have picked a worst spot. I wasn't there five minutes before people started streaming past, laughing and chatting and tapping on tambourines. I sat up and buried my face in my hands, hoping no one would notice me. But a few moments later, I sensed someone kneeling in front of me, and now my hands were pulled away, and a girl my age with china blue eyes stared softly into my face. Her wheat-blonde hair was set off by a crown of yellow daisies.

I shook my head and covered my eyes again, but she pulled my hands away and kissed me on the cheek. Then she placed the daisies on my head.

"I'm Wind," she said. "Do you want to join us?"

I shrugged.

She took me by the hands and pulled me to my feet, which wasn't hard considering that she was a head taller. I saw now that I was in the middle of a procession. In threes and fours, young people were moving toward the center of the park. They were dressed in fringed leather and peasant clothes, like the protestors at the war debate, but they didn't appear to be angry. Instead, their faces were glowing. A few played on guitars and recorders, while others did a sort of loping, twirling dance as they walked.

A lanky boy with a sunburnt complexion swooped down on us. "Who ya got there, Wind?" His flowing ringlets reminded me of John the Trotskyite.

"I'm Margot," I sniffled.

"I'm Jester." Or maybe he said, "Gesture." He handed me a tambourine. "This is yours."

I turned it over in my hand.

"No, you tap on it. Like this." He shook it, making it sound like an armful of castanets. Then he banged it on his head, getting a laugh from the people around us.

"I invited her to join us," Wind said.

"Did she accept?"

"She didn't say anything."

"That's a *yes*!"

Together they lifted me by the elbows and ran with me into the park. I hadn't been picked up since I was a small child, and I let out a stream of giggles.

When they set me down, I asked breathlessly, "What are you protesting?"

"We're not protesting *anything*," Wind said. "We're celebrating."

"Celebrating?"

"Love! Life! Happiness!" Jester waved his arms in big circles.

Wind held me around the shoulders as we walked. "This is a Be-In. Haven't you heard of a Be-In?"

I shook my head.

Jester's eyes grew wide. "To *be* in one, you have to *be* a Human *Be*-ing." He grabbed my hand with the tambourine and banged himself on the head again.

"Then I guess I qualify," I said.

"Of course you do!"

They picked me up again and ran with me deeper into the park. I threw my head back and squealed. And when they set me down, I started twirling and loping with the best of them.

At the center of the park, we all sat in tight circles and sang our hearts out, and as the afternoon wore on, they gave me a new name–Blossom. And Blossom drank sharp-tasting punch and ate chocolate brownies and took deep puffs of a lumpy, hand-rolled cigarette that made her giggle until her eyes ran. She knew it was naughty and that she shouldn't do it and that it wasn't really her, but as the sunlight faded and she got up to skip arm-in-arm with Wind, she couldn't help thinking that this is what she'd wanted, that this was what she'd been working toward all along. And as the two of them swung recklessly round the circle, keeping time to the music, she had the feeling that she was back on the rings again, back on the old maypole-like structure, and with every turn of their dance, another bright metal halo dipped into view, waiting for her grasp.

7. Where or When
Ruth

I WISH YOU COULD SEE HIM. I think you'd like him. So gentle in his manners the way he opened the car door for me and pulled out my chair at the restaurant. He even asked about the children, and smiled when I ran on a little too long. Afterward he held my hand over the wine glasses and smoothed the back with his thumb, his eyes asking the question with such shyness and warmth. I squeezed his hand back. What else could I say?

And now here we are, standing by his bed. He has the same embarrassed look in his eyes, as if he's never been here before. Though I'm the one who's new at this, the awkward stranger in a gentleman's bedroom with her blouse undone. I want to ask him, Is it okay? Do you like what you see?

Instead I take his hand and place it on my breast. It makes me shiver, but I hold it there so he can't take it away. He places his free hand on my other breast and gives it a soft squeeze, as if testing it for ripeness. Then he draws me to him, presses his mouth against mine, tries to light a fire inside. I listen with my whole body. I think I feel something–sparks deep inside–but they fade almost as soon as I feel them.

We break now, and his face colors. But the next moment, he's the perfect gentleman–draws back the blanket and nods toward the bed. And while I finish undressing and slide under the sheet, I watch him pull his clothes off. He has such a fine chest, with small wiry hairs turning to gray in the middle. His shoulders are broad and slightly freckled, and his hips are narrow like an athlete's, though he has the slightest hint of a paunch. I wish he'd stand there and let me admire him, but he climbs in quickly and snuggles up next to me with a boyish grin, an expression so much like yours. He takes me in his arms and nuzzles my neck, and once again I feel something down there–tiny sparks erupting–only fainter this time. It makes me wonder if I'm so easy to be had. For a kiss. For a hug.

Cal pulls away, and when I open my eyes, he's leaning on his elbow, looking so serious. He lifts the sheet and gazes at my body, runs his eyes up and down as if studying a landscape. Where should he put the trees? Where should he plant a rose garden? Would a sundial look nice?

"Do you like it?" I say and feel myself blush.

He smiles shyly and snuggles up against me again. Then he kisses me, devours my mouth, and I kiss him back. Though I wonder if I should be doing more–whispering in his ear or stroking his sides or touching him down there. I run my fingers along his back, trace the knobby bones of his spine. I want to ask him if it's okay, if I'm doing what he wants. But now he slides on top of me and eases himself inside, and he's so strong I have to gasp.

I lift my knees to take him better, and pull him toward me so he doesn't see the tears. He'll think they're not for him, that I don't like him, when nothing could be further from the truth. It's just so nice to be wanted again. To have someone in your arms. And now, once again, the sparks flare up–tiny fireflies deep inside–so faint I barely feel them. Can that part of me still be alive?

He draws his head up, lifts his chest. I place my hands on

his hips to steady him. I want to see his eyes, to see if they're like yours, with that look of innocence and wonder. But his lids are almost shut, as if he's listening to something far away. Something only he can hear.

I wish I could hear it too, but that's the way it is with me. Everything passes over my head–like all those jokes at the troupe rehearsals. Do you remember? How I kept you up at night explaining every last one, until your eyes were closing and you were laughing softly inside your chest. At the funeral, they were telling the same jokes, their faces shining–and I still didn't understand a thing. Though you should have heard them. They couldn't say enough about you. Do you know they named an award after you? A silly little plaque for the troupe members, but they were so proud of it.

Cal says something that I miss.

"I'm sorry." I'm such a poor listener.

He bunches his forehead and tugs at a pillow beside me. "Mind if I put this under?"

"No, of course not."

I need to pay attention–that's what you always said. Always thinking of the next moment, or the one that's past. Never the one at hand. *Little Miss Absent-Minded*, you called me. Though it wasn't *always* my fault. You'd stare at me with those baby blue eyes, and I wouldn't hear a thing.

Cal pushes in deeper, and I cry out. Though I try not to. I don't want to distract him. I want him to lose that sad look in his eyes. Even when he smiles it's still there.

You could be like that. At the most intimate moments, your face would darken, and you'd ask me if it was all right, if I didn't mind the pain. But I just wanted to see you smile, to erase that shadow behind your eyes. Even when we were out for the evening it was there. Even when you played with the children.

Cal shudders now and eases down, and suddenly, he's so

heavy, it's a little hard to breathe. But I don't want him to move just yet. He'll see the tears, and he'll know they're not for him. Even if they're happy tears. Tears of joy. I just wish I could feel it the way he does, though I suppose it's too soon.

Or maybe it's the old problem. What did you call it? *The Slowpoke Syndrome*. Like starting a campfire, you said. Though I didn't mean to be cold. I just wanted to be good for you. Was I? Were you satisfied? Did you get what you wanted?

I smooth the gray hairs on the back of Cal's neck, gently so he won't wake up. I just want to make sure that he's real. He slides off me now half-asleep, and for the first time I notice tiny tucks under his eyes, and I cry harder, but quietly so he won't hear me.

I think you'd have liked him. Such a sweet man. A nonconformist like you. He wears brown-and-white saddle shoes, a tweed coat with leather patches, and a plaid bowtie. And he shaves his head. Not at all what you'd expect in a junior high school vice principal. Though otherwise he's very down-to-earth.

I guess I'm attracted to the characters, as my brother always said. Max never did like the boys I brought home. Did you know you were a problem for him? It took him a while to get used to you. He used to call you a wiseacre, a know-it-all, a college dandy, but now his voice cracks when he talks about you. He misses teasing you about the Dodgers. *The Bums*, he calls them.

I can't stop stroking Cal's neck. I love the way it rumples up. I wouldn't mind seeing it next to me in the morning, though I suspect he'll go back to his wife. I could see it in the restaurant when he talked about his daughters, how he misses them. I don't know how he can live apart from them.

Still, it was nice of Shirley to introduce us, to seat us together at the PTA luncheon. She was very discrete about it. Not at all like your mother.

Did you know Mom brings men home for me? Picks them up on her vacations and delivers them to the apartment. Last week, it was an accountant she met in Las Vegas, a shy, little man named Earl. And the month before, it was a blond man from Sweden–Lars, I think. She met him in Palm Springs. She picks them up like strays and deposits them on our sofa, and then waits for lightning to strike.

Jenny has a fit every time. She bristles as soon as they walk through the door. And if they try to talk to her, she flies into her room.

I just know something happened to her. She wouldn't act that way otherwise. Someone must have gotten fresh with her–a teacher or a man she met on the street–but she won't tell me anything. Runs away if I breathe a word.

Though she seemed okay around Cal tonight. He even made her smile before we left, no small accomplishment. Still, it's hard on her. On all of us. You're still so much with us.

Did you know I feel you in bed some nights? Pressing down on your side. And in the morning, I'm almost afraid to look in the bathroom, afraid of what I'll find.

And always, I see you in the children. So much of you in Margot, that look of cheekiness and devil-may-care. She would deny it to her dying day, but she didn't get it from anyone else.

And with Jenny it's like you never left. I don't know what will come of it. I wish she'd discover boys–or her appearance–which probably amounts to the same thing. But I think it's still a few years off.

And Toby just breaks my heart. To see him in his room all day, playing with his electric baseball game and his trading cards. A boy needs to be outside, to be in the park. I know the other children tease him about his fingers, but it's not natural for a boy to stay indoors. He needs to get some fresh air.

Cal clears his throat. He raises his head and stares at me with his eyes unfocused. Who's this strange woman in his bed? How did *she* get here?

"It's me." I smooth his bushy eyebrows into place.

He chuckles under his breath. "How are *you*?"

"Fine. And you?"

He raises an eyebrow, as if he's thought of something. "Ready for seconds?"

"So soon?"

I didn't think it was possible. But after a little kissing, I help him inside, and once again he's so strong, I gasp in spite of myself. Maybe I'm too small for him.

"Cal, please."

I squeeze his sides, tap him on the chest. It starts to burn, but now he shudders and eases down on me.

"I'm sorry," he whispers. "Don't mean to mess you up down there."

"It's okay." I push him gently with my fingers. "Just move a little, you're heavy."

Already we sound like an old married couple.

He lifts himself off and snuggles up beside me. "I suppose you'll never want to do *that* again."

I stroke his face. "It's all right. I'm out of practice. I...I just need to go slow."

He grins and rubs his nose on my shoulder. A few moments later, his eyelids droop and he's breathing evenly. I wish I could fall asleep like that. I stare at the walls for hours. Though I wouldn't mind staring at *these* walls, at the gray fleur-de-lis pattern with the earth-tone highlights, and the beige, ribbed trim on the bottom half. What do they call it? *You* would know. Wainscoting? And the molding around the edges of the ceiling and the overhead light. So rare nowadays, the way they throw apartments together. Only the swag lamp looks out of place, like a thrift shop purchase. Probably it's a gift from a student–or Cal's idea of a joke.

He never does take himself seriously. I can just picture him walking about the school, herding the students where they need to go, teasing them to move them along a little faster. Or speaking to the teachers and opening with a cute remark. Even then, he probably has that sad look in his eyes. It's so hard on him without his daughters.

I shouldn't be here. The last thing he needs is someone interfering with his life. I sit up and reach for my bra. I'll use that payphone I saw downstairs and call a cab–be home in twenty minutes.

But Cal's arm goes around my waist and draws me back to his warm, furry chest. He puts his other arm around me and holds me so sweetly. And in another minute, my heart settles down. I have to laugh at myself. Where did I think I was going? Like a frightened girl on her first date. And even if I did go home, what would I find when I got there? Just a sink full of dishes and angry looks from Jenny. She'd fume all night until she went to bed.

And anyway, it would have been rude to run off like that after the lovely evening we had. Cal was so thoughtful to take me to that Italian restaurant. Such a cute little place with the exposed brick in the arches and the planters full of pansies and geraniums. With the hanging strings of garlic and peppers. So clichéd, and yet so sweet. He even paid a violinist to play for us.

I wonder if Cal knows how adorable he looks when he tells a story, even if it's a sad story–about all the times he failed to become a principal. All those bitter disappointments. He'd probably hide it if he knew. Men are like that. They cover up the things that make them attractive to begin with.

And you were no different. Showing up on my parents' porch in your Army uniform with that stern look in your eyes. Why hadn't I written to a buddy of yours? you wanted to know. He'd carried my picture all during the

War, and I never once answered his letters. You even took your cap off–remember?–as if it was official business. But you couldn't hide that sheepish look in your eyes.

And besides, it wouldn't have helped. I was fed up with the War, with everyone using it as an excuse, and I wasn't about to put up with one more person telling me what to do.

I told you I hardly remembered your buddy, that he was just a friend of the family on my mother's side. And when you still wouldn't budge, I told you I wrote to whomever I pleased, and if you didn't like it, you could take a hike–or go to hell. It was all the same to me.

You should've seen your face, how your head snapped back and your eyes turned dark. I thought it would send you packing, or at least change your tune. But you still had a trick up your sleeve. You took out that photograph of me and a dark-haired boy necking on Santa Monica Beach. I'd never seen it before–Howie's older brother must have taken it–but when I saw that picture, I cried out. To think someone had carried me across Europe–and in my bathing suit!

My parents came running, so I stuffed the photograph in my sweater pocket and hurried you down the porch steps. They never would have let us go out, not in a million years. They didn't let me date.

"He's an old friend," I called back. "We have some catching up to do."

That's what you wanted, wasn't it? You didn't care about your friend, Howie. You never saw him again. As far as I know, you didn't even write. You were worse than me.

And yet I trusted you, this stranger who'd shown up on my porch, who seemed to know L.A. better than I did. You'd only been in town a few hours, but you took me everywhere–Olvera Street, Sunset Boulevard, Ocean Park–do you remember?–wherever the Red Cars would carry us. And when we got to Angels Flight, you refused to get off.

Each time we came to the end, you said someone had spoiled it for you. First it was a man who coughed. Then a woman with a strange perfume. Then a boy who scratched himself. We had to ride that little cable car up and down the track under a sky full of stars. You sly fox. You just wanted to keep your arm around me, didn't you?

And do you remember the dance hall in Venice Beach? The one with the band that sounded like Tommy Dorsey's? It was so crowded I didn't want to go inside. But you said you'd die of depression if I didn't dance with you, and to make it through the War and die of depression was the cruelest thing in the world. You really took advantage, didn't you?

The place was packed and choking with cigarette smoke, and I was afraid the band would play something fast and I'd make a fool of myself. But they played that same slow tune over and over. *Where or When.* Do you remember? You draped your arms around me and held me close, but you didn't look at me. You were listening to that song. All night long you wore it on your face. I thought you'd forgotten me, that you were thinking about another girl, someone you'd met in New York or Europe. You wore that song even when that fat little sailor tried to break in on us. He was "stinking," as you put it, so drunk he could barely stay on his feet. And yet, he kept following us and pawing me. I told you I didn't want a fight, so you parked me at the bar and told me not to leave. You left me with that ugly little man. And when you returned, you had another girl with you, and for one horrible moment, I thought you were leaving me. But she was for the sailor. She latched onto him like a tiger and wouldn't let go, and as you pulled me back onto the dance floor, I kept looking in their direction, afraid the sailor would follow us. But the girl had him completely occupied. She was all over him, nuzzling his neck, reaching under his shirt, flirting in the most indecent way. You called her the Baby Sitter, remember? She even looked like one–blonde stringy hair, freckly face, skinny as a French fry. I kept asking where you found her, but you wouldn't tell me. You just held me tight and danced to your heart's content. You sly fox. It was a long time before I figured it out. You hired her, didn't you? She was a streetwalker, wasn't she? But your eyes were dreaming again, and you wouldn't answer me. You just kept holding me and dancing slowly with that song on your face. *Where or When.* We stayed so late that we didn't get home until two in the morning.

I never heard the end of it from my parents, not until the wedding six weeks later. And even then, my father didn't want to give me away.

"You hardly know this guy," he said as he walked me down the aisle.

But I felt as if I'd known you all my life, as if I'd always know you. And I still do, even though we can't dance anymore.

Cal wakes up and blinks. He stares at me for a moment, and then lifts himself up on his elbow, and I think now I can get up and use his shower. But he wants to talk. He tells me about the restaurant and how it's finally doing well after several difficult years. And about Emilio, the violinist, and how he misses his family in Ensenada. Cal describes it so sadly, I think he's talking about his own daughters.

Then he draws me to him and kisses me. Kisses my mouth and my neck and my breasts. And to my surprise he's ready again. It's not so bad this time, just burning a little. I stroke and squeeze his sides, pinch him so he'll finish. It takes him a little longer, but now he shudders and eases down on me, and the tears roll down my face like a child. I tug at his sides, whisper in his ear, and half-asleep he rolls off.

But it's your weight I feel, your body that's pressing down. So you have to let go, darling. You have to let go.

I'm too young to be a widow, not even 40 yet. And the children have to get on with their lives. They have to move on as well. So you have to let us go, darling. We'll always miss you–there's no question of that. If I live to be a hundred–if I live to be a thousand. But we can't live in the past. We can't be tied to smoke and ash. So you have to let go, darling. You have to let us go. You have to let go.

Won't you?

8. The Understudy
Margot

SUZIE FARQUHAR WAS THE LAST PERSON in the world I ever thought I'd room with. I knew her in high school as a giggly little blonde who spent most of her time in class touching up her face or making eyes at the boys. Occasionally, she'd pay enough attention to ask a silly question, such as the time in Biology when she wanted to know why it had taken Darwin thirty years to name all of the animals when it had only taken Adam a day. I think Mr. O'Connell said something like, "Adam probably had a Univac," though it was hard to tell in the uproar that followed. I suppose if I noticed Suzie at all, it was only to pass along her comments, which she usually delivered in a whine, as if she were constantly being amazed. Otherwise, I just assumed that she was one of the many characters I'd leave in my past when I went away to college. I never imagined then just how important she would become in my life.

I met up with Suzie again at the beginning of my freshman year at Valley College. I'd been staying at the home of my best friend Jodi Kellerman all summer long, following the big blow-up with my mom, and while Jodi was there, everything was fine. But when she went away to

Radcliffe, things became rather strained in the Kellerman household. Her mom would arch her eyebrows whenever we ran into each other, as if surprised to still find me there. And her father took to putting his arm around me when he came from work, usually after he'd had a scotch or two. "How's my little Margot?" he'd say. He even wanted to kiss me on the mouth, which wasn't exactly the thing you did with your best friend's dad–at least, not in the 1960s.

I'd really had no intention of staying beyond the summer. My plan was to find a place and move out as soon as I could, but I couldn't afford an apartment on my own, and finding a roommate turned out to be harder than I expected. All my close friends had gone away to college– something I was supposed to do–and the places the Student Housing Office sent me to were either filthy and dilapidated or the people were just plain weird. One girl grew marijuana plants in her kitchen and wanted me to take turns misting them. Another, a tall, willowy brunette with purple fingernails and matching eye shadow, told me she'd been a dwarf in a previous life. She had a sneaking suspicion that we'd been brothers. And a third, I'm pretty sure, was a young man dressed in drag. She, or *he*, kept giggling in a deep voice and scratching at his crotch.

After that last experience, I was ready to drop out of school and work full-time just to have a place of my own. But on my way to the Admissions Office, I happened to pass the housing board one last time and spotted Suzie's name printed neatly on a 3-by-5 card with a little heart above the "i." I wasn't even sure she'd remember me– we'd hardly spoken two words in high school–but when I phoned the number on the card, she practically screamed in my ear.

"Margot! You've got to come over right now. I mean it. I thought you were going to Harvard or someplace like that."

"So did I."

"Well, I'm so glad you didn't. Now we can be roomies."

She gave me directions, and fifteen minutes later, I pulled up in front of a faded two-story apartment building done up in pewter gray with a white trim and an outside walkway. It wasn't in the best of shape–the driveway was pockmarked, and the front lawn bristled with weeds–and the mail trough looked like it hadn't been emptied in a week–but as I made my way up the stairs, I felt a flutter run down my chest, the kind I'd always thought I'd experience when I stepped onto some leafy New England campus. Suzie's building wasn't exactly the Victorian dormitory that I'd dreamed about, but if she would have me, I'd have finally a place to stay, and it was enough to send my heart soaring.

I was still making my way along the second story looking for her number when she waved to me from her window. A moment later, she pulled me inside.

"Margot!" she squealed. "Don't you dare make a move for that door. You're moving in tonight."

"Are you sure? Don't you want to discuss the rent and things like that?"

She looked me over as if I was making a joke. She hadn't changed an inch from the Suzie I remembered in high school, all smiles and glowing eyes. I half expected her to ask a silly question–such as, how do you turn on the stove? or, where's the linen closet?–but instead she planted a kiss on my cheek and gave me a big hug, accompanied by a typical Suzie giggle.

"There," she said. "We discussed it. Now go get your things. No, wait, I'm going with you."

And she did, all the way to the Kellermans and back, talking my ear off a mile a minute about how much fun we were going to have. "This is going to be so groovy. We'll be just like sisters."

Suzie was nothing if not sweet–a real lifesaver–but in the back of my mind, I gave it two weeks, three at the most.

We were just so different. I wasn't even sure that we spoke the same language, such as when she promised the first night not to "bogart" anything. Or when she told me, with a suppressed giggle, that she'd been "reincarnated" the week before.

To my surprise, however, we soon fell into an easy rhythm together. Suzie insisted on doing everything as a team–shopping, cooking, even washing our hair–as if we were two girls away at camp. And just like two girls away at camp, we kept each other up at night pouring our hearts out. I thought I'd had it bad, with my father passing away and our house being lost–and the big falling-out with my mom–but it was nothing compared to what Suzie had been through. Her mother was an alcoholic and had deserted the family when she was ten, and afterward, her father and older brother had treated her like slave labor, practically keeping her under lock and key.

"They were so protective," she said. "If I came home even a little late, they'd blow a fuse."

Still, she didn't brood over it. She made it clear that she was putting it all behind her now that she'd left home. In fact, what she really wanted to talk about were boys, especially the cute ones she met at Valley College.

"Can you believe it? So many of them, and they're all so sweet."

She sat up in bed and hunched her shoulders, as if she'd been caught in a fib. It was the same Suzie I'd remembered from Biology class, bubbling over with enthusiasm and hopelessly out of touch.

I assumed that her crushes were mostly one-sided, but not a week went by before a gangly boy with dark wavy hair showed up at our door.

"This is Harris," Suzie screamed, pushing him toward me. "Isn't he beautiful?"

I said that he was, making us both blush. Then I ran off to work, hoping she wouldn't eat him up alive. When I came home around 10:30, they were in the bedroom, giggling in subdued voices.

I slept on the sofa that night, happy for Suzie–and more than a little apprehensive that our living arrangement might be coming to an end.

But a couple days later, another boy showed up–Pete–with muscular arms and a cookie-crumb mustache, and Suzie gushed over him just as she had over Harris.

Then the next day, it was Bobby, with dark curly hair and woolly eyebrows.

Then it was Vin, with a bristling flattop and metallic blue shades.

Then Albert. Then Lenny. Then Harris again.

It got to the point where I couldn't keep track of all the names and faces. But no matter who showed up, Suzie would squeal as if she couldn't believe her luck. Occasionally, she'd go out with the boy to a movie or dinner, but usually she'd just usher him into the bedroom and leave her mark on him, as she liked to put it. And quite often, the boys left their marks on her, affectionate little wings of red that would fade to pink, then plum, then gray before a new one flew into her golden flesh.

"It's so great living with you," she told me after a couple weeks. "No more sneaking around, doing it on the sly."

I'd never seen anything quite like it, and to be honest, it made me very uneasy at first. I thought it could only end in disaster. But the boys were all such gentlemen, polite and considerate to a fault, and Suzie lit up so incandescently when they were around, that I couldn't bring myself to complain. I'd even make myself scarce if someone happened to be over, which wasn't hard, considering that I was away at work or school most of the time.

Though it did take some getting used to, obliterating as it did all my notions about love and romance. I'd always imagined that intimacy was something that happened over time, that two people grew together gradually until they merged as a couple, both physically and emotionally. But Suzie showed me that it could also take the form of spontaneous combustion–and with more than one partner.

And she wasn't the only one. Letters I received from Jodi and other friends away at college talked about boys being sneaked into dorm rooms and weekend trips with a special someone. Even my own mother wasn't playing Old Maid anymore, according to my sister. Jenny would show up at the drugstore during my shift and complain about the men Mom was dating, especially a certain junior high school vice principal that our mother had taken a fancy to.

"He thinks just because they're doing it, he can put his stupid arm around me." Jenny told me this in front of a line of customers at the checkout stand. "It's only because of sex. Stupid, lousy sex." After she had everyone's attention, she added, "You're lucky. At least, you've escaped."

If I *had* escaped, I hadn't gotten very far. I was still living in the same town where I'd grown up and seeing a boy I'd gone steady with since the eleventh grade. Eric went to UCLA now and lived in a fraternity house off campus, but he continued to show up at my door in tattersall shirts and corduroy pants, just as he'd always worn. On our dates, we even went back to the old high school to catch football games, after which he'd bring me home by 11:30, as if my late father were somehow hovering in the background.

I did like him, though. He was a nice, quiet boy with light brown hair and pale, innocent features. And during the previous year, when my life was falling apart, he'd been very patient, listening to one sob story after another.

Still, Suzie must have had an effect on me, because one night while Eric and I were sitting in his Camaro talking, I was overcome by a terrible longing. He was telling me about his fraternity brothers and how they'd taken him under their wings, and as I watched his small lips working up and down, I had this sudden urge for him to close his mouth over my breasts and suckle them ever so softly, ever so tenderly, drawing out an excruciating flush. On an impulse, I bent toward him and crushed my mouth against his, thrusting my tongue inside.

He gagged and pushed me away. "What's got into you?"

When I didn't answer, he laughed and started up the car. As he drove off, he kept gazing at me wide-eyed, as if I'd made a joke. But I couldn't have been more serious. I wanted to get close to him in a way I never had before. To feel something I'd never felt before.

Afterward, I felt terrible about it. I came to the conclusion that some people did need more time to work up to intimacy, and here I was pushing him before he was ready. And still later, when I'd thought it over some more, I decided that he just didn't see me that way. I was a good friend, a trusty companion, someone to take to a football game, and when he found the girl who made him forget himself–probably a sorority sister at a Greek social–he'd drop me like a stone. It put me in such a state that when he phoned the next time, I told him that I didn't want to see him anymore.

"Why not?" His voice grew surprisingly tight.

As calmly as I could, I explained that I was seeing someone else.

He cleared his throat, and after a long silence, he said okay and hung up, leaving me a little shaken myself.

It wasn't altogether a lie. Technically, I *was* seeing someone. Twice a week to be exact, usually while he stood in the front corner of my Art History class. Though I suppose, at one time or another, every girl in Art 151 was attracted to Bjorn Jacobson, the teacher's assistant. We should have been listening to Dr. Atwood's lecture and following his slides up on the screen, but every now and again, you could see female heads turning toward Bjorn's roundish face and silky blond hair. He wasn't even aware of the disruption he was causing. He'd gaze out into the lecture hall as if he were dreaming.

I found out later that he *was* dreaming. When I got to know him better, he told me that during lectures, he liked to mentally create his art projects–sculptures that he made out of brightly painted bicycle parts and machine gears. One day, he brought one to class, a complicated thing about the size of a breadbox, and when I asked him how he could make a work of beauty out of such ordinary objects, a couple girls shrieked with laughter.

Bjorn smiled patiently. "What I'd really like to make out of them is a grant."

I was sure he wouldn't take me seriously after that, but when I scored high on the midterm exam, he invited me to help him grade student papers. I'd mentioned that I might go into teaching, and he thought it'd be good practice.

"I can't stand to read them myself," he warned me. "Most of them sound like postcards sent home from camp."

I thought he was joking, but he wasn't far from wrong. In one of the first papers I graded, a student had written, "The Renaissance artist Mustachio was a very realistic painter. He painted the martyrs on the Cross well-hung."

Another wrote, "We have the Italians to thank for discovering charcoal-obscuro. Thank you, Italians. Thank you very much."

I set the second paper in front of Bjorn. "Is this on the level?"

"She's a poet." He looked up at me without a hint of irony. "They ran her work in the literary magazine."

Bjorn liked my grading well enough to invite me back on a weekly basis. So every Wednesday afternoon, following my Introductory Lit class, I'd make my way across campus fantasizing about the romantic possibilities awaiting me in his tiny office. Usually they involved one or both of us looking up suddenly and seeing the mistiness in the other's eyes, and then running into each other's arms. Though sometimes they were more elaborate, such as Bjorn inviting me to pose for him in the nude and me refusing several times before I finally gave in, with a lot of good-natured bantering back and forth.

Of course, nothing like that happened. When I arrived, he'd hand me a stack of papers, and we'd get down to business like a pair of bookkeepers. Occasionally, one of us would chuckle or groan over something that caught our attention, but otherwise Bjorn just hummed little ditties to himself as he flipped through the pages. It made me wish I had Suzie's art–or was it her artlessness?–so I could ask him the questions that danced through my head. Did he have a girlfriend? Was he looking for a non-artist? Had he really come from Sweden? But I couldn't imagine bridging the gulf between student and teacher. I was afraid he wouldn't invite me back.

Then one evening, Suzie brought home her English professor, Dr. Feldman, or "Eugene," as she called him. He was my English professor too, and as he stood in our living room with his foaming beard and thick glasses, making small talk about the quaintness of student apartments, all I could do was nod in confusion. I stammered something about having to return a book–and spent the rest of the evening staring into a cup of black coffee at a local diner.

It wasn't Dr. Feldman's presence in our living room that unnerved me so much. It was the casual way he and Suzie carried on, as if relations between students and teachers happened all the time and I was too naïve to see it. It forced me to reconsider all those silent afternoons in Bjorn's office. Maybe his way of making a move on a girl was to invite her to grade papers, and if that was the case, then he must have thought I was a pretty cold fish.

When I returned home around eleven, "Eugene" was in our bedroom, talking in a loud voice. He didn't slip out until two in the morning, trying, unsuccessfully, not to wake me on the sofa.

Afterward, I couldn't look at Bjorn the same way. The next time we worked together, my heart wouldn't keep still. I struggled through one student paper after another, and in the middle of a particularly awful one, he came over and put his hand on my wrist. He wanted to draw my attention to a funny comment, but where he touched me, it felt like my skin had been seared.

A few minutes later, he came back and playfully lifted my hand to put another paper under it, scorching my arm all the way to the elbow.

I couldn't work after that. I sat there listening to Bjorn humming away as he scribbled down comments.

"Bjorn?"

"Uh-huh?"

I rose and stood beside him, wondering if he could feel the tension in the room. He dashed off one last comment and looked up at me, raising his eyebrows.

I ran my finger down his cheekbone to his smallish chin. Unlike Eric, he had scarcely any bristle, but where my finger traced a line, it seemed to set off little sparks.

He smiled, causing his eyes to turn a shade lighter. Then he took my wrist and pulled me toward him, and as our faces came together, I lost all sense of where I was. I saw his arm reach out to close the door, and somewhere in the distance, I heard two boys running up the hall. But these were miles away. Up close, bright flashes were going off in my face. Bjorn's hand worked its way slowly up my leg, burning a deep trench, and found its way inside my clothes, causing the floor to shift, as if the room were bobbing over an ocean. I waited breathlessly for him to pull me onto his lap, to put his arms around me–but suddenly, he backed away and gave a hollow laugh. Then he returned to his papers and started humming again.

I stood there turning to stone. When I could catch my

breath, I ran out and didn't stop until I reached the edge of the campus green. I braced myself against the guardrail and gazed out across the rolling lawn as if I were leaning over a cliff. I waited for the slightest sound, the slightest touch, to draw me back. But there was only the shutting of a car door in the distance and the voices of a couple walking behind me. They grew quiet as they passed and then broke into subdued laughter.

I don't know how long I stayed there. Maybe an hour, maybe less. When I finally turned around, the lights were coming on across campus and people were hurrying to their cars. Bjorn was probably on the freeway by now. He liked to leave early to get a jump on traffic.

Back in the apartment, I curled up on the sofa and lay in the dark. Suzie found me there when she came home from work.

"What happened?"

I shook my head and turned away. But she wouldn't take no. She made a bowl of popcorn and plopped herself down by the sofa, and as she munched away, moaning and groaning about how good it was, she got me to gush out a laugh.

"He was just going along for the ride," she said, after I'd come clean. "He's probably undersexed. You know, lacking in hormones."

I grunted, dabbing at my eyes.

"No, I'm *serious*. You have to find someone who cares about you."

"Do *your* boyfriends care about you?" It came out meaner than I'd intended, though I did have my doubts.

"Of course! I wouldn't let them near me if they didn't. And I care about them."

As we sat there munching popcorn, I thought of all the boys who came to our door and how different they were. Some would arrive very businesslike, as if they had better things to do, and others would show up grinning like the cat who'd swallowed the mouse. And still others would show up nervous and short of breath, as if they weren't quite sure they should be there at all. But no matter how they might appear when I opened the door, the moment they laid eyes on Suzie, their faces would glow and their eyes would glaze over, as if they were already in her short, tender arms. It made me realize that they *did* love her, each in his own way. Though it also made me wonder if a boy would ever look at *me* like that.

"Isn't there someone who makes you all mushy inside?" Suzie asked.

I shook my head and blinked away tears.

"There has to be *somebody*! You're just not paying attention."

"I wasn't exactly going to school to find a beau. I think the main point is to get an education."

"So get one. A *real* one."

At Suzie's insistence, we made devil food cupcakes that evening with chocolate frosting and coconut flakes, and in the middle of all the mixing and baking, she got out of me every secret crush that I'd ever had, from the time I tried to sit on my Uncle Max's lap to my high school years, when I couldn't get enough of my math teacher, Mr. Bernstein, with his crinkly blue eyes. She even got me to confess something I'd never told anyone–that I'd been secretly in love with my father's business lawyer for years.

"You see?" she said. "You're not dead."

"And what about you? You didn't have any crushes?"

"Oh," she giggled wistfully. "I guess the mailman. And the man who read the gas meter. But I was only eight."

"*You* started early."

"But they were so easy. All they wanted was a kiss."

The next day, Bjorn raised his eyebrows when I came into class and smiled from a distance. It was a distance because I sat in the back and tried not to look at him. I felt that I'd made a mess of things, that I'd ruined a perfectly good professional relationship without cementing a loving one. But if he'd come up to me and said hello, come up and said anything, we could have gone back to his office and worked it out, one way or another. But he didn't say a word. He just gathered up his papers at the end of class and walked out. It made me feel like one more deluded freshman throwing herself at her teacher.

Suzie kept pushing me to find "a real flame." She'd even have one of her boyfriends bring along buddy now and again, and we'd all go out to dinner together. And I suppose I had other chances. Occasionally, a boy would strike up a conversation in class, or a young man would stop me on campus to get directions. And hardly a day went by at work without a male customer asking for my phone number. But I wasn't very encouraging, and nothing ever came of these encounters. I was just too afraid of what Eric and Bjorn had stirred up in me–of how easily I'd lost control–and I didn't want to risk it again. At least, not so soon–and not with any of the boys I knew.

* * *

With the beginning of the spring semester, however, I did find a flame, and an old one at that. On a whim, I enrolled in a drama workshop, and fell in love with it all over again. Though it didn't start well. On the first day of class, I nearly ran back out. Most of the students were older than me and they looked as if they'd been acting for years. I didn't see how I'd stand a chance among them. But as I was leaving, someone called my name, and suddenly, I was surrounded by four or five faces out of my past. They were all members of the amateur theater troupe my father had started in our living room, and with everyone talking at once, asking about my family and reminiscing about the troupe, even arguing over why it had folded and how to get it going again, I felt like I was back in our old house during one of our rehearsals. I half expected Dad to blink the lights to get everyone's attention.

"You're all making a mistake." This was from a little white-haired man sitting in the front row. "It's not the material or the venue that kills a troupe. It's the lack of funding. In fact, you're wasting your time here. You ought to study science and engineering. That's where the college is putting its real money."

"I auditioned for science once," one of Dad's cronies said, "but I didn't make the cut."

"No wonder," another said. "You make a terrible cadaver."

It went on like that for the better part of an hour. I kept wondering when the teacher would show up, a Dr. Mandeville, but nobody seemed too concerned. Finally, the little white-haired man sighed and placed a stack of sign-up sheets on the edge of the classroom stage.

"Here you go, dears. These are the plays we're putting on this semester. Pick a part that suits you, and we'll have try-outs next time." Then he walked out muttering to himself.

I got the idea that the workshop wouldn't be like any of my other classes. Even to call it a workshop would be misleading. It was more like a time capsule. Outside, the students might be burning their draft cards, smoking marijuana and growing their hair long like gypsies and revolutionaries. But inside, it was as if we'd never left the 1940s. Every Tuesday and Thursday evening at 7:30, someone would plug in a percolator, and while the bracing aroma of coffee filled the room, people would carry on like characters out of an Andy Hardy movie.

"So when you gonna thrill me?" one of the men would say.

"When I find something worth thrilling," the woman would answer.

Even the plays we put on were from my parents' time: *The Petrified Forest*, *Tea and Sympathy*, *The Glass Menagerie*. It was as if we couldn't let go of the past.

Still, I looked forward to that class more than any other. The atmosphere might be from another era, but it was a courtly era, an amusing era, even a tender one–and at the end of each workshop, I always found it a bit of a shock to go back into the world of the '60s.

Of all the people there, I was probably closest to Walt Petersen, Dad's former business lawyer. Just sitting next to him and listening to the soft timbre of his voice brought back some of my old crush. Walt told me that after the troupe had folded, he'd been bitten with the acting bug and had continued performing in little theaters around town. He might have gone on with it, but his wife had forced him to quit. She thought it was hurting the law practice.

"She wouldn't be too happy if she knew I was here," he added with a grim smile.

"But what if you find new clients?"

He chuckled sarcastically and shook his head. I wasn't sure why he found it amusing. Maybe no one ever hired a lawyer from a drama workshop. Or maybe he was too much of an actor to ever do it for an ulterior motive. He certainly had the looks of one. He was short and compact with sharp features, walnut-colored hair and dark, penetrating eyes. And he had the most darling hands I'd ever seen on a man: squarish, well-formed fingers set off by wispy patches of hair on their backs.

Walt was the one who encouraged me to try out for *The Glass Menagerie*. He thought I'd make a great Laura, and I did too, but the part went to a woman in her forties with two teenage sons. Strictly speaking, Lynn Adams was too old to play Laura, and she had the shadows under her eyes to show for it. But she also had strawberry-blonde hair that made her look younger when she wore it in a ponytail, and she had chronic hay fever that gave her the pallor and red-rimmed eyes you'd expect of a sickly 23-year-old.

I did make understudy, however, and it turned out to be nearly as good. The closer we got to spring, the more

Lynn's allergies acted up, making it hard for her to talk sometimes without coughing. So as often as not, Dr. Mandeville would have me stand in during rehearsals.

He could be a tough director. He liked to stop people at their most awkward moments and put them on the spot. The woman who played Amanda, for instance, would sometimes pause in mid-sentence and bunch up her mouth. Walt, who played Jim O'Connor, had a tendency to tilt his head when he got excited. And the man who played Tom would rock back and forth on the balls of his feet. Dr. M never actually corrected these tics, he'd just point them out. "That's it, dears. Don't hide these things. Let's all share them." And afterward, they would either disappear or become part of the character.

I kept waiting for him to interrupt me–I certainly had my share of bad habits–but he only did it once, during the climactic scene when Jim makes a pass at Laura.

"You've got to become a couple," he told us, "if only for a minute."

We did the scene again, and when we still didn't get it right, he made us stay after class like a pair of naughty children.

Walt found it amusing, but I became very nervous with just the three of us. I kept flubbing my lines and missing cues. I took the chewing gum from Walt when I should have refused it. And when it came to the kiss, I was completely undone. Walt wasn't a bad kisser. He smelled nice, like clove and ginger, and he held me close. But when our faces came together, it was just too tentative, not at all the revelation it was supposed to be in the play.

Dr. M took my face in his large, fleshy hands. "Margot, you're anticipating the kiss. You're thinking about it the whole time. You don't *know* he's going to kiss you. You're shocked. You're like a fish that's been hiding in the shadows and you've been yanked into the sunlight. It's so bright your eyes blink." He turned to Walt. "Kiss her *before* the scene. Let's get it out of her system."

Walt wrinkled his forehead as if to say it wasn't his idea. Then we approached and held each other–and kissed. And it was the sweetest kiss I'd ever received, warm and accepting and so unlike the anxious pecks I used to get from Eric. We ran through the scene one more time, and finally, Dr. M let us go.

From then on, he had us kiss before every rehearsal. He explained our little routine to the class, but it didn't stop the teasing. Several of the men offered to coach me, and a number of the women volunteered to warm up Walt.

"I won't act until I've been kissed," one of the men cried out.

Walt took it well enough. When it came time for our little exercise, he'd wink and squeeze my shoulders, and then kiss me as naturally as a husband coming home from work. For me, though, it became something of an ordeal. My mouth would go dry and my throat would tighten up and my heart would beat so wildly, I was afraid Walt would feel it through my blouse. Sometimes just the sight of him at the beginning of class would make my stomach twist into knots.

I probably should have known what was happening. I suppose if Suzie had been around, we would have discussed it and sorted it out, one way or another. But she was living with Dr. Feldman at the time, and days would go by without our seeing each other. Sometimes it got so lonely in the apartment that I'd sing while I made dinner just to keep myself company. And every so often, I'd open the front door, sure that I'd heard a knock. But now that Suzie was going with Eugene, her other boyfriends had stopped showing up, and the walkway would always be empty.

Then one evening, there *was* a knock, or actually a hard rap, and when I opened the door, this strange little man fixed me with a pair of bloodshot eyes.

"Suzie here?" He looked as if he'd spent the night by a railroad track. His clothes were torn and filthy, and his face was horribly sunburnt. He also reeked of alcohol.

"No, she isn't. She doesn't live here anymore." I closed the door about three-quarters of the way. I wondered if I could get the chain back on.

"Her name's on the mailbox." He had a gruff, throaty voice.

"We haven't gotten around to changing it."

"Huh. How 'bout that?" He continued to stare at me.

"Sometimes she calls," I said. "I can tell her you were here."

"Nah, don't bother."

He rubbed his nose hard and made a face that looked like a sneer. Then he lowered his eyes and gazed at my breasts. His mouth dropped open and he stared at me, as if he'd forgotten why he'd come.

"I have to go now," I said. "I've got something on the stove."

I shut the door and locked it, and stood there with my heart in my throat. I couldn't believe Suzie would get involved with a lowlife like that. He must have seen her name somewhere and copied it down, or maybe one of her boyfriends had blabbed about her, and he had to see for himself. After I heard his footsteps down the stairs, I picked up the phone to call the police, but almost as quickly, I put it back down. What could I tell them? He hadn't done anything—except to knock on our door and ask for her, and *that* wasn't a crime. Then I thought of phoning Suzie at work or leaving a note, just to let her know. But in the end, I didn't do anything. I figured it was one of those strange little incidents that happen once and never again, and I couldn't see the point in alarming her.

* * *

Our first performance took place before a small student audience on a Thursday afternoon. Lynn felt well enough to go on, which was a stroke of luck, because I was so nervous, I didn't think I could stand in for her. Even with Lynn, however, the play was a disaster. The cast talked over each other. They answered things that weren't said. They forgot their lines and missed their entrances. During one scene, Dr. Mandeville had to call out directions to the woman who played Amanda. She'd forgotten to come out of the kitchenette at the back of the stage. Walt was so keyed up, he could barely make himself heard. In the middle of his climactic scene with Laura, which should have held the audience spellbound, we could hear chair bottoms flipping up as people emptied the auditorium.

Walt couldn't look at me afterward. He mumbled something about having to get back to his office and hurried away.

Only Dr. Mandeville had a glint in his eye. "At least, we got the kinks out, dears. We'll do better tomorrow. Opening night is always a curse."

But the next afternoon, we were hardly much better. The man who played Tom got his coat snagged on a chair, which was part of the play. However, instead of ripping it, he was yanked backwards onto the floor. It broke up the audience. Then Lynn had a coughing spell that went on forever. The woman who played her mother tried to cover up, but after a couple minutes of adlibbing, *Amanda* looked like she wanted to throw a fit.

Dr. M stood next to me in the wings shaking his head. "They know it's a student production. I'd put you in, but they'd laugh even harder. Just be ready to go on tonight."

For the final performance, we expected a crowd. The student newspaper had written a front-page story about us, and there was a rumor that the honorary mayor of North Hollywood, a famous actor, might show up. So I went home, took a warm bath and drank a cup of hot chocolate. Then I lay down in bed and tried to dream the play into existence. It was a routine that I'd followed all through high school, and it had always worked before. But as I got ready to leave, I was still a nervous wreck. To make matters worse, my car wouldn't start. It coughed and coughed, sounding like Lynn having an allergy attack.

I managed to get Suzie on the phone at Dr. Feldman's place, and she practically took my head off.

"Why didn't you tell me you were performing tonight! I'd have gotten time off from work."

"I didn't *know*. It was a last-minute thing."

When she pulled up in her red Corvair, I apologized again, but she didn't say a word. She just kept her eyes on the road as we drove off. It was so unlike her, I wondered if she was having trouble with Eugene.

I arrived in plenty of time, and just like Laura in the play, I was sick to my stomach. In desperation, I did something my high school drama teacher had warned us never to do–I peeked through the curtains and watched as the auditorium filled up. It looked like we were going to have a capacity crowd. Almost immediately, I spotted the famous actor a few rows back, and next to him, the college president, but these weren't the faces I was looking for. I was hoping that Jenny had gotten word to Mom, and that despite our falling out, she'd show up with my brother and sister. She'd never missed one of my performances before, and it gave me an empty feeling to think that she wouldn't be there tonight. And then, as I was scanning the crowd, I lost all sense of where I was. I imagined I was back in high school, back in our old creaky auditorium, and that if I looked hard enough, I'd find Dad's beaming face with his boyish grin. I even hoped he'd give me a wink and the old thumbs-up. But a moment later, the illusion passed, and I was back in college again, watching a roomful of strangers settle into their seats.

Behind me, the actors who played Amanda and Tom started to bicker.

"Try not to step over my lines," *Tom* said.

"Well, someone has to keep the momentum going. You stand around like you're waiting for a bus."

"Maybe you remind me of a bus. Did you ever think of that?"

"Dears, dears," Dr. Mandeville said. "Put it in the play."

I felt a pair of hands on my shoulders. I thought it was Dr. M, but when I turned, Walt's dark brown eyes peered into my face. His irises were almost iridescent. He drew me toward him and pressed his mouth softly against mine. I'd forgotten about our little routine.

"Cynthia found out," he whispered. "She left and took the kids." His lips were trembling.

The lights dimmed and the crowd fell silent. It was time to go on.

I made my way onto the stage and went through a pantomime of setting the dining room table and lighting candles, and just as I'd done at the beginning of every performance in my life, I wondered what in the world I was doing up there. My arms felt heavy, my ears were stopped up and I had the impression that I was wading through water.

Once again, we were terrible. The man who played Tom walked into me as he came onstage. *Amanda* forgot the names of her children. And for the first time ever, I couldn't remember a line. Dr. M called it out to me from the wings. What made it worse is that I could hear Walt clearing his throat. When I glanced in his direction, he'd be pacing about or scowling at the air in front of him. His character didn't come on until late in the play, and here we were ruining it before he ever had a chance.

Occasionally, the acting would come together, and for a few moments, you could almost imagine that we were a troubled family living in a walkup apartment in St. Louis during the Depression, a family so overwhelmed by our problems that each of us had to escape into a world of our own making. But then the moment would pass and we'd stumble again, and the play would get away from us.

Into this mess, Walt entered and gave the performance of his life. As Jim, The Gentleman Caller, he snowed everyone with his charm and confidence, and won the mother over like a bon vivant. Then, while the others retreated into the kitchenette at the back of the stage, he proceeded to sweep Laura off her feet–poor, crippled, painfully shy Laura. In high school, she'd scarcely been able to talk to him, the most popular boy on campus. But now here he was, years later, sitting in her living room and telling her how pretty she was–and making a pass! And then, almost before she can catch her breath, Jim confesses that he's engaged to be married and hurries away from the dinner party. He leaves Laura crushed and the mother so furious that it tears the family apart.

By the closing scene, when Tom Wingfield tells Laura from a distant city and a distant time to blow out her candles, I could hear sniffling in the audience. And when the lights came on and we took our bows, there were more than a few blinking eyes as the applause rolled over us.

After the final curtain call, Walt embraced me, filling my mouth with his. Dr. M held my face in his hands and gave me a big kiss on the forehead. "A natural! A natural!" The other cast members threw their arms around me, and even Lynn had tears in her eyes that weren't from her allergies.

The entire workshop was invited to the cast party, and as we gathered up our things, Walt offered me a lift, knowing that I didn't have my car. But we didn't make it to the restaurant–at least, not right away. Instead, we drove to his house to see if his wife might call, and once inside, he offered me a scotch, which I accepted. Though that's not what went to my head. He held me again and kissed me, kissed me with his body as well as his mouth, and I felt as if I were no longer a person but a million nerve endings that the slightest breath could unleash. We sat down on the living room sofa and held each other, and as we kissed, his darling hands found their way here and there, making me shudder all over. I nestled against his chest and sighed. He could have done anything he wanted, anything at all. But the minutes passed, and his arms slowly loosened and fell away. When I looked up, he was staring at the window, a distant look in his eyes.

He smiled sadly. "I was hoping Cynthia would call." Then he grabbed my shoulder and gave it a good-natured shake. "I guess you're still Frankie's girl to me. We'd better go. They'll think we got lost."

On the way to the restaurant, we didn't say a word, and as soon as Walt found a parking space, I jumped out and ran inside. A few eyes widened, but most were watching Dr. M do a Greek dance in the middle of the banquet room. Then the man who played Tom sang off key with his arm around *Amanda*. Apparently, they'd made up, though *Tom* looked like he was three sheets to the wind.

Walt came in and winked at me, the way you'd wink at a child who's been allowed to stay up late. Someone offered me champagne, but I shook it off. I realized suddenly that I had nothing in common with these people. Nothing at all. Most of them probably had children my age. Some may have even had grandchildren.

I retreated to the back of the room, but I couldn't escape the feeling that my father might come in at any moment and hoist me up on his shoulder. "Here's my Margot," he'd say. "My little girl."

When the noise level rose again, I slipped out and took a taxi home.

* * *

I stayed away from the workshop for the rest of the school year. I didn't care if I failed, I just didn't want to run into Walt. Dr. M gave me an Incomplete, hoping, no doubt, that I'd show up again. Someone told me he had a role in mind for me for the next semester, but as far as I was concerned, I was through with acting. It was just a schoolgirl thing, something I'd never been particularly good at, and it was time I moved on.

Suzie moved on too. One evening, I came home from school and heard shouts from our apartment. I ran up the stairs and found the strange little man who'd come by a couple weeks before standing in our living room.

"Just get the hell away from me!" Suzie screamed.

He shouted back and slapped her so hard she fell on the sofa. She tried to get up, but he knocked her down again.

With my heart in my throat, I ran inside and grabbed his arm. "Don't make me do something I don't want to do. Don't make me call the police."

His head started back and I thought he'd slap me too. But he dropped his arm and sniffed sharply.

"I don't know what's going on," I cried, "but I think you'd better leave."

My knees were shaking, and I thought if he so much as made a move toward me, I'd faint. But he just looked around, as if he was momentarily confused.

"So that's how it is, Suzie?" he said. "You're not coming home? You don't care how we get by?"

"Yeah, that's how it is," she said between sobs.

"What if I come back later?" he asked.

"So you can beat the shit out of me again?"

He turned to me. "You think that's right? Can't even visit my own daughter?"

I hadn't noticed the resemblance before, but now that I looked, I saw the same rounded chin and upturned nose. And the same startling green eyes. On Suzie, however, it was sweet and fetching. On her father, with his veiny nose and sunburnt face, it was positively grotesque, as if someone had taken a cartoon character and turned it into a monster.

"You're Suzie's father?"

"Isn't he a treat?" she said.

"Well, you bring it on yourself," Mr. Farquhar said. "If

you'd've stayed home and took care of things, none of this would've happened. Did you think we wouldn't find you? Huh? Did you?" His voice started to rise again. "Chasing around with every goddamn prick on the street."

"Mr. Farquhar, please," I said. "I don't think this is helping. I think it's better if you leave."

He nodded obediently, like a child being told what to do. "I'll be back," he said, sneering at Suzie, "now that I know where you are."

"Don't bother," she called after him. "I won't be here."

When he was gone, she cried so hard her face turned a deep red. I sat on the sofa and took her in my arms.

"Suzie, it's okay. Really, it's okay. He can't do anything he wants. You can always get a restraining order."

She shook her head.

"Really, Suzie. I mean it."

"I tried so hard to live on my own, and now he acts like he owns me. Accuses me of everything under the sun and calls me a tramp."

"No, you're not. You're the most precious friend I ever had. And I wouldn't be friends with a tramp."

She cried for a good five minutes.

"And you don't have to go home and be his housekeeper," I said.

She cleared her throat. "That's not what he wants. He wants to get laid." She started crying again.

I stared at her. "Suzie, tell me you don't mean that."

"It's been going on ever since I was twelve." Her voice pitched higher. "With him *and* my brother."

I started crying myself. I laid my head against hers and rocked her back and forth. I thought of all the times she'd been so bubbly and outgoing in high school–and to think it was just a cover-up.

"Didn't you tell anyone?" I asked.

"Once. My sixth-grade teacher. She slapped me and said I had a filthy mouth. She said she never wanted to hear it again."

I kissed her forehead and held her as close as I could.

"What was I supposed to do?" she cried.

She pulled away from me, and I thought she'd break down again. But she rose to a sitting position and cleared her throat, and then she gave me the old Suzie smile. It nearly broke my heart.

"So how come you're not at your drama workshop?" she said.

"I quit. It didn't work out." I managed to smile back.

She closed one eye, as if she didn't quite believe me. But the next moment, she put her arms around my neck and nestled her head on my shoulder. "Did you mean it when you said I was your best friend?"

"With all my heart."

"I wish I had a mother like you."

I laughed. "I'd make a terrible mother."

"Better than the one I had."

* * *

Suzie moved in with Dr. Feldman the next day. She continued to pay her share of the apartment, just in case it didn't work out, and I'd see her every now and again when she dropped by to say hello or give me rent money. She never stayed very long. She was always afraid her father might show up. One time, I suggested that we get another place together, but she just shook her head.

"He'd still find me. It's better this way."

As she got up to leave, she'd always give me a hug and the old Suzie smile, though it wasn't quite the same anymore.

Her father came by a couple days after their fight, and I was able to tell him that I didn't know where Suzie lived. Technically it was true–I didn't have Dr. Feldman's address.

He lingered by the door, as if he didn't believe me, picking at a scab on his forearm. "If you hear from her, would you tell her I want to see her?"

I lied and told him I would, and when he left with his head down, I almost felt sorry for him. He seemed like just another broken-hearted father looking for his child.

After Suzie moved out, the apartment became almost unbearable. Occasionally, Jenny would spend the night when she was "pissed" at Toby or Mom, but usually it was just me staring at the walls, wondering when my life would begin.

One evening, I called Eric's fraternity, just to hear a familiar voice. But when he came to the phone, I couldn't talk.

"Hull-o," he said in his chipper way. "Hull-o." If I had devastated him, it didn't show. He probably had another girlfriend by now. "Hull-o," he said again and hung up.

To ease the loneliness, I took to redecorating. I melted candles over empty bottles and placed them all around the apartment. I hung prints of famous nudes and found a thrift-store lamp with a ruby-colored glass that cast the living room into a deep, sultry red. I hung bead curtains over the doorways and crowded the place with throw rugs and bean bags. And one night, when I felt so empty, I wanted to crawl out of my skin, I lit every candle in the apartment. Unlike Laura, however, I didn't blow them out. Instead, I turned on the red lamp and watched as they burned down one by one. From the outside, it must have looked like I was having a séance or a witch's coven. The light fluttered against the drapes and walls like ghosts, and the flames wavered like tiny demons. But the most gruesome part was the way the wax dripped down, running sometimes like blood, and sometimes like tears, and sometimes, when a flame guttered at the wick, like a wretched little creature burrowing deep inside the earth where no one would ever find it.

9. Pranks 1
Jenny

BY THE TIME I REACHED MY senior year in high school, all I could think of was getting out of the house. My mother was on my case for every little thing. If I was rude to the jerks she dated, if I left the dishes in the sink overnight, if I didn't take a shower for a few days, she'd be all over me for it. I even caught hell for whacking my little brother once when the twerp broke in on me. He'd been sneaking around for weeks, and one night, he finally caught me with my pajamas top over my head. So I let him have it.

"He's just curious," Mom said. She was cradling him on her lap like he was three instead of twelve, holding a towel to his bloody nose. "It's natural for a boy his age."

"Then buy him a *Playboy*."

"Why?" Toby snuffled. "*You'd* never be in it."

I almost whacked him again. Instead, I went to my room and wrote down "June 19, 1969" on an index card and taped it above my desk. It was the date of my graduation, and very soon afterward, I expected to find a job, leave home and put this bullpucky behind me. At least, that was the plan. Along the way, however, I got into this big mess at school and was nearly expelled. There was even talk of putting me in a reform school, which would've been really stupid, but that's how far things had gone.

It all started one morning while I was walking between classes and out of nowhere, somebody gave me a flat. They came right down on my heel and practically took my shoe off. I had to hop to the side of the hallway, while everybody hooted and howled, which was to be expected at my school. The place was full of jerks.

Then it happened again at lunchtime, this time in the middle of the Quad. As soon as I felt my heel go down, I spun around, but nobody was within five feet of me. The people who saw it, though, had these big grins on their faces, as if I had it coming.

Then other things started to happen. Like, I'd walk into my English class and find my desk all covered with wood shavings and bits of lead, as if somebody had taken a pencil sharpener and just dumped out the contents. Or in Algebra, I'd reach down for my book, and my hand would go into something soft and gooey. When I looked down, there was a full chocolate malt sitting in my book rack. Or one time when I got to my hall locker, I found it plastered with Day-Glo stickers in the shapes of hearts and flowers. They were on the inside too, all over my books and sweater and everything. By the time I got home, a few even found their way to my butt.

And it wasn't just *inside* the school. Even *outside* I wasn't safe. Like, I could be walking along the school fence in the morning, and suddenly, I'd feel this squirt of something on the top of my head. The first time it happened, I practically tore my hair apart in the girls' lavatory looking for bird doo. But after two or three times, I realized it had to be water–or perfume. It smelled kind of musky and sweet.

Obviously, somebody had it in for me, though who or why was beyond me. I didn't have any enemies, as far as I knew. I didn't even have any friends. I kept to myself mostly, scrunching down in my desk so the teachers wouldn't call on me. And at lunchtime, I'd eat out in the football bleachers where I could be alone. Of course, that could've just made me more of a target–the hapless loner or the shrinking violet–though I never meant to give that impression. In fact, as soon as I found the bastard, I was going to punch his lights out–or hers. But every time something happened, I'd be surrounded by totally different people. Or there'd be nobody within reach. It was really weird, as if it wasn't a person at all but the world itself jumping out at me.

I started to get really paranoid after a while. Like, if I thought somebody was following too close, I'd slam on the brakes, which caused more than one accident. Or if somebody gave me a funny look, I'd stare them down until they turned away. It didn't win me a lot of friends, but I didn't know what to do anymore. The whole thing was just freaking me out. I even started screaming at the trees when I got squirted in the morning. I mean, like, one morning, I just stopped dead in my tracks and screamed up at the trees, "I know you're up there, so you can cut the crap."

But all that did was crack up these freshmen girls passing by, along with this football player named Reggie, who was in my English class.

"It's the squirrels, Jenny," he said, pounding me on the back. "They're calling to you."

People even started to point me out, as if I was the school freak or something. And I started to wonder if maybe I *wasn't*–if maybe there *was* something wrong with me. Though nothing, *nothing,* compared to what happened during the GAC soccer game.

Every year, the Girls Athletic Club put on this big soccer match, and half the school would turn out to see it. Nobody cared about the game–hardly anybody played soccer in those days–but the girls liked to cut class, and the boys got a big kick out of seeing all these girls running around in their gym shorts. About the only ones who did take it seriously were the teachers. They'd deck out the runty stands on the girls' athletic field in the school colors–royal blue and white–and Mr. Parker, the principal, would get up and put people to sleep with one of his pompous speeches. Even before he was done, a few jerks in the stands would be razzing the players.

My team was expected to win that year, mainly because nobody on the opposing side could run as fast as me or this other girl, Maria. So it came no surprise when Maria scored a goal the first time down the field. I was about to score another one on a free kick, but just as I ran up to the ball, this tremendous fart exploded across the field–and I shanked it.

Obviously, it was from a loudspeaker somewhere, but the people in the stands started going nuts.

"Hold it in, Jenny!" they screamed.

"Watch those beans!"

"Don't play upwind!"

I tried to brush it off and just dig in harder, but the next time I got the ball, the theme from *The Lone Ranger* started booming across the field, and the ball got away from me. The music stopped almost immediately, but as soon as I caught up with the ball again, it came right back on, and once again I lost my dribble. It happened at least three or four times, and then Mrs. Bernstein, the soccer coach, called a timeout and got on the official loudspeaker.

"Would whoever's playing the *William Tell Overture* please stop? This isn't funny."

Naturally, everybody thought it was a riot.

The game got going again, but now I couldn't go anywhere *near* the ball without the music booming across the field like a herd of thundering horses.

People started yelling, "Hi-yo, Jenny, away!"

Or "Where's Tonto? Where's Tonto?"

Even the players got into it. I was setting up for another

free kick, when this girl on the opposing team bumped me as she passed.

"You're such a dumbass," she said.

I picked up the ball and smashed her in the face–and got thrown out of the game.

Though even *that* didn't quiet down the crowd. As I slammed down on the bench, the people behind me were falling over each other. One girl was crying in her boyfriend's lap, she was laughing so hard. And a few rows up to my right, these two jerks just wouldn't give it a rest.

"You're the greatest, Jenny!"

"We love you, Jenny! Just watch those beans."

"And be nice to Tonto."

"Where's Kemo Sabe? You didn't sit on him, did you?"

I knew both of them. One was this blond beanpole of a guy named Cleave, who was in my Biology class, and the other was his pudgy friend Gerald, who I had in English and Algebra. They were both supposed to be geniuses, especially Gerald, but I'd always thought they were creeps.

I kept my head down and pretended not to hear them, but now they started yelling, "We want Jenny! We want Jenny!" And *the crowd* took up the chant.

Finally, I turned around and screamed, "Would you shut your goddamn mouths!"

But all that did was cause another uproar.

I buried my face in my hands and swore I'd never come back to this cruddy place. I'd drop out of school and find a job somewhere. I wouldn't even *wait* until I graduated.

Then it got real quiet, and I could hear Cleave pleading in this innocent voice. "Yes, sir, I do have a class now. No, sir, I wouldn't rather be in Detention."

When I looked up, Mr. Baden, the football coach, was standing over them. He said something and they both got to their feet, and suddenly, the music started up again. You could swear it was coming from the apartment building across the street, though the way it boomed back and forth over the field, it was hard to tell. Mr. Baden craned his head around with everybody else, and while he had his back to Cleave, the jerk reached into his back pocket–and just like that, the music stopped.

Mr. Baden turned back to the creeps. "I guess you boys aren't behind this."

"It's not us," Cleave answered in a breaking voice. "No, sir."

"We wouldn't do a thing like that," Gerald said, as if he was holding his breath.

As soon as Mr. Baden bounded down the stands, the two of them started having fits. They should've been embarrassed. I mean, they had the most idiotic laughs. Cleave's was like a dog, going "yip, yip, yip," and Gerald sounded like a screw rattling around inside an empty can. But they just kept yukking it up like a couple of retards.

Mrs. Bernstein gave me permission to leave before the game was over, but it didn't stop the heckling. For the rest of the day, it was "Hi-yo, Jenny, away!" Or "Watch those beans!" Or "Hey, Kemo Sabe, where's Tonto?" The jerks just came out of the woodwork.

Even on my way home, I got razzed. This Chevy slowed down next to me and backfired, making me jump.

"Excuse *me!*" the driver shouted, which was so funny the guys inside just had to roll around like a bunch of hyenas.

The worst part, though, was Cleave and Gerald, or actually, their stupid laughs. I couldn't get them out of my head. They followed me all the way home and right through dinner and *Hawaii Five-0*. Even at night when I was trying to fall asleep, I could still hear them–like a yelping dog and a screw rattling around inside a can.

I even dreamed about them. I saw them as these two blood red imps perched on my dresser. They had wings like vultures and long curving beaks, and just like my little twerp of a brother, they were trying to catch me when I wasn't looking.

Then I woke up–and I actually *heard* them. Right outside my window!

I got up and peeked through the curtains–and just about died. They were prancing around this huge sycamore tree in front of our apartment building, throwing rolls of toilet paper up into the branches and letting them unwind. And they weren't being too quiet about it either. You could hear their stupid laughs up and down the street.

I dropped the curtains and jumped back into bed. Even in my own room I wasn't safe! I kept waiting for them to go, but they just kept giggling and chortling, as if they had endless rolls of toilet paper. I couldn't believe nobody else had heard them. I mean, they were really loud, like a couple of drunks or something. But it was like one of those nightmares where all kinds of crazy things happen–like, you're walking down the street and bombs are exploding all around you and nobody seems to notice. Only, it wasn't a nightmare. I was wide awake!

I probably should've gone down there and had it out with them, but I was afraid they'd dump a bucket of water on my head. There wasn't much else they *hadn't* done. So I just scrunched down under the blanket and tried to drown them out. I even started to bawl a little. I mean, what had I ever done to these guys? It wasn't like our families were feuding or anything. Or like I'd pissed on their lawns. I hardly even *knew* them.

I figured it would go on and on, and I wouldn't get any sleep that night. But somewhere in the middle of their laughing and prancing around and my bawling and being pissed, I must've conked out. Because the next thing I remember, Mom was shaking me, and the sunlight was pouring in through the open curtains.

"Do you know who did this?" She nodded toward the window.

Outside, the sycamore tree had taken on a whole new appearance. In the morning sun, it was glowing with pastel streamers like some giant flower that had blossomed overnight.

"No, not personally."

"Well, then maybe you can explain it to Mrs. Davenport."

Mrs. Davenport was our apartment manager, and Mom was always afraid that she'd kick us out. She weighed over 300 pounds, and she'd get on your case for the dumbest things, like when Mom left the car in the driveway to unload the groceries, or when Toby slid down the banister on his way out. It was really stupid because we paid our rent on time, but Mom was just paranoid about her. Even now, I could see it in her eyes.

"I'll say something," I said.

"Just make sure you do."

And I meant to, I really did. I was going to pin it on the two creeps. But when I ran into Mrs. Davenport on my way out, she wasn't even pissed. She was pulling the streamers down with a rake, making her huge arms wobble like jelly.

"Why would anybody waste good toilet paper?" she asked me.

I shrugged and kept on walking. I didn't have a clue. I mean, the whole thing was way, *way* beyond me, and I couldn't see the point in taking the blame if she didn't suspect us.

Besides, the only thing I knew for sure was that sooner or later I'd have to confront these jerks or they'd never stop. Already they had half the school laughing at me, and probably even now, they were planning their next prank.

I don't know why I hadn't suspected them before. Gerald had actually bumped into me once in the hallway when I slammed on the brakes, though he'd looked so shocked, as if he'd never touched a girl before, that I couldn't believe he was behind it. And Cleave was always giving me these smirky looks in Biology. Though he *always* looked that way, kind of creepy, so it didn't set off any alarms. Still, I should've been suspicious. And I should've realized it was more than one person.

On the way to school, I kept imagining what I'd do to these creeps when I finally caught up with them, how I'd take them apart piece by piece. And after I was done bashing their brains out, I was going to tell them just what I thought of their stupid games. But when I was right across the street, a car honked, and a couple of guys on the sidewalk yelled, "Hi-yo, Jenny, away!" and just like that, my knees buckled. I realized suddenly that I couldn't fight the *whole school*. I mean, it was like everything had just gotten out of control, thanks to the creeps, and there was nothing I could do about it. I should've turned around and gone back home–just made up some stupid excuse and ditched school–but I was almost there, so I kept on going.

When I got to the main hall, more jerks started to razz me, so I made a beeline to my first class, which was Biology. I expected to find Cleave there–he always showed up early like the teacher's pet–but when I burst through the doorway, the room was empty, except for this couple sitting in the front row holding hands. They looked up and grinned when they saw me. Then the boy covered his mouth and made a farting sound.

"Oh, my goodness!" he said, which so funny they had to double over.

I took my seat a few rows back, but I couldn't sit still. Every time somebody came in, I flinched, thinking it was Cleave. Even when Mr. O'Connell walked in, I jumped a little. Finally, the bell rang, and the jerk still hadn't shown. It was so unlike him, he had to be sick. Or maybe he'd overslept because of his stupid prank the night before. Either way, it served him right.

Fortunately, we had an experiment that day, because I didn't think I could stay in my seat. Mr. O'Connell had us all stand in the back, behind the last row of tables, and then he showed us how to put bacteria into these glass Petri dishes. You were supposed to sterilize this wire loop by running it through a Bunsen burner, and then dip the loop into a vial with the bacteria. Then you were supposed to rub it onto this layer of goo inside the Petri dish. It was kind of neat, actually, and I was starting to get the hang of it, when Cleave walked in with his usual jerky shuffle. He handed a note to Mr. O'Connell, who put it in his shirt pocket without even looking at it.

I couldn't do anything after that. I wandered off to the end of the table and stared down at my open Petri dish. My hands were shaking so hard, I was afraid I'd drop it and ruin the experiment–or get it all over my clothes. And then, while I was standing there, I felt this clammy arm go around my shoulders.

"Hey, Jenny!" Cleave shouted in my ear. "Whatcha got there?" He sneezed right into my dish. "Oh, my God! Germs!"

Everybody thought that was a riot. One boy cried out, "Hi-yo, Jenny, away!"

Even Mr. O'Connell chuckled and shook his head. "Every year there's a jokester."

Cleave backed away with his usual smirky grin, and while he was wiping his nose with the back of his hand, I hauled off and slugged him as hard as I could. His head snapped back, and he fell onto the table, right on top of the open Petri dishes, and then onto the floor, pulling most of the dishes on top of him.

Everybody gasped and jumped back.

Mr. O'Connell shouted, "Don't move! Don't move!"

But Cleave wasn't going anywhere. He laid on the floor covered with goo, thrashing his head back and forth, and crying out, "Oh shit! Oh shit!" He tried to wipe the goo off, but he just smeared it all over himself. After a while, he started to look like part of the experiment, like some giant bacteria that we'd been working on, and that's when

I lost it. I started cracking up and I couldn't stop. My hand hurt where I'd hit him, and people were staring at me, but the more Cleave thrashed about, the more I cracked up.

"Jesus," one guy said. "Don't hyperventilate."

I finally got a bad case of hiccups, and Mr. O'Connell gave me permission to go down the hall for a drink of water, though even then, I couldn't stop. On my way back, a couple teachers stuck their heads out into the hallway to see what was going on. But they really had to see Cleave. He was a scream.

I finally got it under control just before I got back to the classroom. But when I walked in, these two girls were sponging Cleave off like a beached whale, and I lost it all over again.

* * *

Of course, by the time we got to the girls' vice principal's office, it wasn't so funny anymore. We had to sit there until our mothers arrived, which took forever, though it was almost worth it just to see Cleave's mom haul into him.

"Honestly, Cleave, fighting with a girl. Is that how we brought you up?"

Then *my* mother got into it. "I'm sure Jenny had something to do with it."

I could've kicked her. She'd just walked in, and already she assumed it was my fault.

Miss Sturm, the girls' vice principal, smiled grimly, as if we were all her children. "You know, Cleave," she said in this gravelly voice, "you really take a chance when you joke with people that you don't know very well."

He shrugged and looked down at the floor.

"And as for you, Jenny," she said, "why did you think you could settle this with your fists?"

"Because I didn't have a gun."

Cleave's mother burst out laughing. She had the same idiotic laugh as her son, "Yip, yip, yip."

Miss Sturm gave me this steady gaze, as if I was supposed to melt or something.

"I understand that you're not very popular, Jenny," she said. "That you tend to stick to yourself. When I spoke to your mother on the phone, she told me that you've had a difficult time adjusting since your father passed away."

Mr. O'Connell looked at his hands, and Cleave sat up in his chair. He had this bleary look in his eyes, as if he was witnessing a freak show.

"That's got nothing to do with it," I said.

"It does if it gets you into trouble." Then she turned to Mom. "You know, you can get help for this sort of thing."

I couldn't believe it! Cleave and his creepy friend had been dumping on me for weeks, but somehow *I* was the basket case.

Mom said that we couldn't afford therapy, and Miss Sturm said we could go through community agencies.

"There's also special schools," she added, and I knew what she meant by *that*. "It's harder to bring a case of incorrigibility nowadays, but it can still be done."

Then she gave me her steady gaze again. "Well, Jenny, according to the L.A. Unified Code of Conduct, fighting is an expellable offense. But under the circumstances, I think we can let you off with a warning this time. And Cleave, let's keep the jokes to ourselves. Okay?"

He nodded.

His mother stabbed out a cigarette. "Aren't you going to make him apologize to these people?"

"I don't think that's necessary," Mom said.

I gave her a dirty look. Let *him* squirm a little.

"I just hope he doesn't come down with anything," Mom said.

Cleave had about fifty bandages on his face. His cuts were all superficial, but he was making a big show of it.

"Any danger of that, Mr. O'Connell?" Miss Sturm asked.

Mr. O'Connell chuckled nervously. "Oh, I don't think so.

We were using a mild form of *E. coli*. If anything, it'll help his bowel movement."

Cleave's mother yipped again. "That's exactly what he needs."

* * *

In the end, Mom had to pay about $25 for the Petri dishes, a good chunk of which came out of my allowance. But at least, Cleave left me alone after that. He wouldn't even look at me. If we happened to pass in the hall, he'd jerk his head the other way, which was kind of funny in a way. Though it was also kind of creepy, like everything else about him.

Gerald, on the other hand, started giving me these hangdog looks, as if I'd killed his pet hamster or something. More than once, I caught him staring at me in the two classes we had together. He'd look away when I saw him, but in the next class, he'd be staring again. It really started to get to me after a while. In fact, I almost wished he *would* do something. At least with the pranks, I could see them and feel them, but now it was like something was hanging over my head, waiting to fall. Only, it never did. It just kept hanging there.

Then one day, while he was handing out test papers in Algebra, he nonchalantly dropped this crumpled up wad of paper on my desk. I couldn't believe he'd be so brazen about it, especially after what happened to his friend. I didn't do anything, though. I just swept it away like it was a bug.

Then he did it again in English, two periods later. He just dropped this wad of paper in front of me as he walked in. This time, I crammed it deep inside my desk.

But when he did it a third time in English the next day, I stood up to throw it in his face. I didn't care if I *did* get expelled.

"Don't throw it, Jenny," he cried out in a whisper.

Reggie, the football player, cried out, "Oh, *Jenny*. Don't

throw it. Jen-nee!"

The whole class cracked up. I even got a couple "Hi-yo's."

Miss Ringwald slammed her yardstick on her desk. "Is there something you want to share with us, Jenny?" she said.

"No."

I could feel my face burning as I sat down. I took Gerald's wad of paper and crumpled it as tight as I could, imagining it was him. And when I couldn't crumple it anymore, I spread it out on my desk. And that's when I got the shock of my life. He'd written a note.

> Jenny,
> Want to go to the basketball game tonight?
> Nod if you do.
> Gerald

The idiot. He'd put our names on it. I held my head as straight as I could. I figured if I dipped my chin even a little, he'd take it as a yes. And then I remembered the other two notes. I dug my hand into the desk, but the one from yesterday was gone. And God knew what had happened to the other one. It was probably all over school by now.

I slumped in my seat and stared out into space. I couldn't understand why he'd take such a chance. He was supposed to be going to West Point or someplace like that, and here he was risking everything just to get back at me for what happened to Cleave. I was sure we'd both be kicked out if we got hauled into Miss Sturm's office.

I stayed slumped in my seat until the bell rang and the room emptied out. And even then, I didn't move.

"Did you want to see me?" Miss Ringwald said.

"No."

She raised her head. "And you?"

Gerald mumbled something a few rows back.

"Well, then," she huffed in a jokey way. "I guess I'm not wanted here."

After she left, I heard a chair scrape and Gerald's trouser legs brushing against each other. I probably should've just split like everybody else, but I figured we might as well get it over with.

He sat on top of the desk next to mine and gave me an awkward smile, causing his cheeks to dimple.

"So how 'bout it?" he said. "I can pick you up at 7:30."

I brushed some hair off my face. "You know, you're really a creep. And so's your friend."

"We were just trying to make you laugh. You looked so sad all the time."

I kind of snorted. *That* was the last thing I expected. "And I don't appreciate you staring at me."

"Sorry," he said in this tiny voice.

I got up to leave. I figured that was the end of it. It was just another one of their stupid pranks.

He got up too. "It's really a good game. We play Grant. If we win, we go on to the CIF finals."

As if I didn't know that. As if the whole school wasn't plastered with *Beat Grant* banners. "I can read, you know."

"If you want, I can pick you up earlier so we can see the JV game."

"Why do you think I'd even go out with you?"

He shrugged. "I don't know. Do you have a date already?"

That was a laugh. Who'd want to be seen with me?

"How'd you find out where I live?" I asked.

"I do my homework."

"Yeah, late at night."

The dimples formed again. "Did you like it?"

"If you want to know, the apartment manager had to

work all morning just to take it down."

"Sorry." He shrugged again.

"Look, I know you're having your fun, but don't you think it's gone far enough? I mean, it's not funny if I can't laugh along with everybody else."

"Maybe I can make it up to you."

"So that's what this is about."

"No. Not really." He bit his lip.

I hesitated for a moment to see if there was anything else coming. But he just put his hands in his pockets and gave me this innocent look. I couldn't believe it! He was serious!

"I just wanted to ask you out," he said.

I picked up my things and started to leave.

"So is seven-thirty okay?" he called after me.

"Just don't bring toilet paper," I said and hurried out the door.

10. Pranks 2
Jenny

I DON'T KNOW WHY I AGREED to go out with Gerald. Maybe there was a full moon that night. Or maybe I thought it would stop him from staring. Or maybe deep down I really wanted to go. I hadn't been to an athletic event since Dad had taken us to a Dodger game years before, and there was so much talk about our basketball team and how they were supposed to win the city championship and everything that I was dying to see them. I'd even thought of sneaking into the gym and leaving after a few minutes, but I'd have looked stupid on my own. At least with Gerald, I wouldn't be so out of it.

I just wish I hadn't told my mother. She stood there dumbstruck for a couple minutes, as if somebody had whacked her on the head.

"It's no big deal," I said. "This guy just wants to take me to the basketball game. He said he'll pick me up at 7:30."

"A basketball game?"

"Yeah, Mom," Toby said. "You know, with a basket and a ball. You put one inside the other."

"This doesn't concern you." I took a couple steps toward him and he ran around the dining room table screaming.

"Mom! She's picking on me again!"

But she just shushed him. She pumped me for some more information, and then she got on the phone and called every one of her friends to tell them I had "a date." And when she ran out of friends, she called my sister, even though they hadn't spoken in over a year.

"Margot, are you sitting down?"

"Mom, for God sakes!" I threw the spoon into my bowl of Cheerios. "It's just a *basketball* game."

I went to my room and put on a stack of records. As far as I was concerned, I might not even go, even if Gerald did show up, and I wasn't so sure that he would. It could've been just another prank, for all I knew, his way of getting back at me for what happened to Cleave. But just as I was starting to get comfortable, Mom and Margot burst into the room and yanked me out of bed.

"Jenny, into the shower," Mom said.

"But I took one yesterday."

It was like they didn't even hear me. They pushed me into the bathroom, and when I tried to come out, they practically shoved the door in my face.

"Use shampoo," Margot called. "And don't dry your hair."

I thought of faking it, just running the water and slipping out when they weren't looking, but I took a shower anyway. And when I got back to my room, they had a whole outfit laid out on my bed, as if I was some doll they were assembling. Most of it I recognized–like my gray plaid jumper and my sky-blue blouse and my ribbed knee socks–but some of it I'd never seen before–like these velvet barrettes and matching pumps, which Mom must've bought on the sly.

"Mom, this is ridiculous. Everybody's going the way they usually do."

But she just started trying the clothes on me. So I took them out of her hands and dressed myself. Then Margot sat me down away from the dresser mirror and put these giant curlers in my hair. She had this humongous makeup kit that she'd borrowed from a friend, and she went at me now with foundation and blusher and lip gloss and half a dozen other things I couldn't even name.

"You're wasting your time," I said. "I'll just wash it off."

"Hold still. Don't interrupt the artist."

Mom, meanwhile, did my nails. I couldn't bear to watch. Margot had to keep telling me to open my eyes so she could work on them. Then she blow-dried my hair and brushed it out, and when they were all done, they took a couple steps back to check out their work.

They didn't say anything for a moment. They just gaped at me like I was a freak or something. Then Margot clapped her hands and did a little hop.

"An Amazon!" she cried. "I've created an Amazon!"

Mom started to get misty-eyed. She nodded toward my dresser, and when I turned, I saw this strange person staring back at me from the mirror, some blonde junior miss who could've fallen out of a magazine. Then I made a face, and it was me all right.

"Don't scrunch up your face," Mom said.

But I scrunched it up even more. I wasn't even sure I wanted to go through with it. The whole thing was just getting out of hand. I even thought of phoning Gerald and calling it off, but I didn't have his number, so all I could do was sit there and wait–and put up with their stupid questions.

"So what's he look like?"

"Does he live around here?"

"What colleges has he applied to?"

"Do I know his parents?"

"Is he a sosch or an athlete?"

"What kind of car does he drive?"

"He's just *Gerald*!" I cried out. "Gerald Vander Dussen."

"Gerald Vander Dussen." Mom gazed up at the ceiling, as if trying recall that name from newspaper articles or concert programs.

"If you really want to know," I said, "he's one of the guys who teepeed our tree."

I thought that would take the air out of their balloon. But they just made these big eyes at each other, as if they knew something that I didn't. Toby, at least, wasn't around, or I'd never have heard the end of it. The little twerp was spending the night at a friend's house.

Mom tried to get me to eat something, but after a few bites, I couldn't look at food. They were really starting to make me nervous. Also, the closer we got to 7:30, the more I suspected that Gerald wouldn't show, that this was his way of getting back at me for punching out his friend.

But promptly at 7:30, there was a knock at the door, and when I opened it, this strange guy I'd never seen before was standing there. His hair was all slicked back, and he had a pale, squarish face, kind of like George Reeves, the actor who played Superman on TV. And his clothes were all new and spiffy. Like, he had on this silver windbreaker that made him look sort of hulky, along with this rust-and-brown Pendleton, dark walnut pants and gray Hush Puppies. He also smelled kind of spicy, probably from the stuff in his hair. I thought it was a salesman or somebody who'd gotten lost, but then he nodded, and I realized it was Gerald! He must've been surprised too, because his mouth dropped open, but nothing came out.

We stood there gaping at each other until Mom grabbed me by the waist and moved me to the side.

"You must be Gerald," she said in this cheery voice. "Why don't you come in?"

I thought, Oh, God, here we go. But Gerald had done his homework again. Almost before he got through the door, he started telling Mom what a big fan he was of "Mr. Kovacek's architectural style." He even described a couple of Dad's buildings, like this medical plaza on Vineland Boulevard. And while Mom was gaga over that, he told

Margot that he really enjoyed her work in last year's school play and that Mrs. Wilson, the debate coach, said hello. "She thinks you could've gone all the way to the finals, if your partner hadn't gotten sick," he added.

"Did she tell you I made him sick?" Margot said.

"No," he chuckled.

Mom took him aside to ask about his family, but Margot was a real pain in the butt. She kept whispering in my ear, "Ask him if he brought his slide rule. Ask him if he has a ten o'clock curfew. Ask him if he knows my bra size."

I nearly jabbed her in the ribs. "Would you shush?"

Finally, they let us go, with Gerald promising not to bring me home too late, and as the front door closed, you could hear this burst of muffled giggling. It made me wish I *had* sneaked out when I had the chance and just met Gerald by the curb.

Though it would have been hard to miss his car. He drove this humongous white Oldsmobile that took up about three parking spaces. When he opened the door, I felt like I was sliding into a cave. It also had the strangest interior I'd ever seen, with scarlet vinyl seats, a huge wooden steering wheel, Dalmatian shag carpeting–on the floorboards *and* under the rear window–and tiny stereo speakers that hung over the doors like miniature tombstones. And it reeked from the stuff in his hair. I suddenly realized that I didn't know a *thing* about this guy. He could've been a druggie or a sex fiend or a member of some weird cult, for all I knew. Just because we had two classes together didn't mean anything.

"Are we really going to the game?" I asked when he got in.

"Of course." He gave me this wounded look. "And dinner afterward, if you want."

I expected him to go into another speech, like he had in the apartment, but he just turned on the car radio and drove off in silence. I shook my head and stared out my window.

I still couldn't believe it. Only this morning, I was ready to kill this guy, and here I was driving to a basketball game with him. And I had to admit, it *was* a date. I couldn't deny *that* any longer.

"You know, if you wanted to make it up to me, you didn't have to go to all this trouble."

"It's no trouble." He adjusted the rearview mirror. "I *wanted* to do it."

"By the way, I threw away your first two notes. I don't know what happened to them."

"That's all right. I took care of it." Then he clammed up again.

It made me wonder what else he'd taken care of.

* * *

The parking lot was full when we got to the gym, so we had to park on a side street. But even from there, you could hear a faint roar, as if the game had already gotten underway. We hurried to catch the opening tip-off, and when we got inside, it was just chaos.

I'd seen the gym full before—at assemblies and special events—but nothing like this. I mean, the place was just exploding. Everywhere you turned, bodies were flying and people were screaming and gas horns were going off. Just inside the door, the school band was trying to blow a hole through the roof, while down the sidelines, the songleaders were jumping in time to the music, while the cheerleaders shouted through these huge white megaphones. Out on the court, the players were going through their warm-up routines, making the floor shake with every bounce of the ball, and on either side of us—like a pair of towering waves—the entire student body seemed to be crammed into the bleachers. Suddenly, they all let loose with a humongous cheer, and the whole building shook.

I wouldn't have lasted five seconds on my own. Even with Gerald, I nearly beat it out of there. But he took me by the hand and led me to the bleachers, and though it was so jammed, people were sitting on the spots marked "aisle," he found an opening and pulled me up behind him row after row. About a third the way up, some jerk shouted, "Hey, Gerald! Watch out for her right hook!" and the whole section cracked up. Then a couple guys yelled, "Hi-yo, Jenny, away!" and I nearly lost my footing. I wasn't used to the pumps yet. But Gerald held onto me and pulled me along, and somehow we managed to squeeze into this tiny space way up at the top.

"It's better up here," he shouted.

I thought he was joking. The benches were so narrow and they lurched so much, I was afraid any second I'd go tumbling back down. And the noise was just deafening. I mean, it was just bouncing off the walls. I had to cover my ears and bend my head to my chest just to drown it out. Gerald tried to pull my hands away, but I wouldn't budge, not even when this mousy guy in front of me kept flinging himself onto my knees. I'd shove him off, but a couple minutes later, he'd be there again, usually after our team missed a shot or lost the ball.

I didn't see how I'd ever get into the game–or even make it to halftime. But after a while, you just had to. I mean, it just sucked you in. Like, the crowd would do a cheer, "Lean to the left. Lean to the right. Stand up. Sit down. Fight, fight, fight!" and you either went along with it or you got knocked about like a bowling pin. Or whenever a player took a shot, the whole crowd would jump to its feet, and the bleachers just became a trampoline. I mean, it just bounced you up with them. Especially toward the end, when the lead kept changing hands. During the last two minutes, you couldn't stay in your seat if you wanted to.

And when we won on the last play–the last second, actually–the whole place went nuts. Everybody started hugging everybody else. Even *I* got hugged, first by Gerald and then by the mousy guy who'd been flinging himself on my knees. Then the crowd rose up as one and carried us all down to the floor, and as soon as we got there, a rock band started up and everybody began dancing right where they stood.

I was afraid Gerald would want to stay and I'd have to tell him I couldn't dance. But he just led me to the door.

"Don't you remember?" he said when we got outside. "We've got plans."

I didn't know what he was talking about, but he didn't elaborate. He just kept going on and on about the game, as if he was reliving the whole experience. By the time we got to the Olds, he was almost out of breath.

"I shouldn't go to basketball games," he said. "I get too emotional."

"So don't go," I said.

He gave me that wounded look again. "I didn't mean it literally."

We got in without a word, and he drove off in a different direction from the one we'd come. It made me a little suspicious, but after a few minutes, he pulled up in front of a coffee shop and brightened up again.

"What do you think?" He waved his hand at the place as if he'd built it himself.

"Fine." I didn't see what the big deal was. It looked like any other coffee shop, with wall-to-wall windows and a glazed brick trim. Then I remembered that he'd said something about dinner.

When we got inside, we found ourselves in another madhouse. The place was packed, and waiters were running about with their arms overloaded, while all around us, you could hear coins jingling and plates clattering and people talking over each other. I thought I'd freak out again like I had during the game, but after a while, I realized it wasn't nearly as crazy. In fact, it seemed tame by comparison. Like, you could see people with their arms spread out across the backs of the booths, as if they were settling in for the night. Or you could see them lighting up what looked like their second or third cigarette. One old guy near the lobby even yawned, and another, with a salt-and-pepper crew cut, smiled as we passed, and so did the heavy-set blonde woman next to him.

The hostess gave us a booth in the corner, which was kind of neat, but after we sat down, we didn't know what to say to each other. So we just stared out the window into the night, which was even more embarrassing because the glass reflected our faces like a mirror. Who was this couple? I wondered. This guy with his hair slicked back, and this girl with her eyes made up. And why did people keep smiling at them?

The busboy plopped down two glasses of water and a couple straws, and as we started to peel them, I thought I'd break the ice.

"You know, you said something before that really got to me."

Gerald cleared his throat. "What was that?"

"What you said in class today. That I looked sad all the time. Did I really?"

"Not sad exactly. Withdrawn, I guess."

I thought it over for a few seconds, and then I kind of chuckled. "Actually, you guys did make me laugh."

"We did?" He sat up straighter.

"Yeah. When I knocked Cleave down in Biology and he was thrashing about on the floor. That was a scream."

"Oh, yeah." He looked down at his hands. "I heard about that."

Then he clammed up again, and I felt so out of it, I wondered if we shouldn't just skip dinner and call it a night. I mean, just the basketball game by itself was enough. But before I could suggest it, this airy voice floated down as if from a cloud.

"You young people never order the specials, so why don't we dispense with that nonsense? Shall we, hmm?"

I looked up and my arm shot out, knocking the

silverware to the floor. I couldn't believe it! It was like something out of *The Twilight Zone*.

The waiter sighed and bunched up his pant legs. "If you don't like the cutlery, you don't have to *throw* it at me."

As he straightened up, our eyes met, and I backed away toward the window. I would have gone through it if I could have.

"Are you all right?" He pushed my glass toward me. "Here, have some water."

I shook my head. My heart was pounding so hard, I could feel it in my ears. He had the same bored look on his face as when he'd come to our house years before.

"It's clean water," he said. "Straight from the Los Angeles River."

"Didn't you ..?" My whole body was shaking. "Didn't you ..?"

"Didn't I *what*?"

Gerald chuckled. "I think she recognizes you."

"Oh, yes," the waiter said, "I'm quite the celebrity. I used to shun publicity, but now I find I can't get away from it."

"You used to bury people!" I cried out.

Several heads turned, and I could feel my face burning.

The man cleared his throat. "Well, certainly that was *one* of my professions, though we didn't refer to it quite in those terms. My *actual* title was Assistant Director."

"You were at my father's funeral," I whispered in a shout. "You were...one of the attendants." I almost called him "Choirboy," the nickname my little brother had given him. In fact, he still looked like one–round as a ball, with puffy cheeks and frizzy blond hair.

"Young lady, if I had to remember every poor soul I helped to his final resting place, I wouldn't have time for anything else. Now, if you don't mind, I think you came here to nourish yourself, not stroll down Memory Lane. Perhaps a nice fish-and-chips dinner will take your mind off the past. Or maybe you'd like to try our deep-dish shepherd's pie. It's quite delectable, if I say so myself..." His voice trailed off.

I couldn't stop staring at him.

He rested his chin in his hand and squinted at me. "I see we can't get off the subject. What did you say was the gentleman's name?"

"The gentleman?"

"Your *fah*ther."

"Frank Kovacek." I should have made up a name, but I wasn't thinking too clearly.

"Hmm." He raised his head, and after a few seconds, a light seemed to come into his beady eyes. "You do look familiar, now that you mention it. You wouldn't happen to be the young lady who didn't live up to her responsibilities, now would you? The one who went sprinting away from the proceedings and gave us all a merry chase."

"Oh, God." I lowered my face into my hands.

"Ah, yes. Our Little Miss Runaway. The one who went sprinting down the middle of the street like it was an Olympic heat."

"Did she really?" Gerald said.

"We couldn't catch her with the *limousine*."

"She's fast," Gerald said. "She's a star on the soccer team."

"I wouldn't doubt it." The waiter grunted. "I always wondered what happened to our little spoiler. Our Little Miss Runaway. Not only were we late for your *fahther's* funeral, but for the next one as well. In fact, your stunt probably cost me my position at the funeral home–not to mention my marriage." His voice turned so cold, I felt this chill under my skin. "I still haven't gotten back to where I was, by the way, since you *are* so interested. It seems the little woman took the expediency of emptying our bank account before she left, though I don't suppose *that* would concern you too much."

"But you're doing just fine now," Gerald said.

"Well, there are moments—"

"And if you can bring us our food without making speeches, there might be something in it for you. Such as me not reporting this to management."

"And *what*, pray tell, would you report?"

"That you're being rude to a customer."

The waiter's face turned a splotchy pink. He couldn't even blush properly.

"Yes, of course. What was I thinking?" He cleared his throat and took a stubby pencil from behind his ear. "And what would you people like? What delights your young appetites this evening? As if I didn't know."

"How does a cheeseburger, fries and a Coke sound?" Gerald said.

"Greasy and sweet." He grabbed our menus. He didn't ask me what *I* wanted. "Though I must say our cheeseburgers are famous throughout the world."

"Are they as good as the service?" Gerald asked.

"Indubitably." He gave us a curt little bow and left.

"And bring some extra barbecue sauce," Gerald called after him. "And clean silverware for the lady."

"How can you talk to him like that?" My heart was still pounding away.

"Who, Eddie? I tease him all the time. You have to or he forgets himself."

"You come here all the time?"

"Every so often." Gerald shrugged. "Cleave and I used to come here." He looked down at his hands, his pudgy, fumbling hands.

I reached over and gave them a squeeze.

"What's that for?"

"For saving my life."

His cheeks dimpled. "You should hear how Cleave talks to him. He has him running around like a servant."

"Is Cleave still mad at me?"

"I don't know. I haven't spoken to him in a week."

"But you're best friends!"

"That was before he lost my slide rule."

I nearly gagged. I thought Margot had been joking.

"But look at all the nasty things he did for you," I said. "He practically got himself expelled."

"He didn't do it for me. He liked you too."

"What?"

"And he didn't do *all* the work. I poured the pencil sharpener on your desk. And put the chocolate malt in your book rack."

I felt this presence at my shoulder and I shuddered. When I looked up, Choirboy was standing there with this stony look on his face. He put two Cokes on the table, along with clean silverware for me. Then he hopped back and cried out, "Are they coming at me?"

I didn't have a clue what he was talking about.

"They will if you're not careful," Gerald said. "He means the silverware."

Choirboy winked as he left.

"See?" Gerald said. "He's harmless. You just have to keep him in his place. Otherwise, he thinks he's the Lord of Creation."

I took a huge sip of my Coke–and started coughing my head off. It had this sharp undertaste like sour butterscotch.

"Something wrong?" Gerald asked.

I shook my head and gulped down some water.

"I can have Eddie bring you another one. He might have given you one of those flavored Cokes. They have all kinds here."

"It's okay," I wheezed. "I'll manage."

I wasn't too anxious to see the waiter again. Also, I didn't want Gerald clamming up on me. So I asked him to keep telling me about the pranks, and while he did, I just tugged away at the Coke, even though it made my eyes sting and left a glow in the pit of my stomach.

"It was like a contest," Gerald said. "We studied everything you did. We could almost anticipate your actions *before* you did it."

"It's a good thing you weren't *too* crazy about me or I might be dead."

"We considered that."

I should've kicked him, but my legs felt weak all of a sudden, as if I couldn't lift my feet.

Out of nowhere, a second Coke appeared at my elbow, probably left by the busboy, because I didn't see our waiter. This one was even more sour than the last, but Gerald was telling me now about his plans after graduation. So I just kept sipping away, and after a while, the glow in my stomach started spreading into my chest and my arms and even my head. It made the dining room sound distant and muted, though I could still pick up background noises, like plates clattering and coins jingling.

Gerald stared at me as if he'd said something.

"What?" I asked.

"Where you going to college?"

I shook my head. "I'm not. I'm not smart enough." My tongue was so thick, I could barely get the words out.

Choirboy showed up again with some more Cokes.

"Where's our food?" Gerald asked.

"Oh, it's coming," he said. "The cook is putting a special effort into it. In the meantime, to make up for any inconvenience, I'll keep you supplied in Cokes."

"My God, a man of conscience." Gerald's voice seemed to reverberate.

The waiter put his hand to his breast. "My conscience is as deep as the Coke machine."

He smiled at me, and I nearly cracked up. He reminded me of the Pillsbury doughboy with his fat face and frizzy blond hair. I even wanted to poke him in the belly.

Instead, I took a huge pull on the new Coke, and the

glow in my head spread out into the coffee shop. For a moment, the dining room tilted, and then righted itself.

I had a hard time following Gerald after that. I know he said something about going to Annapolis, but his voice got smaller and smaller until I could barely hear it. Then suddenly, our food appeared, and I was staring down at this steaming cheeseburger and all these luscious French fries, along with another Coke. I could almost taste the cheeseburger, it smelled so good, but I couldn't remember what to do with it.

Gerald dug right in. "Aren't you going to eat? Your food's getting cold."

I stuffed some fries into my mouth with my fingers and picked up the cheeseburger without the bun. Gerald didn't even notice. He was going on about this speech he wanted to give at our graduation. I took another huge pull on my Coke, and the glow in my head seemed to cover me like a pillow case.

"I want people to go away with something after I'm finished," Gerald said. He sounded like he was already using a microphone. "You know, more than the usual platitudes."

I laughed, spitting out a French fry.

"It's not that farfetched," he said. "I do have some talent."

"F'r what?" My head tilted forward, heavy as a bowling ball. I thought any second it'd go crashing into my plate.

"For writing. I can be lyrical at times. Wanna hear the opening of my speech?"

"Speesh! Speesh!" I cried out. The words just flew out of my mouth. I raised my glass, sloshing some of the Coke. "Les heara speesh!" Then I started giggling and I couldn't stop. The coffee shop tilted again, and I had to lay my head on the table.

"Jenny, are you okay? Jenny?"

The waiter's voice floated down. "More Coke for the

lady?"

I shook my head, or I thought I did. Tears were rolling down my face, I was laughing so hard, but I couldn't find my hands to brush them away.

Gerald was trying to tell me something. He sounded like he was far away. Then he was right over my ear. "Jenny, are you okay? Is something wrong?"

"Nothin.'" I pushed myself up. "What're you doin' here? Get back on your side."

"Jenny, are you okay? Your face is all red." He sounded really nervous.

"Les heara speesh. Speesh! Speesh!"

Then I did something crazy. I stood up on my seat, pumps and all, and shouted to the whole room. "Lissen, ever'body. Lissen. Gerill wanna maka speesh. Speesh! Speesh!"

I thought Gerald would get up with me–I mean, I *had* everybody's attention–but he just kept trying to help me down. He wouldn't even let me lead them in applause. Then finally, he did help me down, only he helped me too much and I ended up on the floor, *below* the table. He didn't have the strength to pick me up, so these two guys from the next table had to pitch in.

"Is she on something?" one of the guys asked when I was back in my seat.

"Yeah!" I cried out. "I'm on my butt!"

Then I laughed so hard, I had to lay my head on the table again. It was worse than in Biology when Cleave was thrashing about on the floor.

Gerald was over my ear again. "Jenny, do you want to leave?" He sounded really nervous. "We don't have to stay here. We can go somewhere else."

He started wiping my face with a napkin, which cracked me up even more. I was afraid I'd pee in my pants.

"We can go up to the hills and look at the stars," he said.

"The *stars*! They wanna be look at?"

"Sure. They love to be looked at."

"*Why*?" I raised my head.

"Because they're stars. That's what they're for." Gerald's face had turned really pale.

I started singing, "Twinkle, tinkle, little star." Then suddenly, I stopped. "Gerill, I gotta go tinkle."

Only, I couldn't get up. I kept falling back into my seat, giggling like an idiot. Gerald and Choirboy had to lift me by the arms and walk me down the aisle, though even then, I kept tripping over myself.

"Was there something in those drinks?" Gerald asked over my shoulder. I thought he meant everybody else's drinks, because whenever we passed a table, it seemed to go off like firecrackers.

"Oh, you know the Coca-Cola company," Choirboy said. "Always so secretive about their formula.

"You didn't put anything in them, did you?" Gerald asked again.

"Young man, what are you insinuating? Well, here's the ladies' room, Sugar." He pushed me gently in the right direction.

"I'm not Shug'r. Shug'r's my sizzer. I'm *Muff'n*!"

"In that case, good-night, Muffin. Come again."

"Come ag'n!" I cried out. Then I squealed so loud, half the coffee shop turned to look. Only, they weren't smiling this time.

Somehow I managed to pee inside a toilet and stumble into Gerald's car, and as we drove off, I sprawled across the seat singing "Twinkle, twinkle lil' star." Or I'd do the cheer from the game: "Lean to the left! Lean to the right! Stand up, sit down, fight, fight, fight." And every so often, I'd cry out, "Whar the stars?"

"I'm taking you to see them." Gerald sounded really nervous. He even checked my door once or twice to see if it was locked. I tried to check his, but he pushed my hand away.

Then we started climbing this twisty road, and we climbed and climbed, so high that the houses disappeared and we weren't surrounded by anything but these gnarly trees and bare hills. Then Gerald pulled off the road, and we weren't surrounded by anything at all–only sky. But there were precious few stars. And the ones we *could* see, you could barely make out.

"Whar the stars?" I cried. "Who tookem?"

"Jenny, are you okay? I can't take you home like this. I think Eddie put something in those Cokes."

"Who tooka stars?"

"Oh, they're out there. We just can't see most of them. There's too much light pollution."

"Porrution? Qwarboy tookem, din' he?"

"Who?"

"Qwarboy. He tooka stars, din' he?" Then I laughed so hard, Gerald had to hold me up.

"Shh, Jenny, listen. I want to tell you something."

"You wanna maker speesh?"

"No," he chuckled. "I just want to say that I like you a lot. Maybe now's not the right time, but I, um...I just wanted to tell you that."

"I liku too, Gerill. You're very like...lik'ble." The moonlight was shining off his forehead, so I tried to rub it out. Then I tried to rub it off his cheeks, and they dimpled on me.

"I've liked you for a long time," he said. "But I didn't know how to say it."

I rubbed his forehead again, and he rubbed mine back.

"I guess I'm shy," Gerald said. "I'm working on it, but it's hard for me. Especially around girls."

I squeezed his cheeks real hard like my grandmother used to, but I couldn't make the dimples go away. "I'm shy too, Gerill." Then I cracked up and squeezed his nose. I tried to pull it off, but it wouldn't come.

He kind of grunted and pulled my hand down. Then he

did the funniest thing. He covered my mouth with his. So I did it back to him. I mouthed his nose, his dimples and even his forehead, making him giggle. Then we just went at it, mouthing each other all over, and tickling each other wherever we could. Gerald couldn't reach the places he wanted, but *I* could. I got him in the stomach and the armpit and under his shirt all the way up to his plump chest, until he was laughing almost as hard as I was. He tried to fight back, but my jumper straps got in the way. So we got into this huge wrestling match, and somehow we ended up in the back seat with half our clothes flung around the Olds. And while we were horsing around, Gerald stopped laughing and got serious all of a sudden. He gazed at me with this grim look in his eyes, and then he twisted on top of me and started slobbering over my breast, which was worse than the tickling. I was laughing so hard, I almost couldn't breathe. So I chewed on his ear to get back, only I couldn't get a good grip. All I could do was to kind of blow into it, and instead of laughing, he cried out like a little kid and collapsed on top of me. I tried to push him off, but my sides were shaking too hard. So I just laid there giggling like an idiot, and after a minute or two, I could feel this warm damp spot where his trousers pressed against my thigh.

"Gerill, you gotta go wee-wee? You gotta tinkle?"

He whimpered and rolled off.

I finally stopped laughing and gazed up at the sky, trying to make the stars come out. But they wouldn't cooperate. They just got weaker and weaker, as if the night was gobbling them up. Then I fell asleep, and I had one strange dream after another. I dreamed I was a horse that nobody could ride. Then I dreamed I was a songleader, kicking my legs high in the air for everybody to see. Then I dreamed I was Gretel in *Hansel and Gretel*, about to be thrown into the oven by the wicked old witch. Then I was the witch, licking my lips and rubbing my hands. And then I was the oven, or actually, my stomach was the oven, and it was about to burst. And that's when I woke up.

"Gerald, move! Gerald!"

I scrambled out the door and just made it to the side of the hill before I puked my guts out. I must've puked for a good ten minutes, and even then, the spasms just kept coming. I thought it'd never stop. And the smell of Coke was awful, in my nose and mouth and everything. I swore I'd never look at another Coke again, even if somebody offered me one.

Gerald tried to put something on my shoulders, but I shrugged it off. I couldn't stand anything touching me, not until my stomach settled down. And even when it did, I just wanted to kneel there and gaze off into the distance.

"Jenny, we have to get back to the car."

I let him cover my shoulders, but I refused to get up. I didn't feel so god-awful sick anymore–I could even hold my back straight–but I just wanted to stay there and gaze down into the city–down at all the lights that stretched from one horizon to another. It was like I'd found the stars.

"Jenny, we can't stay here."

The headlights of a passing car swept over us, and my teeth started to chatter, but still I couldn't pull myself away. I'd never seen anything like it. It was like a sea of tiny fires. Like the whole earth was winking at me, all these lights gleaming and flickering and pulsating everywhere I looked. In my groggy state, I imagined that these were the souls of the living, and that the stars above were the souls of the dead. And it seemed that the ones above were trying to signal to the ones below, but they never noticed. They never even looked up. They were too busy going about their lives to pay attention, and it made me so sad, I wanted to cry.

"Jenny, please."

I finally let Gerald coax me back into the Olds, and as we started down the twisty road, I put my clothes back on. But

I couldn't get over the lights. Every so often, we could see them peeking through the hillside, lighting up the sky.

Gerald, meanwhile, was quiet the whole time, just closed within himself, even more so than before. When we got down to the Valley, I had him stop at a service station so I could clean up. Then we got going again, and I snuggled against his shoulder until we rolled up to my apartment building.

"Thanks, Gerald. I really enjoyed it." I was still a little groggy, but at least I wasn't wasted anymore.

He nodded without looking at me.

I straightened my hair in the rearview mirror. "Do you want to come to the door?"

He shook his head.

"Okay, then. Bye." I kissed him on the cheek and let myself out.

As he drove off, I waved, but he just stared at the road like he was in a trance.

I expected Mom and Margot to be waiting by the door with these huge grins on their faces. But when I let myself in, they were sitting at the dining room table drinking coffee. It was just like in the old days when they'd stay up late poring over college catalogues.

Mom smiled as I passed, and then made a face. "Whoa!" She grabbed my arm. "What have you been drinking, young lady?"

"Coke."

"And I'm Santa Claus. Don't go near the stove. Here." She held out the coffee pot and an empty cup. "Have some. It's on the house."

"First I have to pee like nobody's business."

I hadn't meant it to be funny, but they both cracked up. Maybe I was still slurring my words.

When I got back, I thought they'd pump me for information. But they just sat there gabbing away, mostly about art–or actually about art doing this and art doing that. It didn't make any sense because neither of them were into paintings and stuff like that. I mean, they might go to a museum once in a while, or check out a special exhibit if it came to town, but that was about it.

And then, halfway through my coffee, it dawned on me that they weren't talking about *art* but a *guy* named Art, and that this guy named Art was getting married in the summer. And it was another few minutes, while I drifted in and out, remembering all the strange and awesome things that happened to me that evening, before I realized that the wedding they were talking about was Margot's.

11. Pranks 3
Jenny

THE NEXT MORNING WAS SATURDAY and I didn't wake up until noon, and when I did, I felt sick all over again. My head was throbbing like this soccer ball that everybody had been pounding on, and my stomach didn't feel so great either. Every time I swallowed something, I could feel it hissing all the way down. And it didn't help that Mom decided to hit me with all the questions I'd been expecting the night before.

"Are you sure all you had to drink was Coke?"

"Mom, I swear. We went to this coffee shop, and that was it. Gerald thinks the waiter put something in my drinks."

"Why would he do that?"

"Because you wouldn't believe who the waiter was. He was one of the funeral attendants for Dad, the creepy, little fat one. And it was like he had it in for me."

"But it's against the law to serve alcohol to a minor."

"Yeah, like I'm really going to prove it. I should just go down there and bash his brains out."

"No, I think you've done enough bashing for one year."

Then my head started to throb, and I had to lay down again. Mom brought me some aspirin and a pot of tea, but the only thing that really helped was to just lay in bed and kind of drift off.

It was hard, though. I kept thinking about the night before and all the crazy things that happened. Like Gerald showing up at our door in his silver windbreaker, or the moonlight shining off his forehead when he told me he liked me. Or I'd think about the basketball game and all the cheers we did, and I could almost feel the bleachers bouncing underneath me as everybody jumped to their feet. Or I'd hear Choirboy's airy voice floating down in the coffee shop, and I'd want to puke all over again–and not from the Cokes either. Mostly, though, I'd think about all the lights below the hill where we parked, how they spread out from one horizon to the other like a sea of tiny fires, and I'd get this hollow, achy feeling in my chest that hurt almost as much as my head. I'd have given anything to go up there again, to sit on the hillside and just take it all in, but I didn't have a car or even a driver's license, so it might as well have been on the other side of the moon.

After a while, I couldn't stay in bed any longer. I just had to get up. So I went into the kitchen to look through the phone book, and right away, I found a couple of Vander Dussens. When I dialed the first number, though, this little girl picked up, and my heart started flopping all over the place.

"Hello?" the girl said. *"Hello?"*

I tried to answer, but nothing came out.

"Hell-oh-o-oh-o-ohhhhh?"

"Hello?" Gerald said.

"Gerald, it's me, Jenny."

"Jenny, listen, I'm sorry about last night."

The little girl piped up. "That's what you *always* say. Every time you go out on a date, you always say you're sorry."

"Franny, get off the line."

"Every time you—"

"Franny!"

The line clicked.

"Listen," Gerald said. "I guess I, um...I guess I lost my head last night. I knew you were...kind of wasted. Eddie must have put something in those Cokes."

"It's okay. I had a *great* time."

"I shouldn't have taken advantage of you."

"You didn't, Gerald. It's *okay*."

"Why don't we, um...just pretend it didn't happen?"

"You mean your little accident."

It got real quiet on the other end.

"That was nothing," I said. "I was puking my guts out."

"Well, let's just say it didn't happen, okay? The whole thing."

"Okay."

"Bye," he said.

"Bye, see you in class." But he'd already hung up, the dork.

I couldn't believe a guy could be so touchy about such things. *I* was the one who should've been embarrassed. I mean, I'd made a complete fool of myself in the coffee shop. They'd probably never let me in there again. And as for the other stuff, it wasn't so bad. It was kind of nice, actually. I never thought I'd let a guy touch me again after this incident I had when I was 15, when this theater manager was all over me during this job interview. But Gerald had touched me, and it wasn't so bad. I could even see him doing it again.

After I got off the phone, I just had to get out of the apartment. So I went shopping for a slide rule to make up for the one that Cleave had lost. I figured it'd be like buying anything else, but the store had so many different sizes and colors that it took me forever. The saleslady who'd opened the display case started taking deep breaths and looking at her watch. So I finally picked out this tiny one that came in a buff leather case and fit in the palm of your hand. It was ivory white with little black lines, and every time I looked at it, it reminded me of Gerald's smile. I know it sounds corny, but *that's* why I bought it.

I spent the rest of the weekend trying to imagine the look on his face when I gave it to him. I could just see his dimples forming and his eyes getting big and his face glowing like it did in the car. I wouldn't have been surprised if he asked me out to another basketball game right on the spot. We could even catch the rest of the season together. And after each game, we could go to the coffee shop and annoy the hell out of Choirboy. And then up to the hill to make out, or just sit there and gaze down at all the lights. I'd even listen to his stupid speech, if he wanted. And when basketball season was over, we could go to movies–or the prom. It wasn't just for the popular kids. We could find our own little table in the corner and laugh at all the snobs.

I hardly slept Sunday night. I kept getting up to check on the sycamore tree–I was sure I'd heard something–but each time, it was just the wind rattling the dead leaves, pulling the last ones off in bunches.

By the time Monday morning rolled around, I didn't know what to do with myself. I wasn't sure I could even last until third period, when we had Algebra together. And then, on the way to school, I saw his Olds go whizzing by, and I knew I'd have to give it to him now. So I went straight to his hall locker, with the slide rule on top of my books, pressed against my chest to quiet it down. My heart was pounding so hard, I thought of just taping the thing to his locker with a note. But then I saw the back of his silver windbreaker, and it drew me toward him like a magnet.

He was waving his arm in big circles, the way you do when you're telling a story and it just takes over your whole body. At least, he'd gotten his spirits back. I remembered how down he'd looked when he dropped me off.

I went right up to him, and I was just about to tap him on the shoulder, when I pulled my hand back. Cleave was standing there! The jerk saw me and nodded in my direction.

Gerald turned and his head started back.

"Hi," I said. "How's it going?"

He shrugged, as if he didn't know why I was asking. "Okay."

"Can I talk to you?" I was dying to give him the slide rule, but not in front of Cleave.

"Well, I'm sort of busy."

He nodded toward Cleave and these two freshmen girls I hadn't noticed before. One was this tall blonde with a bob cut, and the other was this short brunette with granny braids and a peasant dress. They looked like any other tutoring students, and I didn't see what the big deal was. Gerald was probably just being shy–like he told me in the car.

"Did you ever find your slide rule?" I asked.

"No." He shrugged again. "But I have another one. They all work the same."

"Except his." Cleave tapped him on the side of the head. "The battery broke."

They all cracked up like it was the funniest thing they'd ever heard.

"Well, now that that's taken care," Cleave said, turning back to Gerald, "when do you want us to be at your place?"

"Six, I guess." Gerald looked at the girls. "Is that okay?"

"We'll be there," the blonde said. "This is going to be so boss. I've never seen the Stones before."

"Did you really get front-row seats?" the other girl asked.

The blonde kept twisting her mouth at me, as if I couldn't take a hint. I gave her a dirty look right back, and then suddenly, it dawned on me that they weren't *tutoring* these girls. They were all going out together on a double date. It hit me like a ton of bricks. I mean, most senior guys didn't have anything to do with freshmen girls.

I kept staring at Gerald, as if somehow *that* would clear things up, but he just ignored me. I probably should've split–I mean, it was really getting embarrassing–but I couldn't just blow away like a piece of lint, not after I'd said hello.

"I guess I'll see you later." I said it loud enough to get Gerald's attention.

He gave me this puzzled look again. "Okay."

"This is for you." I put the slide rule in his hand. "I don't know how to use it."

His eyes bugged out like I thought they would, but he didn't smile. Instead, his face turned red, as if I'd pulled down his pants or something. I should've just kept the thing–or tossed it in the nearest trashcan–but I wasn't thinking too clearly.

As I walked away, I could feel my ears burning. I was sure the story would be all over school before the day was out. Probably this time, they'd call me Slide-Rule Jenny. Or Jenny the Horse's Ass. Or Jenny the Idiot Who Doesn't Know When to Leave. Though I made sure nobody said it to my face. If anybody so much as looked at me, I stared them down.

When I got home, I threw myself on the bed and just laid there for the longest time. I knew Mom would give me hell for not doing the laundry, but I didn't care. I couldn't see the point of it anyway. Why get all dressed up in clean clothes if we were just going to go out and make fools of ourselves? Something I seemed to be pretty good at.

Gerald and Cleave were probably yukking it up right now with their stupid laughs. This was their best prank by far. They'd really nailed me to the wall. I even thought of dropping out again, like I had during the soccer match, or running away. But then I had a better idea. I would disappear. I mean, literally. I'd just vanish into empty space, and nobody would even know I was there.

I rolled on my back and closed my eyes, and after a few minutes, I could feel it working. My arms started getting numb and then my legs. And then, inch by inch, my stomach and my chest. By the time evening rolled around, I wasn't even a body anymore. I was just a breath of air. A mass of darkness. And soon I wouldn't even be that.

Mom came home and started banging around the kitchen. Then Toby barged in, whining and slamming doors. Normally, it would've pissed me off, but now that I was invisible, it went right through me.

My door opened, and the light came on.

"Aren't you coming to eat?" Mom said.

But there was nothing to answer her, just empty space. So she left, and the night filled up the room again. Through the door, I could hear them talking and clinking their silverware, and later, I heard Mom filling the kitchen sink. But none of it mattered. I was no longer there.

As the evening wore on, it started to rain, first in steady drops and then in gusts, spraying into the room as far as the bed. I got up to close the window, and while I was standing there, I noticed the sycamore bending in the wind below me. I couldn't believe it was the same tree that Gerald and Cleave had teepeed. The leaves were all gone and the branches were dripping, and the two main boughs stood out shiny and pale like a pair of upside-down thighs. It looked so pathetic out there in the rain, I almost felt sorry for the thing. Though the more I stared at it, the more I realized it was a perfect image of me–exposed to the world and helpless to do a goddamn thing about it.

* * *

Gerald shied away from me after that. He'd be polite when he handed back test papers in Algebra, and he stopped staring at me in class. But otherwise, it was like nothing had happened between us, just like he'd said on the phone. At lunchtime, you could usually find him hanging out with Cleave and the two freshmen girls. They'd become a tight little foursome. One time, I saw Cleave playfully ring the blonde's neck, and another time, the girl with the granny braids did a drum roll on Gerald's chest. But I didn't care. I hardly even paid attention.

I still got razzed from time to time by the other students, but as the year wore on, only one or two diehards kept it up, and soon I became as insignificant as ever. Which was fine with me. All I wanted was to be left alone, to become invisible like I had in my room. And after a while, I could feel it working. Like, I'd be standing in front of the bookstore, and the woman at the window wouldn't even notice me–she'd ask the girl behind me what she wanted. Or in class, somebody could be talking to a person in the next row over, and it was like I wasn't even there, as if they were talking through empty space.

Even the school acted like I didn't exist. When the yearbook came out, there wasn't a trace of me in it, not even in the "Late to Class" section for all the dorks who never got around to having their senior picture taken. Mom wasn't too happy about it, but when she called the school, they said there wasn't much they could do now that it was printed.

I suppose I should've been miserable. I didn't have a friend in the world. And things kept getting worse at home. Mom could be touchy as hell when she came back from visiting Margot's future mother-in-law, who was already trying to run her life. And Toby, the little twerp, got caught breaking into a neighbor's apartment trying to steal a girlie calendar. The neighbor didn't press charges, but Mrs. Davenport got all over Mom for it–and she got all over *me*.

"*I'm* not his mother."

"Yes, you are," Mom said. "When I'm not here, *you're* his mother."

She even grounded me for a week, which really pissed me off.

But in spite of everything, I wasn't unhappy. I even had this inkling that things were looking up. I know it sounds strange, and I can't really explain it, but every so often, I'd get this feeling that something was stirring just beneath the surface. Something really neat. I don't even know what brought it on, but I could be walking down the hall at school, or opening my locker between classes, or eating lunch out in the bleachers, and suddenly, I'd feel as if I was going to be hit by another prank. Only, it was something nice, something really awesome. I'd even hold myself still to make a better target. But it never came. It would blow by me, or over me, or through me, as if I really *was* invisible.

And then the thing I'd been waiting for finally came around, though I almost didn't go to it. I found out that we wouldn't be getting our diplomas until *after* our grades were mailed out, and I couldn't see the point in sitting through a boring ceremony just to pick up an empty envelope.

But Mom had other ideas, as always. She roused me out of bed that morning and packed me off to the shower.

"Does everything begin with a shower?"

"Yes," she said. "The world began with a shower."

She started humming and whistling while I got dressed, and Toby whined that he didn't want to go. Then Margot came over and fussed about, as if everything depended on her. It was so much like the old days, I half expected Dad to come waltzing through the living room on his way to the Dart. In fact, as Margot drove us to school, I swore I could smell his Old Spice aftershave in the car.

Then we got there, and the whole scene was just unreal. On the edge of the football field, all my classmates were milling about, covered from head to toe in their graduation gowns. The boys were in royal blue and the girls in eggshell white, and it was so strange to see them like that, I was sure somebody was playing a joke.

Even Toby was impressed. "They look like gifts," he said.

And they *did*–all newly wrapped–to be given to the world, I suppose. Though the funny thing was, they all looked alike. I mean, you couldn't tell the geniuses from the dumbbells, or the jocks from the stumblers, or the snobs from the wallflowers. Everybody just blended in– including me. After I put on my cap and gown and took my place on the side of the field, I waved to Mom in the stands–and twenty parents waved back.

Then the band began to play and we filed into our seats, and I wouldn't have been surprised to see Dad sidling his way through the crowd and waving toward the field like a little kid. But when he didn't show and my family sat there fanning themselves, it dawned on me that Miss Sturm was right. I *hadn't* adjusted very well. I'd been living in my own little fantasy world all these years. I probably didn't even deserve to graduate, if you want to know the truth. I mean, I might've passed my classes, but I hadn't done half the things the other kids had–not by a long shot.

I even started to wonder if I had a right to be there, if the school hadn't made a mistake when they sent me the invitation. But while I sat there feeling out of it, as if I'd crashed a party or something, the strangest little thing happened, and it was like during the basketball game when I got sucked into the crowd. It happened toward the end of the ceremony, after Gerald had given his pompous speech and a boy sang *You're Gonna Hear From Me* and a girl played *The Impossible Dream* on her trumpet. It was after we had officially graduated and switched the tassels on our caps to the other side and Mr. Parker, the principal, got up to tell us that the world didn't owe us a living. It was while he was droning on, and this boy two seats down from me slumped in his chair and started snoring, that I noticed it. The tassel on my cap kept swinging long after it should have, long after the wind had died down and the others had stopped. Even the flags on the platform hung limp, but my little doodad just kept swinging away, tapping me all over the face, as if it had a life of its own.

I finally caught the thing between my fingers and held it for a moment. It was just a bunch of blue and white thread knotted at the top with a silver braid. It hardly weighed an ounce. But when I let it go, it started tapping me again, working its way around my face, pinging me on my eyes and nose and mouth, as if it couldn't resist one more prank. As if it had to play just one more gag or make one more stupid joke. And each time it landed, I swear, it felt like nothing so much as a kiss.

12. The Game Tonight
Toby

TOBY COULD FEEL IT. THERE WAS something in the air. Something in the way the smog hung heavy after lunch, but not too gritty, just enough to make his eyes water and his throat a little husky. Just enough for Mr. Speir, his P.E. teacher, to take it easy on them, ordering one lap around the field and a quick game of volleyball.

Even Miss Stokker, his math teacher, gave them a break. "No homework tonight, kids. I'll be tied up, so you can have the evening off too." Then she giggled, as if it was a joke.

As school let out, the sun bore down on them, but it wasn't an angry sun, a where-have-you-been kind of sun. It was more of a mid-September glow, an Indian summer warmth. Jerry must have felt it too because he whistled as he slammed their locker door shut. Then he wiped his nose on Ellen Forrester's back. She turned and smiled, but he just made a face.

"So," Jerry said as they swaggered down the hall, "think Osteen'll win his 20th?"

"Prob-a-blee." Toby made his favorite throwing motion, a sidearm whiplike action with his elbow and wrist.

"My Dad's taking me to the game tonight," Jerry said.

"Mine too."

They crossed the athletic field, speeding up when a pair of ninth-graders started toward them and slowing down to flush out a scrawny seventh-grader from under the bleachers. At the chain-link gate, where students were lining up to board school buses, Jerry thumbed his nose at old Mr. Hummel. The history teacher turned suddenly, forcing Jerry to open his hand and wiggle his fingers in greeting. Mr. Hummel wiggled his fingers in return, and the boys, when they were far enough down the street, nearly doubled over.

Jerry picked up a rock and threw it at the wheel of a passing school bus. "I thought you didn't *have* a dad."

"I got a dad." Toby hurled a rock that just missed a mail truck. "I'm seeing him tonight."

"No foolin'?"

"Yeah, we see lots of games together. Hey, you know why an umpire dusts home plate with his butt in the air?"

"Uh-uh. Why?"

"'Cause it's a crack-up."

The joke staggered the boys until they reached the railroad crossing a half-mile away. They hunted for the two pennies they'd placed on the tracks that morning, and found them among the ballast stones, pressed smooth and razor-thin. Turning the pieces over in their hands, they couldn't quite believe the faceless, coppery yawns that stared up at them.

At Tujunga Avenue, Jerry gave Toby a shot in the arm. "Okay, Toby Tubby. See you at Chavez Ravine tonight, if you're lucky."

Toby socked him back. "You got it, Jerry Fairy."

"And don't forget to take your radio. You don't wanna miss Scully."

Toby snorted as he turned away. What a dumbass!

He chuckled again a few hours later as he sat on his living room floor tying his sneakers. He *never* took his radio. And he never missed Vin Scully.

Heading out the door, he dropped down the stairs with lightning speed, and was immediately engulfed by the reedy voice of the Dodgers' announcer, droning out of two apartment windows.

"For those of you just joining us, we've barely gotten under way and already Claude Osteen has managed to get himself into a jam."

It was always the same when Toby paid a visit to his dad. He could follow Scully from house to house, from building to building, even on the open street. If he happened to be stopped at a traffic light, one of the waiting cars was sure to be blaring out the game, just as a tow truck did now as it lumbered past his apartment building.

"It hasn't escaped Osteen's attention that Johnny Bench is on deck."

Toby strolled down Huston Street and turned left on Bakman, the game reaching him through open windows. He turned left again on Morrison Avenue, directly into the path of the sunset, and as Vinny led him along, his voice seemed to be coming from the sun itself–from the bright orange smudge it left on the horizon–and the sharp afterglow inside Toby's chest. Yes, tonight would be special. He could feel it.

A wiry man in coveralls nodded at him from under the hood of a '57 Chevy. Scully's voice squawked out of the dash.

"Here's the wind-up and the 1-1 pitch. A slider, low and away, ball two."

Where would his father be tonight? Vinny would find him. He always did. Everyone thought he was talking to the masses, but he was really talking to Tubby. Tubby Kovacek.

We don't know why they call him Tubby, folks, because he's not fat. Take my word for it. He just swings a heavy bat. In fact, you'd have to go all the way back to Pee Wee

Reese to find an infielder of his caliber.

Turning right on Tujunga Avenue, Toby approached an apartment building where three girls from his junior high school were jumping one-legged down the sidewalk. They were too old to play hopscotch, and they made a big show of not taking it seriously, shoving each other off the chalked-in squares and giggling uncontrollably, nearly drowning out Scully's voice from an upstairs window.

"Quite a crowd tonight..."

One of the girls had dark bangs and a creamy white face, and as her hair jostled with her hops, Toby felt his stomach tighten. That very morning, he'd printed her name in the corner of his loose-leaf notebook in tiny letters: *Karen Wheatly.*

"Pee-*yuuu!*" One of Karen's friends was staring at him, her hands on her hips.

The other girls looked up.

"Hey, Three Fingers," the first girl teased.

"Shhh, you guys," Karen said.

"But that's what they call him. Hey, give us the high sign, Three Fingers!"

Laughter peppered the air as Toby hurried away. His left hand throbbed where his thumb and most of his forefinger were missing, the result of a power saw accident three years earlier. But where he felt the taunt most keenly was in his face. The skin across his nose and cheeks flared, as if he'd been sunburnt.

It's incredible how this Kovacek kid can play without a thumb, but he's a pretty tough customer. I don't think anyone can forget what he did in the opener against the Cards.

Down Otsego Street and up Klump Avenue, the gathering dusk sent millions of phantom whirligigs spinning out of control. At a house by an alley, a fat man in a ribbed undershirt sat smoking on his porch, a radio crackling by his folding chair.

"A mile-high pop fly."

The man narrowed his eyes as Toby passed. The end of his cigarette burned a bright red.

Toby chuckled deep in his throat. He had the man's bolo tie sitting in his pajama drawer at home–a classy one too, with a polished turquoise stone set in the clasp–but the man would never know it. He was probably tearing his house apart looking for the thing.

You won't come across a more deceptive base runner than Tubby Kovacek. He can steal you blind, even when you know he's going.

Toby reached the end of Klump and turned up Magnolia Boulevard. He paused by a clapboard house with a shoulder-high wooden fence. Scully had raised his voice.

"There goes Wills! Here's the throw...and he's in there!"

This was the place. Once again, Vinny had found it. As the crowd roared, Toby clambered over the fence and dropped into a patch of geraniums. He found himself in a narrow side yard below the kitchen window. Water hissed into a sink and dishes knocked about. The radio grew louder to drown out the noise.

"That's Maury Wills' 22nd stolen base for the year. Not quite the record pace he was on in '62, but the crowd still loves it."

Staying low, Toby circled around to the back, stepped lightly across a cement patio, and homed in on a darkened room with an open window. He fished inside his jeans pocket for a six-inch metal ruler. Then pushing in the window screen, he pried the hasp over the tiny knob. He waited for another roar from the crowd, and when it came, he pulled back the screen and climbed over the sill.

Inside the room, he crouched again to get his bearings. The heavy odors of cigar ash and shoe leather washed over him, along with the fresher smells of spaghetti, hamburger and fried onions. The door to the hallway was ajar, letting in slats of light around its edges. As his eyes adjusted, he could make out a four-poster bed, an old-fashioned lamp on a nightstand, and a tall dresser with its drawers slightly open.

The running water from the kitchen ceased, and a young woman called out in a giggly voice. An older man answered gruffly. Father and daughter, Toby guessed. He was usually right. He could see them in his mind–an old baldy with a fat face and a big mole on his chin, and a dumpy young woman with kinky blonde hair and big tits. This had to be Baldy's bedroom, based on the cigar odor and the untidy dresser.

There's no fooling Kovacek. For the first half of the season, pitchers threw him fastballs high and inside. Then they tried sliders low and away. But he still hit them over the fence.

Toby entered now into the serious part of his visit. He flattened his back against the wall, closed his eyes and breathed in deeply–and nearly coughed on a whiff of cigar ash. He rubbed his legs vigorously and tried again. And this time it worked. With his heart pumping away and strangers wandering about in the other rooms and Vinny's reassuring patter coming down the hall, Toby could feel the warmth of the stadium lamps blazing down in Chavez Ravine, lighting up the playing field as if it were daytime. He could see the grass shimmering the dark green of 7Up bottles, and the infield standing out a rich caramel brown, the bases anchoring the corners like puffy white marshmallows.

"The Reds' manager goes out to the mound to have a chat with Cloninger."

He could even pick up the scent of peanuts drifting through the crowd and hear his father yelling hoarsely with the other fans–*"Leave him in! Leave him in!"*–just as he had when he'd taken Toby to a Giants game. Osteen was on the mound tonight, but when it was really working, when the radio was blaring away and people in the other rooms were talking back to Vinny, Toby could see Don Drysdale's towering figure slash across the mound with his whiplike sidearm motion. And he could see Juan Marichal, the Giants pitcher, vault his leg straight up into the air and bring it crashing down with fastballs that exploded across home plate. Toby never understood how the Dodgers faced up to such pitches, much less hit them, and yet somehow they did.

"He goes down swinging!"

Even in homes where it didn't quite work, like tonight, where the smells were grungy and the room was a shambles, Toby still had a sense of weightlessness, of sitting on the edge of his seat. It was like putting a Red Hot under your tongue and holding it there as long as you could–or biting down on a sore tooth until you couldn't stand it any longer–and that was like visiting his father too.

"The official attendance tonight is 18,068. A reminder: Tomorrow is Ladies Night. The first 1,000 ladies who show up will get a free Dodgers cap."

And when the action slowed down, as it did now, all he had to do was pay a visit to the concession stand. He picked himself up and glided over to the dresser. The top was a jumble of dirty ashtrays, smelly socks, loose change and eyeglasses, a clutter that would have discouraged anyone else. But Toby was a pro, and within a minute, he'd found his souvenir–a pen with a mercury-like substance in the casing. When he held it in the writing position, the substance crept down, revealing the pale figurine of a naked woman. Jerry had told him about such pens. He said his cousin Michael had one and carried it around as a good-luck charm. Well, now Toby had one too, and as he slipped it into his jeans pocket, he could imagine Jerry's eyes bulging out tomorrow when he showed it to him on the way to school. "Just my luck," he'd say. "Found it under my seat last night."

The pen wasn't his best souvenir–*that* was a white

rabbit's foot with a dab of black on the tip–but it would make a worthy addition to his growing stash of watches, snow globes, earrings, leather gloves, bolo ties, cameo rings and smoking pipes. He'd even lifted a brassiere once for a joke, though his rabbit's foot was his favorite.

"One run in. And Johnson is waving Perez in after him."

He'd nearly been caught taking it. He was in a bedroom like tonight, during a Braves game, and he'd just snatched it off a nightstand, when the overhead light flashed on. He froze, sure that he was trapped, but the woman at the door never looked inside. She just held her hand on the light switch and yelled down the hall.

"You've got five minutes until this light goes out!"

Then she left, and Toby dove under the bed, a little kid's bed, his heart clawing at his throat. From under the blanket's edge, he watched as two small legs in canary yellow sleepers toddled up to his face. He expected the legs to climb over him and onto the mattress, but the blanket lifted, revealing a little girl with whitish bangs and gumball eyes. The girl's head recoiled and her face blanched. Toby put a finger to his lips, but the girl dropped the blanket and waddled back into the hall.

"For Christ sake!" the woman screamed. "What are you doing up again?"

The girl whimpered.

"There's not a goddamn thing under your bed! I'm not going to put up with this crap every night."

The girl whined, and there was a loud crack, followed by the girl's shrieks, and then another crack.

The cries startled Toby into action. He bumped his head against the bed frame scrambling to his feet, and skinned his knee rushing through the window. He banged his knee some more scaling a cinder block wall, but at least he had the rabbit's foot. He held onto it tightly all the way home and throughout the night, waiting anxiously for the police to come. And when the sun filtered through his curtains the next morning and found him still in his bed, still under his covers, he knew it was only because of his new keepsake, the furry little amulet clasped in his hand.

As if to prove him right, for a whole week, the rabbit's foot brought him luck. At lunchtime, he won every game of basketball, making one difficult shot after another. In his homeroom, he was chosen to be flag monitor–something that *never* happened before–and on the way back from the flag-raising ceremony, Karen had actually smiled at him in the hallway. He'd even found a five-dollar bill in the street one afternoon, shortly after he'd socked Jerry goodbye. It was lying in the gutter, staring up into broad daylight, as if waiting for him to come along.

But lately, the rabbit's foot had gotten away from him. He remembered having it when he broke into the fat man's house, the one who'd glared at him this evening. He'd even rubbed it for good luck inside the man's den. But when he reached home afterward, it was gone, along with the blue plastic sleeve in which he'd inserted his name and address. Only a piece of the bead chain still clung uselessly to his belt.

He'd retraced his steps, coming dangerously close to the man's house. But it was nowhere on the sidewalk, and he didn't dare slip inside the house again, not with the man watering his lawn. The loss had nearly brought him to tears, and it still left a sharp ache in the pit of his stomach. Though the truth was he couldn't hang onto *anything*. He was the worst butterfingers in the world. If he grew attached to something, sooner or later, it disappeared on him. It never failed.

He looked up suddenly. The young woman was right outside the door, calling down the hallway to Old Baldy. Her voice sounded familiar, but the words came out garbled, as if she was drunk. Toby shrugged it off. People never entered the bedroom during a game. Besides, it was too early for bed, only the middle of the fifth inning.

He settled back into his corner and lowered his chin to his knees, and within moments, he was under the lights of Dodger Stadium again. The hometown organ poured out *The Yellow Rose of Texas*, and as it sashayed into the second bar, the bedroom door swung open and the woman stepped into the room.

"Do you hafta to listen to the game?" she called down the hallway. "I think you like Dodgers better'n me." Then she giggled.

To Toby's horror, she was naked–without a stitch of clothing. In the dim light from the hallway, her abundant flesh quivered and jounced like a vibrant pink blob. Toby was sure that she'd see him, but she climbed into the bed without looking in his corner and fell onto her back.

And now he had another shock. He knew her! She was his math teacher, Miss Stokker.

"Snookums," she called in a playful voice. "I'm waiting. Don't come make me git you." Then she giggled again.

"Hold your horses," the man answered.

He came in too now, an old baldy, just as Toby had imagined, with a full duffel bag of a belly and a stubby wiener that swung from side to side. The man held coils of rope in one hand, and as Miss Stokker lay in bed, he proceeded to tie her arms to the bedposts.

Toby's lips turned cold. His heart battered against his chest like a dog charging a gate. He was sure he was witnessing a murder, even though Miss Stokker lifted her arms to help and hummed along with the organ music from the radio.

"Is Thomas ready?" she asked in a lilting voice. "Lil' Thomas."

"He will be," the man answered gruffly.

She bent her head forward and stared at the man's crotch. "Hi, you. Wanna wake-up call? A lil' rev'ly?"

The man rose up on his knees. "How's that?"

She twisted her torso. "I can't move."

He busied himself with her legs now, tying them up as well. Toby whimpered silently. He was sure the man would tie him up next.

"Twist now," the man said.

She tried. "Nothing's moving."

"Oh yeah there is."

He ducked his head to her breast, and Miss Stokker gave off a siren burst of a scream. Toby squirted in his pants.

She sighed. "Now the other one. Bite it off."

"You'd like that, wouldn't you?"

The man bent over her chest again, and she groaned low and deep in her throat while her legs stiffened. Toby squeezed his buttocks. He was afraid his bowels would let go.

"Are you ready for Thomas?" he asked.

"You silly boy," she wheezed. "Why don't you...ugh."

The man attacked now with his hips, causing the headboard to rap against the wall, while Miss Stokker gave off short, piercing screams.

Watching from the shadows, Toby squeezed down desperately on the floor against his threatening bowels. He knew what they were doing. He knew that this was what a man and a woman did. He even hoped to do it himself one day. But the man attacked with such fury, and Miss Stokker cried out so piteously, that he wondered if he wasn't killing her after all.

Toby bent his head into his arms and stifled a sob. Already he missed her. He hated math more than any other subject, but nobody had dispensed it with such sweetness, with such a musical hum to her voice. He didn't think he could face the class tomorrow without her.

When he looked up again, Miss Stokker was free of the ropes. She was on her knees now with her back to the man. Old Baldy came toward her, but she squirmed away.

"Not that one," she giggled. "Unless you're not man enough."

The man grunted, and moments later, he was pounding away again, causing Miss Stokker to give off little gasps. Then the man shuddered and sagged and came to rest on her back. He appeared to be dozing. He even snored once or twice.

Miss Stokker leaned on her forearms to support his weight. She elbowed him in the ribs, and when he didn't respond, she elbowed him harder. He awoke with a start and cleared his throat. Then he shoved Miss Stokker roughly onto her back.

She giggled and rose up to say something, but he slapped her head to the side. She rose up again, and he slapped her head the other way.

"Is that the best you can do?" she wheezed.

He punched her in the stomach and bent his head between her legs, and as the muscles on his neck stood out, she sucked in her breath sharply. Her head arched back and her mouth gaped open. The man ducked his head two or three times, and each time, her arms and legs stiffened. Then she shuddered and her body went limp.

The man threw her legs aside. "Christ-O-Mighty!" He climbed off the bed and shambled out of the room, slamming the door behind him.

Vin Scully's voice drifted toward them like smoke from a dying fire.

"Be sure to join us tomorrow night when Sutton goes up against Nolan."

Organ music followed. It was muffled by the door, but Toby could make out the tune. It was the same one his father had sung on the way to the Giants game. Miss Stokker took up the verses now in bright, clear tones, singing with the innocence of a child about sunshine, happiness and love. When the song ended, she swung her legs to the side of the bed and clicked on the lamp, blinding Toby.

"Hi, sweetheart." She hiccupped. "Where'…d you come

from?"

He squirted in his pants. He tried to talk, but he couldn't force the air through his throat. The smell of ripe flesh made it hard for him to breathe.

"Did I...dream you up?" She split his ear with a shrill laugh. Her hiccups were becoming more regular. "You know, you...look familiar. But I can't see a...damn thing without my gl...asses."

She picked herself up and shuffled out of the room.

"Honey," she called to the man. "Snookums. Who's the cute...lil' boy in the bed...room?"

"For God's sake! Give it a rest." He turned up the radio.

"That's Willie Crawford's eleventh home run of the season."

"I think I know...him."

"Yeah, yeah. And I think you're seeing pink elephants again."

"It wasn't pink el...phants. It was rhino...ceri for your informa...tion."

She giggled again and her voice grew faint.

Toby didn't know how he came to be outside in the yard again. Nor how his leg happened to be hanging over the wooden fence, the other one stuck on the wrong side. And he didn't know how it was that he was walking down the middle of Magnolia Boulevard a moment later, toeing his way between the double yellow lines. A pair of headlights veered toward him and away. And then another, with a blast of its horn.

"Get out of the road, asshole!"

But he wasn't sure where the road ended and the sidewalk began. The night had spilled over everything. He had to sense his way from one pool of darkness to another. He tripped over a trashcan, stumbled into a splintery fence. A dog barked. Angry voices shouted. He strained to hear the Dodger announcer, but Vinny's cheerful tone had disappeared, and in its place, new voices sprang up.

"Are you a Communist? Can you sit there and tell me..?"

"Once again, Old Blue Eyes..."

"Opie, is that you?"

"After 23 nuclear tests, the Bikini islands will return..."

"Ve-e-e-ery interesting."

"It's ten till the top of the hour, and here's..."

"That was 'Raindrops Keep Falling on My Head.'"

"And how many times did you get friendly with him?"

"It's going to be another hot one tomorrow."

When he came to, he was standing in front of a Ralphs supermarket on Riverside and Vineland, moving his mouth silently at the customers leaving the store. A young mother giggled as she pushed her toddler past. An older woman sneered. "Get a job," she muttered. But he wasn't panhandling. He wanted their help. He didn't think he could make it home on his own.

After several false starts, he stumbled onto his street, though it looked different somehow. The buildings seemed to have re-arranged themselves into new, unfamiliar angles, and the street lamps rose up taller and sleeker than he remembered. The road itself appeared to have settled into a deep asphalt lake, and even his own building seemed brighter and fresher, as if it had been recently painted, though he knew it hadn't been. It was the same old place that he'd left earlier this evening.

A black-and-white patrol car sat parked by the curb, and as Toby passed it, his heart sank. Once again, he'd missed out on all the fun. Oh, he could make up bullshit stories about the places he'd been and the things he'd done. He could lay it on real thick. But he knew he was just a loser, a coward, a freak with three fingers. No one took him seriously, and no one ever would. He didn't even have the sense to stay home when the real excitement began–when it happened right on his doorstep.

He trudged up the stairs, and as he reached the landing,

he could hear his mother through the kitchen window. By the strain in her voice, he assumed his oldest sister was visiting, complaining once again about her new mother-in-law. Margot had only been married a month, and already the old fatso was driving her crazy.

But when he opened the door, there was no sign of his sister. Instead, a policeman sat by the dining room table, dangling his rabbit's foot.

His mother glared at him. "Where did you get these things?"

She held up a watch and a snow globe. Most of his stash was spread out before her on the table.

Toby shrugged. He couldn't remember all the houses.

She came up to him and grabbed him by the shoulders, firing off one question after another. But he didn't hear a word. He was staring at the policeman, a young man with angular features and slick, dark hair, who resembled the Dodgers' new third baseman, Steve Garvey. The officer rose to his feet, smiling shyly, and as he continued to jiggle the rabbit's foot, Toby knew why he'd come.

It wasn't to complain about the break-ins, which hadn't hurt anybody. And it wasn't to retrieve the stolen goods, which didn't amount to much. It was to take him to the game tomorrow night. Don Sutton was pitching–like Osteen, he was going for his 20th–and the thought of sitting in Dodger Stadium with the lights blazing down and the grass shimmering below him and the smell of peanuts drifting through the air was enough to set his whole body tingling. He went up to the startled policeman and put his arms around him, and though he was Tubby, Tubby Kovacek, it was all he could do not to cry.

13. Mud Wrestler
Jenny

HIGH SCHOOL WAS SUCH A BUMMER, I couldn't wait to get out. I just knew things would get better once I graduated. I even had this wild idea that I'd end up in some paradise with rippling lakes and rolling lawns and awesome sunsets in the background. I probably got the idea from my Dad, who was always telling us stories about his childhood in upstate New York, but I must've taken a wrong turn somewhere, because the farthest I got that first summer was a stupid job in an import store, one of those cheap places where the walls are made of cinder blocks and the merchandise is piled high on rickety metal shelves. The customers would chase you around to ask the dumbest questions, and if you didn't ring them up fast enough, they'd bitch and moan and even growl at you. The worst part, though, was the stock work. Some days, the boxes would pile up like trees until you couldn't see daylight, and then it felt like you'd *never* get out of there.

Probably the only thing that saved me was Gina–or Virginia Lombardo, as she signed her time card. Gina was just a shade older than me, and like me, she'd lost her father a few years before and didn't get along with her mother very well. She was also into sports, so I could actually talk to her about Claude Osteen and Manny Mota, and she'd know what I was talking about. And she could talk to me about wrestling.

Gina had taken up wrestling her last year in high school, and she competed now three or four nights a week in bars and nightclubs. Practically every day, she'd have stories to tell me about the matches she went to and the people she met and the wild things that happened. She'd even show me a hold or two when Patrick, the fat manager, wasn't watching, and at those moments, I could just picture her grappling with another girl somewhere in a makeshift ring. I just had a hard time imagining her apple cheeks and stocky frame in the dives where the matches were held.

"Why can't they hold them at a school or a YMCA?"

"Because girls aren't supposed to wrestle."

"But this is 1969 already."

"Well, you have to go where the action is. It's not going to come to you. Don't you want to broaden your horizons?"

I couldn't see how flopping around in front of a bunch of drunks was supposed to *broaden my horizons*, but she kept working on me to check it out.

And she wasn't the only one. Bea, another cashier, would make a face whenever she heard me say no.

"You should *go*, Hon. It's a shame to pass up an experience like that."

Even Patrick, the fat manager, would put in his two cents. "Hell, *I'd* go if Blondie was on the program. I'd even wager good money."

"Well, maybe *Blondie* doesn't want to be on the program," I said.

He could be such a jerk sometimes.

And then there was my Mom. She didn't want me to go to bars exactly, but she kept dropping hints about my social life. Like, she'd say, "Don't you get bored staying home on Saturday night?"

She probably thought I was hormonally imbalanced because I didn't date. Though I *had* dated once, in high school, and the guy had dumped me like a sack of potatoes. So I wasn't too anxious to get back into it again. And even if I did, I wasn't about to go bar hopping.

Still, I couldn't say no to Gina forever. She was really a good friend. And one day, when the customers were constantly on my case and the boxes had piled up like a cardboard forest and Fatrick kept rubbing his big gut against me every time he had to slip by me at the register to approve a personal check, I suddenly realized that I never saw anything but the inside of this stupid store. It just about freaked me out. I even ran outside for a breath of fresh air, and when I came back in, the first thing I did was to go looking for Gina. I found her in one of the aisles tagging rattan mats.

"So when's the next match?" I said, trying to sound nonchalant. I still wasn't sure I wanted to go.

"Tonight!" Her eyes lit up like candles. "Want me to pick you up?"

"I guess." I owed her a favor anyway. I'd overslept that morning, and she'd punched my time card, which could've gotten both of us fired.

"I'll come by your place at 7:30," she said. "Just wear sweats so no one will ask about your age."

"But I don't want to wrestle."

"You can hang by the bar the whole time. Nobody'll even notice."

When I got home, I told Mom I was going to a Dodger game with some friends from work, and an hour later, Gina and I were roaring down Lankershim Boulevard in her yellow VW Bug. We headed straight into the industrial part of town, and that's when it hit me how insane this whole thing was. I'd nearly been raped once when I was 15, by this half-drunk theater manager who was supposed to be interviewing me for a job, and here I was putting myself in a place *full* of people just like him. I could even picture his bleary eyes and veiny nose as he was bearing down on me, and suddenly, I just wanted Gina to turn around and take me home. But before I could get the words out, she pulled up in front of this one-story building and hopped out.

The place she led me to was basically a hole in the wall. You wouldn't even know a bar was there except for this red neon light that flickered over the entrance. The light was supposed to be a torch, but the bottom part was burned out, so it looked more like somebody's hair on fire. As if that wasn't creepy enough, when we turned into the narrow entryway, this dark sign rose up in front of us.

> *No one under 21 admitted*
> *Minors will be prosecuted*

It stopped me dead in my tracks. I knew we'd be sneaking in, of course, but it never occurred to me that we might get arrested. My mother would have a fit if she had to come bail me out. Also, you couldn't see very far beyond the door–the entryway bent at a right angle–and the smell of cigarette smoke and alcohol really started to spook me. Then suddenly, there was this burst of laughter from inside, and I nearly peed in my pants.

"Gina!"

I thought she'd try to reason with me–tell me how safe it was and all that–but she just backed up a couple steps, grabbed me by the sleeve and yanked me through the door. And just like that, I found myself swimming around inside this gloomy, cave-like place that was choking with cigarette smoke. Rock music started blasting away, just pounding the walls, and the smell of alcohol was so strong, it smacked you in the face. But what really freaked me out were all these scruffy-looking guys with big bellies and raggedy hair. They sat hunched over these little round tables with their mouths open and their eyes all bugged out like they were just waiting to pounce. A few even started howling when we came in, and I nearly peed in my pants again. I was sure they'd be all over us. But Gina led me right by them like it was no big deal and plopped me down on a stool by this long wooden counter. She even ordered a beer and asked me if I wanted one. I was trembling so hard, I could barely say no.

"Are you sure? They don't check here."

I shook my head. I just wanted to disappear. I thought if I stared hard enough at the wooden counter top, I could sink into it. But the problem was, you couldn't ignore the guys. They kept howling and moaning and even laughing out loud, as if they couldn't believe their luck. Then the music stopped, and it got real quiet, except for this one guy who was clearing his throat. Then it started up again, and once again, they started howling and moaning until I couldn't take it anymore. I spun around on the stool–the last thing I wanted was them sneaking up on me–and that's when I saw they weren't even *looking* at us.

They were all glued to the other side of the room, where this gangly woman was prancing about on a stage in practically nothing. All she had on was a pair of jet-black heels and a velvety strap that barely covered her butt crack. She was moving more or less in time to *Wild Thing*, swinging her shoulders and hips and making her long breasts jiggle like salamis. Every so often, she'd come to a dead stop with her back to the crowd and bend over, letting her boobs dangle between her legs, and the guys would moan like they were getting it on. Or she'd sidle up to the edge of the stage and thrust her hip out for one of the guys to blow on it–and the whole room would howl or crack up. It took me a while to realize that she wasn't even pretty– she had this long horsy face and stringy hair that looked like it'd been tie-dyed blonde–but the men couldn't get enough of her. They reminded me of my kid brother Toby, the way he'd gape at all the toy displays around Christmas time.

While all this was going on, a tiny waitress darted about the tables like a moth among grizzly bears, serving drinks and taking orders, though the guys hardly noticed her.

The music changed to *You're the One*, and now the dancer got really crude. She laid down on the floor with her feet toward the audience and spread her legs wide open, as if offering herself up on a platter. The men leaned forward to take it all in. One fat slob even groaned like he was having a bowel movement.

I shuddered and leaned closer to Gina, though she was starting to worry me too. She was taking a good swig on her beer every so often, and I could smell it on her breath.

"You sure you don't want one?" she asked. "It's on me."

"Maybe a 7Up." Though I wasn't sure I could get *that* down. I was feeling more out of it by the minute. "I thought they were going to have wrestling."

"They *are*. Some places have a warm-up show."

This old guy next to her cackled. "That's one hell of a warm-up show." He slapped her on the knee and grinned so wide, you could see the gaps between his cruddy teeth.

I was sure Gina would be offended, but she just smiled and took another swig of her beer.

The music stopped, and there was scattered applause while the dancer picked up bunches of dollars from glass jars on either side of the stage. Then she wiggled her fingers at everybody and slipped out the side.

Another dancer came out now, a short Chinese woman with bangs down to her eyebrows and a pink two-piece outfit. She started dancing awkwardly in place to the Doors' *Light My Fire*, moving much slower than the music.

"How many warm-ups do they need?" I asked.

Gina shushed me, but nobody could hear us. The old guy

had gone up front to get a better look.

The Chinese woman eased down her top inch by inch. She finally pulled it off altogether, and then she laid down on the floor and spread her legs apart just like the other dancer, and once again, the guys started moaning.

I couldn't understand how anybody got turned on by this sort of thing. I felt like a pervert just sitting there. I mean, the whole thing was just so weird, as if I'd slipped into some strange underground world I'd never known existed. Or as if I'd woken up in the middle of a science fiction movie and found out that everybody, including my parents, were actually from Mars.

The Chinese woman danced to a couple more numbers, if you could call what she did dancing. Then she picked up the top part of her outfit and clutched it against her shallow breasts like she was suddenly embarrassed. The men gave her a nice round of applause, while she made these short little bows and collected her tips.

After she left, two guys walked out on the stage dragging exercise mats and started to lay them side by side.

"Hey, now we get to try 'em!" the old guy shouted on his way back to the bar.

The men let loose like a giant fart.

I turned to Gina, but she didn't seem the least bit concerned. She was talking to a slender, dark-haired girl, who must've come in during the show. She was also wearing sweats, and like Gina, she chatted away as if the men weren't there. I couldn't believe it! Here they were about to go up in front of these yahoos, and they acted like it was nothing to worry about.

Gina nodded toward me. "Marilyn, this is Jenny."

The girl held out her hand, which was ice cold from a beer she'd been drinking. *Everybody* seemed to be drinking the bitter stuff, like it was some kind of ticket into the place.

"Steph couldn't make it, huh?" Gina said.

"No, she's down with the flu. And you know how much you can count on Peg and Katie."

Gina shook her head. "They won't let us keep holding these matches if people don't show up."

"We'll just have to go it alone." Marilyn turned to me. "How 'bout you, Jenny? Do you wrestle?"

I shivered all over, and part of my shivering was to shake my head.

Gina answered for me. "She's just checking it out."

"It's really a gas," Marilyn said. "You oughta try it."

"That's what I keep telling her."

The room grew brighter now as these overhead lights came on, and Marilyn and Gina stood up and did some stretches and knee bends. For a few panicky moments, I thought they might go up there and perform the same routines as the dancers.

Meanwhile, the two guys on the stage were hanging a guard net across the front edge. It looked suspiciously like a trap, but when I turned to warn Gina, she and Marilyn were already headed toward the front. I was sure they'd be heckled because they weren't strippers, but the men actually applauded and rose out of their seats. They even crowded around the stage like a bunch of kids, and then money started changing hands. Quite a bit, in fact. More than I made in a week.

Gina and Marilyn did some more stretches up on the stage, and Marilyn ran in place for a few moments. Then they took their positions on the mats, and while the men hooted and howled, the girls bent over and slowly circled each other, moving sideways like crabs. They locked arms, continuing to circle, and then suddenly, Marilyn lunged. And just as quickly, Gina twisted to the side and slammed her to the floor. But before Gina could pin her, Marilyn rolled out from under her and was back on her feet.

I couldn't believe how fast they were–like rabbits. Gina was so much wider, I thought she'd have no problem with

Marilyn. But as they circled again, Marilyn twisted inside Gina and brought *her* down. Then she flopped on top of her in what seemed like a surefire pin. But Gina kicked out her legs and slipped out from under it.

My heart was bopping away like a ping-pong ball. And the men were going nuts, screaming with every move.

"Get her, Honey Bunch, get her!"

"Come on, Baby Doll! That's it!"

"Pin her! Pin her!"

Even the blonde stripper got into it. She stood by the side of the stage in a dressy black pantsuit, cupping her hands to her mouth. "Break her down, Babe! Come on! You can do it!"

Marilyn managed to take Gina down again, but at the last moment, Gina scrambled on top and pinned her for a three-second count–and the room just exploded. It was like Gina had hit one out of the park. Though not everybody was happy. The guys who'd lost money were cussing a blue streak, swearing they'd make it back later.

The girls wrestled a few more rounds, and then they took a breather. And while I was catching my own breath, I heard this kittenish voice next to me.

"You dancer?"

It was the Chinese stripper. She was dressed in a black miniskirt with a lime green poor boy, and she was sipping one of those fancy multi-colored drinks. You'd have thought she was just another woman out on the town.

"No," I said. "I'm a wrestler."

A couple guys turned around to check me out. I felt really stupid, like a piece of meat they were sizing up.

"If I have your breasts, I be dancer," the Chinese woman said.

My ears started to burn. I hated it when people talked about me like that. I asked her where the restroom was, and on the way there, a few more guys ogled me. Maybe they thought I'd dance for them next.

When I got back, Gina and Marilyn were at it again. This time, Marilyn was even more aggressive. She hooked an arm under Gina's knee and drove her one-legged off the mat. But as soon as they got back into position, Gina swept Marilyn's foot and pinned her, and once again, the guys went nuts.

After a couple more rounds, they took another breather, and while Marilyn went off somewhere, Gina showed up next to me, dripping in sweat.

"You guys are fantastic!" I clapped her on the shoulder. "That was amazing!"

"So how 'bout it? Wanna give it a try?"

"No way. I wouldn't know what to do up there."

"Just remember the holds I showed you, and stay low to the ground. And don't do anything half-heartedly. If you're going to attack, then attack with your whole body."

"You make it sound like I'm really going up there."

"No, I'm serious. The owner asked me if you would. Charlie thinks some plainclothes guys might show up tonight, and he's worried they'll ask questions if you're not wrestling."

"Gina!"

"Jenny, it's so easy. Just do what comes natural."

"In front of *these* guys?"

"It's not like taking off your clothes."

"For *me*, it is."

"It'll be okay. Just relax and enjoy it."

I couldn't imagine myself up there in a million years. But just then, these two guys in iridescent suits brushed past us, and my heart started flopping all over the place.

Gina put a beer in front of me. "Here. That's all the preparation you need."

I took a few swigs, and it went straight to my head. I never could hold my liquor. Gina kept telling me that everything was going to be fine. She even showed me a couple holds again, but the room was starting to get fuzzy, and I couldn't feel the floor with my feet. When she had me do some toe touches, I nearly fell on my face.

I started giggling, and now Marilyn came back, and together they pulled me away from the counter. I thought we were going out for a breath of fresh air, but suddenly, I found myself up on the stage with the lights shining in my face. I couldn't see two feet in front of me, but I could feel all those eyes on me, and I could sense the buzz of anticipation.

Marilyn took her position on the mats and waved for me to come closer. I bent over and copied her sidesteps, as if we were circling in a dance. I didn't have a clue what I was doing and started giggling again. Then I lost sight of her–and ended up flat on my back.

"You can do better than that, Blondie!" one of the men shouted.

"Somebody needs practice," another one cried out.

"How 'bout it, Woody? You wanna show her the ropes?"

That brought some howls.

"He don't know no ropes. His old lady took 'em away."

"You go, Brondie!" It was the Chinese woman. "You can do it!"

Maybe it was the beer or a bad case of nerves. Or maybe I just didn't like being knocked over. But whatever the case, when I picked myself up, I was raring to go. Marilyn gave me another wave, and I lunged at her knees, sending her down in a heap. Before I could pin her, though, she spun away and grabbed me from behind, using a hold Gina hadn't shown me.

"Get him, Brondie!" the Chinese woman called. "Get him!"

And now the men took up the chant. "Get him, Brondie! Get him!"

Marilyn tried to turn me over, but she was laughing so hard, she didn't have the strength. So I pushed up with both my legs and pinned her with my back–and the men let out a roar. As I rolled to my feet, I even got a pat or two on the head.

We did a couple more rounds, but Marilyn was so wiry, like an eel, that I couldn't get a grip on her. She pinned me every time.

Then she and Gina went at it, and once again, I couldn't believe how fast they were–like slingshots. Gina won again, and now it was my turn to go up against her.

As we circled, the men hooted, and I could feel the excitement bubbling up from the crowd, running through my arms and legs like tiny electric shocks. I lunged at Gina, but she had even less trouble with me than Marilyn. Time and again, she pinned me, usually after only a minute or two.

Still, I wouldn't quit. I kept jumping up for another round. Finally, they had to drag me *back* to the counter.

When I got there, the bartender set a beer in front of me and winked, and as I downed the bitter stuff, one of the bruisers came over and clapped me on the knee.

"You gotta come back and see us, Blondie," he shouted over the music, which had started up again. "You're not very good, but we like your spirit."

I took another swig, and while the beer danced through my head, I shot back, "You bet. Just watch me."

Already I had stars in my eyes.

* * *

I was hooked after that. Any spare time I had now I spent practicing with Gina in her mom's garage, which she'd converted to a gym. We'd flop around for hours on these two old mattresses, practicing holds and counters and takedowns. And then three or four nights a week, we'd make the rounds at the clubs.

Not all of them had scuzzy dancing like The Torch Light. Some were actually pretty classy. Like Guido's, which served dinner on linen-covered tables and which had a referee for the matches every so often. Or like The Ice

Cavern or Shady Lady, which featured live bands and dancing. Of course, a couple of the places were just out-and-out dives, and probably the worst was The Salt Lick. We'd wrestle there in the middle of this beat-up linoleum floor, while tough-looking bikers hooted and howled and threw dollar bills at us. Though even there, once the matches got started, none of it mattered. All you'd be aware of was the wrestlers going at it and people shouting and your heart bopping away. It was like plunging down a deep hole, or swimming through boiling water, or skating across a frozen lake that was breaking up by the minute. Even when I ended up flat on my back, which was usually the case the first few weeks, I'd still get this awesome feeling, as if some giant had picked me up and flown me to a whole new level of existence.

I didn't even mind getting propositioned, which used to bug the hell out of me at the store. But at the bars, it was just part of the scene. And besides, Gina put up with a lot more crap than I did. She could be swigging a beer after a match, with her clothes all sweaty and her hair sticking to her face, and the guys would still be buzzing around her like flies.

"It's the sweat," she told me one night as we drove home. "It's like an aphrodisiac for them."

I thought she was joking, but she'd been propositioned so many times, she even had names for all the types.

"First you've got the Poppers, the ones who are always popping off at the mouth. They'll shout at you from across the room, things like, 'So, when you coming back to my place to pick up your shorts?'

"Then you've got the Backslappers. They like to pound you on the back, like you're a lodge member or one of their buddies. For them, that's like foreplay.

"Then there's the Foremen. They're a little more subtle than the Backslappers. They'll mosey up to you and stare off the competition, like you're one of their crewmembers, and then they'll stand there all evening protecting their territory.

"The Weepers, on the other hand, just try to make you feel sorry for them. They think if they spill their guts out and tell you all their problems, you'll jump into bed with them.

"And then there's the Confiders. They're another form of Weeper. The Confiders can't stand their wives, or their wives can't stand them, which is supposed to make you feel sorry for them—"

"—and jump into bed," I said.

She smiled without taking her eyes off the road. "Though at least they're not sneaky like the Pulse-Takers. The Pulse-Takers like to hold your hand and stare into your eyes, as if they really care, when all they really want to know is if you're horny or not."

I kind of snorted.

"The Geronimos, on the other hand, don't even wait to find out. They just go on the attack. You can usually tell them by their tight pants."

"Assuming they've got something."

"They usually do." Gina pulled up to my apartment building. "But the ones you really have to look out for are the Barracudas. They'll hang in the shadows for nights on end, and then make their move when you least expect it."

"How many of those did you run into?"

She made a face. "Just one."

"So what happened?"

"Nothing. I don't go there anymore." She reached over and opened my door. "See you tomorrow."

Of course, by then, I'd run into most of the types she was describing and was pretty good at fending them off. And besides, by the time they got around to me, they were usually too wasted to be much of a problem. Like the college boys who could barely write my number down. I don't know why I gave it to them. I guess they were kind of cute with their slurred speech and their alcohol breath, though even when they did call, which wasn't that often, I couldn't see myself going out with them. And *not* because I was hormonally imbalanced or anything, like my mother probably thought. It was just that so many things were coming at me, I didn't know what to make of it.

Like, some nights, I'd feel as if I was being blown about this way and that, with no sense of direction, just totally out of control. And other nights, I'd feel as if I was closing in on something, something really neat, only it was just out of reach, just inches away, and I could never get my arms around it. And still other nights, it'd all be pretty routine–get up and wrestle, and do it again. Though even on those nights, there'd always be a moment or two that got me going, that made me feel as if I was coming out of my skin.

And then, one night, I ran into a Barracuda, and it just blew me away completely.

It happened at The Torch Light, while I was wrestling this older woman named Katie. She'd beaten me half a dozen times with a bear hug, but now I had her in a pretty good headlock, and I was just about to take her down, when out of nowhere, I heard this half-hearted cry, "Hi-yo, Jenny, away!" It jarred me for a second, just enough for Katie to spin around, back-arch me to the mat and pin me like a bug.

I stormed back to the bar. Nobody was supposed to know my real name, let alone this "Hi-yo" crap from high school. Gina handed me a 7Up to calm me down, and just as I was taking a huge swig, this squarish face with glasses rose up in front of me–and half the soda came out my nose.

"I see you've become a star," he said. "You're even on the marquee."

He meant the banner above the door. What it really said was, "Female Wrestling Tonight," but that was his way of laying it on thick.

"How'd you find me?" I pressed a towel against my face. I wasn't used to people showing up from my past. I thought if I pressed it hard enough, he might disappear.

"I've been following your career. You play quite a few venues."

That much hadn't changed. Gerald still did his homework. But otherwise, I hardly recognized him. He was just a shadow of the boy I remembered from high school. His face was pale, almost ghostly, and his hair had thinned out and receded at the corners. What really brought me up short, though, were his eyes. I remembered how they'd shone that night in the coffee shop when he told me about all his great plans after graduation. Now they were just dull and lifeless, like two brown smudges.

"What are *you* doing here?" I didn't mean just the bar. He was supposed to be at Annapolis.

He hung his head. "It's a long story."

Gina grunted. "Does it have a happy ending?"

"I don't know." He bit his lip. "I could tell you about it sometime."

"Assuming I'd be interested," I said.

Gina got up and clapped me on the shoulder. It was her turn to go on.

"What about what's-her-face?" I asked.

"You mean Patty? I haven't called her since I got home. I guess we didn't last beyond high school." He bit his lip again. I was afraid he'd turn into a Weeper right in front of me. "I need to talk to you, Jenny. I feel like you were somebody special, and I wasn't paying attention. I still remember the slide rule you gave me."

That stupid slide rule. I should've thrown it away as soon as he'd given me the brush-off.

"But we're not in high school anymore," I said. "You can't just turn the clock back."

"I know."

"And I'm not the same person I was back then. I'm not even the same person I was last week."

"I'm not either. Maybe we could catch up on lost time."

"Gerald, it wouldn't work."

"It might be interesting."

I told him no a few more times, and finally, he drifted away.

But that wasn't the end of it. It never was with Gerald. For the next couple of weeks, I couldn't go anywhere without seeing his face in the crowd. He didn't call out "Hi-yo" anymore, but I got so fed up seeing his droopy eyes and pale features that I finally confronted him.

"Gerald, look, if I go out with you, will you stop following me around?"

He nodded and hung his head. I shouldn't have agreed to it–he'd really been a jerk–but I knew he'd keep it up until I caved in. Besides, I was dying to find out what happened. He was one of the brightest kids in our class–maybe *the* brightest–and it just didn't make sense for him to be hanging out at bars.

I told Mom I was wrestling that night–she thought the matches were held at the Y–and around 7:30, I went down to meet Gerald by the curb. It was really cold and foggy, and as I stood there shivering, I had the sense that nothing good would come of this. As if to confirm my suspicions, Gerald's white Oldsmobile came rolling out of the fog like some bad memory from the past. When I slipped inside, it was as if time had stood still. Everything was exactly the same as I remembered it–the Dalmatian carpeting, the red vinyl seats, the tiny box speakers over the doors, even the way Gerald turned on the radio and clammed up as we drove off.

We even went back to the old high school, this time to catch a football game, though it was so foggy, you could barely make out the players on the field. They looked like shadowy figures running around on a frosty background. It got so bad, even the cheerleaders gave up and huddled under some Army blankets. We gave up too, finally, and left after North Hollywood fell behind by 21 points.

Then, just as I expected, Gerald drove to the same coffee shop where we'd gone the first time. I wasn't too thrilled about it–there was a certain waiter there I didn't want to see–but I figured Gerald wouldn't be happy until he'd relived the whole experience. Still, as I stepped through the door, I felt like I was passing through a wall of fire, and as we stood around in the lobby waiting to be seated, I kept scouring the dining room, looking for the waiter's frizzy blond hair and bloated face. I had to look high and low because he was only about four-foot-eleven.

"He doesn't work here anymore," Gerald said when he saw me rubbernecking. "If that's who you're looking for."

"Thanks. You could've told me."

"Sorry." He bit his lip. "He was fired months ago. I think he's a messenger now. Or a gofer."

"Serves him right, the bastard."

We got a window booth again, and once again, we ordered cheeseburgers, French fries, and soft drinks, this time from a woman with a face like a bulldog. And then, just like on our first date, we didn't know what to say to each other. So we just sat there hunched over, as if we had these huge weights on our backs, and stared out the window. I noticed in the glass that my eyes could have used some liner and that my hair was sticking out. I brushed it back, but what I really needed was somebody to fuss over me again, like my sister had before our first date.

Gerald still hadn't told me what he was doing home.

"I'm sorry about Annapolis," I said after a while.

"It's okay. I shouldn't have gone." He fingered the silverware.

"But wasn't it neat to be there? Some people dream about it."

"Yeah, I suppose. I should have gone to MIT or Cal

Tech. At Annapolis, they never let you forget you're in the Navy."

"But you *wanted* to be in the Navy."

"I didn't know what I wanted. I'll probably be in the Army next if I don't find another school. It's hard to get enrolled in the middle of a semester."

"You shouldn't have any trouble. You're a good student."

"I *was*. Now I'm just a dropout."

Then he clammed up on me again.

Our food came and we started eating, or at least I did. Gerald just picked at his. He was really on a downer.

So I tried to cheer him up. I told him about my screwy little brother and how he'd been arrested *twice* for breaking into houses.

"Can you believe it? He did it for the thrill."

But Gerald just shrugged.

So I told him about my pregnant sister and how her mother-in-law insisted that she take her temperature every day–up the butt.

"She even wants to help her. And she gets mad when Margot won't let her."

Gerald just made a face. It was like he was determined to be miserable.

On the way out, he stared down at the ground and thanked me for going out with him. I felt like such a wet blanket. Probably all he'd wanted was some companionship, and I couldn't even give him that. No wonder the guys at the bars had to get drunk before they asked me out. I must've come over like the ice queen or something, as if I was totally unapproachable.

"You know what?" I said. "Why don't we go up to the place we went last time? You know, up on the hill where you can see all the lights. I want to see it when I'm *not* wasted."

He broke into a little smile. "You really were, weren't

you?"

"Yeah, like I was faking it. That prick of a waiter put something in my Cokes."

Gerald's eyes bugged out.

"Girls know those words too, you know."

He held up both arms and slipped in through the driver's side.

I thought he'd have us up there in no time, but Gerald actually got lost. For once, he *hadn't* done his homework. He even stopped to get directions from these two weird-looking guys who were out walking. They were dressed in long cloaks, like something out of the Renaissance, and it turned out they were as lost as we were. Though even without the fog, the place would've been hard to find. When we finally stumbled onto the access road, it was just a little cut in the hillside.

We started to climb now, and I couldn't believe how much of the road came back to me–all the twists and turns and the way it swung out to the very edge, where there was nothing but a sheer drop. The higher we climbed, the thicker the fog grew until you couldn't see more than a few feet ahead. It was like we were leaving the earth behind, rising into some strange limbo world. Then Gerald pulled off the road and onto a turnout, and there we were. Though the haze was so thick, you could barely see beyond the hood of the Olds. I mean, it was like smoke. And there was no way you could make out the lights below.

"See?" Gerald killed the engine and slumped in his seat. "Nothing works out the way you think it will."

We sat there gazing into the fog. Except for the hum of the electric heater, which worked even when the engine was off, there wasn't a sound. It really started to creep me out.

"Why don't you tell me about Annapolis?" I said. "*I'll* never see it."

"You mean how I cleaned an admiral's window with a toothbrush?"

"Did you really?"

"Yeah, that was one of the highlights."

"But you were in *college*. It had to be exciting to be around all those bright people."

"College isn't all that tough. Everybody thinks it is, but you can get by if you've got half a brain. All you need to know is how to read and write."

"Well, *I* never made it."

"You didn't even try. You'd probably be a star, if you want to know the truth. You're a hell of a lot smarter than most of the idiots I ran into."

"But they don't accept girls at Annapolis."

"That's probably next."

I gazed out into the fog and tried to imagine myself in a college classroom scribbling away. I'd heard that you had to remember everything or they'd kick you right out. I didn't believe what Gerald said about me being a star, but still, it was nice to hear. Nobody had ever noticed that I had a brain.

I turned to ask if he meant it, but he was lost in himself.

"Hey, Gerald," I said. "Why don't we wrestle like we did last time?"

He squinted at me. "Why don't we *what*?"

"Wrestle."

"We didn't wrestle."

"*Yeah* we did. Don't you remember?" I shoved his shoulder. "Come on."

He grunted and looked away.

"Come on. It'll be fun." I shoved him again.

He made a face and pushed me back.

"Afraid of a girl?" I locked his arm under my elbow and put him in a reverse half nelson. "See if you can get out of *this* one."

Suddenly, he came to life and drove me back against the

seat. "You wanna play rough, huh?" For a chubby guy, he was pretty strong.

Then he reached around me as if he was going to put me in a hold, but instead he pulled up a lever on the passenger side–and the back of the seat floated down until it was level with the one in the rear.

My eyes must've bugged out. "So that's how we ended up in the back!"

He grinned and put his glasses on the dash. Then he threw an arm around my neck and we went at it. He wasn't much of a wrestler–more of a tickler and a groper–but still, he put up a good fight. And anyway, after a while, it became more than wrestling. Our faces came together at one point, and he started nibbling me all over. I laughed and nibbled him back. Then we started making out for real, and I picked up the faintest whiff of cologne, along with this humid, earthy smell that was even sexier. I slipped my hands under his shirt and ran them all through the wispy hairs on his chest, and he put his hands under my sweater and moved them all around, setting off all these little twinges inside. Then we started making out again, and I could feel the muscles in his arms and the tiny bristles on his jaw. And while we were going at it, the strangest thing happened–I felt like I was in the car with Dad, that he was holding me instead of Gerald. I could even smell his Old Spice after-shave and feel his stubbly chin. I pulled back, expecting to see his long, horsy face–but instead Gerald blinked at me. Without his glasses, his eyes were like a pair of tiny dark pools.

He put his hand behind my head and drew me toward him again, and as our faces came together, all these feelings started racing through me. It was like on wrestling nights when I felt like I was closing in on something, something really awesome. Only, it was much stronger, much more intense, as if I could almost touch it. I pulled off his windbreaker, and he pulled off my sweater, and we wiggled out of the rest of our clothes and held each other so tight, there wasn't an inch of air between us—just skin to skin. Then we made out some more, and he rolled on top of me and inside me, and it was so strange, so weird, kind of burning, but also kind of breathless. And suddenly, I started to sense Dad again, as if he was gasping in my ear, wheezing like he did on that God-awful day when we were walking up the front lawn and he was nuzzling my cheek, trying to make it up to me for some promise that he'd broken, some little thing that he hadn't done. He even held the screen door open, "For my princess," he said. But he kept wheezing and gasping, like he was out of breath, and when I brushed past him, he jerked his head back, as if I'd decked him. I thought he was horsing around, but he let out this horrible groan and sank to the ground, and then he just laid there in a sweat. "Dad!" I cried out. I think I even cried it in the Olds. But he just laid there all glassy-eyed, as if he couldn't hear me. As if he was miles away. We tried to lift him, but we could barely sit him up. Mom tapped his forehead and called his name, but he just kept staring into space, as if he wasn't there. As if he'd already left us. He recovered a little when the medics arrived. He even smiled at me as they carried him on the gurney. "Be seein' ya, Muffin," he said. But he never did. They put him in the ambulance and drove off—and I never saw him again.

When I came back to the surface, my whole body was aching. I looked around the Olds, but there was no sign of Dad. Just Gerald breathing softly and the heater humming away.

I started to cry, and Gerald woke up.

"It was my first time too," he said.

The windows had clouded over. So I reached up and rubbed the cold glass with the back of my hand. Outside, there was a break in the fog and you could see a star or two winking down at us. But then the haze rolled in like a thick blanket and sealed us off again.

* * *

After my night out with Gerald, I never quite knew where I was anymore. I could be dragging myself through a day at work and feel like I was fending off drunks at the bars. Or circling Gina during a match and imagine I was flailing about in the Olds with Gerald. Or laying face down on my bed and find myself shivering, as if I was back at the football game, watching the players run around in the fog.

I tried calling Gerald the next day, but nobody answered the first two times. Then his snotty little sister picked up.

"Is this Patty?" she asked.

"No, it's not. Can I talk to Gerald?"

"Who is this? You don't sound like Patty."

"It's Geronimo."

"You're not Geronimo. They shot him down. You're just a girl. Are you sure you're not Patty?"

"You know it's not polite—"

She took a deep breath.

"Listen, could you just get Gerald for me?"

"I can't."

"You can't, or you don't want to?"

"I can't because he's not here. He's in Saint Louis *Obispo*."

"What's he doing there?"

"Applying for school!"

"You don't have to shout."

"Yes, I do. Because you ask me everything TWICE!"

I got the idea that Gerald would be gone for a few days, and I didn't know how I was going to last that long. It seemed like everything just slowed to a crawl. At work, we had so many deliveries, it was like trudging through a swamp. And even wrestling got to be a pain. The bar owners started coming up with all these weird ideas, and they expected us to just go along with them. Like, at The

Salt Lick, they wanted us to wrestle in this inflatable kiddy pool filled with mud. I thought it was a joke, but Gina said we had to do it.

"But it's not wrestling," I said. "It's like we're putting on a show."

"Well, that's what we do. We put on a show. Why do you think they let us hold these matches?"

"But this is *The Salt Lick*, Gina."

"It'll be okay. Just remember to wear your bathing suit."

I did, and just as I expected, the bikers went nuts. They started whooping it up as soon as we got into the mud. Some even poked me in the butt or snapped at my bathing suit bottom, which really pissed me off because nobody was supposed to touch the wrestlers. But every time I looked at Mal, the owner, he'd just roll his eyes along with the other hyenas. He was something of an asshole anyway. The bikers liked to greet him with the raspberries, and as often as not, he'd salute them back with a fart.

When I got back to the restroom, I found out what all the hooting was about. As I peeled off my bathing suit, several curled-up dollar bills fell to the floor, all caked in mud. It was really disgusting, like I'd done it in my pants.

Things got even crazier at The Ice Cavern. Over there, the owner wanted us to be auctioned off like slaves and then wrestle with the winning bidders. When it got to be my turn, I tried to look pathetic, but almost immediately I was "bought" by this shaggy little guy with brick red hair and a goatee.

As soon as we got into the ring, he had his hands all over me. I took him down hard a couple times, and then he started fighting dirty, pinching and scratching and even biting when he thought he could get away with it. I slammed him down again, but from the floor, he swept my legs, knocking me flat. Then he jumped on top of me and started humping away like we were doing it. The crowd thought that was riot. I shoved him off, and while he was on all fours giggling like an idiot, I climbed over his hairy legs and put him in a tight far-side cradle. The more he squirmed, the harder I cranked until I could see his eyes darken and his jaw clench, but I was so pissed, I could've killed him. And then, before I could pin him, the strangest thing happened. While I had him in the cradle, I could feel his heart beating through his back, almost as if it was beating inside me, and I could see these soft downy hairs on his neck and all these freckles spread out across his shoulder blades like tiny pale leaves–and suddenly, I just wanted to bury my face in his neck and hold him for all I was worth. I had to force myself to my feet and stumble back to the bar.

"Hey, she didn't pin me!" the guy cried out.

It got a big laugh from the crowd, but there was no way I was going back in the ring with him.

Gina handed me a beer, half of which I spilled down my sweatshirt.

"Are you okay?" she asked.

I shook my head. I didn't think I'd *ever* be okay.

For the rest of the evening, the shaggy guy kept leering at me from across the room. I tried to avoid him, but whenever he caught my eye, he'd smile and wink, as if we had some unspoken agreement to go in the back and fuck our minds out. And the funny thing was, every time it happened, I'd feel this twinge down my chest, as if maybe we did.

I wasn't the same after that night. If somebody so much as touched me, my breath would catch and this wicked warmth would go flying through me. I even started to wonder if there *was* something wrong with me–if maybe I *wasn't* hormonally imbalanced after all. But then I started to notice it in other people as well, and it just blew me away. Like, I'd see it in Angel, the stockboy, when he carried two giant boxes at once and his face got all flushed and the veins stood out on his neck. Or I'd see it in Bea as she watched him from the cash register with her mouth dropping open and her face turning pink. Or I'd see it in Gina toward the end of the day when her eyes got a little spacey and she had that sad gleam in her cheeks. Or in Patrick when he opened the store in the morning and gazed at me with a sigh. I'd even see it in the customers, the way the women stood in line with tight, little smiles and shiny faces, and the way the men fumbled awkwardly inside their pockets for change. It was like I wasn't surrounded by people anymore but by arms and legs, by mouths and bodies, all waiting to latch onto each other–all waiting to burn into one.

Gerald must've felt it too, because when he came home on Friday, we didn't even bother with dinner or a football game. We just drove straight up to our parking spot on the hill and went right at it. And this time, he made me feel so awesome, like when you're flying down a roller coaster and your breath rushes out and you think you'll never hit bottom, and then you do, only you feel like you haven't, like you still have a ways to go.

I started living for those nights. Patrick could be explaining these new cash registers to us, or Gina could be telling me about a girl who wanted to wrestle, and I wouldn't hear a thing. I'd be thinking about Gerald and the Olds and whether he was picking me up at the store that evening or at my apartment. I even skipped out on wrestling, which didn't go over too well with Gina. We started drifting apart after that, but it was like this thing had taken over my life, and all I could do was tag along and follow it wherever it led me.

And then, suddenly, the whole thing just got old. I don't even know why. Maybe it was the way Gerald's breath could be sour when we made out, or how he took forever to get the condom on. Or how his chubby breasts wobbled over me while we were doing it. Or maybe I just got fed up hearing him complain every night about the tough time he

was having getting into another college. He was afraid
he'd be drafted and end up in Viet Nam.

"I wouldn't last a day, Jen. I'd be one of the first to go."

I know I should've felt sorry for him–I mean, that's what
you expect of a girlfriend–but I couldn't understand why
he didn't just hire a lawyer or run away to Canada like
other guys did. Or why he didn't join the National Guard.
After a while, I stopped listening. I'd just lay there against
the side of the car and watch the lights below. Or I'd think
about Margot and her growing stomach, or about Mom and
her new boyfriend, Steve. Or I'd think about Dad and why
he'd never shown up again. He'd seemed so real that first
night, as if he was right there in the Olds with us, but
afterward, there wasn't even a hint of him.

In fact, the only time he came into our lives anymore was
when we got something in the mail with his name on it.
Mostly it was junk from stores and vendors, but every so
often, there'd be a letter from his old college or some
architecture organization, and just the sight of "Frank
Kovacek" on the envelope was enough to give me a buzz.
I'd even answer the letters from his college, if they weren't
asking for money. Like, once they were doing this survey
on their graduates, so I filled out the questionnaire and sent
it back in. And a couple months later, they mailed us–or
actually Dad–the results. Another time, they wrote about
these scholarships that went begging because nobody
applied for them. So as a kind of joke, I filled out the form
and dropped it in the mailbox. I didn't expect anybody to
take it seriously. I just didn't want the letters to stop.

Gerald went away again for a few days to try another
college, and when he came back, I refused to go out with
him. I just couldn't keep faking it. I mean, it was really
getting me down. He needed a real girlfriend, somebody
who'd listen to all his problems, and it just wasn't me. So I
kept saying no until he hung up.

Of course, that wasn't the end of it. It never was with

Gerald. He kept calling every day, and he even showed up at the store one Saturday morning while I was working the cash register. Between customers, he begged me to go out with him again.

"But it wouldn't work, Gerald. With you, it's affection, but for me, it's just physical."

"That's okay," he said. "I don't mind. It can be physical."

The customers started making eyes at each other.

"Why don't you go out with Patty?"

His cheeks flushed. "I haven't seen her in months. What if we just go to dinner?"

"Because we'd end up on Mulholland."

Patrick came by to approve a check, and while he was swinging his big gut over me, he asked, "Is this guy bothering you?"

"He's okay."

But after he initialed the check, Patrick muscled right into Gerald. "You know, pal, we have a policy about interfering with company personnel."

The customers started cracking smiles. I felt like such a dork, as if I was being fought over by these two chubby Don Juans.

"Gerald, just go," I said. "I'll call you tonight."

I didn't, of course. I was hoping he'd finally give up. But I should've known better. A couple days later, Margot came to the apartment with her mouth all bunched up and this big gleam in her eyes.

"So what's this about you not wanting to go out with Gerald?" she said.

"What!"

"He tracked me down at work. He told me you're the only girl he's ever slept with, and he can't live without you."

"I don't want to hear this." I plopped down on the sofa and pulled Mom's afghan over my head.

"You know what you have to do, Jen?" Margot stood right over me with her big stomach. "You have to date somebody else. As long as you're playing Old Maid, he'll get the idea that you're still available."

"Got any suggestions?"

"You must have a white knight out there somewhere. Anybody'll do, as long as he gets the message."

I thought of all the guys I'd met at the bars, but none of them were exactly dating material. And I didn't want to give Patrick any ideas. He'd already asked me out twice, and he kept giving me these hangdog looks. And there was no way I was going to date the guys who came into the store and asked for my number. Some of them were old enough to be my father. So it looked like I'd just have to put up with Gerald until he went away to school–or until the draft board got around to girls.

And then–wouldn't you know it–it turned out I *did* have a white knight. He arrived in the mail one day in the form of a big fat envelope from Dad's old college, this time with *my* name on it. I thought it was a mistake, but when I opened it, there was a letter inside saying I'd been awarded a scholarship for children of alumni. All I had to do was fill out the enclosed application and send in a transcript of my high school grades.

I was sure somebody was playing a joke–probably some punk in the Admissions Office–and I almost tore the thing up on the spot. But then I had a better idea. I could play along too. So I filled out the forms and sent them in, along with a transcript, and over the next few days, I kept imagining what they'd do to the jerk when they finally caught up with him.

Then a few weeks later, an even bigger envelope arrived. This time it was from the Dean of Students telling me that I'd been officially accepted and that they looked forward to seeing me in August. There were even papers assigning me to a dorm room and a work-study program. I still thought somebody was playing a joke, though if they *were*, they'd gone to a lot of trouble just to put my name on all these official-looking documents. Then I came across this brochure, and on the cover was a picture of these colonial buildings surrounded by rolling lawns and a rippling lake in the background–and it just hit me like a thunderclap. I mean, it was *exactly* the way I'd imagined it, this paradise I was supposed to end up in after high school. I still didn't quite believe it, but when I leafed through the brochure, I found this earth-tone silhouette of a marching band parading across the pages. And though I know it sounds corny, when I saw the band, I thought they were parading just for me, that this was their way of saying welcome–and *that's* when I started to think it might be for real.

I didn't breathe a word to anybody at first. I remembered how people used to laugh at me in high school whenever I opened my mouth. Though I did tell a few customers at the store, some of the friendlier ones who came in all the time, and they were pretty nice about it. They told me that college would be the most wonderful experience I'd ever had and that I should stay in school as long as I could. One woman even said they wouldn't have given me the scholarship if I didn't deserve it.

I think that's what gave me the courage to finally spill the beans, though if I thought my friends and family would be supportive, I was in for a big shock.

"You'll be clear across the country," Mom said. "Why don't you go to a junior college like Margot? Then after a year or two, you can think about transferring."

"Because they're not going to hold the scholarship forever, Mom. They might cancel it if I don't go."

"But how will you stand up to all that pressure?" Margot said. "You've never been a good student."

"I can read and write. I got B's."

I thought at least Gerald would be happy for me. He phoned one day all excited about this appointment he had at UCLA. But when I told him about my scholarship, he really put it down.

"Why'd you want to go to a nowhere place like that? It's not even ranked."

"It's *not* a nowhere place."

"Well, it's your funeral. Listen, I gotta run. They want me there by 2:30."

"So run, dork-head," I said after he'd hung up. I couldn't believe I'd actually slept with the jerk.

The one who really surprised me, though, was Gina. We'd been patching things up lately, even talking about me getting back into wrestling. But when I broke the news, her head snapped back as if I'd slapped her. She even dropped one of the snow globes we'd been tagging, cracking it all over.

"I thought we were a team," she said.

"We *are*, Gina, but I can't stay here forever."

"Why not? This is home."

"*You're* the one who said I should broaden my horizons."

"I didn't mean you should leave." She actually picked herself up and went to work in a different aisle. She didn't talk to me for a week after that, and then only about store-related things.

With everybody working on me, I really started to have my doubts. I even thought of writing the college and telling them I wouldn't be coming in the fall. I figured it would save everybody the trouble of having to send me home after a couple weeks.

But for one reason or another, I just never got around to it. And then, before I knew it, summer had come along, and then August, and then my last day of work.

At closing time, Patrick handed me my final paycheck. It freaked me out so much, I even asked for my old job back.

But he just laughed. "You're fired, Kovacek. Now beat it. And take your things from the lunch room."

I didn't know what he was talking about. But when I

poked my head inside, everybody yelled, "Surprise!" On the big table was this huge white cake decorated with three wild-eyed college guys in a jalopy. They were about to run over this blonde girl who couldn't see them because she was loaded down with a stack of books. Under the girl, it said, "Jenny."

Bea handed me a giant card with a picture of a crocodile sobbing huge tears. When I opened it, a dollar bill fell out–all caked with dry mud.

I shot a look at Gina.

She shrugged and bit her lip. "You left it there." It was the most personal thing she'd said to me in weeks.

Then suddenly, they were all over me. How did I find this college? Where was it located? What was I majoring in? Was I coming home for Christmas? All the attention I'd craved for months just dropped on my head, though I could barely answer them.

Bea was even more overcome than I was. "Every time they hire somebody sweet, they always leave," she practically bawled.

I almost started bawling too. But whenever I choked up, Patrick would pour another round of sparkling cider.

"So where's this place?" he'd say.

"Upstate New York." Though the more I said it, the more I wondered if it really existed.

During the third or fourth round, Gina slipped out the door and headed toward the back. I hesitated for a minute, and then I went after her. I couldn't just leave it like that. But when I pushed open the big delivery door, I got the shock of my life. She was standing on the loading dock, passionately kissing a girl I'd never seen before, a skinny redhead with a pixie cut and deeply freckled skin.

They broke when they saw me.

Gina colored. "This is Stacy. She's my Barracuda."

The girl's mouth dropped open. "I'm your *what*?"

"I'll explain later."

"You *better*."

Gina came up to me now with her eyes down. "Don't hate me."

"Hate you? I thought you hated *me*."

"I just had to figure things out." She searched my face.

"How can I hate you?" I started choking up again. "You're the best friend I ever had. Practically the *only* one I ever had."

"By the way," she said, "I made up that story about the plainclothes guys checking us out the first night."

"I know. I figured it out. Especially since the same guys kept showing up night after night."

We both kind of laughed.

"So don't forget to write," she said. "I'm sure you'll really shine." Then she kissed me on the cheek.

"Hey, watch that," Stacy said.

Gina kissed her too, and they ran down the steps of the loading dock and into the parking lot swinging their arms together.

On the day I left for college, Mom's boyfriend, Steve, drove us to the airport. The place was so crowded, I thought we'd never find our gate. Cars and buses were practically driving on top of each other, and inside the terminal, people were mobbing the escalators going up and down. But eventually we found it, and then we sat around with long faces, as if waiting for a funeral.

After a while, Steve wandered off, and Mom pressed a wad of cash into my hand. It looked like her bowling money for a year.

"I want you to call when you get there," she said. "And at least once a month. Okay?"

I nodded. I realized all of a sudden that I wouldn't be seeing them for a long, long time.

They announced my plane, and Mom told me I'd better go. She said it so matter-of-factly that it sent a chill right through me, as if there wasn't a chance in the world that

I'd change my mind. I hugged them all, including Tyler, Margot's baby, who kept staring at me as if he knew me from somewhere. He was only three months old, and already he looked so much like Dad.

"Try to sleep on the plane," Mom said. "That way you'll be rested when you get there."

I nodded and lined up at the gate with the other passengers. After the airline woman took my ticket, I turned to look back, but they'd all disappeared. It must've been a shock because I started bawling like a baby. I tried to hide it, but the tears just kept rolling down. By the time I slipped into my seat on the plane, my vision was so blurry, the lights on the tarmac looked like darting fish. I rubbed my eyes with my sleeve, wondering what the other passengers must think, but when I gazed at their moony reflections in the window, nobody seemed to notice.

The stewardesses closed the doors, and a few minutes later, the plane took off with a roar, and L.A. became just a bunch of puny lights far below us. Then we climbed through a cloudbank, and the earth disappeared altogether–and that's when it hit me how crazy this whole thing was. Margot was right. I *hadn't* been a good student. I'd actually been something of the class idiot, if you want to know the truth. And to think I could make it at an East Coast college was just insane. And Gina was right too. L.A. was my home. Everybody I cared about was there, and here I was running away from them.

I started bawling again. I kept looking out the window so nobody would notice, but it hurt so much, I didn't know what to do with myself. I even thought of asking to be let off along the way, as crazy as that sounds. Then I remembered I had a round-trip ticket, and I decided that as soon as I got to New York, I'd hop on the next plane home. I even pictured myself climbing the stairs of our building the next day and coming through the front door. Mom and Toby would be shocked, but then they'd realize that I'd come to my senses, and they'd throw their arms around me. It was only after I pictured this scene over and over in my head that I was finally able to calm down.

The plane leveled off now, and the stewardesses started buzzing around the cabin handing out refreshments, though the way they beamed down at the passengers and hovered over them, it was like they were giving out hugs. I couldn't wait for them to get to me, but long before they did, I fell into a deep sleep, and I had one strange dream after another.

I dreamed I was visiting Dad in his home town, as if he and Mom had split up and it was his turn to have me. But the funny thing was, he was my age. I mean, he was a little kid about eight years old, and so was I, and we were best friends. We went camping and fishing and tossed a baseball back and forth, and at night, he told me how much he hated school because the bullies picked on him. I told him I'd take care of them so they'd never bother him again. And then suddenly, we were at a Little League game and he wanted me to come up to the plate and bat. He was an adult now, the coach, in fact, and he stood inside a chain-link fence waving at me to come onto the field. But I couldn't leave my seat in the bleachers. "I need a power hitter," he called. "Mickey can't clear the fences." Everybody was giving me these cold stares, especially Gina and Gerald, because girls weren't supposed to play, but Dad kept waving at me. And then it was winter, and we were little kids again. I'd never seen snow before, but I taught Dad how to build snowmen and scoop out angels in the drifts, and he got so excited, he ran off into the woods as a flurry began to fall. I called after him, but he kept running away on his thin little legs until he grew distant and fuzzy. When I got home, Grandma gave me hell for not going after him. I told her I'd look for him in the morning, but she made me stand by the fireplace in my dripping coat and set a box of rolled-up movie posters in front of me. "I want these tagged before you go anywhere."

Then I woke up in the dark, and for one wild moment I thought I was back on the hillside with Gerald. I even looked around for him, but then I noticed a red light beating outside the window, and I remembered I was up in the air. I checked my watch, and I couldn't believe it. I'd practically slept through the night!

The stewardesses started buzzing around the cabin again, this time giving out hugs in the form of scrambled eggs, rye toast and tapioca pudding. It smelled so good, I felt like an ingrate knowing I'd be going home right away. I also felt guilty about Dad. I kept seeing him as a little kid running off into the snow on his thin little legs, and it made me feel as if I *had* let him get away. I mean, if I *was* staying in New York and going upstate like I was supposed to, at the very least, I'd track down his old neighborhood and all the places he'd been. I might even look up some of his old buddies. But now I wouldn't be doing any of that. I'd just be turning my back on him.

The plane dipped a wing to make its approach, and the sunlight twisted upwards through the clouds like strands of hair. Below us, bars of light reached across the water and glinted off the surfaces of bridges and buildings. As we descended, you could make out cars moving down the roads and boats chugging out in the harbor leaving tiny wakes. It was like watching the world being born, though it also filled me with this sad longing, as if I'd been here ages before and was finally coming home.

Then we touched down and the plane gave off a final blast, and as we started to brake, I wondered if New York would be as cold and impersonal as everybody said it was. I didn't know a soul here. I really *was* flying in on a wing and a prayer. My only connection with the place had been Dad, and he'd left it years ago. Though as we taxied to our gate, I almost had the sense that he was waiting for me, that he was standing in the terminal along with everybody else.

We came to a stop now, and all the passengers jumped to their feet, and I couldn't decide if I should leave or stay. I really didn't know *what* to do. I was afraid I'd even start bawling again. But then the door opened, and everybody started pushing, and I got caught up in this stream of people moving off the plane and toward the baggage area. I figured I'd grab my suitcase and look for a flight home, but after I pulled it off the carousel, I had to exit the terminal. And when I got outside, it was just chaos–all the cabbies yelling and cars honking and people pushing.

So I hopped into one of these burnt-gold taxis standing by the curb–it just seemed like the thing to do–and as we drove out of the airport, the sun rose over the morning clouds, and the day just blossomed into this phosphorescent white. And suddenly, it was like I could see all the possibilities unfolding all around me–not in any definite shape but like these bright, white petals opening up everywhere I looked. I even started to think about staying a few days, just to get a taste of it. I mean, who knew when I'd ever be back here again?

And then I thought, if I'm going to do that, then why not just continue on to the college? I mean, maybe I *was* out of my depth, and maybe I *would* make a fool of myself, but then maybe Gerald was right, and if I put my mind to it, I *could* be a star. It wasn't such a wild idea. I could read and write. And if it didn't work out, at least, I'd go down swinging.

At least, that's what I thought. When I got to the city, though, I wasn't so sure anymore.

14. The Light Theory of Greece

Margot

"YOU KNOW WHAT THE PROBLEM IS? I'll tell you what the problem is. The problem is your life is what you make of it. That's what it *is*. And I'll tell you something else. I never went for psychic-therapeutics, and I did just fine. It's like the man in the parking lot said. He said there's this hospital in Texas where they treat you for cancer, and the first question they ask you when you come in is, 'Why did you choose to get cancer?' That's what they *do*. They ask you when you first come in, 'Why did you *choose* to get cancer?' That's what the man in the parking lot said."

Dorothy smiles at me and sits the baby down on her lap, giving Dr. DeMatteo an eyeful of her American flag brooch with its rubies and diamonds. Then she crosses her legs to reveal her fishnet stockings.

"That's exactly what the man in the parking lot said," she continues. "Margot was changing the baby before we came up, and the man in the parking lot said it's *all* in your head. People *choose* to be healthy."

Dr. DeMatteo smiles politely. He takes off his reading glasses. "Mrs. Winegate, I'm sure that would be helpful if Margot had cancer. But right now you're taking valuable minutes away from her therapy."

"But she's not getting any better! Just yesterday she had another episode. Who in their right mind runs out of the house and leaves a baby locked inside? Does that sound right to you? To leave a baby all by himself?" She laughs self-consciously and nuzzles the baby. "Isn't that right, Monkey Faysh? Yeysh. Mommy left you crying in the howsh yesterday with no one to take care of you."

"We all want Margot to get better," Dr. D says. "But you have to understand that this is only her third session. Therapy takes time."

"But she's got a house to run! And a husband to take care of! And for your information, I think I know a little something about psychic-therapeutics. A friend of mine has a master's degree, and she told me Margot's got postpartum blues. That's what she *said*. Esther Fox in my pinochle group. She said Margot's got postpartum blues and that it's quite common nowadays. A lot of girls have it. Though I don't know why. *I* never had any problems. And Art wasn't easy, believe you me. He didn't sleep through the night the first three months. He was always wetting himself..."

Outside, the eucalyptus tree clatters softly against the windows. It seems so peaceful now, but in another moment, I can imagine the fang-like leaves biting through the glass and the walls bending in and the carpet bulging upward like a tongue. Then the ceiling will close over our heads and the room will swallow us whole, squishing us down into the building's dark intestines.

"Who in their right mind..? Any normal person..."

A truck rumbles down the street, and after it's gone, I hear growling below us like an empty stomach. I draw in my breath, grip the armrests.

"Margot?" Dr. D leans forward. "Are you all right?"

"You'd think she'd know that..."

Even as I watch, the walls begin to shudder. And now the floor rises, and I rise with it, and though I really should stay, I can't anymore. I'm through the door and into the waiting room. Someone calls my name, but the corridor has me now and the walls close in, and it sucks me down one passageway and up the next, scrapes me against the wallpaper, whips me around the corners, drives me past knots of staring faces and widening eyes, sends me flying through the restroom door and up against a porcelain bowl–and leaves me here sprawling, gasping for breath. Though I should have known it would end like this. I should have known I'd be staring over toilet water, waiting for it to suck me down. Waiting for it to pack me in with the rest of the shit.

"Margot! Are you in there?"

The edge of my skin burns. My whole body shivers. I just want it to end. I just want it to be over with.

The door creaks open. Sweet cologne washes over me.

"Margot!"

Why does it leave me here? Why doesn't it take me down?

A large hand lifts my chin, another the small of my back. "Take a deep breath. That's it. You're going to be fine. Just fine. Now let it out slowly."

The door again. A rattle of jewelry. A gust of lilac.

"You see! You see what I'm talking about? This is what we have to put up with. And she seemed like such a nice girl when Art brought her home."

I lower my head to the bowl. I just want it to end. I just want it to be over with.

But the large hands draw me up, raise me to my feet. "Margot, you're going to be fine. Just fine. Take another breath."

"How are we supposed to *deal* with something like this?

The girl can't even sit still."

"Dorothy, please, you're only making things worse."

"*I'm* making things worse. If it weren't for me, she wouldn't even *be* here. I told Art the girl needed help."

"I know, Dorothy. And we're going to help her. So please, wait for us in the office. We'll be right there."

The large hands turn me around and pull me into a wide, firm chest. Is this part of the therapy–hugs and tenderness?

"Margot, you're going to be just fine. There's nothing to be afraid of. You can feel anything you want. Okay? We just want to understand what it is you're feeling. Will you help us?"

I lift my shoulders, press my face into his sternum.

"Will you come back to the office?" He takes my waist and turns me toward the door, as if we're partners in a dance. "It's perfectly safe there. Nothing to be afraid of."

The baby whimpers.

"Shh, shh, Monkey Faysh. Gramma's here. It's okay."

We walk up the corridor with my head on Dr. D's shoulder and Dorothy holding my elbow. From the other end, a mother and a mop-haired boy approach, their faces darkening. As we pass, the mother draws the boy to her side, away from the loony.

Back in the office, Dr. D has me lie on the couch, and the black vinyl cushions enfold me like a downy comforter. I wait for them to wrap me up and seal me off, but they leave me exposed, staring at a pair of Japanese woodcuts on the opposite wall. In one, a fat lord dallies with his geisha. In the other, servants happily prepare a steaming meal. A fierce, snowy mountain scowls down over both scenes, as if it could crush the people at a moment's notice, but they go about their lives without a care in the world.

The sweet cologne floats over me.

"Margot, I think—. Just a minute. Dorothy, *please*."

Words startle up at the edge of the room like a flock of

birds. Nearby, there's a smaller commotion, a gentle rustling. The young blonde receptionist hands me a pill with a paper cup. I drink it down, and almost immediately, I feel as if I'm drifting. It must be psychosomatic–nothing can work that fast. Maybe I'll drift into one of the woodcuts and be done with this business, find myself in a whole new universe.

The big chair next to me wheezes. "I'm going to give you a prescription, Margot. I want you to take it three times a day. More if necessary. Okay?"

I nod without looking up.

"And I want you to phone me if you feel an attack coming on. I'm always available. The phone exchange will put you through after hours." He tears off a prescription and places it next to me. "Feeling better?"

I shrug.

"Now, I could send you home. You've already been through a lot today. But I want you to work through your feelings if you can. Can you do that for me? Do you think you can talk about what happened now?"

My throat twists up and I shake my head.

"Okay. We can talk about something else. Let's talk about your husband. I'd still like to meet him, by the way. I suppose we'll have to schedule an evening appointment when he's not working."

"He won't come." I clear my throat. "Art's like his mother. He thinks therapy is for the mentally deranged."

"But we know better, don't we? We know that most people would benefit from therapy, including your mother-in-law."

I press the heel of my hand against my eyes and stifle a sob. I wonder why he doesn't just lock me up and get it over with.

"So how *did* you meet Art?" He sets a box of tissue next to me on the coffee table.

"It's not very interesting."

"*Everything* you tell me is interesting."

"I met him through my roommate."

"Suzie, the girl you told me about last time?"

"No. Suzie moved up to Monterey." I take a tissue and blow my nose. "She met this wonderful guy named Chad who plays drums in a jazz band." Dr. D holds out the wastebasket, and I drop it in. "I met Art through my second roommate, Beverly. Her fiancé brought him over for dinner one night."

"Tell me about that. What attracted you to him?"

I think about it for a moment, and then I start rambling on about how polite Art was, how he would open doors for me and pull out my chair. But what I see is Art entering our apartment for the first time, tall and awkward with dark, curly hair and woolly eyebrows behind thick-framed glasses. The dinner was so obviously a setup that he had a stunned look on his face most of the evening. And Bev and Lester were terrible. They teased him constantly.

"You're behind schedule," Lester said. "Your mother wants grandkids."

"Well, she'll have to wait," Art said grimly. "I'm not getting married yet."

Bev smiled over her coffee. "Who said anything about getting married?"

Art colored a deep red. I felt so sorry for him. Here he was meeting someone new, and before he ever had a chance to be himself, he was being put on the defensive. Though he did open up later, when he and Lester got into their game of Incoming, pelting each other with bottle caps and napkins and whatever was handy, giggling like little children. And still later, when I walked him to his car, he turned serious again, confiding in me that he wanted to become a corporate accountant with a mid-sized firm. He was so solemn about it, so level-headed, that I had to force myself not to smile. Most of the men in my life weren't happy unless they were setting the world on fire, like my father. But Art didn't seem to have a dream in his head, and for some reason, I found it reassuring.

Suddenly, it's quiet. I must have stopped talking.

"Was he affectionate?" Dr. D asks.

"We didn't kiss for the first few weeks. Bev told me he'd never had a girlfriend before and that he needed time to get used to it."

"When did you decide to get married?"

"You know, I couldn't tell you. We just fell in with the idea. Bev and Lester were planning to get married, so it just seemed natural for us to do it too."

Dr. D nods.

"It was more than that, of course. You have to understand that I had nobody after Suzie left. My father had passed away when I was sixteen, and my mother and I weren't talking to each other. And then suddenly, here were these three people who cared about me. It just seemed like the thing to do."

"How was the wedding?"

"I let Dorothy plan everything. She came up with so many ideas, she just wore me out. She even wanted to pick the gown, but my mother hit the roof. '*She's* not getting married,' she said. '*You* are.' It just wasn't important to me. There was only one thing I cared about."

I stare at the Japanese woodcuts, and the snowy peaks seem to glower over the bamboo dwellings. Once again, I can see Art's startled face when I tell him what I want.

"Art wouldn't talk about it for a week, but I'd had problems with men before, and I wanted to make sure that we were compatible. So I kept pressuring him, and one evening, when Bev and Lester were away at her mother's, he finally gave in. We just took off our clothes and got into bed. He kissed me finally, but his heart wasn't in it. I had the feeling that he was holding me as much to keep me away as to take possession of me. Afterward, he told me I was shaking like a leaf, though I don't remember being nervous. I just remember bumping elbows and knees a lot, and having a tough time finding our places, like raw dancers at a prom. Maybe I was cold."

"And the wedding itself? How was that?"

"It might as well have been Dorothy's. She talked through the whole ceremony. She even pulled me away from Art while we were still kissing, after we'd said our vows, and dragged me around to all her friends and relatives. 'Here's the daughter I never had,' she told everyone. I don't think I had two minutes with my own family."

"At least, you got away for your honeymoon."

"Dorothy almost came with us."

Dr. D grunts softly. "Tell me about that. We've got a few more minutes."

So I tell him how Art's parents drove us to the harbor the next morning to catch the Big White Steamer to Catalina. They'd gone to Catalina for *their* honeymoon, so naturally we had to go there too. On the way, Dorothy gave us last-minute instructions.

"You've *got* to go to the casino. They have a dance hall upstairs and a theater downstairs. And you've *got* to go to the Wrigley estate and the gardens. And don't forget to take a boat ride to see the flying fish. Oh, Sheldon, do you remember the flying fish?" She was practically singing, as if each of these wonders was passing before her eyes.

While we were on the dock waiting to board, however, her mood changed. She grew quiet and her face darkened. Then she broke down, and between sobs, she accused Art's father of never taking her anywhere. "You son of a bitch! You goddamn son of a bitch! That's the last place we ever went!"

Sheldon tried to calm her down. He counted off on his fingers all the places they'd been. "We went to Mexico. We went to Vegas, twice. Last year we went to Desert Hot Springs to see your Uncle Harry. If you ask me, we've been to *too* many places."

But the more he cajoled her, the more she screamed. She even punched him a couple times. Finally, he took out his wallet and looked around for the ticket booth. But just then, the steamer gave off its final blast, and Art and I had to rush on board. We hurried up to the top deck to wave goodbye, but they were still fighting and didn't see us. As the boat pulled away, they looked like a pair of children scuffling on the dock.

We watched the L.A. harbor recede from view, and then we went inside the large dining room and sat by the window. As the ship moved into the main part of the channel, a thick fog rolled in and beads of water formed on the windows. The ship's horn gave off a long, drawn-out moan, and the seagulls cried, and I had the feeling that we weren't off the coast of California anymore, but somewhere in the middle of the Atlantic–or far away in the South Pacific. I squeezed Art's hand, and he smiled. He hadn't been away from his mother half an hour, and already his features had smoothed out and a dreaminess had crept into his eyes. I thought he might be tired from the past few weeks with all the running around before the wedding–and all the lovemaking. After that first night, he'd actually gotten to like it. But he stood up now and waved his arm at the ship.

"Why don't we go exploring? I bet they've got one of those old steam engines from World War II."

"You go without me."

He looked hurt, but it was chilly outside and I wasn't used to the rocking yet. Also, I didn't want this feeling to end, this sense that we were sailing away to some far-off place like Europe or the South Seas.

While he was gone, a small jazz band set up on the dance floor and started playing tunes from the Swing Era, the kind that GIs must have danced to during the War. I could just picture them pouring into a European nightclub with lit cigarettes in their hands and wild looks on their faces. They probably grabbed the first girl they saw and danced their hearts out until they felt like they were home again.

Several older couples got up to dance now, as well as a few young ones, probably honeymooners like ourselves. I wished Art would hurry back, but after the band played several numbers and took a break, he still hadn't shown.

And then I started to panic. I thought he might be locked in a room somewhere. Or that he'd had an accident or fallen overboard. I stood up to go look for him, and just at that moment, he wandered in with his head down.

"Don't leave me like that." I threw my arms around him.

But he pushed me away and sat down with a long face.

"What's the matter?" I sat next to him. "What happened?"

He wouldn't answer me. He just stared at the floor and blinked away tears.

The band started up again, playing that wonderful music.

"Art, dance with me, *please*."

I moved closer to him and held him. I thought I'd embarrassed him by throwing my arms around him, but it turned out he'd had a run-in with one of the crewmen. He tried to get inside the engine room, and the man kicked him out.

I stroked his neck and squeezed his hand, but I couldn't soften the hurt look on his face. It sent me into panic all over again. I wondered why in the world we'd gone ahead without Bev and Lester. Always before we'd done everything together, but they weren't getting married until December, and here we were, flying off on our own. I felt so overwhelmed, I wanted to cry.

The band packed up, and a children's show began. A magician in tails pulled a pigeon from his sleeve, and it caught Art's attention. He went to sit cross-legged on the floor with the children and waved for me to join him. But I shook my head. I was wearing a skirt, and the ship was rocking harder now. I was starting to feel a little queasy. He waved more forcefully, but I just waved back, though I almost cried to see him happy again.

For some reason, I thought when we reached Catalina, the clouds would lift, and the sun would come out, and the steamer would drop us off in a tropical paradise. But Catalina turned out to be as cold and drab as Los Angeles, and the main town, Avalon, was a big disappointment. There wasn't much to it besides a tiny beach and crumbling promenade with two or three blocks of stores and restaurants. Only the big white casino hovering on the edge of the bay gave off a hint of wonder, though it seemed out of place on this scrubby little island, like something left behind by a movie studio. Still, we could have enjoyed ourselves if I hadn't been sick the whole week we were there. The queasiness from the boat never left me, and I couldn't get out of bed without feeling dizzy.

Art was bitterly disappointed. He'd come up with a plan to try a different restaurant every night, and he was dying to explore the island. He finally rented a car so I could go out with him, a cute little thing with tiny wheels and no top, but after we drove it through the streets of Avalon, we found out that you couldn't go very far–only around town. The roads leading to the rest of the island were off limits.

Art returned the car and demanded a refund. But the gray-haired man who operated the rental place refused.

"Didn't you see the sign?" The man pointed to the countertop. "*No refunds. All sales final.* I could have rented that car to another couple."

"Look," Art said. "You cheated us, and I want my money back."

"Whoa! Hold on a minute there, pal. I didn't cheat anybody."

"You knew we could only drive around Avalon."

"Well, where do you want to go? Did you take the scenic tour above the harbor? That's one of the most photographed spots in California."

Art raised his voice. "I said want my money back, and I want it now!"

The man smiled, removed his skipper's cap and mopped his brow. "Sorry, no can do. Now, if you want a discount on a flying fish tour, I can help you there."

"You son of a bitch!"

"Hey, I don't know who you think you're talking to, pal, but you better take it easy."

"Art, please," I said. "It's not worth it. We already drove the car."

"You ought to listen to your lady," the man said.

"Did you hear me?" Art's face was turning red. "I want my money back, and I want it now, you son of a bitch!" He slammed his fist on the counter, shaking the phone receiver off the hook.

The man picked it up and dialed a number. "Hey, Jake. Yeah. How ya doin'? There's someone here who needs a word with you. Just a sec." He held the receiver toward Art. "I got Jake on the line. He's the police. You wanna talk to him? Or maybe you wanna spend the night in jail. That's a spot not too many tourists see."

"Art, please." I grabbed his arm. "People are staring."

He shook me off, and suddenly, I felt so queasy I must have blacked out. I can't remember what happened next. I just remember Art helping me back to our hotel bungalow and laying me down on the bed. And then he wanted to make love. But I was so drowsy and light-headed, I hardly knew where I was. He finally got mad and stormed out.

I thought I'd panic again, like I had on the boat, but I actually found it peaceful to be alone. I could hear the ocean lapping at the shore and a mourning dove cooing in our little patio. Then an evening breeze started up off the ocean, and it shook the palm leaves until it sounded like it was raining. My head even cleared a little, and I could sit up and look out the window. But it didn't last long. The next morning, I was as sick as ever. It was as if my health had disappeared behind the clouds, along with the sun, never to be seen again.

"And the queasiness was Tyler," Dr. D says.

I nod and my face grows warm. "I probably should have figured it out. There were a couple girls in my high school who had the same symptoms, but I couldn't associate being pregnant with the sense of airiness I felt. I thought it was the world pulling away from me, slipping out of my reach, the way Art was slipping away from me. I could feel it in Catalina, and later, when we came home and the doctor gave us the news."

"How did Art react?"

"Like it was my fault. And I suppose I did too. I dropped out of school and worked full-time so he could take extra courses and graduate early. And I tried in other ways to make it up to him, such as calling Dorothy 'Mom,' the way she wanted. But still, we lost sight of each other. We hardly spoke when he came home–we were both so exhausted–and Dorothy phoned every night and told me so many stories about Art that I started to think *he* was the child I was carrying.

"Toward the end of the pregnancy, Art didn't even come straight home. He'd stop off at his mother's for dinner and stay very late, and days would go by without our seeing each other. Though I can't say I blame him. I was pretty grouchy most of the time, and I was never a great cook. Still, it would have been nice to have someone around during the evening. I'd sit in the dark for hours listening to the sounds of the neighborhood–to people walking their dogs, or cars passing by, or a siren in the distance–and I'd wonder what connection I had with any of these things.

"Then somewhere in the middle of the darkness, a tiny face emerged, and it was my father's face, with his prominent chin and wide forehead and sky blue eyes. It was such a shock, you can't imagine–this helpless, little creature who needed me so desperately. I know I should have felt something for him, but he screamed so loud and his lips trembled so fiercely that it just left me numb. I'd ask myself, What did I do to make him suffer like that? How could I have been so heartless? And Art was never around. He'd run away at the slightest fuss, usually to his parents. And then Dorothy would come running over, as if I'd been torturing the baby. But she couldn't be there all the time, and my mother worked odd hours, so I was there mostly by myself with a screaming baby." My voice chokes up and I can't go on.

"And that's when you started having these incidents."

I nod.

"Like what happened today?"

"They're not always the same. A couple days ago, it felt like I was falling, as if the earth was vanishing below me and nothing was holding me up. I almost felt like I was in free-fall. I ran outside and accidentally locked myself out, and a neighbor had to help me back in. And all the time, the baby was screaming at the top of its lungs, as if it was dying. I felt like such a monster."

Dr. D hands me a tissue. "How do you feel now?"

"I don't know. Empty. Like my life."

"Why do you say that?"

"Isn't it obvious?"

"No, not at all. One could say that you've got a beautiful child and a nice little family–and that your whole life is ahead of you."

"But that's what scares me." The tears pour out, and my voice rises. "I just see myself getting deeper and deeper into the future, and I don't know if I want to follow where it leads."

"And where does it lead?"

"I don't *know*." I sponge my nose. "I wish I did, but I don't."

I take another tissue and dry my eyes, and while I'm

sniffling, I have the sense that Dr. D is hovering over me. I wonder if he'll take me in his arms again and press me against his chest. But when I look up, he's still in his chair, his legs crossed at the ankles.

"We'll continue this next time," he says.

Then he stands and helps me to my feet, and as he smiles, his eyes offer twin bouquets of wrinkles.

* * *

Even with the bedroom door closed, I can hear Dorothy on the phone. She's not supposed to call Art at work, but she does anyway.

"You've got your future to think of. And the baby, that poor thing."

As if I'd ever harm Tyler. Though I suppose in her mind, I'm a raving lunatic. On the way, home she insisted on stopping off at the drugstore to pick up Dr. D's prescription.

"Nothing's forever," Dorothy tells Art. "If she's not well, she's not well. It's like I always tell you–you have to close the doors behind you, not the ones in front of you. You can't put your whole life on the line just for this girl. And if you think I'm going to stand by while— What? I can't hear you. She's lying down. The baby's sleeping too. I should go in there and take that poor thing with me. What? Calm down or your face'll break out."

I can just hear Art telling her that it's not legal to take the baby. The idea that it isn't fair probably doesn't cross his mind.

"Well, I don't care what they say," Dorothy says. "No, I said she's asleep. She can't hear a thing. You're just like your father, always shooting your mouth off when you don't know what the hell you're talking about. Now listen to me..."

When I wake up, the house is dark. It must be after eight. I go to the baby's room and turn on the nightlight. His eyes are shut, but he's fussing and his mouth is puckering. I change him and put him on my breast, and after a few minutes, he's asleep again. He'll probably sleep through the night. Like his father, he needs me less and less.

In the dark, I find my way to the living room. The house is so quiet, I feel as if I'm on an abandoned boat that's wandered out to sea. I lift the curtain and peek outside. The street lamp gives off a murky yellow glow, so dreary, it looks like it's warding off people rather than helping them home.

Suddenly, the front door rattles and my heart rattles with it. I'm sure someone is breaking in.

"God damn it!" Art cries out.

His key slides into the lock and the door opens. When I turn on a lamp, he's rubbing his hand.

"Can't you keep the porch light on like a normal person? I almost broke my thumb on the goddamn doorknob."

"I just woke up a few minutes ago. How come you're home so soon? I thought you were eating at your mother's."

"She's too upset to make dinner, thanks to you." He drops his briefcase on the sofa. "You really did it this time."

"Not so loud, you'll wake the baby."

"Do me a favor. Don't have any more episodes in front of her, *okay*? She goes crazy. She's been screaming ever since she got home."

"Maybe she could see Dr. DeMatteo. He says he can help her."

"That's all I need from you–sarcasm."

"I wasn't being sarcastic." I watch him as he rubs his thumb. "So what *do* you need from me?"

"That's a good question."

"Well, when you find out, let me know."

I go into the bedroom and sit on the bed. I have this insane notion that he'll follow me in here and put his arms around me. But a minute later, the screen door slams. He's probably off to Lester's or Bob's Big Boy for dinner, not to be home until late.

The baby fusses again. I'm tempted to go in there and wake him up just for the company, but I can't bear the thought of his screams. So I lie down and try to fall asleep again. The bed, however, won't hold me up. It lets me sink deeper and deeper until I feel as if I'm in a slow-motion free-fall. I sit up to make it stop, and when it doesn't, I go into the bathroom for one of Dr. D's pills.

As I shake one out, I can just picture myself years from now, long after Art has left me, living on stronger and stronger doses. My eyes will become hollow, and my skin will dry out, and I'll look like some discarded rag left on a shelf. I gaze into the mirror, and already I can see it happening. My face looks doughy, and my eyes are full of spider veins. No wonder Art spends so much time away. I'm hardly a sight to come home to.

I drink the pill down, and as I close the vial, it comes to me what I have to do. I don't know why I didn't think of it before. It'll tie up all the loose ends and let everyone get on with their lives. Art can find a new wife, someone who gets along with his mother. And Dorothy can have the second child she always wanted. I'm sure she'd love to raise Tyler. Maybe she'll even lay off Art a little and let him grow up.

I empty the pills into my hand, and with a few mouthfuls of water, I manage to get them all down. Then I shut the medicine cabinet–*close the door behind me*–and gaze at my worn-out face in the mirror. I wonder if it will be as peaceful as it was in Dr. D's office. Maybe I'll go out like a breeze, blow away like the spores of a dandelion. Or end up in one of the Japanese woodcuts on his wall, cooking a meal for a family or dallying with my lord.

My stomach churns slightly, and I think of lying down, but I have to say goodbye to my face. It stares back at me like a slab of flesh, already a useless appendage. Then it fades for a moment, and I feel a slight drowsiness, the first gentle swoop of a long descent. I have to brace myself against the sink.

And when I look up, someone else is staring back from the mirror, someone who hasn't looked that way in ages. Her skin glows like marble, her hair is dark and glossy, and her eyes sparkle in a way I'd almost forgotten. She has the faintest blush on her cheeks, and she can't quite keep her mouth straight, as if stifling a smile. But it's not meant for me. It's for someone else, someone who drinks her in with every pore of his body.

I know where this is from. I've heard the story often enough. The year is 1946, and my father has stumbled onto my mother's front porch in Santa Monica. He's come clear across the country to tell her off for not writing to a buddy of his during the War, which apparently was a major crime in those days. But my mother couldn't care less. She's just told him that she hardly knew the boy and that she writes to whomever she pleases. And if he doesn't like it, he can take a hike–or words to that effect.

Her defiance, of course, is a kind of flirting, and Dad senses it. As he stands there in his Army uniform, it smolders inside his chest and spreads through his body like a slow-building fire, melting the strangeness between them. And now I feel it, burning its way down my gut and into my groin. The skin under my chin flutters, my heart beats wildly. I have to brace myself against the sink again.

And when I look up, Dad is staring at *me* now, taking me in through *my* eyes, which is probably the only way the dead can see us.

"Margot," he calls. "Don't be a sourpuss."

And I know where *this* is from–I can see it so clearly. I'm 16, and I'm standing on the edge of our front lawn, staring into the street as if gazing into an abyss. My arms are shaking from a big fight I've just had with my brother and sister. Someone has made off with an oral report I have to give that morning, and no one wants to own up to it. I've torn the house apart looking for the thing–I know I left it on the coffee table–I always leave my work there–but after a lot of screaming and name-calling, my mother has thrown us *all* out of the house. Jen and Toby grumble their way off to school, vowing to get even, but I can't leave yet–not without my report.

"Margot!" Dad's voice is closer now. He's backed up the Dart to the end of the driveway. "Hop in. I'll give you a lift."

I shake my head. All I can see is Mrs. Nygaard lecturing me in front of the class, her wrinkled face collapsing around her tight bitter mouth. She'll tell me there's no excuse for not being prepared, and then she'll give me an F, ruining any chance I have of getting into a top university.

"Come on, Sugar," Dad says. "The bus won't be here for a few years yet."

I don't know why he's so glib. He had his own big fight with Mom the night before. She told him to stop horsing around with his amateur theater group and put his business back in order or she'd leave him. Though the way he's grinning, you'd think it was just another fun-filled morning. He calls to me again, and I go around to the passenger side, mainly so the neighbors won't see the tears. And when I open the door, my report stares up at me from the floorboard, covered with sawdust. It looks like it spent the night in the garage.

I shoot him daggers.

Dad shrugs. "You said I could read it."

"Not when I have to give it!"

I hop in ready to kill him, but he just whistles a show tune as he backs up the Dart. He even tries to make small talk as we drive off.

"So what'd you think of the Lakers last night. Elgin Baylor's practically automatic from the key."

When I don't respond, he starts cracking silly jokes. "Let's see if the sun is shining on *this* street." He turns right. "Well, whaddya know? There it is. I guess we bring it with us."

I stare out my window.

"So this report you're giving," he says. "It's on depression, right? And you're practicing now."

That almost gets me, but I manage to keep a straight face. "I thought you said you read it."

"I meant to, Sugar. I really did. But it looked so pretty sitting on the sawhorse that I didn't want to touch it. I thought it was you sitting there watching me work."

After a couple blocks, I say, "It's on the Light Theory of Greece."

"How's that, Sugar?"

"My *report*. It's on the Light Theory of Greece–how the Greeks developed great culture in the ancient world."

"Oh, *that* one. Is that like the Heavy Theory of Greece where they eat too much olive oil and spill their guts out?"

I'm almost sorry I told him. "No, it's *light*, as in *daylight*. The sunlight is supposed to be clearer off the Aegean Sea, which is why they developed great culture in that part of the world. At least, that's what Cicero said."

"He did?" Dad cranes his neck. "Where is he? I thought you said it."

"Very funny. Cicero said it 2,000 years ago."

"Well, that's why I didn't hear him. He didn't speak up."

I groan and look out my side. "Can you drive faster?"

"So what's your verdict? You believe that theory?"

"It has its points."

"You know, those Greeks had a lot of strange ideas. They thought that when people died, they became constellations. You could look up in the sky and see your relatives."

"They had to be heroes or legendary figures," I mumble.

"What's that, Sugar?"

"They had to be heroes or legendary figures! They didn't just put Joe Blow up in the sky!"

"Heroes, legendary figures, it's all the same. They were people at one time."

"You know, this is a ridiculous conversation."

"Why? I'm enjoying it."

By this time, I'm hoping he'll floor it. Instead, he does one of those things that always makes me cringe. He spots a pair of junior high school kids out walking and slows down beside them.

"Care for a lift?" he calls through my window.

"Sure!"

They've got to be brother and sister. There's no other way they'd be together. The girl is dressed to the nines in a charcoal drop-waist skirt, gray nylons and matching eye shadow. The boy, on the other hand, looks like he just fell off the turnip truck. His blue jeans are cuffed halfway up his ankles, his red-and-white checkered shirt hangs out the back, and his sneakers look like a dog chewed them for breakfast. He also reeks of pomade. There's so much in his hair that the blond strands clump together, revealing the pale crown of his head.

As they slide into the back, it turns out that the boy's a real talker. Even before the door's shut, he starts rattling away about some car race everyone has to see that weekend or die.

"They say you can't get tickets anymore unless you know someone. And even then you gotta pay a premium. Scalpers got 'em all by now, so it'll cost you an arm and a leg."

"No foolin'," Dad says.

"Yeah. So if you're planning to go, it's probably too late."

"Oh, that's not a problem. I'm entered in it."

"No way!" The kid's eyes nearly pop out.

"Yeah, I'm practicing now." Dad means he's practicing

on Colfax Avenue as he drives us to school, but it goes right over the boy's head.

"Wow! So you must know so-and-so. He's favored to win. Hope you don't mind me saying that."

"Don't mind at all. He's a good friend of mine. I helped him fix his car this weekend."

"No way! And what about..?

"Know him too. We used to train together."

"*Jesus!* And what about..? You can't know *him*."

"It just so happens that he owes me five dollars."

The boy whistles. "So how come I never heard of you?"

"Well, I hate to tell you this, but the really famous people you almost never hear about."

"Don't give me that. You're blowing smoke, aren't you?"

"Am I?" Dad cranes his neck out the window. "Am I blowing smoke back there?" he asks the girl.

She tries to curl into herself, just like I do, but the boy laughs so loud you can almost hear an echo.

"Ha-ha-ha! HA-HA-HA!"

For the rest of the way, the boy tries to punch holes in Dad's story, but he just patches them up without missing a beat. If the kid mentions a driver, Dad knows him from day one. If the kid points out an inconsistency, such as the fact that all the other drivers are at the racetrack, Dad comes up with some nonsense about "gearing down *off* the track." By the time Dad pulls up to the junior high school, the boy's eyes are glazed over with something just short of love.

"Well, see you there," the boy says as he thrusts the door open. "You don't happen to have a smoke, do you?"

"Nope, sorry," Dad says. "I save all my drags for the races."

"Ha-ha-ha!" the kid hollers, causing a few heads to turn. "You're okay. See you later."

"You got it, Butch."

The girl mumbles her thanks and darts away like a mouse that's been flushed out of hiding. She probably tells people that the boy isn't her brother. But the boy drifts away slowly, rising high on the ball of each foot, his head tilted upward, as if he's already dreaming of howling engines and burning rubber.

The scent of his pomade hangs in the car until Dad pulls up in front of the high school, a half-mile away.

"Here you go, Sugar."

I expect him to make another wisecrack, but he turns to me now with the saddest look on his face, as if my leaving will tear his life apart. *He's* the one who caused all the problems, but now I'm supposed to cheer *him* up. Still, I do it anyway. I throw my arms around his neck and plant secondary kisses on his forehead, cheek and jaw, the way I imagine I'll kiss a future lover some day. His head starts back, and I have to laugh at the shock in his eyes. I gather up my things and hop out of the car.

"Go home, Daddy," I say through the window. "Go clean up the mess there."

But he just stares at me with that mournful look, and for some reason I can't turn away. The bell rings, and I'm going to be late, but still I can't leave. And then it comes to me. I know that look. It's the same one he gets whenever he has to give up on another project–when he finally realizes that he'll never be a great writer or actor or entrepreneur, and yet, he can't let go. He's put so much love and effort into it that it's become a part of him. And now he looks at me that way, as if I'm one more hope that will slip through his fingers, one more dream that will never come true.

The memory fades, and it's just me staring at my haggard face in the mirror. My eyes are bloodshot and my hair's a ratty mess, and I have to wonder how I could have ever drawn that look from him. How could he have ever seen beyond this foolish girl with all her petty hopes and needs and wants?

I feel so drowsy, all of a sudden, I could collapse on the floor. But I don't want Art to find me here. So I push away from the sink and head for the bedroom. I'm scarcely into the hallway, however, when I see in my mind Dad's mournful face again, and I realize I can't go through with it. It'd be like destroying him a second time.

I knock over half the bottles in the medicine cabinet looking for the baby's Ipecac. When I find it, I take a good swig and stumble into the kitchen. My eyes are watery and I can barely make out the names in the phone book, but somehow I dial the baby's doctor and fall into a chair. And as I wait for the exchange to reach him, I feel as if I'm sinking again, as if the earth is crumbling beneath me grain by grain and it's only a matter of time until it crumbles away completely and lets me go sailing off into oblivion.

"Hello, Margot," Dr. Peterson breaks in. "How's Tyler?"

My mouth opens, but no words come out. Instead, my stomach lurches and I'm all over the kitchen table.

* * *

It's the old dream again, the one where I'm curled up in the back of the Plymouth, and Dad and Jenny are in the front, chatting away as we drive up the coast. In this version, everything goes wrong. The pier in Malibu collapses the moment we step onto it. The taxi boat picks us up out of the water, but the waves swamp it again and again. When we finally reach the barge, it groans and cracks as we climb up to the deck. On top, it's a different story. People are having the time of their lives, reeling in one fish after another, and Dad couldn't be happier. But as we lower our lines, the feeling comes to me that we're doomed, that despite the bright, cheerful sun and the crystal blue ocean, the barge is going to sink. Dad finds it amusing and calls me a worry wart. Jenny wrinkles her nose in disgust. But I can't ignore the alarm going off, the constant ringing.

I open my eyes. It's the phone. I run into the kitchen and grab it before it wakes the baby.

"Oh, you're still there," Mom says. "I was afraid you'd left."

"I was napping on the sofa."

"Are you all packed? You know, I still don't like this business, Margot, running off with the baby. Are you sure you're well enough?"

"Mom, I'm fine. I took the Ipecac right away. Besides, it's been a couple days."

"And you still haven't told Art?"

"He'll get my note–and the doctor bill. He's never around anyway."

"I don't see why *you* have to leave. Why don't you lock *him* out? Or her?"

"Because Art would never stand for it. He says I'm not friendly enough as it is."

"So where is this place?"

"It's on the way to San Francisco. Suzie said she'll pick me up at the airport. You remember her from the wedding, don't you?"

"All I remember from the wedding is that Dorothy wouldn't leave you alone for two seconds. She wouldn't even let you go to the bathroom by yourself. Well, maybe you're right. If she asks, I'll just tell her to go to hell. It's time *somebody* did. She acts like she owns you."

"Well, there *is* the contract. The wedding contract."

"It's her *son's* contract, and he has obligations too. It's not a one-way street. Look, you don't have to stay in this marriage. It's not supposed to be a living hell."

"I just need to get away."

"What does Dr. DeMatteo say?"

"I haven't told him yet. Maybe I'll phone him when I get there. I don't know."

"Okay, darling. Just take care of yourself. And keep in touch. I want to see the baby grow up."

The doorbell rings two or three times.

"Mom," I whisper. "I have to go. She's here."

I hang up and hurry into the bedroom. The baby is gaping at the ceiling, as if he's been jolted awake. I change him while the front door rattles and the bell rings. It sounds like we're under siege. I get the baby into his jumper and sit with him on the bed, holding him tightly.

Now the back door rattles. "Margot! Are you in there? Margot!"

The baby starts and arches his back.

"Shhh." I put my finger to my lips.

I'm sure he'll howl and ruin everything. But he does something I've never seen before. He breaks into a wide smile, Dad's boyish grin, and I almost laugh and give us away.

Dorothy batters the front door again. It rattles so furiously, I think she's going to break it down. But now the screen door slams, and I hear footsteps down the porch. Moments later, her car starts up, and she drives away.

I put the baby in his playpen, throw the last of his clothes into the suitcase and pull on my sweater. Then I check the stove and the sink and use the bathroom one more time.

At a quarter to three, as if on cue, a car honks. I'm almost afraid to look outside, but when I peek through the curtains, I see the yellow shape of a taxi. With my heart in my throat, I pick up Tyler and step out the door. My fingers are shaking so hard, I can barely fit the key into the lock. When I finally do, someone grabs the suitcase, and I freeze.

"Good morning, ma'am."

He's a short, husky man with a wide grizzled face, and my first thought is, Art's having me watched. But now the man removes his cap to reveal a mop of curly hair, and I realize he's the *taxi* driver.

"Cute baby you got there," he says.

"Why, thank you."

As if reading my mind, he hurries to the cab and puts the suitcase in the trunk. Then he runs around to open our door.

"Is it Burbank Airport you want, ma'am?"

"Yes, please."

I scoot in with the baby, and without another word, the driver shuts the door and goes around to his side. Only when we turn onto the main street do I start to breathe easier.

"So you going on a visit with the little tyke?" the driver asks.

"Yes, we're going up north." I hesitate, and then I add, "To Monterey."

"Yeah? Well, that's real nice up there, all those trees and everything. We went up to Big Sur last weekend, which is just below there, and it was just gorgeous. Especially this time of year with all the ducks flying south."

Tyler grins again, splitting his face in two, and I gush out a laugh.

"What's that?" the driver asks.

"I'm sorry. It's the baby. I've never seen him *smile* before."

"Yeah, they do that. Little tykes like to smile. You take my grandkids, they're five and three and they haven't stopped smiling yet."

Tyler arches his head back and coos, and I laugh again.

"It certainly turned out to be a beautiful day," the driver says.

"Yes," I practically shout at him. "The sun is shining on every street."

"Boy, I can see you're up for this trip."

"I think I am. I've never been out of L.A. before."

"In that case, you're in for a real treat. There's nothing like that part of California. You just gotta watch out for the hippies. They come right up to the car begging for food. *Died-in-the-woods hippies* I call them."

Tyler coos again, grinning his toothless grin.

The driver gazes back in the mirror. "Looks like you got a real optimist there."

"Do you think so? He probably gets it from my dad."

"Yeah? Well, that's a good thing to have. A sunny disposition's a good thing to have. It can really come in handy."

I purse my lips at the baby. "Do you have a sunny disposition?"

He grins again, and I press my nose against his snowy face and feel the gurgling in his chest. We haven't reached the airport yet and already I feel like I'm flying.

15. El Jefe
Toby

TOBY KNEW HE SHOULDN'T CRY. Crying was dangerous. But he couldn't forget the look on his mother's face when she kissed him goodbye that morning. Her eyes had filled with tears, and her nose had turned red, and her skin had grown so tight it looked as if a heavy weight were pulling it down.

He ground his face against the starchy pillow and held his breath, and for a moment or two, he was able to stare evenly across the empty dormitory. But then he thought of his room back home with his team portrait of the Dodgers above his desk, and once again the tears gushed out.

The whole morning had been one long torment, ever since Judge Reynolds had handed down his verdict and waved him out of the courtroom. The deputy who escorted him to the parking lot had handcuffed him to a stocky Latino boy twice his size, and as they waited to board the prison bus, the boy twisted the cuffs so that they bit painfully into Toby's wrist. During the hour-and-a-half ride to the juvenile camp, the boy repeatedly jabbed his heel into Toby's foot.

"You're going to be my girlfriend," the boy cooed,

smacking his lips.

At the corrections camp, they were split up, but Toby's relief was short-lived. The guard who frisked him at the intake room shoved his legs apart when he didn't spread them fast enough, and the gray-haired woman who dispensed the camp clothes dumped his bundle on the counter without so much as a glance. Even the camp director seemed to have it in for him. Mr. Birch led the newcomers to their beds and told the group that he didn't want any shit for the next several months. Toby nodded along with the others, but the balding black man narrowed his eyes at him.

"Everyone's having lunch now," Mr. Birch said, still glaring at Toby. "Follow me if you care to join them."

As the others left, Toby stayed behind. He thought if he could be alone for a few minutes, he could regain his composure. But the tears had come, and now they wouldn't stop, and if the others saw him like this, he knew he was as good as dead. You had to be tough in juvie–his parole officer had warned him–but whenever he seemed to get his emotions under control, his mother's face would appear before him, or he'd remember some item from his room back home, and he'd fall apart. Finally, he just buried his head in the pillow and let his shoulders shake like a girl's.

It wasn't long before the shouts of the other boys reached him. They bounded down the hall and burst into the big room all at once, jarring it awake with their taunts and laughter. As they passed Toby's bed, their voices turned to snickers and meows and the smacking of lips. One or two kneed him in the leg. Another shoved his head into the pillow. A few cursed him, using words he couldn't understand.

Toby knew what was coming. The back of his neck itched where he expected to be grabbed and dragged away. He could almost sense the punches exploding in his face, the kicks slashing into his stomach. His cries turned to wails, and his heart beat so strongly, he could feel it against the bed.

But as the boys filled the room, the noise settled down and the taunts ceased, and he became aware of a gentle hand stroking his hair.

"What's wrong, *chiquillo*? Somebody do somethin' to you?"

Toby ground his eyes against his pillow. When he looked up, he was startled to see a small, olive-skinned boy sitting on the edge of his bed. The boy had sharp, close-set features and jet-black hair that he combed high off his forehead and straight back. He looked to be no more than twelve, but there was a glint of concern in his dark brown eyes that made him seem older.

"You okay, man?" The boy spoke with a strange lilt. "Somebody try to get funny with you?"

Toby rose to a sitting position and dabbed his face with his sleeve. He hung his shoulders and gazed at the floor.

"Just feelin' out of it, huh? You don't like the accommodations."

Toby grunted and shook his head. A tear fell on his wrist.

"Hey, nobody cries here, man. We're one big happy family. Didn't nobody tell you that?"

Toby shrugged. He looked around the room, expecting a throng of jeering faces. But the other boys went about their business as if he weren't there.

"So, what's your name?" the boy asked.

"Tob—." He cleared his throat. "Toby."

The boy's eyes grew large. "You mean like Toby Tyler, the kid in the movie?"

"I guess."

"Aw, shit, we saw him on TV the other day. He was good, man. You know, ridin' horses on his head, doin' back flips, jumpin' through hoops. Can you do stuff like that? You know, ride a horse on your head?"

"I can't even ride a horse sitting down."

"Well shit, neither can I."

Toby chuckled half-heartedly. He wiped his nose with his folded bed sheet.

"Jesus, what happened to your hand!" The boy grabbed Toby's left wrist and bent his narrow head over the missing thumb and stubby forefinger. "How the fuck you do *that*?"

Toby pulled his hand away. "Power saw. I had an accident."

"No *shit*. That musta hurt."

"It was a few years ago."

"Still, it musta *hurt*. People give you a hard time about it?"

"Naw, not really. In school, they used to call me Three Fingers, but then everybody got used to it."

"Three Fingers, huh? I like that. That's a good street name. I'm Rico, like in Ricardo, only shorter, like me."

Toby felt himself warming to this boy. "I had a friend named Ricky once."

"Yeah? Well, I'm better than that Ricky. I'm ten times better than that Ricky. I bet he was a *chingado* anyway."

"Yeah, he was," Toby said, though he had no idea what the word meant.

"So what're you in for?"

"Breaking and entering."

"Yeah? How many places you hit?"

"I don't know. Thirty, I guess."

"Thirty? Jesus, you're a *pro*, man. You fence the stuff?"

"Fence?"

"You know? Sell it through your bro's. That's how you get rich and cover your tracks."

"No, I just did it for kicks."

"For *kicks*?" The boy hung his head in disbelief. "I like that, man. *For kicks*. I bet you got some good stuff too."

"Naw, not really. Nothing great. Maybe a watch or two."

Toby straightened his spine. "I didn't do it for the money. I just kept it in my pajama drawer at home."

"You're funny, man. For *kicks*."

"What about you? What're *you* in for?"

"You name it, I did it. Breaking and entering, armed robbery, assault and battery, possessing a controlled substance. They got a huge rap sheet on me, man, but the judge didn't do shit. The only reason I'm here is because I got too many triple 7's. My PO got fed up with me. He kept telling me to stay away from my gang, but they're my life, you know. I'm nothin' without 'em."

"They got fed up with me too," Toby said. "After my third arrest, the judge said, 'Since you can't live in dee-cent society, I'm prepared to place you in another one where the rules are different.'" Toby did his best to imitate Judge Reynolds' gravelly voice.

"Thirty break-ins. Shit. So you got any sisters?"

Toby shrugged. "Two. They're older than me."

"They bitchen?"

"I don't know. I saw the younger one once."

"Yeah? What's she like?"

"*Big*, man."

"And she just let you stare at her tits?"

"Naw, she gave me a bloody nose."

"Ha! You're funny, man." The boy took Toby's hand and twisted it upwards into a high-five. *"A bloody nose."*

"What about you?" Toby said. "*You* got any sisters?"

"Naw, just me and my parents. Not normal for a *vato*, huh? My father was too busy dealing, and my mother was out trippin'. So no time to make a family. But I don't care. The gang's my family. They look out for me, and I look out for them. So what about your dad? Does he deal?"

"You mean cards?"

Rico bent over, shaking his head. When he straightened up he gave Toby a shot in the arm. "You're a trip, man. No, I mean the good stuff. You know, ludes, smack, bennies. Your dad never told you about that?"

"I don't have a dad."

"Well, you're better off, man. You're way better off. My dad was a *cabrón*, a real good-for-nothing. All he ever did was beat up my mother and pimp for her. He beat me up too when I got in his way, but now nobody messes with me. Not since I made the *barrio*. Little guys don't usually make it, but I wouldn't give up. I just kept coming at 'em. Took care of everybody. That's why they call me *El Jefe*."

"El Hef..?"

"*El Jefe*. The Bossman."

Toby felt a sudden glow in his chest. He wondered if he should tell Rico about his autographed baseball at home with all the Dodgers' signatures.

"So you seen the place yet?" Rico asked.

Toby shook his head.

"What? They didn't give you the guided tour? Well, let me show you around, man. You're gonna like it here."

Their first stop was a tall slender youth with blond curly hair. He stood a few rows away, resting a knee on his bed while he spoke with a pair of smaller boys.

"Hey, Ranger," Rico said. "This is Toby. Three Fingers, on the street."

The youth straightened up and held out his hand. When Toby took it, he twisted their grasp upward like Rico had. "*Que pasa*, Toby?"

Rico bent toward Toby, lowering his voice. "Ranger's head of Vaca-13."

The tall boy lifted his t-shirt to reveal a tattoo of a cow on fire. The flames were a lurid red-orange.

"I got one too," Rico said, "only, it's on my ass where the *rukas* like it."

The smaller boys laughed.

"Is it red like that?" Toby asked.

The boys laughed even harder, making Toby blush.

"Hell, yes," Rico said. "This is the 70s, man.

Everybody's doin' color."

"How long you in for?" Ranger asked.

"Six months."

"Check out his left hand," Rico said.

The tall youth gazed down and whistled. He grabbed Toby's wrist and looked the hand over front and back, just like Rico had. Toby was nearly moved to tears. Most people turned away when they saw the stumps, but these boys actually ate it up.

"How'd you do *that*?" Ranger asked.

"Some dude insulted his *hina*," Rico said. "Then he tried to blow him away. But Three Fingers grabbed the gun."

Ranger pushed Toby playfully in the chest. "Ya gotta shoot first, man. Didn't nobody tell you that?"

Toby shrugged.

The tall youth nodded at Rico. "Tell George to give him the Toshiba." Then he turned back to the smaller boys.

Rico pulled Toby away. "He likes you, man. He never made George give *me* his Toshiba. He's got all kinds of good shit, too. Steppenwolf, Santana, The Doors, you name it."

They entered the cafeteria next, and Toby felt his throat knot up at the sight of the long tables and the glass-and-metal food counters. The room reminded him of his cafeteria at school. It was deserted now except for two boys in white smocks who were pulling trays from the food warmers and stacking them inside wheeled carts.

"Hey, Deej," Rico called to one of the boys. "Toby here needs lunch."

"Well, ain't that too damn bad. Eatin' time's over."

The boy who answered was a rangy black youth with a full mane of spongy hair. Despite his harsh tone, he winked at Toby and proceeded to fill a dish with pork chops, mashed potatoes and green beans.

"Deej gets KP all the time," Rico said, "'cause he smacks."

"Yeah, I'll smack *you*, fuck-face, right upside the head." The youth ladled a generous portion of brown gravy over the pork chops and handed the dish to Toby. "Eat up, Jackson. Good-looking boy like you needs to stay in shape, keep those white limbs strong. I bet that's better'n your mama's cooking."

In fact, it was. Toby's mother worked odd hours and had little time to prepare meals.

After Toby wolfed down his lunch, Rico led him to the combined showers and latrine, where they found a chubby boy with rust-red hair at one of the urinals.

"Hey, Meckles," Rico called. "Show Toby your trick."

Toby followed Meckles into a stall, and while Rico stood guard, the boy pulled down his pants. He lit a match and lowered the flame toward a bush of rust-colored hair. Zsst, a single hair burned down, giving off a dry stink. The boy did it again two or three times.

"Wanna try?" He offered Toby a match. "I mean on me?"

Before he could answer, Rico pulled him from the stall.

"Gotta split, man. Hamie's coming."

Back in the dormitory, a boy named Julio showed Toby another wonder–a wooden crucifix with a lever on the bottom. When Toby moved the lever, Jesus' eyes opened and shut. Then Julio turned the crucifix over, and on the reverse was a demon with an erection. Now when Toby moved the lever, the demon fondled himself.

"You can keep it under your pillow," Julio said. "It'll bring you luck."

"No thanks."

"Well, think about it."

The next boy they met, George, wasn't as generous with his possessions. He made a face as he handed over a cassette player and several audiotapes. "I ought to make you pay, man. If it wasn't Ranger, I would. Usually it's a buck a day."

Then George motioned for Toby to come closer to his bed. He lifted his pillow to reveal a row of crudely rolled cigarettes. "How 'bout some smokes? Good price today."

Toby shook his head. "I don't smoke."

"Well, how 'bout some grass?"

"Grass?"

"Yeah, you know. Reefers?"

"Weed," Rico explained. "Pot. What Mary and Juan do together."

Toby still didn't understand.

Rico leaned close and whispered, "Marijuana."

Toby shuddered and shook his head.

"Well, shit," George said. "You gotta like something."

"He's new, man," Rico shot back. "Give him a chance."

As Rico pulled Toby away, he said under his breath, "George's sister sneaks him all kinds of shit. They caught her stuffing it in Frito bags, so now she puts it down his pants when she comes to visit."

A bell rang, and Rico clapped Toby on the shoulder. "Hey, you're in luck, man. Wait'll you see Miss Marpleton. You'll get a hard-on just lookin' at her."

He led Toby down a hallway and into a classroom. At the blackboard, a young moon-faced woman was erasing the previous lesson, using wide circular strokes that made her full breasts bobble under a tawny knit blouse.

"Hey, guys," she sang as they entered. "Just sit anywhere."

Toby followed Rico to the back of the room and settled into a desk covered with deep knife cuts and graffiti. He tried not to stare at Miss Marpleton's breasts, but he couldn't take his eyes away. To his embarrassment, they started floating toward him like a ship with two prows, gently rising and falling. When they were nearly at his face, a slender hand reached down and startled his chin.

"You must be one of the new boys." She drew his head upward into a pair of amber eyes.

Toby hoped she wouldn't ask him to stand.

"He can't talk," Deej said. "I fed him my pork chops."

The class broke up.

"What's your name?" the Miss Marpleton asked.

"Three— I mean, Toby."

"You like to write, don't you, Toby?"

He lifted his shoulders.

"Well, you like to read, don't you?"

"I guess."

"Who's your favorite author?"

"I don't know." He could feel the whole class staring. His penis was throbbing.

"Hmm." The teacher released his chin, which continued to tingle from the pressure of her hand. "Well, who's your favorite hero? It can be anybody. Even someone from a comic book."

"Superman, I guess. 'Cause his can fly."

"Hey!" Deej called out. "That's *my* hero."

"We can share," Miss Marpleton said. "In fact, it'd be neat if two of you wrote about the same person."

She smiled at Toby, and his heart turned over. As she walked back to the front, the seat of her tartan skirt bunched from side to side.

"I want everyone to write a couple pages about someone they admire," she said. "Let's take ten minutes. Just write whatever comes into your head. Pick anybody you want, and tell me why you admire that person." She wrote the word *admire* on the blackboard. "It doesn't have to be a public figure. It can be a character from literature or someone you know. Okay?"

To Toby's surprise, there was no groaning or slouching. The boys immediately hunched over their desks and began scribbling away. He followed their example, and though he'd never liked writing, the words poured out of him. He wrote about the brother he'd always wanted, the brother he could pal around with and tell jokes to and go places with.

The brother who wouldn't get bent out of shape like his sisters did when he played a practical joke or when he came home late from school. If he had a brother, they could go fishing every week or camp out in the Sierras or take in Dodger games. And no matter where they went, they'd always get along because his brother would know all kinds of things, like what bait to use and how to sneak into a movie theater and how to act around a girl. And Toby could ask him anything–whatever popped into his head–and his brother wouldn't laugh or call him names. He'd just give him the answer. And now that he was in juvie camp, it was like he had *fifty* brothers, and he was going to make the most of it, really get to know these guys. Maybe he'd even take up smoking or get a tattoo. He didn't write *that* down, but he thought about it, and it made him laugh inside. His sisters would have a cow apiece when he came home and blew cigarette smoke in their faces. Or when he lifted his shirt to reveal a tattoo of a blue shark with purple fins.

At dinner, Deej came up to him and set a package of ready-made vanilla pudding on his tray.

"For my friend," he said. "Keep that for a good time."

"Hey, I saw him first," another boy called out.

Rico elbowed him. "You're a hit, man. They like you."

Later, in the TV room, Ranger stood up to make an announcement. "This is Toby's first day, so he should pick the first program."

A couple boys groaned, but most clapped and whistled.

"Right on, Toby," someone called out.

Dorsey, the parole officer in charge, grinned and wagged his head slowly. "That's right, fellas, spoil the new kid."

"So what'll be?" Ranger asked.

"*Petticoat Junction*," Toby said.

His cheeks flushed as soon as the words came out. He wished he'd picked something more tough-sounding, like *Gunsmoke* or wrestling, but the boys settled in to watch without complaint, and when the train rolled down the tracks at the end of the episode, they let Toby choose the next program as well.

Before lights-out, Toby lay in his bed listening to George's tapes on the cassette player, pumping his feet in rhythm to Santana's *Black Magic Woman*, a recording that he'd always wanted. The voices of the other boys reached him in muted tones, and despite the hum of the fluorescent lights overhead, he had the feeling that he was in a cabin somewhere high in the mountains, snug under a blanket with a crackling fire nearby. He chuckled to himself when he remembered what a crybaby he'd been that morning. Hell, these guys weren't so bad. You just had to know them, that was all. Julio had even come by to offer the crucifix again. And George had slipped one of his funny cigarettes under Toby's pillow. "It's free, man. On the house. Introductory offer." Even the stocky boy who'd given him a hard time on the bus looked away when Toby caught his eye. The fatso wasn't even tough, just big and stupid.

From across the room, he heard Deej complaining to Dorsey. "But you *said* we could."

The parole officer held up both hands. "I never said you could order pizza. Maybe tomorrow night."

Pizza? Here? Even at home his mother didn't have pizza delivered. Toby shook his head. Six months in this place would be more like a vacation. The schoolwork was easy and the chores were a cinch. After classes, he and Rico had spent maybe twenty minutes distributing clean laundry. They'd even played a joke on the fatso who'd bullied him, giving him underwear two sizes too small. The best part, though, was that Toby would have all kinds of stories to tell when he got out. None of his friends had been in juvie. They hadn't even been arrested, the sissies.

Rico came by. "Hey, Three Fingers, tomorrow we play softball, and Ranger wants you on our team. You can hit, can't you?"

"I played clean-up in Little League," Toby lied.

"*All right!* Just remember, if somebody gives you a hard time, you come to me, *El Jefe*. I'll take care of 'em."

Five minutes later, the lights went out, and as Toby nestled into his pillow, he imagined himself stepping up to the batter's box and cracking a line drive over Deej's surprised head. He'd never actually played in Little League, but he could still swing a mean bat, even with one thumb. They didn't call him Tubby Kovacek for nothing.

In his dreams, however, it wasn't Deej's face that came to him but Miss Marpleton's. She stood over home plate with a softball bat in her arms, still wearing her tartan skirt and knit blouse.

"Here, Toby," she called, lifting both arms, as if she wanted a hug.

He tried to put his arms around her, but she vanished– and the next moment, he was in the classroom, writing away at his desk. Miss Marpleton leaned so close, one of her breasts grazed his cheek, and his penis began to grow.

"Now get up and read it," she chirped.

Toby shook his head. His penis was growing like Pinocchio's nose, pushing up against the desk in front of him.

"Don't you want to share?"

He shook his head again. The other boys grinned while his penis grew and grew until it knocked against the blackboard on the front wall.

"You see?" she cried out, turning toward the noise. "You just have to try."

And now they were alone again. She smiled at him and pulled her knit blouse over her head. Toby's heart beat faster. He expected her boobs to flop out as his sister's had, but instead, a pair of tiny bull's-eyes dangled on springs where her breasts should have been. She giggled and drew his head to her flat, bony chest.

"Don't tell anyone," she whispered. Her words singed his ear. She even called him Three Fingers.

Toby woke up. Rico was kneeling beside him, whispering so close, he could feel his breath.

"Three Fingers, you gotta come. Ranger wants you to do the Vaqueros."

"Do what?"

"We only got a few minutes. *Vamanos*, man."

Still drowsy, Toby let Rico pull him out of bed and into the laundry room next door. In the dim glow of the emergency light, he could make out three boys standing side by side in their underwear. As he entered, the nearest boy yanked down his briefs, and his penis sprang out like a stiff cigar. Toby chuckled, thinking it was another trick, like Meckles with his matches, but the boy wasn't smiling.

Rico pushed Toby down in front of the boy. "We gotta do it quick, man. Dorsey ain't gonna snore forever."

The boy pulled out a thumb-sized screwdriver and pressed the tip next to Toby's eye. "Suck hard, asshole, or this one comes out first."

Toby's heart stopped. He realized what the boy wanted.

"I can't. I ..." His jaw was shaking. "I don't know how."

The boy lifted Toby's upper lip and jabbed the screwdriver upward. The pain blinded him, causing his head to drop.

The boy yanked him up by the hair. "Start sucking, asshole."

"It's okay, Three Fingers," Rico said. "You can do it."

The boy grabbed Toby's lip again, but Toby covered the screwdriver with his hand and nodded quickly. He reached for the boy's penis. He was trembling so hard, he had trouble getting it into his mouth. Then he couldn't form a seal with his lips–the inside of his mouth was too sore.

"Ouch!" The boy thumped Toby's head with the screwdriver handle. "Don't bite, *puta*, just suck."

"Hurry, Three Fingers." Rico knelt beside him. "Pretend

it's a Popsicle. That's it."

Toby managed to move his head back and forth over the boy's member. His face felt numb, and tears rolled down his cheeks. He thought he might still be dreaming, but the screwdriver bit into the skin by his eye, and the boy's smelly penis filled his mouth.

"That's it," the boy breathed. "Don't stop."

Toby's nose was clogging up. He wasn't sure how much longer he could continue. His jaw ached and his lips were trembling, but he was afraid the boy would put his eye out. The screwdriver bit deeper as the boy started to moan. Then it fell away as the boy's penis throbbed and shot a warm, slimy liquid into Toby's throat, making him gag.

The boy pulled back, a little winded. "Oh, you're good, *puta*." He shivered and held his breath for a moment. Then he hammered Toby with the screwdriver handle, knocking him to the floor. "Just don't bite."

Rico helped Toby to his knees. "Hey, Three Fingers, you didn't tell me you were a pro. Now we gotta do Javier, then David."

The second boy came forward, yanking down his briefs.

Toby reached for the boy's penis, tears streaming down his face. He managed to get the boy's member into his mouth, but the ripe flesh turned his stomach, and hot, stinging vomit shot up through his mouth and nose.

"Motherfuck!" The boy jumped back. "Goddamn motherfuck. All over my fuckin' leg."

Toby heaved again, splattering the floor.

The boy cuffed him on the ear, knocking him into the mess. Then he kicked him in the tailbone and in the back of head. "Goddamn motherfuck."

"Watch it!" Rico cried out in a thin voice. "Don't hurt the merchandise."

"Is that the best you Vacas can do? *Shit*, man."

"Hey, we gave you first shot."

"I'll cut his fuckin' dick off."

"He's new, man. Give him a chance. He knows his stuff. You saw what he did for Gabby." Rico's voice was growing fainter. "You gotta give him a chance."

"What's going on in there?" Dorsey's deep bass echoed in the big room.

"Javier wet his pants," Rico said.

Laughter broke out unevenly.

"I don't want no horsing around now," Dorsey said. "It's late."

There were a few more titters and a couple taunts, followed by a stern warning from the parole officer. Then the boys settled down, and the dormitory grew quiet.

As the night turned cooler, the walls cricked slightly. Here and there, the silence was broken by the twang of bedsprings or a dreamy whimper. Occasionally, a snuffling breath would take up a rhythm and then cease after a minute or two. But otherwise, the peace that descended over the juvenile camp was as gentle as it was absorbing, and not even the startup of Dorsey's ponderous wheezing seemed capable of disturbing it.

In the laundry room, Toby lay in his mess, gazing across the floor. A quiet sob rocked his body. His upper lip was swollen, and his head and tailbone burned. He wanted to pour out his grief, as he had that morning, but the tears wouldn't come. Instead, an emptiness filled his body, a feeling that he'd been hollowed out and pumped up with air. He slowly drew in his breath and closed his eyes.

And when he opened them again, it seemed as if several minutes had passed. His cheek was numb from the cement floor, and the back of his throat felt raw. He tried to move his legs, but his tailbone cried out. He didn't think he could get to his feet.

A hand shook his shoulder. He squirted into his briefs.

"Hey, you did great, *chiquillo*," Rico whispered. "Don't worry about Javier. He won't do nothin'. He's just talk. Tomorrow, Ranger wants you to do Deej. So bring the pudding he gave you, okay? He likes to do it up the ass. And Wednesday, we want you to do the H-Street Gang. They'll get you some neat stuff when you get out. They'll even get you laid, man. I mean, real pussy." The boy giggled softly. "But you can't stay here. If Dorsey finds you, it'll be the shits. No TV, no pizza, no fuckin' nothin'. So I brought you your sheet to clean up. I can't stay." He buffed Toby's head and left.

Toby continued to lie on the floor, gazing into his mess. A tear oozed from one eye into the other. He understood now what his life would be like for the next six months–and the price he'd have to pay to survive. He could see it in the puddle in front of him, which seemed to grow even as he stared at it, filling up with spit and vomit and burnt pubic hair and the slimy stuff that came out of their dicks. He stifled a cry and peed into his briefs, emptying his bladder until the urine trickled off his leg. Then he closed his eyes again.

And when he woke up, the moon was beaming through the window, cutting a silver-white path across the floor and through the crosshatch bars that divided the room in half. The moonlight came to rest on a stack of bulging laundry bags on the other side, making their grotesque shapes look almost human. Toby wondered why he couldn't he slip through the bars like that, melt through the window and disappear into the night.

He sat up stiffly and wiped his face with his sheet. A stab of pain shot through his tailbone, though the back of his head wasn't so bad anymore, just a little sore. Only the inside of his mouth felt tender when he touched it with his tongue. He drew his knees to his chest and held himself still, trying to catch any stray noise that might wander in through the open window. But the only sounds that reached him were Dorsey's snoring in the big room and the creaking of a bed or two. They were all asleep, the bastards, deep into their dreams. Probably for them, Miss

Marpleton had real breasts, big pillowy things they could play with all they wanted. Probably for them, they got pizza *every* night, and if someone got in their way, they just beat the crap out of him. He understood now the look of fear in the stocky boy who'd bullied him. He was probably next.

Toby tried to summon up his mother's face, but instead the image of his public defender came to him from the morning, a strapping black man in a three-piece suit. The man had drawn Toby to his side as he made his case before the judge.

"Your honor, you simply can't put a boy like this into the system. He won't last a week."

Judge Reynolds had shaken his fat chins in annoyance. "Counselor, I think after three arrests, Mr. Kovacek has preyed on our society long enough. Let's see how tough he is in a place where they aren't so lenient."

Toby grunted at the judge's words. He thought he was a sissy, a scrawny little white kid who couldn't take care of himself. But he didn't know him, that was all. He just didn't know him.

And it was the same with these guys. They thought they could push him around and make him do whatever they wanted, but they just didn't know him. They didn't know who they were dealing with. He'd just have to show them, that was all. Make them think twice before they stuck their dicks inside him again.

The room wobbled as he got to his feet.

He'd just have to teach them a lesson. Do something that would knock their socks off, like going in there and waking up Dorsey. Then for sure they wouldn't get no TV, no pizza, no fuckin' nothin'. And they could kick him in the head a thousand times for all he cared.

He walked around the room chuckling to himself. Wouldn't that be something. Wouldn't that be a kick in the pants. They thought he was just a faggoty little punk they could push around. They didn't know he was really Tubby, Tubby Kovacek.

He quickened his pace to a jog, holding out his arms as if he were flying. Then he stopped to pick up his sheet and tied it around his neck. And when he started jogging again, it flowed behind him like a cape. Now he was Super Tubby. *Super Tubby Kovacek.* He could bend their necks in his bare hands, make them all crap in their pants.

He laughed and jogged faster, and came to a skidding halt as the moon flashed by. He backed up a few steps–and there it was, catching him in the face, smiling at him.

Come to me, it said. *None of the others can, but you know how.*

Damn right. Damn fuckin' right.

He stepped out of his soggy briefs and scampered up the crosshatch bars. Even without a thumb, he could be fast when he wanted to, faster than any of these bastards. He tied the loose end of his sheet to the uppermost bar and hung out with an arm and a leg dangling. Let them try to catch him now. Their dicks weren't *that* long.

He laughed so loud, it echoed against the walls. Maybe he'd give his Tarzan yell and wake them all up. Wouldn't that be something. Wouldn't that be a kick in the pants.

He looked for the moon. He had to bend now, but there it was, still smiling at him.

Come to me, it said. *None of the others can, but you know how.*

Damn right. Damn fuckin' right. He crouched against the bars and flung himself as hard as he could, and for a brief moment, as he went flying, his head grazed the ceiling. Then the sheet caught and yanked him back, dropping him down with a snap.

16. Sweetheart of the Ardennes
Ruth

I PROBABLY WON'T SLEEP TONIGHT. Never do anymore. Just lie here until the darkness lifts and then stumble my way through work. I should do like Alice says, *follow the flow*–give out the numbers and let the voices carry me.

Mom, you have to find something new. You can't be an operator all your life. You have to uproot yourself and start over.

Margot would map out my whole life if I let her, put me on an airplane and set me up in a new town somewhere. Though it's certainly worked for her. You could see it in her eyes, how they've gotten their luster back. And her complexion, smooth as the baby's. Probably from the climate up there in Monterey.

You really oughta try college, Mom. It's a gas.

And Jenny you wouldn't recognize. So grown up now, the way she carries herself.

I shouldn't think about them or I'll cry. The place was so full when they were here, and now it's empty. I suspect

Margot's right. I need to move on, find something new. I just keep thinking I have to be here for Toby when he gets out. For my baby...

Everybody's going back to school, Mom. Even Jodi's mother.

Jenny lit up when Margot said that, as if she could just picture me in a classroom.

You'd be really good, Mom.

Though I think it's passed me by. I think my days as a student are over. *You* were the educated one in the family. The one with the college degree.

It was all my mother's doing.

That's what you always said. Still, it couldn't have been easy. Working nights on the loading dock, and struggling to stay awake in class the next day. How did you do it?

I just did what I was told.

I'll probably stare at these walls forever. Though I do feel a little heavy. Almost like I'm drifting. Must be from the rice pudding.

She wanted me to be an "ahkitek." She couldn't even pronounce it.

Oh, Frank, you'd never forgive me. We tried so hard after the police came. But he wouldn't listen. He just wouldn't listen...

If she'd wanted me to be an engineer, I'd have been an engineer.

To die like that. All alone. My poor baby. Is he with you? Do you go fishing? I feel so heavy all of a sudden. Like I'm drifting. Maybe I'll fall asleep for once. Get some rest before I go to work...So heavy now...Must be from the rice...From the pudding...

...

It wasn't your fault. The little runt never did develop a sense of self-preservation.

I'm so sorry, Frank.

He's okay. He's with me now.

What do you do all day?

There is no day–or night. We go fishing and camping. You should see your son. He's become quite the fisherman. The trout scatter when he approaches.

How sweet.

He has a girlfriend, too. A little towhead named Ginger.

I'm no good at this. I wasn't cut out to be on my own.

You were always the strong one.

Not true.

You carried me even before we met. Just ask Howie Cavanaugh, the fella you got all steamy with on the beach.

I hardly knew him. Our mothers were best friends growing up in Philly. He came out with his brother for a few days, and we went to the beach.

Good thing you didn't go camping.

How do you know we didn't?

Oh, I knew *everything* about you. Howie made sure of that. From the moment we met at the training camp in Devon, it was Ruthie this and Ruthie that. Everything reminded him of you–the English countryside, the double-decker buses, the fog. He even compared you to the ladies of the night. Quite favorably, I might add.

How flattering.

Well, this was during the War, Kitten. Most of us had never been away from home. We were like kids in an amusement park, and the ladies were one of the main attractions. They were very polite, by the way. Very proper and British.

Did you ever?

With the ladies? No, it wasn't for me. It was too cold and rainy there–too strange. If one of them came up to me and said, "How about it, ducky?" I'd pull down my cap and hurry away.

I can just see you.

What do you see?

You didn't have a sweetheart back home? Someone

waiting for you.

Not really. The girls in my hometown were so conventional. They just wanted to settle down and raise up a husband and have some kids along the way. There may have been one or two, but they were out of reach.

I smell a secret.

You've never asked before.

So I won't now.

Howie had someone, though. He had *you*. He had you on the brain and he couldn't get you off. You should've heard him crossing the Channel. Drove us all nuts. "I'm coming back to you, Ruthie." Over and over. "I'm coming back to you." And he carried that photograph everywhere, the one of you two smooching on the beach. It damn near broke his heart that you didn't write. I know *he* wrote. I helped with the letters.

So that's *why they sounded so good. Literary almost.*

Well, thankee, ma'am. I've turned out a few good lines in my day. Then you did read them.

And took them to school. You can't imagine what it did for my status, to have a beau in the Army.

"Then why didn't you—?"

I don't know. Howie was so serious. I was only 17.

Even *I* started thinking about you. You became our pet project. Everything we did was to get back to you.

I find that hard to believe.

It wasn't all that unusual. Most fellas had someone they were getting back to. One B-17 pilot wore his mother's panties under his cap.

Did it help?

Hard to say. His plane was shot down, but he survived. Spent the rest of the war in a POW camp.

Didn't you get sick of me?

On the contrary, you kept us going. We decided that you didn't write because you were in Europe. So when we scouted a town, we kept an eye open, and damn if we didn't see you now and again. You'd be turning a corner, or entering a shop, or disappearing down a country road into the fog, always one step ahead of us. We figured it was only a matter of time until we caught up with you. Howie even showed your picture around to the locals, and almost always, there'd be someone who'd nod his head, as if he'd seen this dame.

I'm surprised Howie didn't wear it out.

The photograph? He kept it under plastic in his ID packet. He thought it would lift the spirits of the MPs when they asked for our papers.

Wasn't that Betty Grable's job?

You were our Betty Grable. I remember one MP got very jealous.

"You guys in G2 get all the girls." He couldn't have been more than 18.

"What?" I said. "You didn't get one? They passed them out as soon as we landed. Some MPs got two."

You should've seen the kid's face. "Hell, no. All I do is stand here and freeze my ass off." He was guarding a command post near the front.

"At least you're not in a foxhole," I said.

"Yeah, I won't get trench dick."

Such language.

It was Army talk. You couldn't say hello without swearing. The kid was actually giving us a test. It was during the Battle of the Bulge, and hundreds of Jerries had slipped behind our lines dressed up as Yanks. And they didn't just look the part. They actually sounded American. You could strike up a conversation with a fella you thought was from Jersey, and two minutes later, you'd be dead. So the kid was under strict orders. He had to ask questions that only a Yank could answer.

He asked us, "Who does Joe DiMaggio play for?"

Howie answered, "The Phillies."

"Okay, smartass," the kid said. "Who does Mickey

Mouse like to screw?"

"Your mother," Howie said.

The kid gave us a dirty look. "You guys are gonna freeze your asses off if you don't cooperate."

Was it cold?

It was colder than cold. I've never been so cold all in my life. It was snowing on and off, and freezing up constantly. Most of the time, I wore two pairs of woolen socks and a scarf my mother sent me, and I still couldn't keep warm. Even the locals complained, so we didn't horse around long. We told the kid what he wanted and hurried inside the command post. And while we were in there, another Jeep pulled up.

"How 'bout them fucking Yankees!" one of them shouted.

We could hear everything. The plumbing was backed up, so they had to pry the windows open.

"You like Goofy? He's my favorite. So's Donald. Fucking Donald!" He practically gave the family tree.

What was wrong with that?

Where'd these guys get off being so happy? Nobody wanted to be there. People were freezing their behinds off and getting shot.

Well, it didn't take long to find out. Howie and I were walking back to the Jeep when the command post blew. Then the guard station went. The MP's face was practically torn off his head. We all hit the ground, and so did the loudmouth who'd driven up after us. He wasn't ten feet away from me. According to his chevrons, he was a staff sergeant, but there was something funny about the way he lifted his head, sort of stiff and straightforward. Not the way a GI would do it, which was more rangy and rubbernecked.

I wasn't the only one who noticed. A captain came walking toward us with a gash in his forehead. He was the only brass to survive. He just happened to be outside taking a leak.

"You better get down," the loudmouth said. "Might be more coming in. Probably 88s."

The captain shook his head. "I don't think so."

He walked right by us and picked up a chair. He motioned for the loudmouth to have a seat. Then he had the men round up the other three who'd driven up with him.

"Okay, let's continue the questioning." The captain stood behind the loudmouth with his hands on his shoulders. "What position does Bobby Feller play?"

The man laughed. "Wherever the fuck he wants. What is this? We already passed our test."

"Who does Fred Astaire dance with?"

"The girl next door. Shirley Temple."

The captain picked up a hatchet that had fallen nearby. "Finish this sentence. 'We have nothing to fear but...'"

"The fucking Germans."

"Was ist Ihre Einheit!"

The man smiled at us. "Somebody wanna translate?"

The captain brought down the blunt end of the hatchet on the man's head. He hit him so hard, one of his eyes fell out.

"Was ist Ihre Einheit!" he asked again.

Before the man could answer, he brought the sharp end down.

The GIs dragged the body away. They put a corporal in the chair next.

"Was ist Ihre Einheit?" the captain asked.

"You got me, Mac."

The hatchet came down again.

He didn't have to ask the third. The soldier wet himself and started crying. He wasn't more than a kid, probably younger than the dead MP. He said he'd been raised in Chicago and was visiting family in Germany when the War broke out. He got down on his knees and begged for his life, but the captain shot him anyway.

The last one made a run for it. He didn't get far. The men all but shot his head off.

Then it was quiet–and the snow started coming down. It didn't let up for the rest of the day.

That night, we stayed at a new command post about a mile down the road, on a ridge overlooking the Ardennes Forest. Around ten o'clock, the weather finally cleared and the moon came up, and it turned out to be one of the loveliest nights I'd ever seen. Drifts covered the forest like a blanket, smothering everything under a layer of snow, and the trees glittered in the moonlight as if they were made of glass. It was like something out of a fairy tale, and so still, you could hear yourself breathe. Though you had to wonder where it all came from. How could so much beauty rise up out of this hell?

I was gazing out the window, trying to make sense of it, when I saw your face in the glass. I'd only seen you in profile before, kissing Howie on the beach, but you were staring at me, as if you were right outside the cabin. I moved in for a closer look, and at that moment, the captain walked in and cleared his throat. It must've looked like I was trying to kiss the glass.

"Feeling lonely, Kovacek?"

"Don't know what I feel, sir."

"We'll be home soon. The Jerries stuck their necks out this time. They never should have left their fortifications. Now there's nothing between us and Berlin."

I knew what he meant. We all thought the same thing– that the way home was east, and if you wanted to make it back, you had to cross the Rhine. And God help you if you didn't have a return ticket.

I never saw your face again, not in the window or in the towns. And Howie never mentioned you after that. He handed me your picture the next morning.

"Here," he said, "give the broad hell for me, will ya? I'm

through."

And from that moment on, we both knew we'd make it. Howie because he was pissed, and me because I'd made a promise. That's how business was done during the War, Kitten. That's how you calculated your chances.

I carried you all over the Ardennes after that, and later across the Rhineland and back into Paris. I can't tell you how many girls I kissed along the way. In Paris, they'd throw their arms around you, as if it was a game. I even slept with one or two out of loneliness and cussedness, but it didn't change anything. You were my sweetheart now. You were burned into my brain, as if you'd been there all my life. It was probably the only reason I kept my sanity.

Did you have it when you showed up on my porch?

Well now, that's debatable. I'd taken a Greyhound cross-country, which was bad enough. But when I got to L.A., it felt like I was in a foreign country again. I hardly recognized the place with all the changes after the War. I found myself doing what I'd always done when I was back in the ETO, back in the Jeep with Howie–I scouted the town.

So that's *how you knew L.A. so well.*

But I went about it as if there were still a war on. I kept asking myself, Where's the high ground? What would make the best cover? Where would the Schu mines be hidden? Then I saw your face, and I realized it was all a waste of time. I was in friendly territory.

I wasn't too friendly.

Compared to what I'd been through, you were hospitality itself.

But you gave me hell for not writing Howie.

Just a cover-up. I couldn't throw myself at you.

So what'd you think of this dame when you finally caught up with her? Was she what you imagined?

Even better. I couldn't believe my luck. I had to pinch myself. And what about you? What'd you think of this broken-down soldier who turned up on your front porch?

I left home with him six weeks later, didn't I?

To get away from your parents.

Partly.

You know, I still can't make it without you.

But you're no longer here.

That's the way it is, Kitten. We leave that indelible mark on each other. Like it or not, you'll always be a part of this old heartache.

Same here, I'm afraid.

And I'm not the only one. You should hear the songs they write about you up here. The men march through the corridors singing your praises.

Don't make me laugh.

Laugh all you want. We've named about 300 stars after you.

Out of how many?

Billions. But it's the thought that counts. I visit them every so often just to keep warm. In fact, as far as I'm concerned, you're still the cream in my coffee–and my hot toddy at night, if you get my drift.

Oh, Frank, don't tease me.

Who's teasing? How 'bout we get the old campfire going? Bring back some of the old magic.

Now you're being ridiculous.

I've never been more serious.

Just like you to lead me on.

So whaddya say, Kitten?

In your dreams.

Where else?

Note from the Author

Thank you for reading *After Dad*. If you enjoyed it, please write a review at Amazon, Barnes & Noble, GoodReads or the book review site of your choice.

RC